Col

Colin University
© 2018 Mark A. Roeder

Cover Photo Credit: Konstantin Kirillov on Dreamstime.com.

Cover Design: Ken Clark

ISBN-13: 978-1983902949

ISBN-10: 1983902942

A Special Thanks to My Patrons

Books do not make authors rich. Often, they don't even pay the bills. This book was made possible in part by my patrons on Patreon.com: Cassandra Anker, Albert McCann, Bryan Grasso-Shonka, Robert Beemer, Stefan Woollard, Victor Freeman, Luke Horn, Mark Andrews, Robert Powell, Daniel Harrison, Jaime Vidal, John F Callow, John McGrath, John Smeallie, Donald Covert, and John McGrath.

Patrons get the inside track on my novels, sneak peaks, and other perks. You can become a patron for as little as $2 a month. For $10 a month, you get a copy of every ebook I publish on the day it is released. For $20 a month, you even get to create a minor character for a novel. Even if you can't become a patron, check out my page because some posts are public.

Check it out:
https://www.patreon.com/user/posts?u=8324548 or go to patreon.com and search for "gay youth novelist".

Acknowledgments

No book is without error, but there are a number of individuals who help me remove as many as possible before publication. Ken Clark, Jim Adkinson, Jim Hertwig, and David Tedesco have all put a lot of time and effort into proofreading this novel. Ken is also responsible for the great cover, in fact nearly all the covers of my books.

Other Novels by Mark A. Roeder

Also look for audiobook versions on Amazon.com and Audible.com

Blackford Gay Youth Chronicles:

Outfield Menace

Snow Angel

The Nudo Twins

Phantom World

Second Star to the Right

The Perfect Boy

Verona Gay Youth Chronicles:

Ugly

Beautiful

The Soccer Field Is Empty

Someone Is Watching

A Better Place

The Summer of My Discontent

Disastrous Dates & Dream Boys

Just Making Out

Temptation University*

Scarecrows

Scotty Jackson Died... But Then He Got Better

The Antichrists

Bloomington Boys—Brandon & Dorian*

Bloomington Boys—Nathan & Devon*

Lawn Boy

Bloomington Boys—Scotty & Casper*

Bloomington Boys—Tim & Marc*

Brendan & Casper

Someone Is Killing the Gay Boys of Verona

Keeper of Secrets

Masked Destiny

Do You Know That I Love You

Altered Realities

Dead Het Boys

Dead Boys of Verona

This Time Around

The Graymoor Mansion Bed and Breakfast

Shadows of Darkness

Heart of Graymoor

Come Back to Me

Skye & Colin

Marshall Mulgrew's Supernatural Mysteries

Christmas in Graymoor Mansion

The Fat Kid

Brendan & Casper: Older & Better

Light in the Darkness

Bloomington Gay Youth Chronicles

A Triumph of Will

*Temptation University**

The Picture of Dorian Gray

Yesterday's Tomorrow

Boy Trouble

The New Bad Ass in Town

*Bloomington Boys—Brandon & Dorian**

*Bloomington Boys—Nathan & Devon**

*Bloomington Boys—Scotty & Casper**

*Bloomington Boys—Tim & Marc**

Peralta's Bike Shop

Hate at First Sight

Colin University

A Boy Toy for Christmas

*Crossover novels that fit into two series

Other Novels:

Benji & Clyde

Cadets of Culver

Fierce Competition

The Vampire's Heart

Homo for the Holidays

For more information on current and upcoming novels go to markroeder.com.

Follow the author on Twitter @markaroeder

Chapter One
Bloomington, Indiana
August 2010

Heads turned as Skye drove down 10th Street in his 1935 Auburn boattail speedster. It was an amazing car once owned by Clark Gable and later James Dean if you can believe it, but it totally lacked storage space. There wasn't even a back seat. My duffle bag was stuffed between my legs and my backpack was on my lap. The few other things I had packed were stuffed around me. I felt like a sardine crammed into a can.

There was a traffic jam on Sunrise Drive, which led down to my dorm, so Skye turned into a parking lot across 10th Street. We didn't need a close spot. Unlike most people I saw pulling trunks and toting boxes into the dorms, I didn't have much to carry.

After Skye snagged one of the few remaining parking places, I climbed out of the car, stretched, and shouted: "I am so glad to get out of this car!"

"I should've taken Marshall up on his offer to use his hearse. There would have been plenty of room for you to stretch out."

"Hmm, let's see... arrive for my freshman year at IU in a hearse or a vintage automobile once owned by movie stars..."

Skye laughed.

"You don't think anyone would be impressed by Marshall's hearse?"

"I'm not so much concerned with impressing anyone as I am with not being pegged as a freak on my first day."

"Hand me your duffle bag and laundry bag. I'll help you carry your stuff inside."

"You know you could leave the Auburn with me if you're feeling guilty about abandoning me in Bloomington without a car."

"I'm not feeling guilt at all. None whatsoever."

"Grr."

"You really think I'm going to leave my beloved Skyemobile with you?"

"Hey, it was worth a shot."

When the light changed, we crossed 10th Street, along with several others, and then walked down the sidewalk along Sunrise Drive. There were cars parked in every available space, and the sidewalk was crowded with students and their parents carting packing boxes and bags into the dorms. Teter Quad was located to the west and my residence, Ashton Center, was to the east. Ashton was actually a complex of smaller dorms and buildings. My room was in Hershey Hall.

Skye and I entered Hershey and walked down the hallway to my room. I had already obtained my key-card during freshman orientation. I unlocked the door and we entered.

"Wow, small, but at least you have it all to yourself," Skye said.

"I would have preferred a roommate."

"You'll have plenty of opportunities to interact with others here. You may be glad to have a space of your own, even if it isn't much bigger than a closet."

"There's more storage space than I need," I said indicating the built-in bookshelves and closet by the door.

"You'll be glad to have the storage I bet."

"It's going to take a while to get used to this. It's not a fourth the size of my bedroom back home, but I'll be spending most of my time on campus anyway."

"True. Ready to go shopping?"

"Yeah."

"Have your list?"

"Of course."

"Let's hit Target first and then Kroger," Skye said.

We made our way back outside and dodged students and parents as they packed belongings into the dorms. We returned to the Auburn and Skye pulled out onto 10th Street. He drove past Ashton and then other dorms. The street took a sharp left and we passed through a narrow tunnel, far too quickly. My heart raced with fear.

"If I did that while driving this car you would kill me," I said.

"That's right," Skye laughed.

"Did you notice all the girls checking you out?" I asked.

"I'm accustomed to being admired. When you're as gorgeous as me it's bound to happen." I laughed. Skye wasn't as conceited as he pretended to be. "I think they were looking at you, Colin, at least I noticed a couple checking you out and a couple of boys too."

"What can I say? I'm even more gorgeous than you," I said, trying to top Skye's pretend conceit.

"Nope, sorry. You are only the junior version."

"Wrong! I'm the young and hot version. You are the old and busted version."

"Hey. I'm 30."

"Yeah, like I said, old and busted, a has-been."

"I can still kick your butt."

"Yeah? You think so old man? Want to take it to the mat?"

"Nah, I'd hate to embarrass you."

"Yeah, right."

"I'll try to come down and catch some of your wrestling meets and I'll definitely make it when IU wrestles Notre Dame. That's a quick trip from Verona."

"I'll warn you. I have my eye on your college record. I mean, since I beat your high school record..."

"I'm very proud of you for that."

I smiled. Skye meant it. Skye was my uncle. He was more the age of a big brother, but he felt more like my dad.

Skye drove to Target on 3rd Street. We had to park quite some distance from the store because the parking lot was crowded.

"Damn, I thought everyone was on campus. I guess I was wrong," Skye said.

We walked across the parking lot into the store and grabbed a cart. I pulled out my list.

"We'll get the groceries at Kroger. We'll definitely have to make a trip back to your dorm when we're finished here," Skye said.

"Yeah, especially since I need a dorm fridge."

Skye followed along as I pushed the cart. I had brought clothing, my new iPad, and toiletries from home, but I needed the aforementioned fridge, a toaster, washcloths, towels, soap, laundry detergent, and a whole list of other stuff. I wasn't even sure it would all fit in the car. Skye helped me make a few decisions on what to purchase, based on his years of living in a dorm at USC back in the olden days. The mini fridge took up most of the cart and the rest quickly filled.

"I don't know if all this will fit," I said as we headed for the checkouts.

"Oh, it will fit, but you may have to walk back to campus."

"It's actually close enough that if I ran I might beat you there," I said.

"It will be a tight fit, but we'll manage."

Every checkout was open, but we still had a fairly long wait in line. After Skye paid for my stuff, I wheeled the cart out to the Auburn.

"This is not going to fit," I said.

"Have faith. Get in."

I climbed into the passenger seat. Skye handed me bags, which I packed in tightly around my legs. When all the spare legroom was taken, he put the fridge on my lap, then proceeded to stuff bags around me.

"I can't see," I said laughing.

"You don't have to see. You're not driving."

Skye kept stuffing bags around me.

"There, it all fit and you don't have to run to campus."

"I can't move," I said.

"Just be glad you didn't have to ride like this all the way from Verona."

Skye climbed in and navigated his way out of the parking lot. I couldn't see anything in front of me, only to the sides. I was glad the Auburn was a convertible.

Skye scored a parking spot on Sunrise Drive fairly near Hershey Hall, which was a good thing because we had much more to carry than before. Skye reached in, pulled the fridge from my lap, and then pulled out bags until I could climb out of the car.

Skye picked up the fridge box again.

"Load me up," he said.

I did, then grabbed as much as I could, but there were still bags in the car.

Someone was kind enough to open the door for us when we reached the dorm. We walked to my room where I put down enough bags to unlock the door. I let Skye enter first, then followed.

No one had messed with my stuff when we returned to the Auburn. One bad thing about the car is that there was no way to lock it. There wasn't even a top. Luckily, the skies were clear because if it rained we'd get wet.

After our second trip inside I realized Skye might have been right about storage. The stuff I bought at Target covered my bed and desk. I unpacked my fridge and plugged it in so it could begin getting cold and then we returned to the Auburn.

"Hey, can we take some photos of your car?" a couple of cute college boys asked Skye when they realized he owned it. They had been checking it out as we approached.

"Sure, so ahead. Get in if you want."

Skye was very proud of his Auburn. It was his baby. I had stood beside him in shock when he purchased it at a vintage car auction for nearly half a million dollars! It was a beauty with a red leather interior that complemented the pale-yellow body. What I liked best was the boattail that tapered to a point. Most people would have kept such a car in a garage, but Skye drove it all the time, except when the weather was too cold or wet.

The guys took their photos, gushed over the Auburn, and thanked Skye. We climbed in and waved at them as we set out once again.

"You know if you had a normal car we could have done all this in one trip," I said.

"Would you rather I have a normal car?"

"No. I'm just saying."

"What if I drove a hearse like Marshall?"

"Actually, I like his hearse, but it's not the kind of car I want to drive or even be seen in during college."

In a few minutes we passed College Mall and headed a couple of blocks south. The parking lot in front of the strip mall that included Kroger was even more crowded than the one at Target. We parked fairly far away from the store, but we didn't care.

"Wow, this is huge," I said as I entered the store with a shopping cart.

"It's not quite like the little grocery in Verona. Is it?" Skye asked.

"Twelve of them would fit in here. I bet this is four times the size of the Kroger in Plymouth."

I had a list, but also planned to grab things I thought I might need as I spotted them. As we walked through the crowded aisles I picked up cereal, Pop-Tarts, honey-roasted peanuts, milk, Fuji apples, bananas, cheese, and other items. I didn't buy much in the way of junk food because I tried not to eat too much of it. I needed to keep in shape for wrestling and I wanted to remain in my weight class. I was absolutely not going to put on the "freshman fifteen," the weight Skye had warned me that most college freshmen gained their first year.

"Are you sure this is enough?" Skye asked when we headed for the checkouts.

"Yeah, I have my meal plan at school so I'll eat mainly on campus. Most of this will be for breakfast."

We checked out. Between the two of us, we were able to carry everything back to the car without taking a cart. I climbed in with my bags. Once I was situated, Skye handed me his. My side was cramped, but I had a lot more room than I did after our Target run. I could even see where we were going.

We had to park a good distance away from Ashton this time, but we didn't have as much to carry so it didn't matter. Once back in my dorm room, I put the milk, cheese, and the few other items that needed to be kept cold in the fridge.

"We need to head to The Tudor Room soon. Our reservation is for 12:30," Skye said.

"Yeah, let's find the restroom and then head out."

The nearest restroom wasn't too far down the hall. It was clean, but looked as if it had been built long ago. I liked the pale green tile of the walls. We used the restroom, washed up, and then headed out once more.

This time, Skye headed down to 3rd Street and drove along the southern edge of campus. It was far less crowded than 10th Street where many of the dorms were located. Once we reached Indiana Avenue and drove up the eastern side of campus, I was in more familiar territory. I had visited Bloomington with Skye and Marshall while I was still in high school. We even stayed on campus in The Biddle Hotel for a night.

Skye parked the Auburn on 6th Street and we walked across Indiana Avenue onto the campus once more.

"Now this is familiar. We were here not quite three years ago. Right?" Skye said as we followed the path between Dunn Meadow and the stream known as the Jordan River (don't ask me why it's called that, I have no idea).

"Yeah, that was a fun trip, but we didn't get to stay long enough."

"You're only saying that because you wanted to make out with more college kids."

"Well *someone* kept interrupting me."

"I won't be around to interrupt you now, but remember to save some time for studying."

"I'll probably be so busy with classes and wrestling I won't have time to make out."

"You have to learn to budget your time. I had a reputation as a party boy at USC, but the truth is I made sure I finished my classwork first."

"That's what I plan to do. I hate having stuff hanging over my head."

We followed the sidewalk as it passed the Indiana Memorial Union, better known as the IMU. The building was huge. It was the largest student union in the world. The Biddle Hotel, a Burger King, and several other restaurants were inside. We entered through the revolving doors of the hotel lobby and walked up the stairs.

"I forget which floor the Tudor Room is on," Skye said.

"Yeah, I hear the memory begins to fail for the elderly."

"Keep it up and I'll get a room and stick around to ruin whatever fun you try to have."

"I take it back! I take it back!"

After walking down a long hallway, we rode an escalator up to the next floor and I confidently led the way to the Tudor Room. We walked inside and up to the podium.

"We have a reservation for Mackenzie at 12:30," Skye said.

The hostess led us to a small table by a window that looked down over a large patio outside. We remained at the table only long enough to place our drink orders before we headed for the buffet.

"It's a good thing you made a reservation. This place is packed," I said.

"I made this reservation weeks ago. Sometimes us old people have good ideas."

"Yes, I suppose I'll be wise when I'm thirty."

I chose grilled chicken with green chili, farfalle with butternut squash, spinach, and artichokes, and Tuscan lentil soup as well as some bread and cheese from the salad bar.

Our Diet Cokes were waiting at our table by the time we made it back. We sat down and began to eat.

"I love the food here. Marc is so lucky to live close. He can walk here anytime," Skye said.

"So can I now."

"Sure, rub it in."

"I doubt I'll be here much. I'll be eating on the cheap."

"If you need money, you tell me."

"Thanks, but I'm good for now."

As my Mom and step-dad's only heir, I actually had quite a bit of money. I wasn't rich by any means, but the sale of the house and most everything in it gave me a lot of cash. I wouldn't actually have control of my money until I was twenty-one, but I didn't need it. Skye had insisted on paying for college. I did have a wrestling scholarship that paid for quite a bit of it, but Skye was putting out thousands more. Skye was always there for me.

We talked and laughed as we ate. There were some hot college boys eating with their parents, and a number of other students eating alone. A couple of the boys kept checking us out. There were some hot college girls too. I noticed a table of three girls stealing glances of us, but mostly of Skye. They were out of luck with Skye because he only liked guys. I liked both girls and guys.

We hit the dessert bar next. I had chocolate cake, a no-bake cookie, and carrot cake. Skye had key-lime pie, pecan pie, and a big chocolate chip cookie. We had hot tea to go with our dessert.

I was eager to get back to my room, but I lingered with Skye. It would be quite a while before I saw him again. It was going to feel odd not seeing him every day as I had for years, but then I guess it was like that for all kids going off to college.

When we could eat no more, we left The Tudor Room and walked back toward the car. Some college boys were playing football in the meadow. Maybe I'd have a chance to join a game later.

"Your mom would be so proud of you," Skye said as we walked once again between the Jordan River and Dunn Meadow.

"I hope so."

"She would be, Colin. I am sure of it."

"Thanks," I said, blushing slightly.

"I will warn you now, if I don't get a phone call or a text at least once a week I will come down and do my best to embarrass you."

"Oh no. I'm not giving you the pleasure. I'll keep in touch."

"Good because I'll want to know how wrestling practices are going."

"Missing your glory days, are you?" I asked.

"Just a bit. Part of me wishes I was just beginning college too. Those were good years for me. Now is good too, but sometimes I miss it."

"I'll do my best to have fun for you."

"You're so gracious. Do you need anything else?"

"I think I'm stocked up. If I've forgotten something, I'll deal with it."

"Okay, let's go pick out a bike."

We walked the very short distance to Peralta's Bike & Skate Shop. Marc Peralta, who was from Verona and had attended IU, owned it. We'd visited Marc and his shop when we were in Bloomington a few years before.

The bell rang on the door as we entered.

"Hey guys," Marc said.

"The place looks busy," Skye said.

"Yeah, it's like that at the beginning of the fall semester. So, are you moved in yet?" Marc asked me.

"Moved in, but not unpacked."

"We've come to find a bike for Colin," Skye said.

"Well, I do have plenty of those. I'll give you the Verona boy discount and this weekend everyone who buys a bike gets a free

$25 gift card for Dagwood's.   It's a great sub place just across Indiana Avenue from campus."

"I like this. Skye pays for the bike and I get free food," I said.

"How do you plan to use the bike?"

"I'll mostly use it to get around on campus and maybe to ride to Kroger or the mall."

"A road bike will be best. Mountain bikes are great for riding on rough terrain, but a road bike performs best on city streets and sidewalks. I have single-speed and multi-speed bikes. The multi-speed bikes are easier to ride, especially for going up hills, but a single speed is better for exercise."

"I want a single speed. It will help strengthen my legs."

"Are you sure?" Skye asked.

"Yeah."

"Okay then. What do you recommend in a single speed?" Skye asked.

"The best single speed I carry, without getting into the big bucks, is the Schwinn regulation Little 500 model. It's a great basic bike and will easily last you all through college. I carry quite a few in stock. Most of the riders buy from me. Try this one out," Marc said eyeing me.

I straddled the bike. It was the perfect height and the seat was comfortable. I got off and lifted the bike. It was light enough to carry if necessary.

"I like this one. I don't think there is any need to look further," I said.

"Okay, we'll take that one then," Skye said. "He also needs something to lock it up and I think a flasher would be a good idea for night riding."

It took a few more minutes to pick everything out, then Skye pulled out his credit card and paid.

"Come and see me sometime, Colin. Remember, if you ever have any kind of emergency, call me. I'm almost always in Bloomington. My number is on the receipt and the card I put in your bag. Add it to your phone. If you have any problems with your bike, bring it back in."

We talked a bit more, but the shop was busy and Marc was needed so we said our goodbyes and then departed.

"I think I'll ride back to the dorm. There is no way we can get this bike in the Auburn," I said as we walked down the sidewalk beside Indiana Avenue.

"That's true. Have you thought of anything you need that we didn't buy?"

"I think I have it all. Thank you so much, Skye."

We hugged.

"I'm going to miss you, but I'm excited for you," Skye said.

"I'll miss you too," I said, getting a little closer to tears than I thought I would.

"Call me in a couple of days and let me know how you're doing. Let me know if you need anything and put Marc's number in your phone. You never know when you might need someone here in town to help you."

"I will."

"Have fun and try not to do all the things I did in college." Skye grinned.

"Oh, I made a list. I'll try to surpass you."

"Oh lord. Goodbye, Colin. I love you."

"Goodbye. I love you too."

We hugged again, then I walked my new bike across Indiana Avenue while Skye walked back to the Auburn. I suspended the shopping bag from the handlebar and then set out for Hershey Hall.

The Schwinn was harder to petal than other bikes I had ridden in the past, but that's what I wanted. My legs would get a good workout whenever I rode to class. I needed to remember to register my bike so it would be easier to get back if it was lost or stolen.

I rode through campus as students and families explored. I was one of a few thousand new freshmen who didn't know his way around yet. I did have a slight advantage. In addition to the freshman orientation tour I had also explored campus when we stayed here overnight during my high school days. I knew the IMU fairly well and also had a general idea of the location of many of the main buildings. I intended to scout out the location of my classes before next Monday.

I was able to reach Hershey much quicker by bike than was possible by car. Being able to ride across campus instead of following the streets was quite an advantage. I locked my bike up in one of the racks outside of my dorm and went inside. I wanted to explore, but I decided to get my room in some kind of order first. At the least, I wanted to make my bed in case I got busy with something later and didn't come in until late.

My room was too quiet, but there was a lot of noise from the hall as more students moved into the dorm. I still wished I had a roommate, but maybe Skye was right. I might be thankful later to have my own quiet space.

Sheets, blankets, and a pillow were among the things Skye had purchased for me at Target. We had none to bring from home because we lived in Graymoor Mansion, which was officially a bed & breakfast, but was actually more of a hotel. Housekeeping provided all of our bedding at home. I made my own bed every morning, except on Thursdays when housekeeping changed the sheets. I was going to miss having someone else do my laundry.

I headed out as soon as my bed was made. The rest could wait. I had very little to do until Monday when classes and practices began and I was eager to explore.

I began right in Hershey Hall and soon discovered that there were washers and dryers right in my dorm, which would be convenient. I quickly found my way into Barnes Lounge, which was attached to Hershey. It had a pool table, TVs, tables and chairs, vending machines and more. I continued exploring, got lost, then figured out where I was again. One thing I didn't find was anywhere to eat, but I knew there were cafes and restaurants in some of the dorms and other buildings. I'd just have to figure out where.

I walked outside, which is where I truly wanted to be on a hot August day such as this. There were buildings in every direction, but also large open green spaces in between and lots of trees. What had attracted me to IU on my first visit was the fact that it felt like a big park. It was a truly beautiful place and I loved beauty in all its forms.

I spotted more beauty almost immediately. There were hot girls and hot guys everywhere. That's something else that attracted me to IU on my first visit. I smiled remembering how I had managed to pass myself off as a college boy even though I was still in high school. Skye and Marshall caught me making out with a girl and later with a boy and ruined my fun both times, but they didn't know about the other girl and the two guys I'd met while on campus. I had a long make out session with the girl and another with a boy from France. I also hooked up with a hot lacrosse player in his dorm room. What Skye didn't know couldn't hurt me.

I wasn't sure if I was more interested in girls or guys. Sometimes, I was more into one than the other, but then after a while my preference changed. It had more to do with the individuals I met than anything. Sometimes, pure lust was the dominant factor. Other times, it was more about personality.

Boys were easier to get. While I was almost certain girls were every bit as horny as us guys, most were less willing to hookup for the sole purpose of getting off. There were exceptions, but most girls wanted more. That was okay when I wanted more too, but sometimes I just wanted to have sex and then go and do my own thing.

I didn't spend much time thinking about my preference. If I ended up with a girl, fine. If I ended up with a guy, that was fine too. As a college freshman one thing I did not want was a serious relationship. While I had no intention of becoming the campus slut I wanted to be free to hook up if that's what I desired.

I eyed a few girls and a few guys as I walked around the 10th Street dorm area. Better still, quite a few eyed me. I was accustomed to drawing a lot of attention. Most people found me attractive. I personally sometimes thought my nose was too small and my mouth too big, although other times they seemed okay. My body was my best feature. I had been active since I was a boy. Even when I was very young, Skye showed me how to do pushups. I got involved in sports as soon as possible and worked out with dedication. In my middle and high school years I played football and wrestled. In recent years Skye had trained me in hand-to-hand combat and sword fighting. I was muscular, defined, and had only 4% body fat. I was also well proportioned. One of the things my uncle had taught me is that more isn't always better. That went for muscles as much as anything else. My muscles were for actual use, not a bodybuilding competition, so I had avoided getting big for the sake of being big.

I wandered past the Wells Library and into the Arboretum. I thought the Arboretum should have more trees, considering its name. There were several of them, but most of the area was open spaces of grass. There was a stream that led to a small pond in the middle, where at the moment a pair of ducks swam near the water-lilies that grew at one edge. There were a few kids sunning on the grass, plus other students and parents strolling and admiring the trees and flowers.

Brendan, my high school football coach, said that the football stadium was located in this space decades ago, well before his own time. It was hard to believe that the Arboretum was man-made. It had a somewhat landscaped look because of the sidewalks running through it, but if I didn't know better I would have thought it was here since the beginning. Even the limestone and iron fence that surrounded the area on three sides looked as if it was a part of a park and not the remnants of the days when this was the stadium.

I wandered into a more familiar area of campus and soon spotted the IMU. I didn't enter the building, but instead walked down the same sidewalk Skye and I had earlier. Dunn Meadow soon appeared and as I had hoped a few guys were playing football. It wasn't the same group I'd spotted earlier, but that didn't matter.

I walked up and watched a play. The "quarterback" didn't have a bad arm on him, but the ball wobbled a lot. His receiver caught it and raced for the goal, but didn't make it far before someone grabbed the shirt that hung from his shorts.

"Can I join?" I asked when the play was over.

"Sure. Hey, I'm Quinton. You can be on our team since we're uneven. Tuck your shirt into your shorts. We're playing flag football."

"I'm Colin."

The other guys nodded to me and I nodded back. I joined my team and faced off against our opponents. When our quarterback yelled *hike,* I pushed past the other team and broke into the open. The quarterback spotted me and threw. His pass was off, but I managed to snag it. I raced toward the goal and made it most of the way there before my shirt was pulled from my shorts. I circled back around to the boy who had nabbed my shirt.

"You're good. I'm Shane."

"Thanks. You're fast. I'm Colin."

The teams lined up again and this time my team scored. On the next play, I snagged the shirt of the player who had the ball just before he could score. It was a very casual game, but it was a chance to run and play with other young guys.

I was hot and sweaty in no time at all, but I didn't mind. I actually liked to sweat. The only problem was that sweat ran down my forehead and into my eyes making them sting. Even that didn't bother me much. It was worth it to play.

I had a blast. I loved football and was looking forward to watching the IU games. I played in high school, but I was a better wrestler than I was a football player so wrestling was my main focus. I was actually a good enough player that I might have made the IU team, but when IU offered me a wrestling scholarship I accepted. I was breaking with the long-standing football tradition of the Verona boys. The Gaylord brothers, Brendan, Shawn, and Tim had all played football for IU. Brendan was even the quarterback way back in the day.

A new boy joined us after a few minutes and from the moment he did it was hard to keep my eyes off him. He was quite good looking with longish blond hair and pale blue eyes.

Being blond myself, I was not especially attracted to blonds. I had always thought guys with dark hair were so very sexy. This blond boy was different. I felt an immediate attraction to him and had difficulty keeping my mind on the game.

Even so, I had an extremely good time playing. This game had none of the seriousness found on the football field back in Verona. It didn't much matter who won. It was more about making a good pass or catch and zigzagging through the opposition without losing your shirt.

When the game ended over an hour later I was breathing a little hard and extremely sweaty. I had no doubt my face was red because it tended to get that way after heated exercise. I could feel my hair plastered to my face. I definitely was not looking my best, but I did not want to let the blond boy with the pale blue eyes slip away. At a school as big as IU, I might never see him again if I let him get away from me.

He smiled at me shyly as I walked toward him.

"Hi. I'm Colin," I said.

"I'm Haakon."

We gazed into each other's eyes and I immediately felt something click between us. I could tell from his accent that he wasn't from the U.S., and he sounded Scandinavian, maybe Sweden or Norway.

"Would you like to do something or go get something to eat?" I asked. I had never been the shy type.

"Yes, I would like that very much. I do not know my way around well. I'm from Norway and have only been in the U.S. a few days."

How about that? I had nailed it.

"I would love to show you around, although I'm not familiar with everything on campus either."

"Could we meet somewhere in a few minutes? I am very sweaty."

I laughed. "We both are. I could use a shower. What dorm are you in?"

"Forest Quad."

"I'm in Hershey Hall in Ashton. Why don't we go clean up and then I'll meet you in the lobby in Forest?"

"That sounds good," Haakon said, smiling.

"What made you want to come to IU?" I asked as we began walking east across campus.

"I wanted to attend an American school and my parents agreed to send my brother and me to school overseas for one semester each. When I began to research schools, I liked this one best. It's highly rated."

"Is your brother at IU too?"

"No. He is at the University of Oslo, where I will finish school. He will come to the U.S. next semester. I think he will come to IU, but he hasn't decided yet. We were going to come together, but our mother could not stand for both of us to be out of the country at the same time."

"I suppose I can understand that."

"Hamlet and I are close. It is more difficult to be away from him than it is from the rest of my family. I already emailed him and sent him a few pictures of campus."

Hamlet, that's an interesting name, but then so is Haakon.

"I'm very close to my uncle, Skye. This will be the first time in a long time that I've been away from him for a long period of time, but he's less than four hours away."

"What about your parents?"

"My mom and step dad were killed in an auto accident a few years ago. I have no idea where my father is. He left when I was so little I don't even remember him."

"I am sorry."

"I live with Skye. He's always been like a father to me, although now that I'm older he seems more like a big brother."

"It is good you have someone."

"Yes. I miss him but I am very excited to be here. I come from a small town so I'm thrilled to be where there is so much to do and so many people."

"I am from a *very* small town so I know what you mean." Haakon grinned and my heart beat a little faster.

We soon reached Jordan Avenue.

"I'm going this way, but I'll see you in a few," I said.

We parted. I began to run. Since I was meeting Haakon in his dorm I needed to hurry.

It did not take me long to reach Hershey. I stripped in my room, then realized my soap and shampoo were still sitting in one of the Target bags. I rummaged around until I found them, washcloths, and a towel. I needed to get organized. My room was already a mess.

I wrapped the towel around my waist and walked down the hallway toward the bathroom. A couple of guys checked me out, but then guys who didn't know me usually did when I was shirtless. It didn't mean they wanted me. I was unusually well-built for my age so I tended to attract attention. When girls looked at me when I was shirtless, it usually meant they were attracted to me, but it was different with guys. Boys who had no sexual interest in other boys still checked them out. It was more a competitive thing that anything.

I entered the bathroom. At one end were separate shower stalls and hooks for towels. I hung up my towel and turned on the showerhead in a stall. The water was soon steaming. I entered with my shower caddy.

I closed the curtain more to keep water from getting out than for privacy. I was accustomed to communal showers. I even preferred them for the wide-open space.

27

I worked my vanilla and brown sugar shampoo into my hair. It smelled good enough to eat. I rinsed it out and put in the matching hair conditioner, which smelled even better. I quickly lathered up with my favorite Irish Spring soap and then rinsed off. I usually liked to linger in the shower a little, but I didn't have time now.

I stepped out, dried off, wrapped my towel around my waist and headed back to my room. A couple more guys checked me out, as well as a mom who was helping her son move in. I smiled to myself after I passed her. Older women were always eyeing me. I wondered what thoughts went through their mind when they did so and if they thought about me later.

Once in my room, I hurriedly changed into khaki shorts and one of my dressy tank tops. Okay, I know a tank top does not sound dressy at all, but there are different types. I had everyday tank tops I wore for working out, but also better-made tops of thicker cloth that had a more tailored look. Believe me, if you saw the two types modeled together you would see the difference. I put on my gold chain and sprayed on a little Burberry Brit cologne. I quickly combed my hair and I was ready.

I did not want to get hot and sweaty again, so I walked toward the southern part of campus at an easy pace. It was not difficult to get sweaty on a hot summer's day like this one. The late afternoon temperature had climbed into the low-90's. I loved it!

I followed a wide sidewalk that led past the Jordan Avenue parking garage and then angled off onto a sidewalk that went southeast, passing Read Hall on the east side. I could already see Forest Quad up ahead. I didn't know the location of all the buildings on campus, but I had studied the campus map from orientation and I remembered a good deal of it.

Forest faced 3rd Street, so I walked around the building and entered the lobby. It was much larger than the one in Hershey, but then Forest was several times bigger than Hershey Hall.

I didn't have long to wait before Haakon arrived via the elevator. He looked extremely handsome wearing a bright blue polo shirt and cargo shorts. I loved his slightly curly blond hair.

"Hello again," Haakon said.

"Hey. Shall we go?"

Haakon nodded. We left the lobby and walked down the sidewalk that bordered 3rd Street.

"What parts of campus are you unfamiliar with?" I asked.

"Almost all of it! I took the tour, but there was too much to take in and I was overwhelmed with being in a new country so far from home."

"That would be overwhelming. I live in Indiana, although in the northern part of the state. I'd like to check out the HPER if you don't mind. It's one of the gyms on campus. We can explore on the way."

"That sounds very good to me. So I guess this is as far as the university goes in this direction," Haakon said, pointing to the homes across the street.

"Yes, Forest Quad is on the far southern edge. The Memorial Stadium, Assembly Hall, and the baseball and softball stadiums are at the northern edge of campus several blocks north. There are some dorms almost that far up too. My dorm, Hershey, is in the southern part of campus, but getting close to the center."

"I know I will get lost at first."

"You and a few thousand others I bet."

Haakon smiled. "Yes, I forget I am not the only one who is new here."

"Probably a fourth of the students are new and there are lots of students from other countries. I've already heard languages while walking around that I couldn't identify."

"I am good with languages."

"You certainly speak English well."

"I think I may want to be a translator. I speak Norwegian and the languages of the countries near Norway. I know some German and Italian. I am working on my English. That is one reason I wanted to come to school here. English is a very difficult language to learn."

"I've heard that."

"Yes, it often does not follow its own rules. It is very confusing sometimes."

"Well I am very impressed with anyone who speaks more than one language. I am terrible with foreign languages."

"I am good with them. When I make a mistake, I would appreciate if you would correct me so I can learn."

"I will, but so far I haven't heard any mistakes."

We soon turned to the north and followed the sidewalk along Jordan Avenue. We paused in front of the Simon Music Building to gaze the fountain in the stone-paved plaza out front that shot water high into the sky. I loved the sound of falling water.

We walked on, passing Read Hall on our right across the street, then the Musical Arts Building, and then the Delta Gamma Sorority House with the Jordan Avenue Parking Garage just across the street. A couple of sorority girls eyed us. Haakon sighed and looked away from them quickly.

"Are you okay?"

Haakon gazed at me anxiously. "I hope you're okay with it, but if not, I might as well find out now. I'm gay," Haakon said.

"Good."

"Good? Americans seem to me very... unaccepting. I am surprised by your reaction."

"You are right about Americans. There are many truly ignorant and small-minded people here, but I am not one of them. I'm bi and my uncle is gay."

Haakon smiled. "Wow. That is wonderful."

"I'm open about being bi. I see no reason not to be. I don't announce it to everyone I meet, but I make no attempt to hide it."

"I hope this doesn't make me sound conceited, but the girls here are always looking at me. It's not so bad back home, but here they cannot seem to keep their eyes off me."

I laughed. "That could make you sound conceited, but I can understand where that would be a problem for you."

"I don't know how to handle the unwanted attention. I don't want to make them feel rejected."

"Most of them are probably just looking. They're interested, but probably won't approach you. You're merely eye candy for them."

"Eye candy?"

"Scenery they enjoy. Like when you check out a guy, even though you probably won't hit on him."

"Oh okay. I think I understand."

"When a girl acts too interested, tell her you're gay. She won't feel rejected."

"I suppose I am making it into a problem when it isn't. It's just that I am not accustomed to so much attention."

"I'm sure blonds are much rarer here than in Norway."

"You are blond."

"True, but the vast majority of guys here have brown hair. Blond hair is a novelty so blonds get more attention."

"Ah."

We crossed over the Jordan River as we walked beside busy Jordan Avenue. A campus bus stopped to let off riders. It was the third bus I'd seen on our walk. I definitely wasn't in Verona anymore.

We passed the rear of the IU Auditorium and then turned to the left. We entered another small park-like area. To our left was the auditorium and to our right was a hillside that led up to the parking area for Wells Library. Roses and other flowers covered the bank. More roses grew in flowerbeds around a bronze of Hoagy Carmichael sitting at a piano writing music. He held a real yellow lily in his hand.

"I read somewhere that it's a tradition for the statue to always have a flower in his hand. Apparently whenever one dies, someone comes along and replaces it," I said.

"You know a lot about IU."

"I don't know a lot, but I visited here when I was younger. My football coach went here and told us stories about when he played ball for IU. There are many others from my hometown who went to school here as well."

"So coming here is a tradition?"

"I guess, although my uncle went to the University of Southern California. I considered it, but ever since I visited the campus I was drawn to IU."

"What is it like being bi?" Haakon asked.

"I think it's rather like being gay or straight. I'm attracted to some individuals, but not others. The only difference is that the sex of the individual has nothing to do with it."

"I have always liked boys," Haakon said.

"There are a lot of hot boys here."

"Yes, I have noticed."

Haakon and I smiled at each other. We entered the fine arts square. In the center was Showalter Fountain. Several students were gathered around it, sitting on the benches placed near large flowerbeds while others sat on the edge of the fountain itself. The fountain depicted Venus, surrounded by dolphins. The sound of the falling water was cool and inviting. I felt like jumping in.

The IU Auditorium faced west toward the fountain. To the south was the Lily Library and to the north the Fine Arts Building. I didn't actually know the name of all these buildings, but each was clearly marked.

As we left the square, we passed the IU Art Museum. Woodburn Hall, one of the academic buildings was across the street to our left. Our destination was located just past the art museum. We had finally arrived at the HPER.

We entered through one of the doors on the south side and immediately stepped into a large gym. It was an old gym with a wooden floor, but the floor was so polished it shined. A few guys played basketball and a couple of girls ran around a track. To our left were entrances to locker rooms and a station to check out sports equipment.

We walked across the edge of the gym and then up a short incline. We found ourselves in a long wide hallway. Another hallway soon branched off to the right with stairs leading down to a men's locker room. We walked on past vending machines and entered an area with a group of tables and chairs. Across was another entrance to the building and behind was a wall of windows. We stepped up to the windows and looked in. Below was a large pool.

"So that's where the pool is," Haakon said.

"One of them anyway. There's an outdoor pool and another in the main gym. I think there are others too."

"I thought this was the main gym."

"No, this is the old gym. The main one is the SRSC, the Student Recreational Sports Center. I haven't been inside yet, but it's big."

We continued down the hallway, but soon came to classrooms. I knew there was a weight room somewhere in the HPER, but I'd probably use one of the weight rooms in the SRSC instead.

We backtracked and walked out the main entrance. We stood upon the terrace for a few moments and looked out over tennis courts in front of us and a large athletics field to our right.

"This place is enormous," Haakon said.

"Very true. There are large parts of campus I haven't entered yet."

"Is it always so hot here?"

"It's often this hot in the summer this far south in Indiana. The temperature can get over 100. It's a little cooler up north where I live, but not much."

"When I left home it was about 62. The hottest it usually gets in August is maybe 75."

"I don't know if I could stand that. If that's as warm as it gets in August it must be very cold in the winter."

"Yes, and our winter lasts a very long time. I like the warmth here, although today there is too much of it for me."

"I'll take you somewhere cooler or at least out of the sun," I said beginning to walk south toward the IMU. "Do you play any sports?"

"In the summer I like rowing and football. In the winter I skate a lot."

"Will you be on any of the IU teams?"

"No. Part of my agreement with my parents is that I focus on my studies so I won't be on a team, but I will play when I have the chance as I did today."

"Today was a blast. I love football. I played in high school."

"Are you on the IU team?"

"No, but I'm on the IU wrestling team."

"You look like a wrestler. You have a lot of muscles."

I smiled. "I wrestled and played football in high school. I also do gymnastics and have trained in self-defense and sword fighting."

"Wow. Now I feel lazy."

"You aren't. It's just that I'm a very physical sort of guy."

Haakon raised a blond eyebrow. "Oh really?"

"Yes," I said, gazing back at him. I wanted to kiss him, but I thought it too soon. I didn't want this to be only a hookup. I figured we could at least be friends and maybe more, although I wasn't looking for much more than friends. Then again... but there was no reason to think about it now.

"Don't get me wrong. I have other interests. I love movies. The whole film business fascinates me."

"Maybe you should be an actor."

"No, I don't have the talent for that, but I'm leaning toward being a stunt man, stunt coordination or trainer."

"That sounds much more exciting than being a translator but I love languages."

"If you love it, then it will be exciting for you," I said.

"I do get ridiculously excited about speaking other languages."

"See? I was right."

I led Haakon around the IMU. We stopped for a moment to gaze at Dunn Cemetery because it was such an unusual site on a college campus. Marshall had told me the campus grew around it and that it wasn't actually part of IU, which explained the chapel.

We continued on until we reached the old part of campus, which I knew fairly well because I had explored it when I visited in high school. Soon, we were walking in the shade of Dunn's Woods.

"Oh, this is much cooler. I like it. I did not expect to find a forest on campus."

"I was surprised too on my first visit."

"This would be a good place to read or study."

"There's something I want to show you then," I said.

I led Haakon off onto another of the brick paths that ran through the woods and headed for the northeastern edge. Before long, we emerged from the edge of the woods. Before us stood the small limestone pavilion known as the Rose Well House.

"My football coach told me this is his favorite place on campus. When he went to school here, he often came here to study or read."

"Oh, I love this. I think I will do the same."

We sat down on the benches that lined the interior.

"I've been told IU has a lot of little hidden places like this, not that this one is hidden. Maybe I should say unexpected."

34

"I enjoy exploring with you. You are a great tour guide."

"Well, I've shown you most of what I know, except for the IMU. Much of the rest is as new to me as it is to you. Are you hungry?"

"Yes."

"Good because I am. Let's go get something to eat."

"As long as it is not too expensive. I have to be careful with my money."

"Me too. There is a Burger King in The Commons. Want to go there? Oh wait, do you know what a Burger King is?"

"Yes, we have them in Norway, but there everything is made of fish."

"Really?"

Haakon began laughing. "No. I am putting you on."

"I feel like an idiot for believing you. I'll get you back for that sometime."

"I will beware. I love Burger King."

"Let's go then."

We stood and walked toward the IMU.

"So this building is the student union?" Haakon asked.

"Yes, and it's huge. It actually has a hotel inside if you can believe it."

Haakon eyed me.

"Are you trying to get me back already?"

"No. I swear there is a hotel inside. I stayed there for a night. There is lots of stuff inside. Come on, I'll show you."

We passed through one of the south entrances, turned right and walked down a wide hallway. "There is the Starbucks," I said, pointing to the left as we continued on. Moments later we entered a large room with lots of comfortable chairs and sofas. "This is the South Lounge. I'm told it gets pretty crowded."

"I like the fireplace."

"Yeah, there is always a fire burning even on hot days like this. It would be a great place to sit in winter."

We exited the South Lounge and walked down another hallway.

"Beyond those doors is the Tudor Room. It has a great buffet. I ate there when we visited a few years ago and my uncle took me there for lunch today. You have to try it."

We continued on. The hallway curved sharply to the right.

"The main bookstore is there," I said, pointing to the right. "It's located on two levels."

When we reached the stairs, I took the flight going down.

"That is Sugar & Spice. It has great cupcakes and huge Cokes."

"I think you do know everything about IU!" Haakon grinned.

"No, but I explored the IMU a lot when I stayed in the hotel you don't believe exists," I said. We followed the hallway around Sugar & Spice and then on. "This is The Commons. There are two parts. The first is actually called The Food Court, but we want the actual Commons because it includes... Burger King."

The Burger King stood before us. We joined the small line.

"Wow, I can't believe there is a Burger King right here and I think I spotted a Pizza Hut in the first section."

"Yes, and Charleston Market, a salad place, and a sushi place. Downstairs is the Dunn Meadow Café and around the corner is the Baja Fresh Mexican Grill. There are places to eat in several of the dorms and in other buildings too."

"You're a great tour guide."

"I'm not as knowledgeable as I sound. I haven't been to most of the restaurants and I don't know exactly where they are."

We worked our way to the front of the line. We both ordered Whoppers, fries, and a Coke. Less than two minutes later we walked toward a table along the side of the narrow dining area with our trays.

"Mmm, I have a weakness for fast food. I don't get much of it back home. The closest fast food restaurant is several miles away," Haakon said.

"It's the same in Verona. We have a great burger place called Ofarim's, but the closest McDonald's is in Argos ten miles away and the closest Burger King is about fourteen miles away. I love being able to walk to so many restaurants, although this is the first time I have done so. I haven't even finished unpacking yet. I couldn't stand staying in my tiny dorm room. I had to get out and explore."

"Yeah, me too, except I quickly got lost and ended up by the field where we played football. I am glad I did because I met you."

"I'm glad we met. I don't know anyone here yet. I don't even have a roommate," I said.

"I have one, but he does not speak much English and no Norwegian and is always staring at his phone."

"A lot of people become obsessed with their smart phones. I suppose I do at times, but not too often. Where is your roommate from?"

"China. He seems nice enough, but I don't think we're going to be friends. He doesn't seem interested in spending time with me. Perhaps that is a good thing since we live together. We will probably get tired of each other sharing such a small space."

"Yeah. It might work out for the best if you're friendly, but not actually friends who hang out. You can hang out with me and I'm sure you'll meet lots of others."

"Yes, and even without knowing anyone there are guys to hang out with. I stopped to watch the boys on the field play football and they invited me to join. Everyone is very friendly here."

"Yes, Bloomington and IU have a reputation for that."

We carried on a conversation as we ate. I could feel a friendship developing between us. I did not want to screw it up by turning this into a hookup. As much as I wanted to get it on with him, I knew that if it happened we would be much less likely to become friends. If we hooked up I might not even see him again and I had a feeling we could have a lot of fun without getting naked. There was also the possibility of becoming friends with benefits later too.

"I'm actually eager for classes to begin. Does that sound weird?" Haakon asked.

"No. I'm eager myself. Everyone tells me college is much different and better than high school. But, I'll admit, I'm more eager for wrestling practices to begin."

"You must be very good to make a university team."

"I was one of the best wrestlers at my high school. Actually, I was the best, but the competition here will be much tougher. I'm looking forward to that. I love a challenge."

"I'm rather competitive myself. I'm too competitive at times."

I laughed. "Me too, but I'm mostly competitive with myself. The one guy I truly want to outperform is me. I like to pit myself against guys who can beat me because it makes me that much better."

"I like that philosophy, although I must admit I'm more focused on beating whomever I am completing against. Sometimes, I get extremely angry when I lose. I have to be careful or I can be a little childish." Haakon grinned.

"Losing can be hard, especially when there is a lot at stake. I've seen wrestlers cry when they lose matches during sectional or regional competitions."

"Did you ever cry when you lost one of those?"

"No, but I never lost." It was my turn to grin.

We continued talking as our Whoppers and fries disappeared. The Commons wasn't too crowded. I knew it would be once school started, but for now we could easily sit and talk.

"Can I have your number? I'd like to hang out again sometime," I asked when we were nearly finished.

"Actually, no. You can't."

"Oh. Okay. I understand. This afternoon has been fun at least," I said, feeling the sting of rejection. I didn't really understand. I thought we were getting on great.

"Oh, you misunderstand. I would like to hang out more, but I can't give you my number because I don't have a phone yet. It is cheaper for me to buy a phone here, but I haven't been able to do so yet. The process is confusing."

"I can help you with that," I said, instantly feeling a hundred percent better.

"Yeah? I'm not sure how different things are here."

"What kind of phone do you want?"

"Cheap! I need one prepaid. Your phones come with contracts here too I imagine?"

"Yes, most do."

"I definitely must have a prepaid phone then. I will return home in December and will not be back."

"Yeah, you definitely don't want a two-year contract. We can probably get a pretty cheap prepaid phone at Target in the mall. We can go there next if you want."

"That would be great and then I will give you my number."

"Sweet. Are you ready to head out?"

"Yes," Haakon said, stuffing the last two of his fries in his mouth.

We dumped our trash and put away our trays.

"There is one thing I want to show you here in the IMU before we go. It won't take long," I said, walking back the way we had come.

We walked down the hallway past Sugar & Spice once more and then past the escalator and stairways. We continued on until we came to another lounge on our left. I led Haakon through the lounge and down the wide stairs.

"This is the lobby of The Biddle Hotel. See, I was not putting you on. It does exist."

Someone was checking in even as I spoke. They stood at the front desk with their luggage.

"Okay, I believe you now."

"Let's go get your phone."

We walked out the revolving doors and then to 7th Street. It was a short walk to the nearest bus stop near the corner of 7th and Woodlawn. The campus buses did not go to College Mall, but we only had to wait a few minutes before a city bus came along.

"All this is IU," I said indicating both sides of the street as the bus moved up Woodlawn Avenue. "Everything here is too," I said as the bus turned onto 10th Street.

"It seems almost too big."

"Up that way are more dorms, the outdoor pool, Assembly Hall and the football stadium," I said, pointing up Fee Lane. "To the left is the Kelly School of Business and on the right is the Wells Library."

"Are you sure this is your first year?"

"Yes. I was so excited about coming I spent a lot of time browsing the university website and looking things up online. I have been here once before so that helps too. My dorm is down that way," I said as we passed Sunrise Drive.

We didn't leave IU behind until we reached the Bypass where the bus turned right. It was a quick trip from there to the bus stop near College Mall.

We got off the bus, then waited for the light to change so we could walk across College Mall Road.

"There are places to eat everywhere here," Haakon said, noting the Fazoli's, Applebee's, and Casa Brava, which were all in view.

"Yeah, this is the east side. I don't know it very well, but this is the main business area of Bloomington I think. There is also stuff on the west side, but I'm not sure what. Downtown has restaurants too and there are a bunch just beyond the west side of the campus.

We walked across the parking lot and went in the entrance near Sears.

"Wow. I have never been in an American shopping mall before."

Haakon was interested in everything as we walked slowly through the mall. I imagined that many, if not most of the stores were new to him. I noted an Abercrombie & Fitch and an Old Navy store among others. After we turned to the left, I spotted an Aeropostale, which was my favorite clothing store. I resisted the urge to go in. The last thing I needed was to spend money on clothes. I had more than enough already.

Before long we reached the mall entrance to Target, which was to the left. There were more stores further up the mall, including Hollister, American Eagle, and Macy's, but exploring that section could wait for another time. We were on a mission.

I entered Target for the second time that day. We turned left toward electronics and began to browse phones.

"Do you want a smartphone or more basic?" I asked

"I want a smartphone if we can find one that doesn't cost too much."

The selection was limited so it didn't take long to consider the options.

"I think this one would be best. It's a little small, but it's much cheaper than the others and it works with Net10. Let's check out the data plans."

I grabbed a brochure and read.

"Oh, this is good. It has unlimited calls and texting. It also has unlimited data, although it runs at a much slower speed after the first 2 gigabytes. You can use the campus Wi-Fi so that won't be a problem. I recommend this phone with Net10. The plan will cost $30 a month and it's prepaid with no contract."

"That's one then," Haakon said.

"Are you sure? You're the one who will be using it and paying for it."

"I'm sure. You obviously know what you're doing. At home I'm on a plan with my parents so I don't know anything about plans."

"This one should be great. It's the one I would get if my uncle wasn't paying for my phone. Need anything else while we're here?"

"There are some things I'd like to get."

"Let's do it. Grab a cart."

I smiled as Haakon bought some of the same things I had earlier, including Pop-Tarts. He was from Norway, but we weren't that different. We wandered through the store as Haakon picked up supplies for the coming days.

"Oh! I need some of those!" I said, when Haakon stopped to buy hangers. "I totally spaced on hangers when I was here with Skye earlier."

We spent about a half hour in Target and then checked out. It was a good thing I only needed hangers, because Haakon had bought enough it would take both of us to carry it all.

"We should come and explore the mall more sometime," I said as we walked back the way we'd come.

"I'd like that. I guess we could have before we went into Target, but my mind was on a phone."

"We don't have to do everything at once. I should get back anyway. I have plenty that I need to do in my room."

"Me too."

We walked back to the bus stop. This time, we got on one heading downtown because it would go right past Forest Quad. It was only a few blocks and we could have easily walked there it if wasn't for all the shopping bags.

"I'll help you carry these up to your room," I said as we got off the bus.

"Thanks. I didn't realize I was buying so much."

"You should have seen all the stuff I bought in Target earlier today. I'm amazed it fit into my dorm room."

We entered the lobby of Forest Quad. Haakon pulled out his card and swiped it so we could use the elevator. We rode up several floors before getting out. I followed Haakon to his room. The door was open and his roommate, a slim Asian boy sat at his desk. He was so engrossed in his IPad he didn't even look up.

"See what I mean?"

I sat with Haakon on his bed as he dug out his phone. Luckily, I had a pocketknife or I don't think we could have gotten it out of the plastic clamshell. Once we did, I sat and waited while Haakon set up his phone and his account.

"There," he said after a few minutes. "I can now give you my number."

"Shoot."

I punched it into my phone, then sent him a text.

"Now you have mine as well."

I once again wanted to kiss Haakon, but I didn't want to rush into anything. Our friendship seemed to be developing nicely as it was, and I had hopes for the future.

"I should get back to my dorm. If I don't finish unpacking I won't be able to find anything," I said.

"Same here," Haakon said, indicating his mostly full suitcases.

"Let's do something again soon."

"Definitely," Haakon said.

I left his room and walked down the hallway to the elevator. I rode down to the lobby and then walked outside.

I returned to Hershey by the same route I'd used earlier in the afternoon. I liked Haakon a lot, a little more than I wanted if that makes any sense. I did not want to get involved in a serious relationship, especially at the very beginning of my freshman year. Then again, how serious could a relationship be with a boy who was leaving the country in a few months and would likely never return? I was concerned about nothing. I could relax because a serious relationship wasn't possible with Haakon. We could likely become good friends, hopefully friends with benefits, but nothing more.

It was nearly 9 p.m. when I walked into my room. Clothes were strewn on my bed and bags from Target and Kroger were everywhere. It looked a bit as if a mall had exploded. Before beginning to put things away and organize, I set up my MacBook, signed into the Wi-Fi and played an episode of *Cheers* on Netflix. Skye had convinced me to watch it a few weeks before. I was not enthusiastic at first, but it made me laugh so hard I fell off the couch. I now watched it whenever I got the chance. I especially liked Cliff and Norm.

I began with my clothes. I pulled out the hangers I'd purchased on my Target run with Haakon and began to hang up my shirts, jeans, and sweat shirts. I moved on to putting away my boxer briefs and socks. I was glad to have quite a bit of storage because my clothing took up more space than I expected.

Next, I turned my attention to the shopping bags strewn about the room. I tackled them bag-by-bag, trying to organize and put things away as I went. I also reorganized as I went because some of my original choices didn't work so well. It was approaching 11 p.m. before I had everything put away and organized. I even ended up moving my bed and desk. I went through five episodes of *Cheers* before I sat down in my desk chair.

I wasn't a sloppy type of guy or a neat freak, but I was going to have to keep my tiny room in order for it to be livable. Even a small mess would look huge in my broom-closet of a dorm room. I was always organized, mainly because I hated it when I couldn't find something. Not being able to find what I was seeking pissed me off almost as much as a Wi-Fi connection that didn't work right. The connection in Hershey was great. It handled Netflix with ease.

I knew I should sleep, but I couldn't yet. I thought about hitting one of the gyms, but they were likely closed at this hour and I wasn't up to a workout anyway. I opted for a nighttime walk around campus.

The night air was quite warm, but not humid. I loved heat, but wasn't a big fan of humidity. I knew I could expect more humidity than we had up north, but the warmer winter temperatures would more than compensate me for sticky weather.

August was one of my favorite months. It was consistently hot. If I had my way it would be August all year 'round. I suppose I would miss fall, snow around Christmas, and the freshness of spring, but I will be willing to give twelve months of August a try.

I walked north up to the SRSC, then west to North Jordan. I turned right and strolled past the frat houses. The houses were impressive, at least from the outside. There were at least a dozen along North Jordan, more down on 3rd Street and a few scattered elsewhere. I hadn't given much thought to fraternities, but frat boys appealed to me. I was sure I'd get my chance to meet some.

I turned left onto 10th Street, walked past the outdoor pool and then down Fee Lane past Briscoe, McNutt, and Foster Dorms. Foster was like Ashton. It wasn't a single dorm, but rather a complex of dorms. Attending a school this large was going to be quite a change from Verona High School.

I walked across the Arboretum and deeper into campus. When I reached the far side of the art museum, I discovered something cool. A large tower projected a changing pattern of lights in every color of the rainbow on the wall of the museum. Several kids were laying on their backs with their legs stretched up the wall watching the lights. I joined them.

"Sick. Isn't it?"

I turned my head to see a handsome boy with dark hair smiling at me.

"Yeah. I didn't know this was here."

"Someone in my dorm told me about it. I'm Orion."

"That's a cool and unusual name. I'm Colin."

"Freshman?"

"Yeah."

"Me too. I'm from Fort Wayne."

"Yeah? I've been there. I love Cebolla's. I'm from a little town called Verona. It's near Plymouth."

"Yeah, Cebolla's is the best Mexican restaurant in Fort Wayne. What are you studying or do you know yet?"

"I haven't picked out a major, but I'm interested in sports fitness. I want to be a trainer and maybe a stunt man in films or even train actors to do stunts."

"You look like you'd be good at anything physical. I bet you do sports."

"Yeah, I wrestled and played football in high school and I'm into gymnastics. I'm on the wrestling team here."

"I wrestled in high school, but I won't be on any teams here. I was good enough for high school, but not good enough for college level."

"I hope I haven't taken on more than I should. I love to work out, swim, do gymnastics and self-defense training. If I didn't have classes I might have time for everything."

"Yeah, I hear the classes get in the way of all the fun. I almost went to a party up in the Villa's tonight, but I don't even know where the Villas are yet."

"Yeah, I'm still finding my way around too. I was out exploring when I found this."

We talked with each other and a few of those near us as we watched the lights for several minutes. College felt different from high school. There weren't any defined groups here as far as I could tell. In high school I was one of the jocks, but I'd never liked the separation between groups. Here, we were just all college kids. It was a definite improvement.

"Ugh. My feet are going to sleep," Orion said squirming around and away from the wall.

I got up too. "I think the back of my head is getting flat," I said, rubbing it.

"Wanna go sit by the fountain?" Orion asked.

"Sure."

We walked the short distance to the fountain and sat on the edge. There were a few others sitting or walking around enjoying the night and the sound of the falling water.

"You have incredible hair. I've always had a thing for boys with blond hair."

I grinned. Orion was hitting on me. There was no doubt about it. I didn't mind. He was hot and I was worked up from spending time with Haakon and seeing so many hot boys on campus.

"Thanks. I sometimes wish I had dark hair. I feel kind of... pale."

"No. You look amazing. You are the hottest guy I've seen here so far and that's saying something."

"So I take it you're gay."

"Yeah."

"I'm bi."

"Cool. Bi boys are the hottest."

Orion gazed at me a moment and leaned in. When I didn't pull back he kissed me and we began to make out right there on the edge of the fountain.

"You're a great kisser too. Some guys are no good at it," he said when our lips parted.

"It's the same with girls. It's really disappointing when I begin to make out with one and she's horrible."

Orion moved in again and we spent the next few minutes making out. Orion also ran his hand up my arms and felt my biceps.

"Damn, you're built. You drive me crazy. Maybe we can go somewhere... darker," he said quietly.

"I have a single room."

"Yeah? Can we go there?"

"Yes."

We stood. It was a good thing it was dark because I was seriously hard. The bulge in my shorts was noticeable even in the light of the street lamps. It would have been obvious if it was daytime.

We walked over to Ashton and entered Hershey Hall. I unlocked my door with my card and we entered.

"You are so lucky to have a single," Orion said.

"I wanted a roommate, but there are advantages, I said, closing the drapes.

I turned to Orion, pulled him to me, and kissed him more deeply than I had sitting on the edge of the fountain. He immediately began running his hands over my chest and feeling my pecs.

"Your body drives me crazy," Orion said.

I kissed him again and then he pulled my shirt over my head.

"Damn! You're gorgeous, Colin."

Orion leaned in and licked my chest. He licked all over my pecs and sucked on my nipples. I was so hard I feared my shorts would rip from the strain.

Orion licked down over my abs and kneeled in front of me. He unfastened my belt and worked my shorts loose. He pulled them and my boxer briefs down and then swallowed me.

I gasped as his lips closed around me. I'd received plenty of head, and it always felt so good I had to fight to maintain control. Well, it was almost always good. Like kissing, not everyone was talented.

Orion moved his head up and down and then pulled my scrotum into his mouth. I moaned. It felt even better than his lips on my penis. Not many guys licked and sucked my balls, and only one girl had ever done it, but it turned me on so much it was a struggle not to bust.

I was so turned on I knew I couldn't hold back a moment longer, so I reached down and pulled Orion up by his shirt. I pulled it over his head and kissed him again deeply. As I did so, I began to stroke him.

I nibbled on his ear lobes and then bit my way down his neck to his shoulders. I licked his chest and sucked on his nipples, making him moan. Orion had a nice body. He wasn't built, but he had some nice muscles. I pushed him back on my bed and pulled down his shorts and boxers. I leaned in and engulfed him.

Orion squirmed and moaned. Before long he began to grunt and groan. He throbbed in my mouth and then busted his nut.

The moment he finished, he sat up and dropped to his knees. He drew me into his mouth and went at it like he was starved for my penis. I didn't try to maintain control. I watched as he swallowed me over and over, then I moaned loudly and filled his mouth.

Orion stood and then we kissed.

"That was freaking hot," he said.

"I agree."

We pulled up our shorts and put on our shirts. We never had taken off our shoes or socks. Orion walked toward the door, stopping to kiss me once more.

"Goodnight," he said.

"Goodnight."

I yawned. It was past one and I felt like I could sleep now. I was mellow and content as I always was after sex. I stripped, climbed into bed, and in a very few minutes fell asleep.

Chapter Two

I woke up late the next morning, which was perfectly fine because classes and wrestling practice didn't begin until Monday. I stumbled down the hallway in a towel and came to life in the shower.

It was after 11 a.m. by the time I was dressed so I ate only a single Pop-Tart for breakfast and then headed out.

I hopped on my bike and rode up to the SRSC. I absolutely had to work out and I was eager to check out the sports center. I found a bike rack when I arrived and locked up my bike. I climbed a long flight of wide steps to the front entrance and entered into a large lobby area. At the other end of the lobby were the glass doors of the rear entrance. I turned left, showed my student ID to the attendant and began to explore. The SRSC was much bigger than the HPER near the center of campus. I found a series of small rooms that each contained a racquetball, squash ball, or volleyball court, then more small rooms with treadmills and other cardio equipment. I soon came to a larger room, more of a small gym really, where an instructor was leading a group cardio workout.

As I continued to explore I discovered a large gymnasium with multiple basketball courts. Far above I could see an indoor running track. Across from the gym, I discovered my main area of interest, a very large room filled with weight equipment. I didn't enter just yet because I wanted to see what was on the next floor.

I climbed the stairs again. Off to the right was the running track that I had viewed from below. I entered a vast room to the left that was filled with exercise bikes, treadmills, and every piece of cardio equipment one could imagine. The room was actually twice the size that I first thought for what I had taken for a large mirror across the room was actually the entrance to another room, just as large and just as filled with equipment.

I climbed on an exercise bike and began to pedal. As I warmed up I looked around. There had to be well over a hundred different pieces of cardio equipment in this area and just as many in the one I'd walked through getting here. I thought the little room I'd passed downstairs was the cardio area of the SRSC. This place was awesome!

I remained on the bike for twenty minutes or so, then climbed off to explore the rest of the top floor. I soon discovered another large and mostly empty room with mirrors along the walls where a yoga class was going on.

I walked back down to the second floor. I noted a large bank of small lockers. There were such banks of lockers on each floor and I'd spotted a sign that indicated the main locker room was in the basement.

I entered the weight room, also much larger than the one downstairs. The equipment was impressive. I recognized many of the same machines we had in the gymnasium at Graymoor Mansion. There were a lot more machines here, at least a hundred, but then the student population at IU was huge.

I felt very much at home on the machines. I worked out daily at home and intended to do so in Bloomington as well. Most of what I loved to do required me to be fit and I just plain loved working out. Marshall said it was a sickness that I caught from Skye. I was going to miss Marshall, but I'd see him on trips home. Unlike Haakon, I didn't live far away.

There were quite a few other students in the weight room, but I was willing to bet the SRSC would be far more crowded once the semester got going. I hoped it wouldn't become so crowded that I had to wait for machines.

It took me over two hours to complete my workout, but I was in no hurry. I felt energized as I left the weight room. I didn't depart from the SRSC quite yet. I wanted to get a look at the pool.

I walked downstairs and descended still further so that I was one level below the entrances. I soon found a doorway that led into the pool area. Before me was an Olympic size pool. I didn't pay too much attention to the pool for a few moments because the swim teams were practicing. The boys were wearing Speedos that left little to the imagination and the girls wore close-fitting swim-suits that showed off their bodies. My shorts grew a little tighter in the front as I subtly checked out the swimmers. I love the slim smooth bodies of the guys and the girls...mmm.

The scent of chlorine tinted the warm, moist air of the Natatorium. I wasn't quite finished checking out the swimmers, but I began to notice other features, such as the enormous banners depicting famous IU swimmers like Mark Spitz.

Beyond the end of the Olympic size pool was the diving pool. It was much smaller, but far deeper. What I noticed most about the diving pool were the diving platforms, the tallest of which was frighteningly high above.

I passed a whirlpool and then climbed a set of stairs that took me to the balcony level. Here a set of glass doors led me right back into the lobby. The building so was vast I hadn't realized I was so close to the entrance.

On my next trip I'd rent a locker for the semester and bring along my swimsuit and shower supplies. I hoped to spend a lot of time in the SRSC. It would be my home away from home.

I climbed on my bike and rode toward the heart of campus. The one-speed was much harder to pedal than a multi-speed bike and I could feel it working my legs. The bike was giving me a little trouble as I pedaled uphill, but in time I'd grow to handle hills with ease. I liked to push myself physically and this was one more way to do it.

I made my way back to Woodlawn Avenue, crossed 7th Street, and then rode down onto Dunn Meadow where I stopped and placed my bike in a rack by the IMU. I noticed a lot of activity on the north side of 7th Street and also up by the HPER. Something was going on. I locked up my bike and went to investigate.

I crossed 7th Street and headed toward a booth decorated with a piñata and colorful streamers that stood in front of one of the homes that had been converted into a university building. A large sign in front of the building read La Casa Latino Cultural Center. Hispanic music played and a wonderful scent filled the air. As I drew closer I discovered the source. The center was giving away free sopapillas. I was hungry so I eagerly accepted a small paper bowl of the triangular shaped pastries sprinkled with powdered sugar and drizzled with honey. I browsed some of the displays while I was there then walked toward the next booth.

Even before I read the sign I knew the next house was the GLBT Center. A rainbow flag hung out front and streamers in a rainbow of colors decorated the booth. I had spotted the center during visit in my high school years, but hadn't gone inside.

I picked up some literature on glbt campus groups and then walked up onto the porch where free books were lined up on the railings. I went inside to see what the center had to offer.

There was a lobby area off to the left and offices to the right as I walked down the hallway. Further on I discovered a library in a large room on the left. I entered and gazed at the books and DVDs lining the shelves that covered the walls. There were fiction and non-fiction titles and all of them were on glbt topics. I doubted I would have much time to read once school started, but if I did any reports or papers on glbt subjects this was the place to come.

"Help yourself to sandwiches and we have chips, soft drinks, and M&M's," said a kind-looking man about the age of Sean's dad.

"I definitely will. Thanks."

"I'm Doug Bader. I'm the director of the center."

"I'm Colin Stoffel. I'm a freshman."

"Welcome to IU. If you want to check items out of the library, all you need is a photo ID to register. We offer free HIV testing once a week and counseling services. It's also a nice place to come, relax and meet people."

"Thanks."

"If you need anything, just ask one of the staff."

Doug moved on to greet other students. I grabbed a small sub sandwich, a bag of chips, and a Diet Coke and browsed titles as I ate. There were some books I wouldn't mind reading if I had the time and some movies I wanted to watch too.

I noticed a couple of boys eyeing me as I looked around. Since they were in the center they were likely gay or at least bi. Another boy was dressed so flamboyantly he almost had to be gay. Either that or he had a thing for neon colors. He wore short shorts and a tight shirt that revealed his slim abs. Every piece of his clothing, including his shoes were in neon colors. His hair was unnaturally blond. I admired his boldness. When he looked at me I smiled and nodded to him. He openly checked me out.

After I finished my sandwich, I grabbed a cup of M&Ms and headed outside. The boy dressed in neon followed me.

"Hey," he said as I stepped off the porch. I turned to greet him.

"Hi."

"I'm Dylan!"

"I'm Colin. Are you a freshman?"

"No. I'm a sophomore at Bloomington North. I'm still in high school."

"I thought you looked a little young, but some guys do. I like your outfit. It's very bold and no one can say it isn't colorful."

"Thanks! Are you checking out all the open houses?"

"Yes. I didn't know this was going on, but I intend to check it all out. It looks like most of it is up by the HPER and art museum."

"Mind if I tag along?"

"That would be cool. I only arrived yesterday. I haven't met too many people yet."

"Great, I came to check things out, but mostly to check out college boys," Dylan said as we began walking up the street toward the HPER.

"It's good place for that. There are thousands of us."

"You are by far the hottest I've seen."

"Thanks. You're very cute and I admire your bold attire."

"Are you gay?"

"Actually, I'm bi."

"Cool. I'm gay, although I probably didn't need to tell you that. With me, it's totally obvious!"

I laughed. I loved Dylan's enthusiasm. If nothing else he was entertaining.

"Well, between your clothes, your hair, and the fact you were in the GLBT Center I figured you were gay, but I wasn't sure. Sometimes the most obviously gay guys aren't."

"No one would guess you're gay... I mean bi. You look like a jock."

"I am a jock. I'm a sports freak and I have other interests."

"I hope one of those is high school boys," Dylan said, batting his eyes in an exaggerated fashion.

"Well, a lot of them are too young for me. Some are even illegal."

"I'm sixteen so I am perfectly legal. Do you hook up a lot?"

I wasn't sure I was comfortable with the direction of our conversation.

"Well... I don't know if I'd say a lot. I hook up... enough."

"There is no such thing as enough. Oh! Can I do a selfie with you?"

"Sure, why not?"

Dylan moved in close beside me, put his arm around me, and snapped a photo of us with the camera on his phone. He ran his hand down my back and slightly grazed my butt as he pulled his arm away. He showed me the photo.

"We look fabulous!"

I smiled. It was impossible not to like this boy.

"You must work out. You have an incredible body. Can I feel your abs?"

"I guess." I raised my shirt and Dylan ran his hand over my abs.

"They're so hard. You have muscular everything. I bet you're hot in bed."

"I work out and I wrestle. I played football in high school too," I said to answer his question and get away from his "hot in bed" comment.

"Oh! That's sooo hot! I love jocks! I know a lot of them at North... intimately."

"How is it at your school? I mean... do guys give you trouble or do you dress more conservatively there?"

"I dress the same everywhere, except at school no one is allowed to wear shirts that show their midriff. No one gives me trouble. The jocks look out for me. We have an arrangement. I do favors for them and they protect me."

I didn't ask about the favors. I was almost certain they were sexual. Dylan was an interesting guy.

I was amused to watch guys stare at Dylan when they first noticed him. A very few wrinkled their noses, but most were merely surprised by Dylan's unnaturally blond hair and neon outfit. Two different girls asked to take his picture. Only one guy was an asshole and he was older than college age. He sneered at Dylan and looked like he was about to say something unkind when I put on my badass expression and stepped toward him. He turned and quickly left.

"Thanks!" Dylan said.

"I don't like people like him and I hate bullies."

"I bet you have no trouble taking care of bullies," Dylan said.

"None at all. My uncle trained me as a fighter."

"I think I'm in love," Dylan said, putting his head on my shoulder for a moment.

I laughed.

"I admire strength," Dylan said.

"I'd say you're strong yourself."

"Me? I'm a wussy."

"No one who dares to go around in tight, bright neon clothes can possibly be called a wussy."

"Too flamboyant?"

"I'd say it fits your personality perfectly and in case there is any doubt that is a compliment."

"I considered wearing my tiara and neon yellow feather boa, but I thought that would be too much." Dylan laughed at my somewhat shocked expression. "I'm kidding. I don't have a boa or a tiara. Boas are too puffy and I think tiaras should be earned."

"So tiaras are like trophies?"

"Yes, you have trophies?"

"I have a few, mainly for wrestling."

"So you're good?"

"Yes."

"Very good?"

I nodded.

"I'd love to see you wrestle."

"Come to a meet at IU and you can."

"Are the other wrestlers hot?"

"I don't know. We haven't started to practice yet, but I imagine most of them will be hot."

"Oh, that almost makes me wish I was a jock, but I'm not that fond of physical exertion or sweating."

"I'm afraid those are required."

"Figures!"

A lot of guys would have been uncomfortable being seen with Dylan, but I was not one of them. I believed everyone should be themselves and Dylan was doing exactly that. I was too, but it didn't take much courage to wear a tee-shirt and running shorts.

College kids handed us flyers as we approached the booths by the HPER. Some were ads with coupons for places like Pizza X and Dagwood's. Others were about upcoming events and clubs on campus.

"There's a horse!" I said, shocked. It was true. A horse stood on the grass on near the HYPER.

Dylan laughed. "Have you never seen a horse before?"

"Yes. I'd ridden horses, but I didn't expect to see one here."

"The equestrian club brings one every year."

"So you've been here for the open houses before?"

"Oh yeah. I come every year. I have been fond of college boys since I was very young."

I grinned. I was not surprised.

My favorite thing about the booths was the free food. Dylan and I picked up bottles of water, slices of pizza, cookies, and popcorn. I had no need to worry about lunch. By the time we finished walking around I was sure I wouldn't be hungry. No wonder there was such a crowd. Free food always attracts college kids.

The area had a carnival-like atmosphere. There was even a climbing wall, dunking booth, and games involving throwing Frisbees as well as a basketball game.

"I want to try the climbing wall. You in?" Dylan asked.

"Sure."

We finished our pizza as we waited in line and set our water and popcorn off to the side when our turn came up to be strapped into harnesses.

"I like this. It's kind of kinky," Dylan said, causing the boy who was adjusting his harness to both blush and laugh.

I began climbing the wall and made steady progress, but it was quite a bit harder than it looked. Dylan surprised me by quickly passing me. He climbed like a monkey! I paused and watched him for a moment before resuming my own climb.

The wall seemed a lot higher while I was climbing it than it did from the ground. I almost felt as if I was scaling an actual cliff. I thought climbing the wall might be fun, but it was more exhilarating than I'd imagined.

I reached the top, then slowly climbed down. Dylan was already on the ground watching me as one of the boys manning the wall took his harness off. I was soon on the ground beside him.

"Where did you learn to climb like that?" I asked as we walked away to explore other areas.

"I occasionally have to run from bullies. I'm fast, but the quickest way to lose them is by scaling tall fences. They usually give up when I go over a fence."

"Does that happen often?"

"No. Like I said, the jocks at school look out for me, but they aren't always around, especially when I'm away from school."

"If I saw someone chasing you, I'd kick his ass," I said.

"And I haven't even done you any favors... yet," Dylan said, wiggling his eyebrows.

"You don't have to buy protection from me."

"I like to do favors for hot guys."

"Isn't it nice to just hang out sometimes?" I asked.

"Yeah, although I prefer sex."

I smiled and shook my head. "Come on, let's check out some more booths."

"Hey, will you do some pull-ups for me?" Dylan asked as we reached a large tree with a low branch that was perfect for pull-ups.

"I suppose."

I jumped up, grabbed and branch, and performed a few quick pull-ups, but then stopped when I saw Dylan stagger.

"Hey. Are you okay?" I asked, jumping down and quickly stepping to his side.

"I almost passed out."

"What's wrong? Too much sun?"

"Too much sexiness. You were so freaking hot doing pull-ups."

I would have thought Dylan was putting me on, but he actually looked as if he might yet pass out. I had to keep from laughing. Did I actually have that much effect on him?

"I'm better now," he said after a few more moments.

"Perhaps we should get out of the sun for a while."

"No. I'm fine and it wasn't the sun, big boy. It was you."

Dylan was fun and while I wasn't usually attracted to flamboyant types, he was quite attractive. I was quite sure that Dylan would do anything I wanted if I took him back to my dorm room. I was slightly tempted, but a part of me would have felt I was using him. I had a feeling a lot of guys did. I don't think he minded, but I didn't want to join that crowd. I felt it would be better for each of us if we didn't have sex. There were other ways to have fun and I was having fun now.

A few minutes later, Dylan talked me into getting in the dunking booth. The temperature was soaring so the thought of being dumped into cool water was inviting. I climbed into the tank and situated myself on the narrow bench.

Dylan did his best to dunk me, but he couldn't hit the target and I doubted his pitches were hard enough even if he had managed.

"Nice try, Dylan!" Dylan stuck out his tongue at me.

Next up was a frat boy wearing a Kappa Sigma shirt. His first pitch was very close, but he missed.

"Is that all you've got? I know toddlers that throw harder than that!" I shouted as he was getting ready to throw again. He actually had to pause because I nearly made him laugh. He missed on his next try. "Come on, you're embarrassing the Kappa Sigs!" His final attempt was so close it actually nicked the edge of the target, but only barely. "So much for the frat boy. Let's get someone up here with a real arm!"

I enjoyed taunting those who tried to dunk me. It made those watching laugh and those throwing baseballs at the small target try even harder. Five kids in a row failed.

Next up was an athletic looking girl who I found quite attractive. She took careful aim, but missed.

"You throw like a girl!" I called out.

She shook her head. "That's it! You are going in!" she said, pointing at me. I laughed as she made her next pitch, but my laugh was cut short as the bench disappeared beneath me and I plunged into the tank of water underneath. It was colder than I expected and I gasped.

I came up with water streaming off me. I climbed out of the tank as those gathered around cheered for the girl. I grinned at her as I climbed down the ladder at the side of the tank. She laughed at me. I was completely drenched.

Dylan joined me as I peeled off my wet shirt and wrung it out. He gawked at my bare torso for a few moments with his mouth hanging out.

"Oh my gawd, how can anyone be that hot?" he asked, causing some of those near us to laugh. "I have to get a photo of you."

Dylan pulled out his phone and quickly snapped pics of me, then he insisted we do another selfie.

"Here's your phone and wallet," he said after he finished his mini-photo session. I had given them to him before I climbed in the tank to avoid ruining them.

We each grabbed another bottle of water and slice of pizza, then walked to the Showalter Fountain and sat on one of the benches facing the fountain. I spread my shirt out to dry on the hot concrete beside the bench.

"I'm glad I met you. This has been a blast," Dylan said.

"Yes, it has. That's something I think I'll like about going to school here. Is isn't difficult to find someone to do something with."

"A lot of guys don't want to hang out with me."

"It's their loss. You're fun."

"Wow, you think I'm fun and we haven't even been naked together."

"There are lots of ways to have fun."

"Yes, but those that involve getting naked are the best."

"Sometimes, but many of those relationships don't last long. I hooked up with a boy last night and I may never see him again."

"Oh! Was he hot?"

"Yes, but that's not the point. I met another boy yesterday. We didn't hook up, but we exchanged numbers and I think we'll become friends."

"With benefits?"

"Maybe. Hopefully, but even without benefits I like spending time with him."

"Is this a rejection?"

"No, but I think we might be better off not hooking up."

"You're killing me! Do you know how super incredibly fantastically unbelievably hot you are?"

"I'm aware that I'm attractive, but plenty of guys are."

"No guy can possibly be as hot as you."

I tried not to laugh, but I couldn't help it. Dylan was quite serious. "I'm not that hot, Dylan."

"Oh, but you are. I will do anything you want. *Anything.*"

"Hand me your phone." Dylan did so. I messed with it a few moments and then handed it back. "There, you have my number. I don't want to hook up with you, but I would like to hang out sometime. I will warn you that, when school starts, I will be extremely busy. It might even be a couple of weeks before I have any time at all, but I promise we can hang out again if you want."

Dylan sighed. "Well, I'll take what I can get, but my offer remains."

"I will keep that in mind."

"At least I get to look at you. You're beautiful."

I blushed slightly. "You are very attractive too, Dylan."

"Yes, I am! I'm fabulous, but I'm not a Greek god."

"I'm not either, at least I don't remember reading about me in history class and I don't think there is a single temple dedicated to me."

"There should be!"

"You're crazy, Dylan."

"Hi."

I looked up. A boy wearing a Phi Delta Theta tee-shirt gazed down at me.

"Hey."

"We're having a rush party next week. I'd like you to come," he said, handing me a small flyer.

"Okay, I might. Thanks."

"Please do. You look like Phi Delt material. We're one of the highest ranked fraternities on campus. We also throw great parties."

I nodded. The boy walked away.

"I notice he didn't invite *me*," Dylan said.

"You are in high school."

"He doesn't know that."

"I'm sure he has a good idea. You look too young to be in college."

"I think he was intimidated by my fabulousness."

"You know. I think you might be right."

Dylan and I spent another hour at the open house, then he walked me back to the IMU where I'd left my bike.

"Are you sure you don't want me to come back to your dorm room?" Dylan asked as we stood by the bike rack.

"I'm sure. I think we should just be friends."

"Can I at least get a kiss?"

"Okay," I said grinning.

I had barely given Dylan my answer when he pulled my head down to him and kissed me deeply. His tongue was in my mouth so fast I didn't have time to prepare myself. Dylan ran his hands over my chest and groped my pecs as he kissed me. I managed to pull away after several moments, but it wasn't easy. He left me speechless.

"I'm good at other things too, *very* good. Remember that."

"Text me sometime," I said, unlocking my bike.

"You can count on it."

I climbed on my bike.

"Later, Dylan."

"As soon as possible," he called out as I pedaled away.

I wanted to get in a good ride while I had the time, so I rode my bike down the path by Dunn Meadow and then turned north on Indiana Avenue. I decided to ride around the main part of the university which was bordered by Indiana Avenue, 6th, Woodlawn, 10th, Jordan, and 3rd back to Indiana. Quite a bit of IU was outside that area, but within it were most of the classrooms and main public buildings.

The sun was hot on my bare chest and back and I was already beginning to sweat. I couldn't have asked for better weather. I was still growing accustomed to my new one-speed, but I was already learning to adjust. One very cool thing about Bloomington is that there are a lot of bike lanes, even on major streets. I could ride and not be quite as concerned with traffic as usual, although I was still careful.

There was a ton of activity around campus. There were cars everywhere, so many in places that I made better progress than they did.　There were also college kids all over the place.　A few were still moving into dorms, but most were out walking, running, and playing around on the grass.　I passed several fraternity houses on 3rd Street.　Smoke wafted from grills by a couple of them and frat boys partied.　I thought about the invitation I'd received. I wasn't much interested in joining a frat. There was no way I'd have the time, but I might attend the party just to see what it was like.

In a few minutes I had completed the loop.　I continued on, but this time headed straight up 6th Street, past all the booths, then around the Showalter Fountain, and along the left side of the IU Auditorium.　This was the shortcut back to Hershey.

I was tired when I reached my room and the cool air felt wonderful. I hit the showers because I was extremely sweaty. I'd had a great day so far and it wasn't over yet.

Chapter Three

I slipped my backpack over my shoulder and headed out to my bike. My free time was quickly slipping away and I needed to make a Target run. I could have taken the bus, but I figured traveling by bike would be faster and I wanted to get in some riding time.

Target and the College Mall weren't all that far from my dorm. A quick ride down to 3rd and then another eight blocks east and I'd be there.

It was another fine and hot August day. Classes started tomorrow. The few days I'd already been in Bloomington were a whirlwind of activity. I'd caught a showing of *The Social Network* in The Whittenberger Auditorium with Dylan, had lunch with Haakon at Dagwood's, worked out, swam, and scouted out the location of all my classes and that was only the beginning!

I parked my bike in a bike rack near Target and ran the cable through the bike frame and backpack and locked them up. A trip to Target was rare for me when I lived in Verona, but this was my 3rd trip in less than a week.

I walked inside, picked up a basket, and headed straight to the area where the soap and shampoo were located. I bought a pack of Irish Spring soap, Herbal Essence rosemary & herb shampoo and matching conditioner, and a stick of Right Guard sport gel antiperspirant to keep in my locker at the SRSC. I didn't need to worry about towels because I could pay a small extra free and use those provided by the SRSC.

I had everything else I needed, but I wandered over to the grocery area and browsed. I didn't want much junk food in my room because I tried to stay away from it for the most part. I purchased some walnuts and dried pineapple. I already had a large supply of Pop-Tarts. I didn't need much food in my room because I intended to mostly eat on campus.

I checked out and carried my two bags out to my bike. I stuffed the bags in my backpack and zipped it up. I climbed on my bike and rode around the north side of the mall to Fazoli's. I had timed my trip so that I could have a late lunch while I was on the east side.

I locked my bike to a tree and took my backpack in with me. I scanned the menus and then ordered three cheese tortellini Alfredo and a drink. I took my number and then filled my cup with ice and diet Coke and took a seat at a booth that gave me a view of the Steak 'n Shake across College Mall Road.

My order arrived in no time at all. I loved Fazoli's breadsticks, but wasn't able to get them often when living in Verona. The closest Fazoli's was about an hour away in South Bend. Here, it was a short bike or bus ride from my dorm. I planned to come here often, but then I would probably eat on campus most of the time. That is what IU needed; a Fazoli's in the IMU!

The food was delicious and the breadsticks better. I took some more when a Fazoli's guy came around with the basket. I ate enough breadsticks that I knew I couldn't finish my pasta, so when I refilled my drink I asked for a to-go box and a bag.

When I finished eating, I packed up my leftovers, which included a couple of breadsticks and then walked back out to my bike. I tied the bag around one of the handlebars and took off. I cut through Eastland Plaza to the west of the mall instead of riding up busy 3rd Street. I passed The China Buffet, another restaurant I intended to visit when I could. Like Fazoli's, it was inexpensive and good. I intended to watch my money closely. Skye paid my tuition and all my school related bills and he gave me an allowance for food and other necessities on top of my meal plan at IU. I was not going to ask for more if I used up my allowance. I had money saved up and didn't want to dip into that unless it was a must. When I was twenty-one I would have quite a bit of money with the inheritance from Mom and my step dad, the funds from the insurance, the sale of the house and everything else still sitting in a trust fund.

I stopped in at my dorm to put my leftovers in the mini-fridge, then headed for the SRSC. I rented a locker and paid the towel fee for the semester. One nice thing about the SRSC was that I could check out any sports equipment I wanted for free. I thought I might give racquetball or squash a try when I had some spare time in the future.

I descended the steps all the way to the bottom level and walked to the locker room. I found my locker, put away my shower supplies, and changed into loose running shorts and a tank top.

I climbed the stairs up to the level that held the weight room and entered to begin an intense workout. At home, I often did a split-routine, hitting specific muscle groups one day and another group the next. Today, I did it all because tomorrow I would have no time for the SRSC. Between classes, assignments, and wrestling practice I would be swamped.

The weight room was more crowded than it had been before. More freshmen had undoubtedly discovered the SRSC and others who had focused on all the other campus activities now turned their attention to the gym. I didn't mind. There were plenty of machines and I was performing such a variety of exercises that if the machines I wanted were occupied I could vary my usual order and not waste any time standing around.

While I didn't fail to notice the sexy college boys around me, I was in the weight room to work out. I was all business while I was lifting. Concentration was crucial. I wasn't even aware of those around me while I was actually performing an exercise. Only between sets did I take notice.

A boy caught my attention as I stepped away from the lat station. I didn't notice him because he was hot. He wasn't. He was very average and even a little pudgy. I noticed him because he was straining his guts out on a bench press machine near me.

"Hey, you're going to hurt yourself," I said.

He released the grips and sat up quickly, looking slightly alarmed.

"You are trying to use way too much weight. You obviously can't handle that much. You'll injure yourself."

"I have to get in shape. I'm tired of being flabby and weak."

"Well that's not the way to do it." The boy blushed. "Listen, it's great that you want to get into shape, but you're trying to do too much too fast. You won't last a week if you keep it up. Start with a weight you can handle, one that doesn't feel light, but also isn't too heavy for you. When you get used to it, add a little more weight. When you get used to that, add more. Over time, you'll get stronger."

"I saw you doing bench presses earlier. You were using over 200 pounds."

"Yes, but I didn't begin with that. I didn't even begin with weights. I started with pushups. I got to where I am now by taking very small steps. You can't rush it."

"How long have you been working out?"

"Hmm, probably since I was twelve and I did pushups and ab crunches starting when I was about eight."

"Wow."

"It takes time. Working out should be enjoyable. You're turning it into an unpleasant ordeal. Don't push yourself so hard."

"Okay, thanks."

I moved on. I kept an eye on the boy as I moved from machine to machine. He seemed to be heeding my advice. Most young guys had an interest in working out, but most didn't have a clue about how to do it properly. I was truly lucky I had Skye to guide me from the time I was young. I had never thought of it that way, but I'd had my own personal trainer my entire life.

I was in the weight room for nearly three hours. As I began to leave a slim guy with curly brown hair approached me.

"Hey, I'm Travis. I'm with Zeta Beta Tau. Are you a freshman?"

"I'm Colin and yes."

"Are you on any teams?"

"I'm a wrestler."

"Awesome. We're having a rush party on Wednesday night we'll also have a booth at the Greek fair on Tuesday in Dunn Meadow. You should check us out. We're looking to add more athletes to our fraternity. You're exactly the kind of guy were looking to add to the brotherhood."

"Okay. Thanks," I said, taking the small flyer Travis handed me.

I left the weight room and headed for the locker room. That made two invitations I'd received to frat parties. I thought potential pledges applied to frats. I didn't know that frats pursued pledges. I wasn't much interested. If I had more time, I might have given joining a fraternity some thought, but I doubted I'd have time to breathe once school started.

I stripped in the locker room, stopped and picked up a towel and washcloth and took a quick shower. Despite the fact that the SRSC was busy, the showers were nearly empty. The hot water was relaxing after my intense workout and acted like a massage for my tired muscles. I felt much better just getting the sweat off me. I much preferred to smell like Irish Spring instead of sweat.

I rinsed off and then retrieved my towel. I dried off and then walked back into the locker room. As I changed into my swimsuit I spotted a boy checking me out. I pretended not to notice and even turned away from him as I put on my swimsuit so he could check out my ass. I headed for the pool pretending to be oblivious. I never minded if guys checked me out. In fact, I liked it. I guess I'm an extrovert or perhaps even an exhibitionist.

The warm moist air and the scent of chorine reminded me of the Natatorium in Graymoor Mansion as I entered the SRSC Natatorium. Whoever was in charge had wisely divided the pool into lanes that cut across the width instead of the length of the pool, making for shorter, but a far greater number of lanes. Most of the lanes were taken, but there were a few left. I lowered myself into one of the free lanes and then began to swim laps. I wasn't an expert swimmer, but I loved to swim. It was a good way to wind down after a workout and I loved the clear, blue-tinted water.

I kept doing laps until I grew too tired, then climbed out and headed back to the locker room. I took yet another shower to wash off the chorine, but I could still faintly catch its scent as I put on antiperspirant at my locker. I liked it. I thought of it as cologne.

Dressed once again, I headed out to enjoy my last day of freedom at IU. I wanted to make the most of every moment.

***

My eyes popped open when my alarm went off on Monday morning. I retrieved my shower caddy, wrapped a towel around my waist, and headed down the hall to the bathroom. The shower helped wake me up and I was eager for the day to begin by the time I returned to my tiny room. I dressed, then toasted two Pop-Tarts for breakfast while I made a mug of tea in the microwave.

I was accustomed to eating most of my meals in the large dining room in the Graymoor Mansion Bed & Breakfast where I lived with Skye, so eating alone in my room was a bit lonely, but I knew I would be surrounded by others most of the day.

After breakfast, I grabbed my backpack, which was already loaded with the few books I'd need before I returned, and then walked out to my bike.

I had a short but nice ride over to Ballantine where my first class met. Campus was crowded with students heading to classes and various destinations.

I parked my bike in one of the many bike racks near Ballantine. There must have been fifty bikes there already. I went inside and walked straight to the large lecture hall for my English Composition class. I had scouted out the exact location of all my classes so I wouldn't get lost. I was glad I did because a few of them weren't so easy to find.

College was completely different from high school. For one thing, my first class today didn't start until 9:30, which was a vast improvement. For another, this class at least was far larger. There had to be nearly two hundred students in the hall and more were entering. Other differences soon made themselves apparent. Instead of our professor, a teaching assistant, or T.A. entered, introduced himself, and handed out a syllabus. When our professor arrived, he began with a summary of what we'd cover during the semester and covered the requirements, which included reports, essays, and a research paper.

My next class was in Woodburn Hall, which wasn't that far so I walked. I planned to hit the IMU for lunch after class so it was easier to leave my bike by Ballantine.

One thing I missed about high school was having a locker, but then some of my classes were in far distant buildings so I suppose a locker would have been of limited use. My second class was much like the first and my workload increased. A few girls eyed me as well as the T.A. and another student.

It was a little early for lunch when class ended, but I walked toward the IMU anyway because I knew there might be quite a line. I considered Burger King, but then decided that I was more in the mood for Pizza. There was a Pizza Hut in the food court. That was another difference from high school.

I was right. There were already lines in the food court and a lot of tables were taken. The wait wasn't too bad. I picked up one of the individual pizzas available at Pizza Hut and then walked over to the fountain and got myself a huge Diet Coke. I waited in line again to pay and then made my way to one of the hundred or more small two-person tables that were closely squeezed together. There were even more tables in The Commons just beyond the wall and I was willing to bet all would soon be filled.

My pepperoni pizza was so much better than what passed for pizza at Verona High School that there was no comparison. I felt sorry for my former classmates who were still stuck back in culinary hell.

"Mind if I sit here?"

I looked up. An athletic guy wearing a Sigma Alpha Mu tee shirt gazed down at me.

"Have a seat," I said.

"I'm Bryce."

"I'm Colin."

"It's nice to meet you. I'm with Sigma Alpha Mu. Have you thought of pledging a fraternity?"

"Not really, although I have been approached by a couple. Is that usual?"

"Figures. No, it isn't. Most potential pledges come to the Greek fair or show up at the rush parties. I'm not surprised other frats are after you. The moment I spotted you I knew you'd be great Sigma material."

"I doubt I'll have time for a frat. I'm on the wrestling team and I have a serious training program of my own I intend to maintain."

"Pledging takes some time, but we work around those with commitments to a sports team. After you're in, fraternity functions don't take up a lot of time and most are optional. There are a lot of advantages to joining a frat."

Bryce mentioned quite a few as we sat and ate. He made some good points, but I wasn't sold.

"We have our rush coming up on Thursday. Please stop by. At the very least it's a great time and you'll meet a lot of the brothers."

"Okay, I might check it out, although I expect this week to be crazy."

"Great. Keep us in mind. So how do you like IU so far?"

"I love it, except I have a single room and I would have preferred a roommate."

"I don't hear that often. You can always switch next semester and if you join a frat you can have a roommate." Bryce grinned. "Okay, I'll stop with the sales pitch, but I have to try. You'd be a great addition to Sigma."

"For all you know I could be stupid. I could bring your G.P.A. down all by myself."

"No one gets into IU by being stupid and I'm a good judge of character. Last year, I recruited a diver who will likely be in the Olympics and a guy who is close to being a genius. When I see a prime candidate, I move in. I wouldn't want you to get stuck in one of those other inferior fraternities." Bryce laughed. I liked his sense of humor.

"If I told you I'm bisexual would you still be interested in me for Sigma?"

"Yes. Are you?"

"Yes, I am."

"It's cool. I think most guys are bi, especially if they've been drinking. One of our brothers has a boyfriend who is in one of those other inferior fraternities and everyone is fine with it."

"That is a point in your favor."

"Great. We would really like to have you. Sorry, I said I'd stop."

I laughed. "I won't hold it against you."

"So, you're a wrestler? You look like you'd be good at it. I wouldn't want to face you on the mat."

"That's what I hope my opponents think. I can't wait to get started here. I love a challenge."

Bryce and I talked while we ate. True to his word; he didn't mention Sigma again, not even when we parted. I could tell he was dedicated to his frat. I liked the idea of a fraternity, but I didn't think it was for me, at least not this school year.

My afternoon was busy. I had two classes after lunch, then I hit the library to pick up a couple of books I needed for assignments. As soon as I made it back to my dorm room, it was time to leave again for wrestling practice. I walked to the nearest bus stop and caught a campus bus.

A lot of guys back at VHS would have envied me if they knew where I was headed. The wrestling team practiced in Assembly Hall, the home of Indiana University Basketball. I actually wasn't a big basketball fan myself. My interests focused more on football, wrestling, and baseball, although I admired the skill of basketball players. Perhaps my lack of interest in basketball had something to do with my lack of skill. I was an okay basketball player, but not great. At 6'2", I was as tall as Skye now, but that wasn't tall for a basketball player. There is no way I could have made the IU team. Anyway, the basketball crazed boys back at my old high school would have gone nuts if they knew I would be using the same locker room as their beloved Hoosier players.

Assembly Hall was impressive. Soaring windows were the main feature of the front façade and when I entered, the lobby area was filled with light. Sports memorabilia and enormous pictures of great IU athletes were on display. Two ramps led to the upper level, but I followed the signs that led me out onto the floor of the basketball court. I gazed up at the thousands of seats that rose up and up to dizzying heights. The interior was sort of shaped like a large oblong bowl with the basketball court at the bottom. At the moment, nearly the entire wooden floor was covered with the biggest wrestling mat I had seen in my entire life. There was plenty of room for four matches to go on at one-time in the four circles on the mat.

I joined the other guys who were sitting in the seats on the edge of the floor. More boys joined us as the starting time for practice neared. I counted 27, including myself. IU had a much bigger team than VHS, but that was to be expected. Most of the guys sitting around me were seriously buff. I did not stand out here as much as I did back in high school.

Our coach and assistant coaches approached and everyone grew silent.

"Freshmen, welcome to IU wrestling; the rest of you, welcome back. Each of you freshmen was the top dog at your high school. That's why you're here, but college wrestling is a whole new match. Everyone here was at the top in their high school as well, and so were the wrestlers on the teams you will be facing on the mat. You will be competing against opponents who are tougher than any you've faced before. You will be challenged in ways you never have been before. To succeed, you must become more than you are now. This is a tough program and I expect nothing but the best from you. If you can't come in and give your best every single day then you don't belong here."

The coach continued on. I liked him. He didn't try to be a bad ass or intimidate us, but he made his expectations clear.

Those expectations were high and I was eager to meet them, both for him and myself.

"Now, I'm going to take you to the locker room where you'll pick up your singlets and locker assignment. Keep in mind that you are in IU basketball territory. This is their home, so treat it with respect. Most of our meets will be held in the Intercollegiate Athletics Gym across the bypass off 10th Street, but we practice here. I do not want any complaints from the basketball coaching staff. Understood?"

"Yes, sir," echoed off the nearest walls.

We followed coach through a doorway and then through the hallways until we reached a large locker room. A long table was set up where the team managers handed us our new crimson & cream singlets and our locker assignment.

I stripped and then slipped on my singlet, although singlets fit so tightly it would be more accurate to say I squeezed into it. Wearing a singlet was about as close to being naked as was possible while still wearing clothing. The outline of my dick clearly showed, but I gave it no thought. I was used to it.

As they stripped and dressed it was more evident than ever that my teammates were ripped. Wrestling against these guys during practices had to make me a better wrestler. This was the perfect environment for me to hone my skills.

"Hey, I'm Evan," said the boy with buzzed blond hair dressing next to me.

"I'm Colin."

Evan was shorter than me, but probably weighed twenty pounds more, and it was all muscle.

"Can you believe the size of that mat out there?"

"Yeah. Everything is bigger here."

"You got that right," said an older boy with spiked black hair as he grasped his bulge.

"Hey, don't be intimidating the freshmen with your horse cock, Blake," said another wrestler. "A big dick is all he's got. He's a pussy on the mat."

"Fuck you, Fletcher."

"Hell no! I'd never walk right again if you stuck that thing in me. I told you before, you gotta stick to those loose whores you fuck."

All the guys laughed. Blake truly was hung. I'm not sure I'd ever seen a dick that big before. I wondered if it intimidated his opponents... or his girlfriends.

I walked back out onto the floor where the coaches paired us off to evaluate our abilities. Four pairs of us were on the mats at once and a coach observed each pair. I was paired with a sophomore named Jackson who was roughly the same size as me. The coach guided us through a series of moves and made notes as we performed them. After more than thirty minutes he sent us back to our seats.

"Damn, you're good," Jackson said.

"Thanks. I'm eager to see how I stack up against the rest of the team."

"From what I've seen, you're better than the sophomores and most of the juniors."

"The question is, am I better than the opponents I'll face in meets?"

"True. True. It's a long time until our first meet."

"So, you were on the team last year?" I asked as we sat and observed those on the mat.

"Yeah. Practices are intense and we spend a lot of time in the weight room. No matter how good you are now, I guarantee that when the first meet comes around you will be a shitload better. I thought I was good and I couldn't believe how much I improved."

"Great. That's exactly what I want."

"We were a tough team last year. I hope we will be again. See the black guy on the mats now? That's Norman. He's a senior this year. He's being considered for the Olympic team."

"No shit? He must be good."

"He's gone undefeated in his weight class."

"Damn, he's huge. He's shorter than me, but look at those muscles."

"Yeah, I've seen guys almost cry when they have to wrestle him. He's quite a nice guy off the mat. I wouldn't be surprised if a few guys almost cry when they have to face you. You have a great balance of build and size. You're really tall for a wrestler."

"Yeah," I said, laughing. It was true. Except for Norman, everyone else was under 6', most of them well under.

"This first day is mainly evaluation of you new guys. The coaches are noting strengths and weaknesses so they can develop individual training programs. It's a lot like having a personal trainer. The coaches truly care about everyone reaching their full potential. They're strict, but fair and they're not jerks."

"That's good. I have a low tolerance for jerks. From what I've seen so far these are coaches I'm eager to work with."

"Tomorrow is when practice truly begins. Most practices you'll be in the weight room or on the mat. I have a feeling you'll love it."

"Yeah, I'm not much for sitting and watching, although I pick up moves by observing."

I was called to the mat again later, shown a "new" move, and asked to put it into practice. It was simple for me because Skye had taught me the move two or three years ago. Skye could easily have been a wrestling coach himself. Being trained by him gave me a distinct advantage now.

We hit the showers after practice. It was the first time I got a good look at most of my teammates naked. Norman was built almost like a body builder and all the guys were ripped, but the most astonishing sight was Blake's penis. He caught me looking, but instead of pretending I wasn't checking him out I looked directly at him and said, "Whoa." He laughed.

"Blake is way too hung for a white boy," Norman said as he soaped up near me.

"You know all the new guys have to take it up the ass from Blake, right?" Fletcher asked.

"You're full of crap. If the new guys had to take it from Blake, there would be no new guys. No one could survive that," I said.

Fletcher laughed. "You're probably right."

I had some seriously hot teammates, which was hardly a surprise. I was subtle about checking them out, except for Blake. I wasn't the only new guy staring at his enormous dick. I had no problem with anyone knowing I was bi, but I didn't think it was cool to be too obvious about checking out guys who might have zero interest in other males. Besides, these were my teammates and I generally avoided hooking up with teammates.

I returned to the locker room to dress. I felt completely at home here, even though today was the first time I had entered.

This locker room was nicer and larger than any I had seen so far, but they were all basically the same.

"Hey, have you thought of joining a fraternity?"

I looked up at Blake as I tied my shoes.

"Not really."

"I belong to Phi Sigma Kappa. We're having our rush party this Thursday. You should come."

"Don't do it, Colin. Blake only asked you because you're good looking. All the guys at Kappa are good looking. I think it's actually a whore house," Jackson said.

"Shut it, Jackson, but thanks for saying I'm good looking."

"Oh damn, I meant all the guys at Kappa are good looking, except Blake. He only got in because he's hung."

"Too late. Your compliment has already been noted and accepted," Blake said.

"Noooo!" Jackson wailed, causing the other guys to laugh. "Be wary, Colin. I hear part of the Kappa initiation is taking it up the ass from Blake."

"Hey, I didn't believe it in the showers and I'm not believing it here for the same reason."

"Come if you can. I think you'd be good Kappa material."

"I might. Yours is actually the 7th invitation I've received."

"Damn!" Blake said. "Just remember, Kappa is the best!"

"He's not biased at all," Norman said.

"We throw a great party if nothing else. A lot of people come to rush who aren't interested in joining. We generally let them if they bring a girl."

"I might come. I'm still finding my way here. I'll catch you guys later," I said standing and departing from the locker room.

I followed the hallways back to the front entrance. I walked across the parking lot and crossed 17th Street to the nearest bus stop. In a few minutes I was back in my dorm.

I was hungry, but I had a lot of assignments so I pulled out a book and began reading and taking notes. I wanted to get a chapter or two out of the way before I ate, then I'd return and work until I turned in.

I had never been the studious type and yet I was interested in just about everything. Those who assumed I was nothing but a dumb blond jock were sorely mistaken.

I worked for nearly two hours before hunger forced me to push my texts to the side. I walked over to Wright Quad where one of the closest dining rooms was located. I was surprised by its immense size when I entered. The room was vast; probably four times the size of the Tudor Room.

I was faced with a difficult choice. The dining room was a food court similar to that in IMU or a mall. Italian, Mexican, burgers, salads, sandwiches and more were offered. I decided on Mexican and was soon seated with a plate of burritos, Spanish rice, and refried beans. I wasn't sure about the quality of the food, but one taste was enough to tell me I had nothing to worry about.

Three girls seated nearby eyed me. All were rather attractive and I didn't mind the attention. I smiled when I caught them looking and soon they brought their trays to my table.

"Mind if we sit here?" the tallest, with auburn hair asked.

"Not at all."

"Do you live in Wright?" one asked.

"No. I live in Hershey in Ashton. It's a small dorm with no dining areas."

"I didn't think I'd seen you around. Are you on the wrestling team?"

"Uh, yeah. How did you know?" She pointed to my shirt. I had forgotten I'd changed into a comfy IU Wrestling tee-shirt before I started studying.

"Oh! I thought you were psychic for a moment."

"You look like a wrestler. You're built like one."

"I wrestled in high school and played football."

"You're not on the football team here too?"

"No," I laughed. "I don't think that's even possible, although our meets don't begin until November."

"What are you studying?"

"This year I'm getting freshman courses out of the way, but I intend to get into sports fitness with some drama thrown in. I intend to be a trainer and I'd like to work in films doing stunts and training actors for hand-to-hand combat, fencing, sword fighting, and everything related."

"Oh, that sounds exciting!"

We kept talking and by the time I left I had three new numbers in my phone. I definitely wouldn't mind hanging out with those girls again. They were witty, funny, and sexy. I briefly considered hitting on them, but since there were three that would have been difficult. I wouldn't have minded taking all three of them back to my room, but most likely they would have been insulted by such a suggestion. I couldn't hit on any one of them without hurting the feelings of the others, so I postponed any potential action. I truly needed to get my ass back to school work anyway.

It was difficult to avoid the temptation, but I returned to my room without a girl. My schoolwork had to come first. Skye had warned me about all the temptations of college life and how I could find myself in trouble if I didn't have self-discipline. He didn't tell me not to hook up or party, but he did say that I should do my work first and then have fun. He also warned me against working too much. Breaks were helpful and even necessary. It was true. I was a lot sharper and more focused after I returned from supper, although part of that might have been than I was no longer starving. I trusted Skye when he gave me advice. He always told me the truth. He'd hooked up and partied a lot during college, but he also graduated with a 3.8 GPA.

I worked until a little past midnight, taking small breaks to keep myself sharp. I considered going out for a walk or even a bike ride after I quit for the night, but I needed sleep. Tomorrow would be another busy day.

Chapter Four

Haakon and I walked up the steps of Zeta Beta Tau, one of the fraternities that had invited me to their rush party. I wasn't much interested in joining a frat, but I wanted to see what it was all about. Haakon was equally curious, or perhaps more so. When I invited him, he jumped at the opportunity to check out an America frat party.

I didn't know much about frats. I'd watched *Animal House*, but I doubted it was terribly accurate. For the sake of the frats I hoped not.

We stepped inside to a fairly calm atmosphere. I didn't spot John Belusi anywhere. There was music playing a bit loud, almost everyone was drinking beer out of red plastic cups, and some of the guys were getting friendlier with the girls than the girls wanted, but this was no *Animal House*.

Haakon and I soon had red plastic cups pressed into our hands. I sipped at mine since I didn't much care for beer. Haakon wrinkled his nose when he tasted his and I laughed.

"Don't like beer?" I asked.

"Oh, I like it, but this is not good beer. The Germans have the best beer."

"I actually don't care much for beer myself."

"That's because you probably haven't tasted good beer. You should taste what my father buys. It is from Germany."

I had forgotten that drinking was acceptable at a much younger age in Europe. It was no wonder Haakon knew beer.

"Hey, Colin. I'm glad you could make it."

I turned to see a boy I vaguely recognized as the one who invited me to the party.

"Yeah, I thought I would come and check it out."

"Who is your friend?"

"I'm Haakon."

"It's nice to meet you. I'm Travis. Any friend of Colin's is welcome. Let me show you guys around."

Travis did just that. The party was in the lounge, but he also showed us an impressive game room complete with a pool table, a Foosball table, and other games in addition to a few sets of tables and chairs. Next, we walked through a large kitchen where three kegs sat on the counter and then toured the upstairs. The bathroom was as nice as the one in Hershey and the rooms were much larger. It was an impressive house.

"Zeta has a lot to offer. Living in the house is much better than life in the dorms, plus imagine having a group of guys who will always have your back. We work together and help each other out. Our cookouts and parties are legendary and there are always lots of girls."

Travis introduced Haakon and me to a few of the brothers, gave us both an application, and then turned us loose. We remained several minutes more, mostly because I didn't want to appear rude by leaving too quickly, although there were so many people I didn't know if anyone would notice.

"You ready to get out of here?" I asked when I figured we had lingered long enough.

"Yeah."

The music and voices faded as we walked out to the sidewalk. We crossed 3rd Street and stepped onto campus.

"Are you planning to pledge?" Haakon asked.

"No. I mostly just wanted to check out a frat party. You?"

"No. I think I only received an application because I was with you."

"Oh, I don't know about that. They seemed genuinely interested in you."

Haakon shrugged. "It doesn't matter. I want to experience dorm life in an American university. I can't do that if I join a fraternity."

"You could probably join and still live in a dorm, but you won't be here very long anyway."

We walked along the edge of Dunn's Woods in the moonlight. Insects called out from the darkness under the trees and I caught a glimpse of something scurrying around the trunks of the oaks and maples. The air was faintly scented with the blossoms of a plant I couldn't identify.

"This is lovely," Haakon said as we neared The Rose Well House.

I gazed at Haakon. He was so very handsome. The time had come to discover if we could be more than friends.

We stepped into the Rose Well House. I drew near to Haakon and he gazed at me expectantly. I leaned in slowly, giving him plenty of time to back away or put his hand on my chest to stop me. Haakon didn't stop me. My lips met his and I kissed him for the first time.

We broke our kiss for a moment as we gazed into each other's eyes, then I pulled him to me once more and kissed him more deeply, before releasing him. We sat on one of the built-in benches along the walls.

"I have been waiting on you to kiss me," Haakon said.

"You could have kissed me."

"I was afraid you were not attracted to me. You're so incredibly hot you can have anyone."

"Thank you, but I'm sure there are those I cannot have. You are incredibly hot as well, Haakon."

"Not like you, but there is no point in arguing. Can I ask you something?"

"Anything."

"Is it confusing to be bisexual?"

"No. It seems rather natural to me. Guys and girls are quite different, but they both have something to offer."

"Do you think you would like someone who is both male and female?"

"I think I might find that confusing. I don't think I would be attracted to someone who was both. I love girls and I love guys, but a mix of the two doesn't appeal to me. Perhaps it should, but it doesn't."

"Well, I am glad you like guys."

"I'm glad you do too."

"What if I only liked girls? Would we still be together now?"

"Yes. If you only liked girls, I would have contented myself with being your friend. I like you in ways that have nothing to do with physical attraction."

"I am the same with you, although I have a strong attraction to you."

"Good," I said and then pulled Haakon to me again. We made out for a good long time as we sat in The Rose Well House. I do not know if anyone walked past as we kissed, but it didn't matter. I did not care. I enjoyed making out with Haakon more than I'd enjoyed anything in a long time.

"I should get back to my room. I still have some work to finish before bed," I said reluctantly after we had made out for several minutes.

"Me too. I think the professors are trying to kill me. My reading assignments alone take hours!"

"I know what you mean. I don't think I'll be doing any reading for fun for a while. By the time I finish what I have to read for classes I don't want to read anymore."

We stood and began walking.

"Perhaps this is premature to discuss, but since I will only be here for one semester I don't want to get too serious with anyone. You're incredible Colin, but come December I leave and am unlikely to return to your country."

"I understand. To be honest, I don't want to get serious with anyone either right now. I hadn't planned to date anyone period, but then I met you. I want to date you, but I also want to be able to see other guys and girls and hook up with them, and like you said, you will only be here a short time."

Haakon nodded. "If I met you in Norway I would like you for my boyfriend, but since I met you here... we can date and see others too. I really wouldn't want to give up the other possibilities here. I like American boys."

I grinned. "Me too, but lately I've grown rather fond of Norwegian boys or at least one of them."

Haakon took my hand and we walked through campus together until we parted on the far side of Jordan Avenue to return to our dorms.

I liked where things were going with Haakon. I liked that we knew exactly where we stood with each other. I even liked the fact that he was only here for a few months. That might sound odd, but I had a feeling I could actually fall for him and I wasn't ready for that. I didn't want that serious of a relationship during college. Knowing that he would be gone before Christmas would help keep things from becoming too intense between us. It was insurance against losing control of my feelings and following a path I was not ready to follow.

***

I rode my bike down 3rd Street. It was one of the busiest streets around campus during the day, but in the late evening there was far less traffic. I had finished wrestling practice less than half an hour ago. Most of today's practice had taken place in the weight room. My upper body was especially tired, but my legs not so much. It was the perfect time to get in a good ride and give my legs more of a workout.

Physical activity was a great counterpoint to sitting on my butt in classes and studying in my room. I had not attended IU long, but I had already developed a good balance of the intellectual with the physical. I was also quite pleased with my academic progress.   I had not only kept up with all my assignments; I was already working on projects that were not due until the end of the semester. I had a couple of chapters to read yet before the end of the day, but there was plenty of time yet and after wrestling practice and a long bike ride I would be quite ready to sit down and read.

I turned and rode all the way up Indiana Avenue, then cut across 17th Street into the parking lot on the south side of Memorial Stadium. I rode around the stadium examining it from every side. If I had chosen a different path, I could well be attending football practice in the stadium instead of wrestling practice in Assembly Hall. I didn't regret my choice to focus on wrestling, but I wished I could have done both. That was the problem with life. There was never enough time to do everything I wanted.

Quite a few Verona boys had played football for IU. Brendan, my football coach at VHS, had actually made it as far as quarterback. As far as I knew I was the only Verona boy to wrestle for IU. I preferred to go in a new direction.

My stomach grumbled and I realized I had not eaten since lunch. Considering how much I liked to eat, I was amazed that I actually forgot to do so at times. This had been a busy day. I attended classes, did some research in the library, made out with a girl in a lounge in Wright Quad, and attended wrestling practice.

I rode back down to 10th Street and then headed downtown. There was still plenty of light and it would be a perfect opportunity to sit in the covered outdoor eating area in front of The Scholar's Inn Bakehouse. I had not been inside since I was there with Skye and Marshall back in my high school years. It was odd, but that seemed so long ago.

The Bakehouse was on the square at the corner of 6th Street and College Avenue. I parked my bike in the rack out front and went inside. The Bakehouse hadn't changed. There was a long counter on the left side of the old store building and booths, tables and chairs taking up the rest of the space. A counter that ran along the northeast corner looked out onto 6th and College. It would be a great place to sit in cold months, but today I wanted to dine alfresco.

I gazed at the menus written on chalkboards above the baskets that held different varieties of bagels and breads. After some deliberation, I decided on the three little pigs scramble, which included bacon, ham, sausage, caramelized onions, tomato bruschetta, and cheddar, plus toast.

I took my number, filled a glass with ice water, and walked outside to find a table. Nearly all of the tables were taken, but I snagged one recently vacated.

I sat and sipped ice water for a few minutes while watching the constant flow of traffic. City and campus buses, delivery vans, cars, trucks, and bikes flowed past. Bloomington was a surprisingly busy town.

"Mind if I sit here?"

I looked up. A boy dressed in tight fitting biking shorts and a matching top gazed at me.

"No. Have a seat."

"Thanks. There are no outside tables left. I wanted to talk to you as well."

"You wanted to talk to me?" I asked, confused. I had never seen the boy who sat down across from me before.

"I noticed your bike. It's Little 500 regulation. Are you on a Little 500 team?"

"Oh! No. I'm not. I picked that bike because it would work my legs better than a multi-speed. A friend of my uncle owns a bike shop in town. He recommended it."

"Peralta's?"

"Yeah."

"So are you interested in biking or bike racing?"

"Well, I like to ride. I've never given thought to racing."

"You should."

"I don't think I'd have the time to get serious with it. I'm on the wrestling team at IU."

"Have you pledged a frat yet?"

"No. I'm not very interested in fraternities. I'm sure a lot of them are great, but it's not for me. I'm too busy."

"It's something you should consider. Being a member of a fraternity can be a great experience."

"This sounds like a sales pitch," I said smiling.

"Okay, you caught me. I'm a brother at Alpha Alpha Omega. I spotted you and your bike and thought you might be Alpha material. The more I talk to you, the more certain I am I was correct and that Alpha could do a lot for you. I think you'd be a great addition to our Little 500 team."

"I wouldn't have the time for that. Wrestling takes up a lot of my free time and I don't want to give it up."

"Oh, we wouldn't want you to give up wrestling. We work around team members who are on a sports team. One of our riders last year was on the lacrosse team and another on the soccer team. I'm Grant."

"I'm Colin."

My food arrived and Grant's arrived right after. My scramble was excellent. I'm not sure how many eggs were in it, but it was plenty big. I loved the toast, too.

"Can I talk you into checking out Alpha and meeting some of the guys?" Grant asked.

"You mean a rush party?"

"No. Ours was last night. I mean come and look around. I'll be your personal tour guide."

"I don't know..."

"It won't hurt to look."

"How diverse is Alpha?"

"Very. We have an Asian brother, another who is black, and one is even from Russia. Two of our brothers last year dated each other. We don't actually make an attempt to be diverse. We look for whomever will be a valuable addition to Alpha. Our black brother, Aaron, has the highest GPA on campus. He's a great guy too, but you can see why any fraternity would want him."

I nodded. "Good. I'm bi and I don't have much patience for intolerance."

"You won't find any at Alpha. No one who is intolerant gets in. There were a few problems in the past but that was years ago. We could ride over after we finish eating. Please?"

"I suppose, but I don't have a lot of time. I have work to do yet."

"Great. You won't be sorry. I promise."

"Just remember that I'm not that interested in joining a fraternity. You are actually the eighth guy from a frat who has approached me."

"Really?" Grant asked, laughing. "I'm not terribly surprised. You're fit as hell so you've got to be a great athlete."

"I do okay."

"I bet you do better than okay. I'm not terribly athletic, except for biking. I have a bit of an obsession for biking and especially bike racing."

"It's good to be passionate about something. I love wrestling, football, martial arts, and anything physical."

"I can tell you're a physical guy merely by looking. You have an incredible body. Please don't think I'm hitting on you. That's merely an observation and I'll admit there's some jealousy in there too."

I laughed.

We kept talking as we ate. I liked Grant. He was interesting and had a nice sense of humor. I had looked forward to dining alone as I watched passersby and enjoyed the warm evening, but eating with Grant was even better. That's one thing I loved about Bloomington. Finding someone to hang out with was never a challenge.

After we finished eating, we dumped our plates, glasses, and silverware in the bins inside we came back out to the bike rack. Grant unlocked a bike that was identical to mine, except his had seen far more use.

We rode down College to 3rd, where we turned left and headed back toward campus. Only a few minutes later we coasted into the parking lot of Alpha Alpha Omega.

The house was impressive, which wasn't unusual for a fraternity house. Many of those in Bloomington looked like large mansions. I followed Grant inside to a large lounge furnished with comfortable loveseats and chairs, an enormous TV, and an entire wall dedicated to The Little 500. Grant took me toward it first.

"Wow, Marc is in a lot of the photos."

"Yes. Marc Peralta is an Alpha legend. He's a friend of your uncle?"

"Yeah, we had supper with Marc and Alessio when Skye brought me down to drop me off for school. He's really cool."

"Well, if you were trying to get into Alpha, a recommendation from Marc Peralta would give you an automatic in. Of course, since I'm trying to sell you on Alpha, you don't need it."

"This is impressive," I said pointing to the wall and the showcase filled with Little 500 trophies.

"We've won the Little 500 more times than any other group. We don't win every year, but we are always a force to reckon with. We are considered the team to beat."

Grant gave took me through the large kitchen, a large dining area, and other rooms on the first floor, then we went upstairs.

"Here is our bathroom," he said as we stepped in. It looked like a dorm bathroom, only not as big and much, much nicer.

"Wow. This makes the bathroom in Hershey look truly pathetic."

"It was completely renovated two years ago. One of our alumni runs a wholesale contractor business and he donated all the marble, the fittings, and basically everything you see. The brothers considered separate shower stalls, but the communal showers make the space seem larger and some guys, like Federico like to show off," Grant said as a tanned, buff boy walked past us dripping wet to take his towel from a hook. Federico flipped Grant off. "Hey, is that anyway to act when I'm trying to talk Colin into pledging?"

"I wasn't flipping him off, only you. Hi, I'm Federico," he said, extending his hand.

"I'm Colin." Federico had a very nice body. He was muscular with great definition and a thick uncut penis. He made for good scenery.

"You should consider Alpha. All the guys are great here, even Grant." Federico smiled. I liked him.

"I'll show you my room next so you'll get an idea of the accommodations. The seniors have the best rooms, but there are no bad rooms. I actually kept the same room I had last year because I like the view."

Grant led me into a room that was far larger than mine in Hershey. He shared with an Alpha brother, but there was still plenty of room for two. A huge window looked out over a large side yard toward a frat house across the street.

"This makes my room look like a closet. I have a single and it's very, very small."

"Yeah, I was in Forest Quad for a very short time last year. I was attracted to Alpha by its Little 500 reputation, but the rooms were an excellent bonus.

"The main asset of Alpha is the brothers. We truly are like brothers. I'm an only child, so that's a big deal to me. We help and support each other and have a great time together. We throw great parties, and ours are more about the food than the alcohol, unlike most fraternities'. There is always a keg at our parties, but we're best known for burgers and brats. A few of the brothers don't drink at all and even those who are the heaviest drinkers aren't stupid about it."

"That's cool. I avoid drinking most of the time since I'm a bit of a fitness freak. I have no objection to others drinking, but I don't because it works against my goals."

We soon left talk of the fraternity behind and talked instead about wrestling, bike racing, workouts, and girls.

"I should head out," I said after an hour.

"Give me your number."

"Sure." Grant handed me his phone and I punched in my number.

"You will be hearing from me. Please think about joining Alpha."

"I will. I'll admit you have changed my opinion from definitely not wanting to join a fraternity to maybe."

"That's good. I hope that maybe will change to a yes."

"It's possible, but I can't say it's likely."

Grant walked me out. I returned to my bike, pushed it across 3rd Street onto campus and then rode back to Hershey Hall.

I had something thinking to do. I had zero interest in joining a frat when I arrived on campus a few days before, but life in a fraternity was different from what I'd imagined, at least at Alpha Alpha Omega. The nice rooms and the fact I'd have a roommate were big draws, but the idea of living in a house with guys like Grant was even more attractive. There was the Little 500 tradition at Alpha too. I had never participated in a bike race and I loved new challenges. Pledging was something to consider. My main cause for hesitation is that I didn't want to overload myself. I had a tendency to try to do too much and I already had quite a full schedule.

I put the topic aside and studied for a quiz I had tomorrow. I liked to study for tests and quizzes right before I went to bed because I knew my mind would keep working on the material even while I slept. I thought of it as painless studying.

***

I faced Norman on the mat. He was in a weight class considerably higher than mine. I would never face an opponent who outweighed me by so much in a meet, but the coaches pitted me against him during practice. I wasn't quite sure why unless it was to see how I performed.

Practice halted as we faced each other. The entire team stopped what they were doing to watch.

Norman and I circled, looking for an opening. I dove in and went for his leg. He staggered, but I could not take him down. He grabbed me, but I slipped away before he could get a good hold.

I watched for my chance and tried to come up with a way to take him down. I knew a great many moves I could use, but I was limited to those legal in wrestling. When we came together, trying to move Norman was like trying to move a mountain. He was incredibly strong and his mass was so great that I was sure it alone defeated many opponents.

Norman took me down on the mat and for a moment I thought it was all over, but I maneuvered out of his grasp and pounced. For a few moments, I had him, but then he broke free.

I wasn't going to give up. I kept trying, but my chances of success were slim. Norman nearly pinned me more than once, but each time I escaped. I never came close to pinning him, but I performed much better against him than I expected.

Norman pinned me in the end. No one was surprised, including me.

"I think you broke the record," Norman said as he nodded at me with approval.

"Record?"

"For staying on the mat with me without getting pinned." He looked over at one of the coaches who held a stopwatch.

"He lasted forty-four seconds more than anyone else," the coach said.

"You're good," Norman said, pointing at me.

"Thanks."

"That was impressive," Jackson said as Norman stepped away. "I wrestled Norman once and he pinned me in three seconds."

"I felt like I was wrestling a mountain," I said.

Jackson laughed. "You went after him like you intended to pin him."

"I intended to, although I didn't like my chances. I don't like to lose."

"Taking as long as you did to lose to Norman is winning."

"I suppose I can look at it that way."

Lasting as long as I did against Norman must have been a bigger deal than I thought for several guys came up and expressed their admiration before the end of practice. I could tell the coaches were quite pleased as well.

I showered after practice even though my plans involved getting sweaty again. The sights in the showers and locker room here were even better than they were at VHS and the scenery there was rather... stimulating. I don't think there was a guy on the IU wrestling team that didn't interest me, but hooking up with teammates could be tricky. I had no plans to put the moves on any of them. There were plenty of opportunities for sex elsewhere.

I sent a text as I stepped out of Assembly Hall, then caught a bus and rode to the SRSC where Haakon and I had arranged to meet after I finished wrestling practice.

I arrived first so I waited in the lobby area. I didn't mind. I was sure my body would benefit from a break since I'd had quite a workout on the mat.

Haakon arrived in only a few minutes.

"Wrestling practice, then a workout? You like to torment yourself. Don't you?" Haakon asked.

"Ah, this is taking it easy compared to what I do at home."

"Who are you? Superman?"

"No, but I used to suspect my uncle was a superhero. I still think he might be. If not, he comes close."

"He's a stud, huh?"

"He's more than that." I pulled out a photo of Skye and myself taken shortly before I left for school and showed it to Haakon.

"Damn! He's hot!"

"I won't comment on the hot part, but he has an exceptional body."

"Mmm, if he was my uncle..."

"If he was your uncle you would not be thinking what you are thinking now."

"I don't know. I think I might!"

"Well, he is my uncle and I don't think about him like that. We're very close."

"I can understand that. I can also see where you might suspect he's a superhero.

"It's not only the way he looks. He does amazing things."

As we showed our IDs and headed downstairs to the locker room, I told Haakon about the accident that took my mom and step dad away from me and nearly cost me my life.

"He pushed the car out of the lake by himself," I said.

"Seriously? He pushed an entire car that was filled with water out of a lake?"

"Yes, it was completely submerged, several feet down and several feet away from the shore."

"Damn. Maybe he is a superhero."

"He is to me, but I don't let him know that," I said grinning.

Haakon and I stripped and changed into workout clothes. I let him use my locker. Haakon looked very good wearing nothing but boxer briefs and looked nearly as fine once he'd pulled on his shorts and sleeveless shirt. I wore my usual loose shorts and tank top.

"I usually do come cardio first, then hit the weights."

"Sounds good."

We headed far upstairs to the vast cardio room that contained stationary bikes, treadmills, and more.

"Oh man, I have to try one of these curved treadmills," Haakon said.

"Okay, let's do it."

We climbed on treadmills side by side. While most treadmills were flat, these were shaped like a smile, low in the center and curving up at the ends. I had run on them before and much preferred them over the more common design. Running on them felt more natural and was easier on the knees. I liked that most of the treadmills and most of everything else in the cardio area was human powered. Only a few of the machines were plugged into the walls.

"Oh yeah. I love this," Haakon said as he ran beside me.

"Yeah, these are great, but they're no good for racing. I raced a guy for twenty minutes the other day and never could pull out in front."

Haakon rolled his eyes, but smiled.

We soon moved onto the weight room. Haakon looked especially sexy while working out. I caught glimpses of his muscles bulging as he lifted and the sight made me breath harder. I had always been attracted to strength. Haakon wasn't nearly as built as me, but he looked fine and he could handle some serious weight.

We headed for the showers when we finished in the weight room. I shared my shower supplies with Haakon, which was a good excuse to shower side-by-side even though there were plenty of free showerheads available.

I enjoyed the opportunity to view Haakon naked. I appreciated the beauty of both the male and female form, but I truly think the male form was the more artistically pleasing of the two. Haakon had a truly beautiful body with a smooth, sculpted torso that tapered to a narrow waist. He had a perfectly shaped, rounded ass and strong thighs with well-developed calves. He looked especially sexy as he soaped up in the hot, steamy shower room. My eyes were on him more than they probably should have been, especially since we weren't alone in the showers. I didn't care. Haakon knew I was attracted to him and I feared no one.

We rinsed off, turned off the water, and then shared a towel. We dressed and then headed out of the SRSC and walked to the nearest bus stop.

"Would you like to come to my room for a while?" I asked.

Haakon gazed into my eyes. We both knew what I was asking. "Yes. I would like that very much."

I wanted to kiss him right then and there, but the bus pulled up and we climbed on. We sat together as the campus passed by outside the windows. A few stops later we got off the bus near Ashton Center.

"Wow, your dorm is small compared to Forest," Haakon said as we approached Hershey Hall a short time later.

"Yeah, it wasn't what I was expecting, but it's in a good location. Prepare yourself. If you think the dorm is small, wait until you see my room."

A couple of minutes later I opened the door to my room and we entered.

"Okay, this is small, but you do have it all to yourself."

"True and there are advantages to that," I said, closing the door.

I gazed at Haakon, pulled him to me, and kissed him. We made out for several long moments and then I pulled his shirt over his head.

I ran my hands over his chest, then leaned down and licked his pecs. I ran my tongue over his nipples, causing him to moan.

Haakon grasped my chin and pulled my lips to his again. He kissed me deeply, then pulled my shirt over my head. He pushed me back on my bed and began to lick all over my torso. It turned me on like mad.

Aggressiveness aroused me, whether I was with a male or female. One of the hottest sexual encounters I had with a female was with a girl who shoved me down on my back and rode me hard. I was very forceful myself and the best sex always occurred when my partner was equally aggressive.

Haakon was obviously as turned on as I was. We had never gone further than making out and groping, but now he went for my shorts and within moments I was naked.

I wasted no time in stripping him naked too. I had seen him nude, but now I could feel what before I had only gazed upon. I loved his smooth, soft skin, and hard muscles.

Haakon and I were all over each other. We didn't go all the way, but we did plenty. Haakon was amazingly talented at giving head. He took me right to the edge a few times before letting me explode in his mouth. Our moans and groans filled the room and I was certain the guys on either side of me could clearly hear us through the walls. I didn't care.

Over an hour later, we lay back panting.

"Now that is my idea of a workout," Haakon said.

"It's definitely my favorite workout."

"We must do this again."

"Yes, soon and often."

Haakon grinned and kissed me.

"I hate to hook up and run, but if I don't get up I'll fall asleep."

"I know what you mean."

We stood, dressed, and then I kissed Haakon deeply at the door.

"I'll see you soon," he said.

"You can count on it."

My phone rang not five minutes after Haakon departed. I didn't recognize the number, but I answered.

"Colin, it's Grant. I was wondering if you'd want to come over to Alpha. We're showing a movie I'd like you to see."

"Hmm, is it a documentary of the greatest accomplishments of Alpha Alpha Omega or a recruitment film?"

Grant laughed. "No, but I think you'll like it. It was filmed in Bloomington. There will be popcorn, chips, and soft drinks. I promise there will be no sales pitch."

"Sure. Why not? I'm caught up on my work. A movie would be good."

"Okay, cool. We're going to start soon, so get here as quickly as you can."

I put on my shoes, climbed on my bike, and cut across campus to Alpha. It was a short trip by bike.

Grant spotted me as I entered the lounge and walked to me.

"I'm glad you could make it on short notice. Let's grab some drinks, popcorn, and chips before it starts."

Alpha had an actual popcorn machine on wheels like those found at carnivals. It was good stuff with plenty of butter. Grant and I sat down as the film started.

I hadn't seen *Breaking Away*, but I'd heard about it from Marc and I recognized the main character, Dave Stoller, from the photograph on the wall in Marc's store. I recognized a few of the locations in the film. I had walked through some of them earlier today.

I have to admit I got into the movie. It was a good thing because if I didn't like it, I could never have told Marc. The Little 500 scenes at the end especially drew me in. It made me want to race.

"You tricked me," I said when the movie ended. "That was obviously propaganda designed to make me want to race and therefore join Alpha Alpha Omega."

"Perhaps I have an ulterior motive, but it is one of my favorite movies."

"I have to admit. Part of me does want to race. Not that I'm interested, but what is pledging like?"

Grant smiled. "Since you asked... it's a little rough, but not bad. It was rather an ordeal in the past, but it's been toned down. We aren't allowed to do most of what was once done to pledges. If we did, we would lose our charter. Hazing is out and I'm glad. As a pledge I didn't want to endure it, but as a brother I think the pledge period is much better without it. There is no hazing and nothing sexual, but pledges are basically slaves for the brothers. Each pledge is assigned a big brother. He has to clean his room, make his bed, and serve him in other ways. My big brother made me run to McDonald's for him in the middle of the night and get him a Big Mac. There is also a day you aren't allowed to eat anything unless a brother gives it to you. That sounds bad, but it's an opportunity for the brothers to get to know the pledges. We nab pledges and take them out to eat and we pay. It's not a bad deal when you think of it. There is always a party during the pledge period and the pledges do all the work. Like I said, pledges are mainly slave labor for a few days."

"I'm sure I could handle that. My problem would be time. That's one of the objections I have to joining a fraternity."

"After the pledge period, there isn't much demand on your time. Most fraternity activities are things you'll want to participate in. We always work around class and sports schedules, even for pledges. I'll be honest; we *really* want you, but we go out of our way to work around the schedules of all pledges."

"I'm leaning more toward pledging than I was. I'm not saying "yes" but I'm closer than I was before you tricked me into watching *Breaking Away.*"

"I'm sneaky that way. I promise, if you join Alpha you'll love it. We have never had a brother leave. We're one of the few fraternities that can say that. We have had pledges quit, but very few. You could fill out a pledge application while you're here. You won't be under any obligation."

"I suppose I could go that far."

"Awesome! I will be right back."

I smiled. Grant seemed truly excited. I didn't say so because I didn't want to give Grant false hope, but I was leaning heavily toward pledging. The more time I spent with Grant and the other brothers, the more I liked the idea. Living in Alpha House was a plus too. I could even have a roommate.

"Here's the application. It's fairly simple. In Alpha, the brothers get to pick who they want as their little brother. If you pledge, I'm picking you. Since I recruited you, I should have no problem getting you."

"That would be great."

I filled out the application and gave it back to Grant.

"We announce on Thursday who has been accepted, but you will have no trouble getting in. We have a meeting where we discuss candidates and vote. Each year, we receive a lot more applications than we have spaces, so we have to turn down a lot of applicants, but you're a recruit, which is almost always an automatic acceptance."

"If I decide to officially pledge, I won't hold it against you if I'm not accepted."

"Good, because I pity the guy who pisses you off."

"It takes a lot to get me angry. I don't like bullies, but otherwise it's hard to get on my bad side."

We talked a few minutes more and then I departed. I would make my final decision on Thursday, but at the moment I was leaning heavily toward joining Alpha. Things could change quickly in only a few days.

It was quite late by the time I returned to my room, so I checked some emails, then undressed and climbed into bed. Tomorrow would be another busy day at IU.

Chapter Five

"I am so glad you showed me this place. I've walked past, but I figured it was way too expensive," Haakon said as he sat across from me at a table in The Tudor Room.

"With our student discount for coming in after 1 p.m. it's not much more than eating at Burger King since the price here includes everything and it's so much better, although I love Burger King."

"It's much quieter and we don't have to worry about not being able to find a table either."

"True, although it can be very crowded at times. That's why I made a reservation."

"I'm so glad I met you."

"Just because of my restaurant knowledge, huh?"

"That's merely a bonus. You love sports as much as I do, you're strong, ridiculously hot, incredible in bed, intelligent, funny, and kind."

"I'm beginning to think I should pose for a statue."

"I meant every word."

"I feel the same way about you."

"It makes me wish I lived in the U.S. I can't talk you into moving to Norway, can I?"

"It's too cold for me and I could never live that far away from Skye."

"I know what you mean. It's difficult to be away from my family, even though I know it's only for a few months."

"Things are as they are, so we should enjoy what we have. Even if we never meet again after you go home, even if we don't even keep in touch, we still have now. One of the many things Skye taught me is that now is the most important time."

"You must have an incredible relationship with him."

"I do. It isn't perfect and there have been some rough patches, especially early on, but he's like a father, brother, and friend all at once. I never knew my biological father so Skye has always been like a father to me, even when he was very young. He never really knew his father either. I think he wanted things to be better for me than they were for him."

"I think you are lucky."

"I am and so are we."

"I would feel even luckier if we were both free after lunch and could go to your room."

"Me too, but it's not too difficult to enjoy what we have, especially this grilled chicken, tortellini, and loaded potato soup. I plan to hit that dessert bar hard later."

"It's a good thing you are very active."

"True, but I'll be starving before I eat again."

"Have you decided whether you are going to pledge Alpha yet?"

"Yes. I'm going for it. I think I'll be sorry if I don't. I've done very well keeping up with my coursework and I've even worked ahead on papers and reports. I'm confident I can also handle the added load of Alpha. I want to ride in that bike race and if I practice this year, I'll have a good shot of making the team next year."

"You want to do it all, don't you?" Haakon asked, grinning.

"I would love to play football, join the swim team, and try lacrosse. Soccer would be good and... yes. I want to do it all."

"My goals are far more modest, but when I return to Norway I plan to join a sports team. I am rather fond of hockey."

"Oh, yeah! I'd love to play hockey too. It's wonderfully violent... and rugby. I wish we had rugby here."

"Calm down, Tiger."

"It is good to dream."

"It is also good to get more loaded potato soup."

"I like the way you think, but I am moving on to dessert."

We split up. I returned with a small slice of vanilla cake with buttercream icing, a no-bake cookie, and a macaroon all on a small dessert plate. I made another trip to get another cup of hot jasmine green tea.

"That looks good," Haakon said.

"It is. There is also some peach cheesecake I have to try."

I enjoyed myself a lot as Haakon and I ate and talked in the Tudor Room. The food here reminded me of that in The Graymoor Mansion and made me feel at home.

I sampled the peach cheesecake before I was finished and ate another no-bake cookie. We paid at the counter and then stopped by the tiny Tudor Room restroom before departing. After we'd both washed our hands, I shoved Haakon up against the wall, kissed him deeply, and pressed myself against him.

"I think you like to torment me," Haakon said when I pulled back.

"Yes, but I'm also tormenting myself and mostly I love kissing you. Come on. We both have class soon."

"Thank you for lunch," Haakon said as we stepped out into the lobby area of The Tudor Room.

"You're welcome, but you paid for your own."

"I mean for showing me this place. I will be back."

"In that case, you are welcome. I'll see you later."

"The sooner the better."

We walked out of the Tudor Room and headed in opposite directions.

Lunch with Haakon was a nice break. I'd had two classes this morning and I had another coming up very soon. After that, it was off to the library to do a little research, then back to my room to study before wrestling practice. After that, I'd grab something to eat, work out, swim if I had time, and then go back to my room to do whatever work I had not yet finished. Not every day was quite so packed, but most days were rather similar to this one.

***

"For the next week, you belong to us," said Flynn, the senior in charge of Alpha Alpha Omega pledge week. Some of the pledges were obviously intimidated by him, but not me. "Your big brother owns you, but any brother may call upon you to perform tasks for him and you will serve the house as a whole as well.

"Tomorrow night, we are having a party. You will show up promptly at 6 p.m. to clean and set up the party. You will be shown what to do during the party and you will do the cleanup after. This Saturday, we are having a car wash in the parking lot to raise money. You will all be here at 10 a.m. and you will remain all day until we see fit to dismiss you. I suggest you wear a bathing suit because you will get wet.

"The only individuals who will be excused from helping with the party or the car wash are those who have sports practices or class commitments and the second those commitments are completed you will come straight to Alpha to do your part. You must arrange in advance with your big brother to be excused. Those of you who are excused from a part of any required activity will put in double the effort when you arrive. Is that clear?"

"Yes sir!" we answered in unison.

"This week you must prove to us you are worthy to be admitted to Alpha Alpha Omega. Not everyone makes it. We accept only the best. When the week is concluded we will vote on you. One blackball is all it takes to toss you out so you'd be wise to please all the brothers."

I watched Flynn as he continued talking. He had broad shoulders and a muscular build. He had unusually dark red hair and piercing blue eyes that gave him a fierce appearance. He was a great choice for intimidating pledges and keeping them in line.

After our group meeting was over, we were handed over to our big brother, which in my case was Grant. He took me upstairs to his room and introduced me to his roommate, Damon, a slim sophomore with brown hair and eyes.

"Starting tomorrow, you will come in the morning and make both our beds and pick up any mess you find," Grant said. "Since you'll miss out on some of the set up for the party, you can make it up by cleaning up after Damon too."

"Yes sir. What time in the morning?"

"The time is up to you, but not before 9 a.m. or after noon, unless you have classes that make it impossible."

"I can do it."

"We won't make a mess for you, but I expect the room to be in perfect order."

"It will be sir."

"I know I can count on you and you know, I'm getting hungry. I need something from McDonald's."

Grant and Damon placed their orders and Grant handed me a twenty. The nearest McDonald's was over by the mall, so I went outside, climbed on my bike and took off. Luckily, they did not order drinks or I would've had to take a bus.

I arrived at McDonalds only a few minutes later, placed the orders at the drive-through, and was soon on my way back. I rode hard since the distance was not great and I covered the few blocks quickly. I made much better time than the cars and buses on 3rd Street because the bike lane wasn't clogged with traffic.

I walked inside Alpha house and up to Grant's room. The door was open. I walked in and presented Grant and Damon with their orders and then gave Grant his change.

"Very good. That was quick. I could grow to like this," Grant said with a grin.

"Will there be anything else, sir?" I asked, feeling somewhat like a butler.

"No, you may go. I'm eager to see what you do with our room tomorrow."

I headed out. Being a pledge was slightly demeaning, but every member of the fraternity had been a pledge at one time or another. It was my turn to suffer and the suffering wasn't at all bad.

I had an hour between classes the next morning, so when the first ended I hopped on my bike and rode to Alpha. I went straight upstairs to Grant's room. The beds were unmade and the same general mess I had observed the night before was still there, but Grant was true to his word. They had not gone out of their way to make a mess for me to clean up.

I made the beds, picked up the dirty clothes and placed them in Grant and Damon's laundry bags. Luckily, the dirty clothes were near the beds so I could tell what belonged to whom. I picked up the trash off the floor, the desks, and wherever I found it and put it in the wastebasket, then I dumped it into a trash bag I had brought with me. Next, I pulled a can of Endust and a dust rag from my backpack and dusted the desks, bookcases, and other surfaces. That was not strictly required, but I intended to do this shit right.

Before I departed, I straightening things up and did some minor organizing to give the room a neater appearance. I glanced around the room before I departed. It looked much better than when I entered and likely better than it had for some time.

I packed up my cleaning supplies, grabbed the trash bag, and headed outside. I tossed the bag in the large garbage bin at the edge of the parking lot, climbed on my bike, and headed to class.

I could see the advantage of having a pledge to use as a slave for a week. I tended to keep my room in order, but it would have been nice to have someone come in and clean while I was gone, go out and get food for me, and perform whatever minor task I wished.

My pledge duties meant I would have no spare time today. After my second class, I went straight to the dining hall in Wright Quad, picked up a grilled chicken sandwich, a salad, and some iced tea, then sat by myself and read. I remained in the dining room reading until it was time to depart for my afternoon class. Today, and likely all week, I would have to study whenever and wherever I had the chance. I had a good block of time after my next class, but once wrestling practice began I would be busy until late tonight.

Wrestling practice was strenuous, but was a welcome respite from classes and studying. I had read so much I thought my head might explode.

"You are going down, Colin," Evan said as I took my position on the mat.

"You keep dreaming about that," I taunted.

Evan was a freshman as well. He was shorter than me, but muscular enough that we were in the same weight class. We constantly talked shit to each other, then laughed about it.

Evan was a fierce wrestler and I always eagerly anticipated wrestling with him. He had skills and some unusual moves. Struggling against him made me a better wrestler, but he had yet to pin me.

I twisted and turned and slipped from Evan's grasp, but before I could grab him he was gone. Evan was rather talented at escapes and I had been keenly observing him to learn his secret. Before long, I had him and took him to the mat. Getting him on his back was no easy task, but I coolly kept maneuvering him.

I forced Evan onto his back. He nearly escaped from me, but there was no escape for him. I pinned him, then gave him a hand up.

"Damn, wrestling you is like wrestling with a Vulcan," he said.

"A Vulcan?"

"Yes. You are maddeningly calm. Nothing rattles you and you never lose your cool. You're also unnaturally strong."

"We superior beings are like that. As a mere mortal, you would not understand."

"Uh huh."

"Well I am superior to you."

"You keep telling yourself that, Colin," Evan said as he patted me on the back.

"How many times have you pinned me?" I asked.

"I'm letting you pin me. The coaches said I should build up your confidence."

"You keep telling yourself *that*, Evan."

"I will pin you someday. It is my lifetime goal."

"I suggest you pick an easier goal because it will *never* happen."

"Jerk."

"Weakling."

"Okay, if you two are finished flirting it's time to hit the weights," Blake said.

"Flirting? With that?" I asked, wrinkling my nose.

"You wish you could have some of this," Evan said.

Blake shook his head in frustration and we headed toward the weight room with the rest of the team. I loved wrestling practice.

The moment I showered and dressed after practice, I headed straight outside, climbed on my bike, and pedaled south toward Alpha. I usually took the bus to practice, but I wanted to make it to Alpha as quickly as possible because the other pledges were already setting up for tonight's party. Riding my bike was much faster.

"It's about time you got here, slacker," said Slade, one of the other pledges.

"Yeah, Slade has been hard at work in the *five* minutes he's been here," said Wes, another of us.

"Tennis practice," Slade said, grinning slightly.

"So what needs to be done?"

"I'm glad you asked. Since you have muscles we saved all the heavy lifting until you decided to show up. We were instructed to clear out the middle of the room and arrange the furniture near the walls."

"Okay. Let's do it!"

"You don't have to be so enthusiastic, Colin. None of the brothers are watching right now," Wes said.

"Didn't you know about the spy cameras?" I asked.

"Seriously? There are cameras in here?"

"Yeah, and I'm sure one of the brothers is watching our every move and listening to everything we say."

"Oh shit. I am so fucked."

I began laughing. It took him a few moments, but Wes realized I was putting him on.

"You asshole!" I laughed harder.

"Come on. Let's get to it."

We moved all the sofas, loveseats, and easy chairs to the sides of the room. When we did so, we discovered a large amount of dust under each, which we swept up. We worked well together, moving from one task to another. The lounge quickly took shape.

"Not bad," Flynn said when he walked into the room with Federico.

"I want you and you in the kitchen with me," Federico said, pointing to two of the pledges.

"You and you come with me," Flynn said, pointing to Wes and me. "The rest of you dust every surface in the room, place four trashcans in here, set up a long table in front of the trophy wall and then report to the kitchen for your next task.

"Yes sir!"

Flynn led us outside to a large van parked in the lot. We all climbed in and he started it up.

"We're picking up two kegs, then we have to make a run to Kroger for ice and soft drinks. You two get to do all the lifting."

"I'm sensing a pattern here," I said.

"We try to get all the use we can out of our pledges. You'll get your chance next year if you get in."

Our first stop was at Big Red Liquors, which had locations all over Bloomington. Wes and I waited in the van since we weren't old enough to go in, but Flynn soon motioned for us to get out as an employee brought out a keg on a dolly. He placed it behind the van and then went back for another.

Wes and I squatted down, grabbed the keg, and lifted. It was damned heavy. We maneuvered it up against the seats and then hopped out to load the second keg.

"Secure them with these straps," Flynn said.

We set to work and soon had the job done. We climbed back in the front and Flynn headed for Kroger.

"Okay, Colin, fill a cart with two-liter bottles of soft drinks. Get a mix of different kinds and make sure you get 7Up or Damon will scream in your face for a good five minutes. Wes, you fill another cart with ice and then both of you meet me back here."

Our task did not take long but when we returned, Flynn was waiting on us eating a chicken leg.

"Okay, let's go."

We went through the checkout, then Wes and I pushed the carts out to the van and loaded everything into the back.

We were soon at Alpha once more. Flynn parked, told us to take everything to the kitchen, then departed.

We took the ice in first. That task alone took several trips, then we took the soft drinks. Our last task was carrying in the kegs and it was not easy. Wes and I were both strong, but the kegs were heavy. I'd guess they weighed somewhere between 150 and 200 pounds each. Getting them inside and to the kitchen was a struggle, but we accomplished it.

"How do you get the kegs in when you don't have pledges to do it for you?" I asked Flynn, who was standing in the kitchen.

"Oh, we use the dolly. It's easy."

Wes and I groaned. Flynn laughed.

"You're sadistic. You know that, don't you?" I asked.

"Hey, no trying to score points by complimenting me, Colin."

"Grr."

When the party began later, our job was to replenish whatever was running low, empty the trash as the bags filled, and make sure there was a constant supply of beer.

Tonight's party was a get together with Alpha's sister-sorority, Delta Omega Omega. There were a lot of hot girls at the party, but as pledges we were not allowed to speak to them unless they spoke to us first. We were not allowed to touch them or dance with them. We were at the party strictly as servants. It was a little like working for a catering service without getting paid.

I enjoyed myself for the most part, although it was more work than I would have thought to keep the party well supplied with drinks and snacks.

I was tired when the party ended, but the pledges were not finished. We had to clean up everything, put everything away, and move everything in the lounge back to its original position. It was past 3 a.m. when I rode my bike back to Hershey Hall.

I was hurting the next morning when I woke up. My body cried out for more rest, but I had class. I forced myself to get out of bed, then wrapped a towel around my waist, grabbed my shower caddy and headed for the showers.

The hot water helped to bring me back to life, but I was still dragging when I dried off and returned to my room to dress. This was going to be a long day. I hoped I did not fall asleep in class. It's a good thing I didn't like alcohol. I could imagine what I would've felt like if I also had a hangover.

I was reasonably awake when I walked into my first class, but I wasn't at my sharpest. I took more notes than usual because I doubted I would remember anything.

I nearly forgot I was meeting Haakon for lunch in The Food Court of the IMU. That's how tired I was. Perhaps something to eat would help. I couldn't remember if I had eaten breakfast or not. I was starving so my guess was not.

"You look like hell," Haakon said when he spotted me.

I grinned. "I look that good?"

"What are they doing to you at that frat?"

"I was up until 3 a.m. helping with their party and I had a strenuous day yesterday. I've been kind of out of it today. I think I forgot to eat breakfast."

"You also forgot to shave."

I raised my hand to my chin and felt the stubble.

"Crap."

"Oh, you look sexy."

"You already said I look like hell."

"You're also sexy. What should we eat?"

"I could go for a pizza."

"Me too. You sit right here, or better yet get some sleep and I will get us both pizza."

"I think I love you."

Haakon smiled and departed. I put my head down on the table and fell asleep.

A hand shaking my shoulder awakened me.

"Here is your pizza sleeping beauty."

"Oh, cool. How much do I owe you?"

"You can buy next time, but I'm afraid you'll have to pay the delivery charge with sexual favors."

"Mmm, yes, but not today."

Haakon laughed. "You are tired."

I bit into my pepperoni pizza from Pizza Hut. I'm not sure when I'd tasted anything so wonderful.

"So you helped with a party; does that mean you don't have any sexy hazing stories?" Haakon asked.

"Nope. Hazing is out. Basically, we are slave labor. It's not bad, but I learned yesterday that beer kegs are very heavy."

"Just remember that this time next week you will be a member of Alpha Alpha Omega."

"Only if one of the brothers doesn't take a dislike to me and blackball me."

"They can do that?"

"Yes, although I think Grant might kick the ass of anyone who blackballed me. Then again, he probably wouldn't know who did it. I'm guessing it's a secret ballot."

"Since Alpha approached you, I don't think you have much to worry about."

"If they do, they do. I'll admit, I do want in, but if I don't make it I'm sure I'll live."

"So I won't have to hold your hand while you cry?"

"Jerk."

Haakon laughed. "You should get some sleep."

"I might work that in before wrestling practice and if I can't I'll go to bed early tonight. I should have more time to spend with you after this is over, although I want to ride with the Alpha Little 500 Team."

"I don't think you're going to have much time for me, but that's okay. We will merely have to make the most of what time we have." Haakon rubbed his foot against my leg and even in my semi-exhausted state it made me want to jump on him.

"I think you enjoy tormenting me."

"A little, but sometime when you're good and rested you can take your revenge on me." Haakon leaned over and whispered how into my ear. His words nearly made the front of my shorts rip from the strain.

"I wish I was rested up now!" I said.

"It wouldn't matter. I have class in a few minutes."

"Grr."

Haakon and I had a great lunch. By the end I was beginning to come back to life. After he departed, I stopped by a restroom on my way to class and checked myself out in the mirror. The dark areas under my eyes made me look a bit like a raccoon. At least the stubble on my chin didn't show much. That was one advantage of being blond.

I was semi-alert in class. The moment it ended I headed for Hershey Hall. I set my alarm and lay down on my bed. I must have fallen asleep instantly because when my alarm went off I couldn't even remember putting my head on the pillow.

I felt rested when I awakened, but oddly enough, wrestling practice is what truly energized me. It might have had something to do with my hunky teammates and what Haakon whispered in my ear at lunch. I also vaguely remembered a dream that featured Haakon. I couldn't remember much about it other than he was naked and it was a *very* good dream.

Being a member of the IU wrestling team was making me a better wrestler. To be honest, I was not learning many new moves. Skye was such an accomplished wrestler that even what was new to the team was not to me. What truly helped me hone my skills was wrestling against a wide variety of excellent wrestlers. Competition in high school could be intense, but the guys I had wrestled in high school could not match the skills of my IU teammates.

I did not hit the SRSC after practice. Instead, I returned to my room, gathered the books I needed, and then rode to the IMU and sat at one of the outdoor tables on the large patio on the north side of the building.

A fire was going in the fire pit and the scent of the wood smoke wafted over the patio. I enjoyed the outdoors while I worked on my assignments for the day. It was very restful. I wanted to remember this place for future study sessions. I loved being outside.

When I grew hungry, I walked up the wide stone steps and entered The Commons. I ordered a Baja burrito and a Coke from Baja Fresh and took them back outside to my table. The burrito was delicious and had plenty of cheese and guacamole. It came with chips & salsa.

I read while I ate, partly to cover more material, but also to avoid eye contact with girls who were seated near me. I was in a rather worked up state, but the last thing I needed was to hook up. The girls were checking me out and I knew that something might happen if I allowed myself to so much as look at them.

My apparent disinterest must have been enough to discourage the girls because they made no effort to speak to me and departed before I finished eating. I was relieved and yet disappointed. A fantasy of taking them both back to my room played out in my head until I forced my mind back on task.

Reading became more difficult as the light failed. I moved in very close to the fire where others were sitting quietly and managed to read a while longer by the firelight, but after a while I was forced to give it up. I packed up my books and rode my bike back to Hershey.

I finished up my assignments in my dorm room. It was still early when I did so, but I forced myself to climb into bed. I lay there for a quite a while unable to sleep, but I kept my eyes closed and allowed random thoughts to flow through my mind. Within a few minutes, I was asleep.

Chapter Six

I reported to Alpha with the other pledges at 10 a.m. on Saturday as ordered. Our first task was to make large signs reading "Alpha Alpha Omega Car Wash – Donations Accepted."

While a couple of the guys put up the signs where they could easily be seen from 3rd Street, the rest of us carried hot water in buckets, attached long hoses to spigots, and gathered rags, brushes, and other car washing supplies.

I had come dressed in a tank top, running shorts, and sandals because I knew I was sure to get wet. The morning was warm and somewhat humid, promising a rather hot day. As the first car pulled in, I pulled off my tank top and tossed it on the grass so I wouldn't get it soaked.

Our first customer was a Camaro containing two rather sexy college girls. I sprayed the car as soon as the girls stepped out and off to the side, then Slade, Wes, and I set to work with soapy rags. The other pledges stood back and waited for another customer.

I pretended not to notice as the girls checked me out, but Damon noticed and soon walked over to me.

"Colin, let one of the other guys take over. I want you to stand out by the street and hold up a sign for the car wash."

"Why do I feel like I'm being pimped out?" I asked, grinning.

"Because you are."

"I feel so cheap," I said, then laughed.

The girls followed me as I walked the short distance to the edge of 3rd Street. I stood shirtless in the sun holding the sign over my head and occasionally moving it around.

"So you're an Alpha brother?" one of the girls asked.

"I'm a pledge. The Alpha brothers are basically using us as slave labor to raise money."

That's a good idea, especially with you out here. Are you a football player?"

"I'm on the wrestling team."

We continued chatting while I flashed my sign. More cars began to pull in. The girls reluctantly departed when their car was finished. Before long, there were as many cars in the lot as we could handle, so Damon pulled me from sign duty for a while and I returned to washing cars.

I noticed that all the guys were shirtless now. The day was beginning to warm, but I had a feeling Damon had instructed the other pledges to peel their shirts off. We were definitely being pimped out.

We had an extremely busy morning. We took turns breaking for lunch at midday. The brothers had kindly provided soft drinks and sandwiches from Subway. I had my break at about 12:30.

"How are we doing?" I asked Grant.

"Incredible. We've taken in over $600 this morning."

"Seriously?"

"Yes. I am a genius."

"So this was your idea?"

"The car wash, yes; using shirtless pledges to bring in business was Damon's idea, although to be fair I was going to have you guys strip your shirts off as soon as I came out. Our team had car washes in high school and we always did better when we were shirtless. It brought out some girls and even more older women and gay guys."

"Sex sells."

"Yes it does, and you're doing particularly well."

"Yeah?"

"Most of the money is coming from cars you wash."

I laughed. "What can I say? I'm glad to be of service."

"Hmm, maybe we should run an escort service, but that would be getting dangerously close to prostitution. I doubt the national council would appreciate it."

"Yeah, it's best to stick to low level pimping."

"Get back out there as soon as you can and use that bod to make us money," Grant said with a smile.

"I'll consider you my pimp."

"Okay, as long as I don't have to wear ridiculous pimp clothes."

"Hey, if I'm being pimped out, I think you should dress for your part." I grinned as I pictured Grant wearing an outrageous long fur coat and an oversized lime green hat.

"It's not happening. What?" Grant asked when he noticed my smile.

"I was picturing you dressed as a pimp."

"Gee, thanks."

"Anytime."

I finished my sub and rejoined the crew. There were only two pledges on each car now because there was a line of cars waiting. The drivers were a mix of college girls, older women, a few older men, and even a few high school and college boys. Some were only there to get their car washed, but most were probably more interested in the boys washing their cars.

Max and Riley were a constant source of amusement. They squirted each other with the hoses whenever possible and got most of the rest of us too. They seemed more like high school boys than college boys, but then all of us pledges had only been out of high school for a few months.

Two very old ladies sat off to the side ogling Wes and me as we washed their car. They made no secret of checking us out. I even heard one comment on Wes's fine ass. I nearly laughed, but managed to control myself. Wes grinned at me. He'd heard them too. He wasn't the least bit bothered by it. Like me, he found them brave and amusing.

"What do you think?" I asked as I walked toward them after we'd finished.

"I think you are the hottest young man I have ever seen in my life and your buddy isn't bad either. If I was sixty years younger I'd be all over you."

I grinned. "Thanks, although I did mean the car."

"Do you really think we care about the car?" asked her friend.

I laughed. I really liked these old ladies.

"Unfortunately, we're too old to do anything but look," the first said, standing up with some difficulty. She reached in her wicker purse and handed me a fifty-dollar bill.

"Thank you very much," I said, offering her my arm. She took it and I helped her back to her car. Wes escorted her friend to the passenger side.

"I hope you don't mind two old women checking you out."

"I'm flattered and you're not that old."

"Oh, I am. Enjoy it while you've got it. I had fun when I was your age. To be honest I was considered a bit loose and I'm not one damn bit sorry. If I had it to do over again I'd be much looser." She laughed and so did I.

"Oh, I have a lot of fun."

"I bet you do. A boy with your face and body can probably have anyone he wants."

"Honestly? Yes." She smiled. "You have a great day," I said, kissing her cheek.

"Oh, I will now. I'm going to tell all the ladies at the club that a handsome young man couldn't resist kissing me."

I noticed Wes gave his old lady a kiss on the cheek just before he helped her into the car as well. We waved as they departed.

"Hmm, I wonder if my grandmother is like that when she's out and about," Wes said.

"You never know. Weren't they awesome?"

"Yeah. They were sweet, and talk about brave!"

"I don't know if I would have the nerve. Come on, the next car awaits. Maybe some more grandmother's will check us out."

Wes laughed.

The weather in the afternoon could best be described as broiling. The temperature climbed into the high 90's and it was unusually humid. I made sure to keep sunscreen on, but I was already fairly well tanned so that helped protect me from sunburn. I didn't mind at all when Riley or Max sprayed me with the hose. It was a perfect day to get wet.

"Marc!" I said as he climbed out of his vintage blue Camaro. His husband, Alessio, exited from the passenger side. Both were in their 40's and they looked fine.

"I was told you had pledged Alpha. I must say I'm pleased."

"I wasn't going to join a fraternity, but one of the brothers convinced me to come and check out the house and meet some of the guys. He hooked me with Alpha's Little 500 tradition."

"So you think you want to race?"

"Yes, I do."

"That's awesome. We'll have to talk bikes and racing sometime."

"Don't do it, Colin. He will never shut up," Alessio said.

116

"Oh, like you aren't as into it as I am."

"I love your car," I said.

"I have a thing for Camaro's."

"We will make it shine," I said.

"Good, although I really came to pick up college boys."

"Sure you did," Alessio said, patting him on the back.

"Actually, hooking up with one of these college boys would probably kill me." Marc laughed.

"And if it didn't, I would," Alessio added.

Marc and Alessio wandered off to talk to some of the brothers. Marc was a legend at Alpha and both he and Alessio were quite involved with their old fraternity, so all the brothers knew them.

"So you know them?" Wes said as we sprayed the Camaro and began to wash it with soapy rags.

"Yeah, they are friends of my uncle. They're really cool."

"I assume they are a couple."

"Yep."

"I think gay guys have it easier sometimes," Wes said.

"How so?"

"I feel like I can't be myself around girls. They expect me to be a jock, which I am, but I like to cook, I love art, and I'm kind of a sensitive guy."

"You sound like a girl's dream."

"Not really. Girl's talk a lot about wanting a sensitive guy, but act sensitive around one and she loses interest. I figure gay guys can more easily be themselves."

"Maybe, but I can't really say. I'm bi."

"You like guys and girls?"

"Oh yeah! Right now, I'm especially interested in a guy I met here, but I'm attracted to girls too."

"Here? Is he a brother?"

"No. I meant here at IU. He's from Norway."

"You must get tons of sex."

"Honestly? Yes."

"I'm jealous."

"You don't look like you'd have any problems."

"Ah, well. You know how girls can be."

"True. They aren't as easy as guys. At least most of them aren't."

"Older women can be easy. My first was an older woman."

"Yeah?"

"Yeah. I was sixteen and she was thirty-five and recently divorced."

"I bet you enjoyed that."

"Yeah. Actually, it was the perfect way to lose my virginity. I was rather uncertain of my abilities. She guided me when I got lost without judging me. I think it was much better than it would have been with a girl my age."

"You might be right. I've always been very confident, so I don't know."

"You're lucky. I was not confident at all, but my affair with her ended that. Ever since I have been a love machine!"

I laughed.

"I'm glad your confidence has improved. I've never had a problem with it. My mom taught me not to fear failure. She said that if there was something I wanted to do, I should try even if the odds were I'd fail. It often takes several failures to achieve success. A point proven the first time I stood up for a gay boy who was being bullied."

"What happened?"

"I got my ass kicked."

"That had to suck."

"Yeah, but I actually achieved my goal of rescuing him and it encouraged me to truly learn how to fight. That's when my Uncle Skye began to seriously train me."

"I bet you don't get your ass kicked anymore."

"It's been a long time, but anyone can get their ass kicked. I try not to be overconfident. That's my problem. Sometimes, I'm a little too sure of myself and that can be dangerous."

"Yeah, I guess so." Wes gazed at me for several moments as he absentmindedly washed the Camaro.

"What?" I asked.

"I'm not hitting on you or anything, but... how did you get a body like that? I'd kill to look like you. Do you work out all the time or what?"

I grinned. "I think you want some, Wes."

"Noooo," Wes said.

"I'm messing with you. I work out a lot; some in the SRSC, but mostly doing other things. I'm on the wrestling team here. In high school I wrestled, played football, trained with my uncle Skye, and did gymnastics. If I get into Alpha I'm going to try to make the Little 500 team."

"I don't have the time to be that active. How do you have time to study?"

"I carefully schedule my time. School is my top priority, but I try to work in as much of everything else as I can. I've started using a lot of spare bits of time to study. When I have ten or fifteen minutes I use them. It helps."

"You must be smart too."

"I am not as dumb as my blond hair would have you believe."

Wes laughed again. We finished washing the body of the car and scrubbed the tires with brushes. The next step was rinsing the car off with the hose. I gave myself a good spray before I started. The cool water was refreshing.

After rinsing the Camaro, we dried it with a shammy so it wouldn't spot. I think the proper name for the super absorbent cloth was chamois, but this was Indiana, a state where even some Old English words were still in use.

"Wow, it looks like new," Marc said as he returned.

"If you and the Camaro would like to be alone for a few moments we can all step away," Alessio said. Marc stuck out his tongue.

"I would not mind a car like this myself. I tried to talk Skye into letting me use the Auburn for school."

"I'm sure that went well," Marc said.

"He said he'd buy me a Yugo. I looked it up online because I thought he was making it up, but it's a real car. Several sites referred to it as the worst car in history."

"That sounds about right," Alessio said.

"Skye thinks he's funny sometimes. I hope to get a car for my sophomore year. I had a junker, but it died. I would not have trusted it on a trip to Bloomington anyway."

"Tell Skye I said he has to buy you a new Lotus," Marc said.

"Yeah, like that will work. I don't expect anything cool. I'll be happy with anything that looks decent and runs well."

"Well, the looks decent part rules out the Yugo."

"No kidding. Those things were ugly."

"Hey, you have my number. I know you're busy with pledge week, but when things calm down call me and we'll get together and talk bikes and racing. People are waiting so we'd better not keep you," Marc said, handing me a bill with Benjamin Franklin on it.

"Thanks. You're very generous."

"We like to support Alpha. Besides, I stole it out of Alessio's piggy bank."

Alessio rolled his eyes, then smiled as they climbed in the Camaro and drove away. I took the money over to Damon.

"Wow. A hundred? How did you get this? Have you been flirting with the older women?"

"Yes, I have, but this is from Marc and Alessio."

"Oh, okay. They are always helping us out. This car wash is raising a lot of money. I think we should make it an annual event."

We kept washing cars until dark. There was never a time when there wasn't at least one car in the lot getting washed. I got hit on by a couple of much older women and an older guy who offered to give me a personal tip. I had the feeling I could make a bundle as an escort. I actually didn't see much wrong with that, but it wasn't for me.

I was extremely tired at the end of the day. I rode my bike slowly away from Alpha and toward my dorm. I felt like I'd just finished an intense workout session. My muscles were actually sore.

When I arrived at Hershey Hall, the first thing I did was take a shower to wash away all the sunblock and sweat. I felt and no doubt smelled much better when I returned to my room.

I made myself a mug of tea in the microwave and sat down to make some headway on my reading assignments. Doing nothing but sitting, drinking tea, and reading was relaxing after all those hours in the hot sun. I went to bed early. I was wiped out.

***

Haakon jumped into the pool and swam to me. We had finished our workout upstairs in the SRSC and now it was time to relax.

"This pool is one of the best things about IU," Haakon said.

"It's great, but I actually have one at home."

"Well, not all of us live in a hotel!"

"There are advantages. The scenery is much better here," I said, indicating some hot boys standing by the side of the pool.

"You don't have good scenery in your pool?"

"Not enough. Mostly it's older men who aren't in good shape and boys who are too young to be interesting. There are a few hot guys, but not enough."

"I think you are merely greedy."

"Yes, I am! Mmm, this water feels great. This is the first chance I've had time to relax in days."

"Pledge week is tough, huh?"

"Yeah. I have classes and wrestling practice and I try to work out, but I think every member of Alpha has called me and placed a take-out order. One of them did it at 2 a.m., but he was drunk. I'm not sure he even remembers."

"I'm glad I'm not a pledge."

"It sucks in some ways, but mostly it's okay and sometimes even fun. I'm not looking forward to tomorrow."

"Why not?"

"It's fast day. We're not allowed to eat anything an Alpha brother doesn't give us, but Grant says none of the pledges will starve."

"Damn. I guess that means we can't meet for lunch."

"Yeah. I do not want to sit in The Commons or a dining hall when I can't eat anything."

"It will all be worth it I'm sure."

"That will be my mantra tomorrow."

I gazed at Haakon. I wanted to kiss his soft red lips. I was tempted to do so right there in the pool, but I wasn't sure the other swimmers would appreciate it.

Haakon and I gave log rolling a try a few minutes later. The log was made of foam that reminded me of the material used to make kick boards. It was large enough to stand on, but it was quite difficult to balance. Haakon and I both fell into the water on our first attempt. We remained on the log for several seconds on our second try. By the third attempt we were beginning to get it down. The trick was to keep rolling the log underfoot while maintaining our balance. We considered ourselves a success when we remained on for a full minute-and-a-half.

We had a lot of fun watching others as we waited for our turn. No one was good at log rolling and most were terrible. Everyone laughed at those trying to stay on the log. It was an event where failure was the rule.

After we'd had our fill of failure, we returned to swimming. We swam a few lengths, but mostly we messed around and talked.

"Let's go back to your room," Haakon suggested with a very slight grin that promised a very good time.

"You have the best ideas."

Haakon and I climbed out of the pool and walked to the showers. We quickly washed off the chlorine, then dried and dressed in the locker room. The sight of Haakon's naked form made reaching my dorm room as soon as possible of the utmost importance

The bus ride took forever. Actually, it was probably only ten minutes, but it seemed like forever. I was in such a hurry to get inside my room I put my card in backward, but soon the door was unlocked and then relocked behind us.

Haakon and I ripped off each other's shirts and aggressively made out as our hands roamed everywhere. We kicked off our shoes and tore through each other's shorts. As soon as we were naked, I shoved Haakon onto his back on my bed and explored his torso with my tongue, returning often to his lips to make out with him for a few moments before returning my attention to his chest and abs. Haakon writhed and moaned as I sucked on his nipples.

I drew Haakon into my mouth and made him moan even more. I worked him into a state of torturous need, then returned to his torso before he lost control.

Haakon shoved me off him and onto my back. He explored my body as I had his and soon I was the one moaning. I loved Haakon's aggression. The best sex was rough, intense and just short of being a battle for dominance. Haakon was a strong and assertive partner. He loved to struggle and wasn't afraid to use muscle to get what he wanted. Far too many guys, and girls for that matter, were too submissive. I preferred sex with someone as forceful as me.

Our breath came hard and fast and our bodies were damp with sweat. I slipped away from Haakon for a moment and opened the drawer where I kept condoms and lube. When I was ready, I pounced on Haakon. He wanted it, but he didn't give it up easily. He struggled against me as I forced him onto his stomach and held him down as I slowly penetrated him. He groaned with passion as I buried myself inside him.

Haakon's struggles subsided as I took him and he began to moan, groan, and push himself back against me. I flipped him over onto this back, pulled his legs over my shoulders, and entered him again.

I had incredible control and could keep going and going. I watched Haakon for signs he couldn't take it anymore, but the rougher I was with him, the more he seemed to like it.

I couldn't resist leaning over and kissing him as I made him whimper, moan, and groan. He kissed me back hungrily.

I kept going and going until Haakon began to moan louder than ever. I went at it harder and faster and watched as he began to climax. That sent me over the edge. I buried myself in him and released my pent-up passion.

I rolled off Haakon and lay beside him on the bed. My chest heaved and I fought to catch my breath.

"That was incredible," Haakon said.

"Damn, you're sexy," I told him and then gave him a quick kiss on the lips.

"We have to do it again!"

"Now? Are you trying to kill me?"

Haakon laughed. "Uh no, not now. I don't think I could handle it again now. I am going to be sore tomorrow, but it will be pleasant reminder of this evening."

"I'm glad I met you," I said, kissing him again.

"Not as glad as I am that I met you. That was the best sex I've *ever* had."

"It was close to the best sex I've ever had."

"Close huh? What was the best?"

"Well, there was the time I was with three girls and then there were those two male gymnasts. I can truthfully give you the award for best solo."

"You know, if anyone else told me about hooking up with three girls at once or two gymnasts I'd be certain they were lying, but I have no doubt you're telling the truth."

I grinned. "I am and you're incredible. Let's shower. I can't stand the feel of lube once I'm done."

Haakon and I wrapped towels around our waists and then walked out into the hallway. Three guys clapped and cheered for us, making Haakon blush slightly and me laugh.

"You think they heard?" he asked.

"Yeah, there are no secrets in the dorms. You're so cute when you blush."

"Grr, stop."

Haakon and I entered a shower stall together. The hot steamy water and our soapy bodies worked us up again, but we contented ourselves with only a little making out. Soon, we rinsed and dried off and headed back to my room.

"I could really fall for you if I wasn't returning to Norway so soon," Haakon said as he dressed.

"Yeah, if I let myself, I could fall for you too. I hate that you'll be here such a short time and yet that acts as a safety net. I do not want a serious relationship right now."

"Me either, but if we met in a different situation, things could be very different."

"True, but I like what we have now. I say we make the most of it."

"I agree. Hopefully, you'll soon be up for a repeat of this evening."

"Oh, I will be, very, very soon."

Haakon kissed me and then departed.

I felt totally relaxed and mellow as I always did after sex. I could probably have gone right to sleep, but I wanted to get in some studying. Sleep could wait.

It was a very good thing I wasn't desperate for sleep because my cell phone rang. Grant ordered me to pick up six pizzas from Little Caesar's on 3rd Street and deliver them to the house.

I couldn't ride my bike and taking a bus would be slow, so I set out from my dorm and ran toward 3rd Street. I kept an easy pace, but still covered the distance quickly. Only a few minutes later I arrived at Little Caesars.

With the stack of pizza boxes in hand, I walked at a brisk pace toward Alpha, which was a few blocks distant. A few minutes later I entered and found Grant and a few of the other brothers in the lounge.

"That was fast," Grant said.

"I ran to Little Caesar's. I figured it was much faster than taking the bus."

"Good job. Remember, tomorrow is fasting day."

"I won't forget."

"Take a piece with you. You've definitely earned it."

"Thanks."

As I departed, Riley entered carrying three two-liters of Coke. I wondered how many other pledges were making deliveries to Alpha tonight.

I crossed 3rd Street and entered the old part of campus. Dunn's Woods was dark except for a few areas illuminated by lampposts along the brick pathways. The croak of a few frogs and numerous insects broke the silence.

I stopped and sat in The Rose Well House for a few minutes. The quiet was a nice change from my dorm, which could be quite noisy.

I smiled as I sat there. So far, college was going well for me. Before coming to IU, I wondered how I'd handle not being one of the most popular guys in school, but I found it didn't matter. Everyone was generally nice here and being an unknown among thousands wasn't all the different from being popular in high school. I liked it better in fact. I'd always thought the social hierarchy at VHS was bullshit. Everyone had value.

My studies were going well and wrestling practice was incredible. The facilities were amazing and there were so many guys here with similar interests. Even when I went to the SRSC alone to work out, I wasn't truly alone because I was surrounded by a lot of guys like me. There were tons of hot boys on campus and loads of hot girls. I could probably have hooked up every night if I wanted, but I didn't have the time and too much of anything was not good.

As if all that wasn't good enough, I'd pledged a fraternity, picked up a new interest in bike racing, and I'd met Haakon. I wasn't sure if I was glad or not that he was only here for a few months. Part of me wanted him as a boyfriend, but another part was glad that wasn't possible. I wasn't going to waste time pondering it. He was here until December and then he would be gone. Nothing would change that. The fact that a long-term relationship with Haakon was impossible was a disappointment, but even more of a relief. I truly did not want to get into a serious relationship at this point in my life.

I stood and walked on, passing the bronze statue of Herman Wells where it sat on a bench. My football coach, Brendan Brewer, had actually known him. Now, he was a legend who appeared in paintings and statues. Wells Library, the main campus library, was named for him too.

Campus was much quieter at this hour. I walked past the Showalter Fountain in the center of the arts square and could near nothing but the sound of falling water.

The noise level grew as I neared the dorms. I could hear voices and laughter, but not nearly so much as during the day. Inside Hershey I could hear more voices and music, even when I entered my room and closed the door behind me.

The hour was growing late now, but I still studied for a while before stripping and climbing into bed. I smiled as I caught the scent of Haakon's cologne on the sheets and then quickly fell asleep.

Chapter Seven

I was not eager to begin fasting day. I was usually starving before lunchtime arrived and what if I had to go longer before I could eat? I wasn't sure how I'd make it through wrestling practice if I was truly hungry. I could cheat without anyone knowing, but I wouldn't do that. Doing so would violate my personal principles.

My stomach was already grumbling as I wrapped a towel around my waist and grabbed my shower caddy. I opened my door to discover a small box with a card on the top. I opened the card and read, "Little Brother, I thought you might find this of use. Meet me at The Tudor Room at 12:30. Grant."

I opened the box and smiled. Inside was an apple, a banana, a granola bar, and a small package of trail mix. I was saved!

I walked to the showers still hungry, but with a much better outlook for the day. I smiled when I noticed a boy checking out my butt as I hung up my towel. I wasn't quite an exhibitionist, but I liked being checked out by guys or girls. Not many girls had a chance to check out my ass, but they often checked out my chest when I was shirtless. It was one of the benefits of being in shape.

I loved my morning shower. Some people couldn't get going until they'd had their coffee, but I didn't feel right until I'd washed my hair. I loved the scent of the vanilla and brown sugar shampoo as I worked it in. I was always aware of scents and selected things like shampoo, cologne, and soap with great care. There were many scents I loved; the scent of autumn, the chlorine scent of a pool, daffodils, and even the scent of hot tar on a blacktop road on a summer's day. I doubted most guys paid much attention to scent. Perhaps it was a part of being bisexual. While I was generally very masculine, I possessed a great appreciation for beauty, loved flowers, and loved nice scents. I'm sure I wasn't alone among males, but these were thought of as feminine traits. I was glad to have that side of myself. I liked who I was, all of me, including those parts that were not so masculine.

I sniffed my Irish Spring as I lathered up. I don't know if the soap had anything to do with Ireland other than the name, but it was my favorite. Showering with my brown sugar and vanilla shampoo and Irish Spring was like visiting a spa.

I rinsed and exited the stall and walked toward my towel. The boy who had checked out my butt was finished with his shower too. I took an extra-long time drying my hair with my face covered to give him an opportunity to check me out all he wanted. I pretended not to notice him gazing at me as I dried off my arms and torso, but eventually our eyes met. I expected him to quickly look away, but he didn't. I liked that he possessed the courage to look me in the eye. I winked at him.

Nothing more happened between us, but he openly watched me as I dried off. I smiled at him as I departed and headed back to my room.

I quickly dressed, made my bed, and then ate the banana and granola bar Grant had given me. I stuffed the apple and the trail mix in my backpack for later.

I would have no problem making it through the morning now and since Grant told me to meet him at The Tudor Room, I could look forward to a great lunch. I knew he would not be so cruel as to lead me on.

I climbed on my bike and rode over to the bike racks near Ballantine. It was a good central location for most of my classes, although quite far from Assembly Hall.

My first class passed quickly. I had nearly an hour before my next, so I walked the short distance to The Rose Well House and began one of my reading assignments. Using what spare time I could for studying was more necessary now than ever. I never knew how much of my time the brothers of Alpha would demand.

"Hi."

I looked up. A nice-looking girl with auburn hair gazed down at me.

"Hey."

"Do you have your essay finished?"

"Essay?"

"For English Comp. We're in the same class."

"Oh! Sorry, it's a huge class. Yeah, I finished it a few days ago," I said.

"You're lucky, as well as cute. Mind if I sit?"

I grinned. "This isn't actually my property. You're free to sit anywhere you wish." She sat right next to me.

"I'm Scarlett."

"Like in *Gone with the Wind*. I'm Colin."

"I love that novel," she said.

"I liked it."

"You've read it? You don't look like the kind of guy who would read *Gone with the Wind*."

"Yeah, I have. What do I look like I'd read?"

"Sports Illustrated."

"Well, I read that too."

"I'm not surprised. You're very fit. You have nice arms."

"Thanks."

"Call I feel?"

"Sure."

Scarlett ran her hand over my bicep.

"Flex it for me?"

I did and Scarlett gripped my bicep. She was not an ordinary girl. I liked her forwardness.

"It's hard as a rock."

"Thanks."

Scarlett gazed into my eyes. I knew what she wanted. I leaned in and kissed her. She responded and slid her tongue into my mouth. We began making out in earnest.

Scarlett ran her hands over my chest and down over my abs. I thought she was going to grope me and if she did she'd find something else rock hard. Instead of moving her hands lower, she slipped then under my shirt and ran her hands over my bare torso.

We kept making out. I loved the scent of her perfume, which reminded me of rose and honeysuckle. She created a desperate need in my shorts that was both painful and pleasurable. We made out for a good fifteen minutes before our lips parted.

"I have to get to class. I hope to see you again," she said as she stood.

"I'd like that." I did not stand. I couldn't.

Scarlett stepped away. I watched her as she walked up the steps of Wiley and entered. I loved college. This could not have happened in high school.

I returned to my reading with some difficulty. I was still worked up and it was not a feeling conducive to studying. I somehow managed, but my thoughts kept going back to Scarlett and the things I'd like to do to her. At least when I stood up to walk to class my passion had cooled enough it was no longer obvious. I couldn't have walked across campus right after we made out for sure. I smiled. This was turning out to be a great day.

I was starving by the time my second class let out. That was not at all unusual but I was thankful Grant had invited me to The Tudor Room. Otherwise, I would have been starving with no prospect of eating for perhaps the rest of the day. I had the apple and trail mix in my backpack, but those wouldn't go far if they were all I was getting until tomorrow morning.

I didn't have a lot of spare time before meeting up with Grant, but I plopped down in a worn wingback chair by the Whittenberger Auditorium and worked on an essay.

Just before 12:30, I put away my notebook and walked down the hallway to The Tudor Room. Grant was approaching from the direction of the South Lounge.

"Please tell me you're taking me to lunch," I said.

"Are you willing to beg?"

"For The Tudor Room when I'm starving? Yes!"

Grant laughed. "Well, you don't have to beg. That's why I told you to be here."

"You're a great big brother."

"You're a great maid. My roommate and I will miss the cleaning service after pledge week."

"Your room looks better than mine, although I tend to be neat and organized."

"Me, not so much, but I don't have tell you that. Be thankful Federico is not your big brother. He's a slob. Come on."

Grant led me inside. We walked up to the podium. He'd made a reservation. We were escorted to a table along the wall looking down on the patio outside The Commons. Our server arrived and we both ordered Diet Cokes.

"Let's hit the buffet," Grant said. "Have you been here before?"

"Yes, a few times. I love it and today is the best day ever to come here."

"See, I said you wouldn't starve."

"I am going to stuff myself. Thanks for the food this morning. I still have some of it in my backpack. You wouldn't believe the calories I burn."

"I can imagine."

We went straight for the hot bar. I selected ham with Dijon honey glaze, chicken with choron sauce, and penne pasta with artichoke and wild rice.

"I love eating here. The price is actually very good considering it includes everything. I can spend nearly this much at Burger King downstairs," Grant said.

"Yeah, I plan to come here about once a week. I usually grab something in my room for breakfast so that cuts down on my expenses."

"There are a lot of events on campus that offer free food. That's how they attract crowds. I've known guys that survive mostly on free food. Most college students tend to be poor."

"I'm lucky. I have a partial scholarship, and my uncle pays for everything so I don't have to work on top of everything else. He does not want me to work. He said I should focus on school and wrestling."

"He sounds great."

"He actually is. He's part dad and part brother. We're really close. I think one reason is that both of our fathers took off when we were young. Skye was like a dad even when he was in high school. After my mom and step dad were killed in an auto accident, he became my official guardian."

"That had to be rough."

"Yeah, without Skye I'd be living with my grandmother. She's fine, but I much prefer Skye. He never treated me like a kid, even when I was one. He makes his expectations clear and he's reasonable, especially when it comes to sex. He never told me I couldn't have girls or guys over. Instead, he warned me that I'd damn well better use protection and that I shouldn't do anything stupid."

"Oh man, that is so much better than my parents, especially my mom. If they knew the girls I did in high school they would have shit a brick."

I laughed. "Skye said he understood what it was like and he knew I was going to have sex. He never interfered. My main problem was that the guys I brought home were often more into him than me!"

"You've got to be kidding. I would kill to look like you."

"You haven't seen my uncle."

"He's that hot?"

I nodded. "Before you ask, no we have not messed around."

"Okay. I'll admit I was going to ask. Is he bi or..."

"He's gay."

"Have you ever thought about it?"

"Well..."

"You have!" Grant laughed.

"I thought about it a little when I was younger, but not much even then. We were so close it would have been weird."

"When I was about fourteen I wanted my older sister."

"You pervert." I laughed.

"I was such a horn dog at that age I would have fucked any female who would let me, but I was too chicken to ask."

"That's a rough age."

"Yes, overpowering lust and no outlet."

"Well, there's one."

"Yes, and I availed myself of it a few times a day."

I laughed again. I laughed a lot when I was with Grant.

"You probably don't think about girls at all now, right?" I teased.

"No more than 10 or 12 time a day or maybe... hour, but life is easier now. It must be nice being bi."

"It doesn't suck."

"That would open up a lot of opportunities. I almost wish I was bi, but the attraction to guys isn't there."

"Yeah. Sexual attraction is either there or it's not."

"True. Like you. You're probably the hottest guy I've ever known. I recognize that, but I'm not attracted to you."

"Come on. You can admit it. You want me."

"I actually don't."

"Well, I am insulted," I said, crossing my arms.

"Yeah, right."

"It's nice to have relationships that don't involve physical attraction. It can complicate things."

"True. I'm glad I'm not attracted to guys because it could be awkward living in a frat. I'm not saying you'll have any trouble with that, but I don't want to be attracted to my Alpha brothers."

"It's a matter of not acting on attraction and setting priorities. Like you, you're very attractive, but I don't want that kind of relationship with you. Since you're not into guys it definitely wouldn't work, but I prefer to keep things simple."

"Maybe I could use you as bait to attract girls, but that's no good since you like them too. It's truly not fair that you're bi. You would be so useful if you were gay."

I raised my eyebrow.

"I didn't mean it that way!"

I laughed again. "I don't think you need me as bait, but I'll give a girl up to my big brother now and then."

"I knew I liked you. I'm sure you get as many girls as you want."

"Hey, I haven't messed around with a girl since... this morning."

"Grr."

I told Grant about Scarlett.

"That's it. I should have let you starve today."

"I'd say I'm sorry, but I'm not."

We kept talking while we ate. I had more ham and tried the Italian wedding soup, but I didn't eat too much of either because I wanted to save room for dessert. I could only eat so much even when I was willing to stuff myself.

The dessert bar was probably my favorite part of The Tudor Room. I had a slice of lemon cake alongside a small piece of key lime pie. In addition to my Diet Coke, I had a cup of jasmine green tea. I wasn't big on green teas, but I loved jasmine.

Grant hit the dessert bar hard, so I didn't feel at all guilty when I returned for a slice of blackberry cheesecake, strawberries, and a lemon bar. The slices weren't especially large so I wasn't indulging myself quite as much as it sounds, but it was rather more dessert than I usually ate.

We were both truly stuffed by the time we finished. I knew I wouldn't have to worry about hunger all afternoon. I was certain I'd be starving again after wrestling practice, but I still had my apple and trail mix. Even if that's all I had for the rest of the day I'd be okay. I'd be hungry, but I could live with that until tomorrow.

"Thank you so much for this, Grant," I said after he paid and we stood near the doors.

"It's what big brothers are for. Next year, you can bring your little brother here on fasting day, if you 're lucky enough to get one and you survive pledge week."

"I think I'll survive. I should be okay unless one of the brothers takes a dislike to me."

"That is not likely."

"I hope not. I wasn't interested in joining a fraternity at first, but I truly want in Alpha now."

"I knew I could turn you. I'll see you later, little brother. I have class."

"Later and thanks again."

I walked outside and used what time I had left before class to study in Dunn Meadow. I pulled off my shirt, leaned back against my backpack, and read while I enjoyed the warmth of the sun.

I felt a little too relaxed so I set the alarm on my phone in case I fell asleep. Otherwise, there was a real danger I'd doze off and awaken sunburned and late for class.

Some guys were playing Frisbee at the other end of the Meadow. I was aware of their voices, but otherwise paid them no mind. I would have liked to join them, but I needed to keep up with my work in case an Alpha brother demanded I make a McDonald's or Taco Bell run for him. There would be time to play in the future. Being responsible wasn't always fun.

"Mmm. Mmm. I want to lick you."

I looked up. Haakon stood looking down at me.

"You're the 5th guy who has said that in the last half hour."

"I think you're lying, but then again I wouldn't be too surprised."

"I'm lying. What's up?"

"I'm on my way to class."

"I need to head to mine soon. I'll walk you."

I stood up and pulled on my shirt. Haakon leaned in and we shared a brief but passionate kiss.

"How is fasting day going?" Haakon asked.

"Great, thanks to Grant. He took me to The Tudor Room."

"Oh, I think fasting day is a fraud. It's more like stuff yourself day."

"It was at lunch. The object isn't to starve us, but to let the brothers get to know the pledges better."

"So do you know Grant better now?"

"Yeah, especially after we hooked up in a restroom after."

Haakon eyed me for a moment.

"Liar."

I laughed. "Yeah, but I did learn he's straight."

"Oh, so you hit on him huh?"

"No. It came up in conversation. He is rather attractive."

"Ah, so you plan to hit on him."

"Grr. You are having way too much fun at my expense."

Haakon laughed. "You know as well as I do there is no such thing as too much fun."

"Or too much sex," I said as a girl walked near. She grinned and I wiggled my eyebrows.

"Are you flirting again?"

"Me? I saw you staring at that boy's butt a few feet back."

"That wasn't flirting. He couldn't see me checking out his ass. Here is where we part. I'll see you soon I hope?"

"You can count on it."

I watched Haakon for a few moments as he walked away; talk about a nice ass. Mmm.

I was getting hungry again as wrestling practice approached so I ate my apple during the bus ride to Assembly Hall. I could not afford to be weak during practice. The guys I faced on the mat were formidable.

I stripped in the locker room and then pulled on my singlet. I wondered who had designed singlets. They hugged the contours of the body so tightly it was almost like being naked. Most of the guys didn't wear a jock and the outline of their dick was clearly visible. It was easy to tell if a guy was cut or uncut by checking out his bulge; singlets were that revealing. I was so accustomed to wearing one I wasn't the least bit self-conscious. I usually wore a Speedo while swimming and that was as revealing as it was possible to get without being naked.

I was paired with Jackson for the day. We were in the same weight class and both 6'2" so we were a good physical match. I was more skilled, but I'd found I could learn something from every opponent and teaching Jackson moves give me a workout.

Jackson had size and the muscles, but I was considerably stronger than him. A lot of guys had commented over the years that I was stronger than I looked. I had a feeling that was largely due to my genes. Skye was far stronger than he looked too, even though he looked exceedingly strong.

I couldn't wait for our first meet, but it was still weeks away. My need for competition was well satisfied in practice. We were a team, but when we faced each other on the mat we did not hold back because each of us was determined to win.

By the time practice ended my singlet was soaked with sweat. I clung to my body as I peeled it off. I grabbed my supplies and headed for the showers.

I loved to work up a good sweat, but I also loved to wash the sweat away when I was done for the day. I loved the feel of the soapy washcloth as it glided over my tired muscles. It was relaxing and felt almost like a massage.

I let my eyes roam as my teammates soaped up around me. The showers were a gay boy's dream. I had enjoyed the sights in the locker room at VHS, but what I saw there was nothing compared to the sights here. Most of my teammates had chiseled bodies that would make a straight boy drool and Blake had that enormous cock. I didn't know Blake's sexual orientation, but I wondered how many hooked up with him just to experiment with his enormous dick. It was actually too big. I was mostly a top, but even if I was a total bottom I don't know if I would have had the courage to bend over for that. I laughed.

"What are you laughing at Colin?" Fletcher asked.

"You do not want to know."

"You're just a little bit scary. You know that, right?"

"Yeah, I'm scary, especially to those face me on the mat."

"You really need to work on your confidence, Colin. Have some faith in yourself," Evan said, then laughed.

"When you've got it, you've got it," I said, flexing my pecs and biceps."

"Ego alert!" Blake said.

"Hey, we all have our shortcomings," I said.

"You certainly do," Blake said, staring at my dick.

"Hey! I am plenty hung. I just don't have a freakishly huge cock like you."

"Who does?" Evan said.

"I hear Blake is a virgin because no one can take that thing," Norman said.

"You heard wrong," Blake said.

"Seriously, Blake, has anyone ever taken the whole thing?" Norman asked.

"You mean besides your mom?"

"Ha ha."

"Only one girl has ever taken it all."

"She must have been a slut."

"Let's just say she was experienced. Man, that felt good. You guys with tiny peckers are lucky."

"Hey!" Evan said.

"Don't take it personally, but you all look like you have pencil dicks to me."

I laughed. It was probably true.

I rinsed off and left the intellectual discussion of the showers behind. Today's conversation was actually quite tame. I'd heard things in locker rooms and showers you would not believe.

I was getting hungry as I walked to the bus stop nearest Assembly Hall. I hated to think how hungry I'd be if I hadn't eaten that huge lunch in The Tudor Room. I still had my trail mix, but I intended to save it since it might be all I got until breakfast tomorrow.

I returned to my room and worked on my assignments. I knew an Alpha brother could demand my presence at any moment so I wanted to make sure I had my work done.

My phone remained silent for the next two and a half hours. I completed all my assignments and even put in a little extra work on a research paper that was coming along nicely. I almost couldn't believe I actually had free time.

I thought about eating some of my trail mix, but decided to save it for later. I wasn't starving yet and I might well be before I went to bed. I drank some water, which was allowed, then went outside and got on my bike.

I would have liked to take a long bike ride, but considering the calories I would burn up this was not the time. Instead, I took a more leisurely ride through campus and soon ended up at Dunn Meadow where a football game was in progress.

"Can I play?" I asked as I approached during a lull.

One of the guys took one look at me and said, "Hell yeah, we're short a man. You're ours!"

I laughed and walked over.

"I'm Ash."

"Colin."

The guys introduced themselves. This was obviously a pickup game.

"You know much about football?" Ash asked.

"I played in high school."

"Great, you are our quarterback then. Anyone object?"

Everyone shook his head.

"You sure? I'm actually more of a wrestler."

"You're the only one of us who has played real football."

"Okay then."

I quickly outlined a simple play. It wasn't much, but this was a casual game with only six guys on each team.

It had been a while, but I still managed a perfect spiral. Unfortunately, Ash let it slip right through his fingers. It was a sign of things to come. As the game progressed it became apparent that was I not only playing with amateurs, but amateurs who were especially bad.

Ash quickly earned the nickname Butterfingers. He was rarely able to catch the ball and could not maintain his grip on it when he did. I showed him how to cradle it against his chest, but even that didn't help him. Another player, Tad was nicknamed Trip after he tripped over his own feet, not once, or twice, but three times!

The game was a travesty of errors. I never laughed so hard in my life. I was actually sacked once because I was laughing so much I couldn't throw the ball. Normally, I do not laugh at others for lack of athletic ability, but everyone was laughing, especially at themselves. We had a blast.

It was half an hour before we scored and nearly an hour before the other team made a touchdown, but scoring was not the point in this game. These guys were clearly here to have fun. The guys began to show off when a small group of girls began to watch and became more inept than ever. I thought they were putting on for a while, but then realized the girls made them nervous.

"Ash, have any of these guys ever played football before?" I asked.

"No, most of us are physics majors. See Booker over there? He thought a football was supposed to be round."

"So I'm basically playing football with the cast of *The Big Bang Theory*?"

"Yes."

"Then I'd say you guys are doing pretty well."

Ash laughed. "Not what you're used to, is it?"

"No, but it's been a long time since I've had this much fun and I love football."

"So you don't think we're sad and pathetic?"

"I didn't say that," I said, then grinned. "No, I don't think you're sad and pathetic. Everyone has their strong points. If you want to see sad and pathetic, put me in a physics class."

We continued. I couldn't find a receiver on the next play so I tucked the ball against my chest and ran down the field. Two of the physics boys tackled me and bounced off. I laughed so hard I couldn't run. They pounced on me and with the help of two more guys took me down.

We played for another half hour or so, then the game broke up.

"Hey, would you like to go get something to eat?" Ash said.

"I can't."

"Oh, okay," he said, looking a bit like a puppy who had been scolded.

"I would like to some other time, but I can't now. I'm pledging Alpha Alpha Omega and we're not allowed to eat anything today unless one of the brothers gives it to us."

"Oh. Okay."

"Here, give me your phone and I'll give you my number." I punched my number in then sent a quick text to myself with his phone. Mine chimed. "There, I'll be busy this week, but I should have some time next week."

"Thanks. It must suck not being allowed to eat."

"It hasn't been so bad. My big brother in the frat took me to The Tudor Room and I ate the entire buffet. I'm exaggerating, but I ate a lot. I am getting really hungry now."

"So you have to starve until tomorrow?"

"Maybe, but I do have some trail mix my big brother gave this morning. I think I'll survive."

"You frat guys do some odd things."

"I'm only a pledge. I may get into Alpha, but it's not a sure thing."

"So do they make you guys stand around in your underwear while they yell at you?"

"No, it's nothing like that. That might have been part of pledge week way back, but that kind of thing isn't allowed. We're basically used as servants." My phone rang. "I have to answer this. It could be one of the brothers."

"Colin, report to the house now," said a voice I didn't recognize, but was loud enough even Ash could hear it. Whoever it was hung up.

"See what I mean? I have to go, but I had fun. We'll get together soon."

"Later, Colin."

I hurried toward my bike. I liked Ash. He was different from most of the guys I knew. He certainly was not athletic and I admired his courage in giving football a try.

I hopped on my bike and took the quickest route to Alpha. I hoped my summons meant food, but for all I knew whoever had demanded my presence wanted me to wash his car.

When I arrived at the house, two brothers I had not met were waiting on me. One of them checked his phone.

"Five minutes, not bad. I'm Grayson. This is Rhett. Follow us."

I did as I was told. They led me outside to a Mustang convertible that looked like it probably dated from the 1990's. I climbed into the back seat. It was not roomy. Grayson started up the car and we drove toward the eastside, hopefully toward food.

"Has today been rough?" Rhett asked. I noticed he had a southern accent and I wondered if he'd been named after Rhett Butler in *Gone with The Wind*. Hmm, I'd met Scarlett earlier, now Rhett. What were the odds?

"Not as rough as I expected. Grant took me to The Tudor Room."

"I think he has a hard-on for you. We've been threatened with a beating if we blackball you so we thought we should meet you."

"I don't think I'm his type, but he has seduced me into wanting to race in the Little 500."

"Yeah?" Grayson said. "You ride?"

"Some, but not enough. If I'm accepted into Alpha I plan to ride with the team this year and set my sights on racing next year. I'm on the wrestling team and I keep in shape, but cycling is a fairly new area to me."

"He seems okay so far; don't you think so, Rhett?"

"So far," he said. I thought I could detect a smile in his voice.

"I think we should bump him up from McDonalds to Five Guys."

"Oh, I love Five Guys!" Rhett said.

I liked where this was going, although I had never heard of Five Guys. As long as there was food there, I didn't care.

Grayson turned south on College Mall Road and drove past the mall. Kroger came into view. As Grayson turned I spotted Five Guys. It was definitely a restaurant. I had been very close to it before, but had never noticed it since it faced away from Kroger.

We got out and I followed the guys inside. Perhaps it was because I was extra hungry, but the scents inside made my mouth water.

"Order whatever you want. It's on us, which may never happen again."

"Thanks. You are my new best friends."

I ordered a bacon cheeseburger, fries, and a drink. The burgers at Five Guys came with as many toppings as one wanted for free, so I added mayo, pickles, lettuce, tomato, grilled mushrooms, ketchup, mustard, relish, onion, green peppers and barbeque sauce to mine. That was most, but not all the available toppings.

When we'd all ordered, we took a booth.

"I am starving. I burned up a ton of calories during wrestling practice and then I played football on Dunn Meadow, which was probably not the brightest idea."

"How good are you at wrestling?" Rhett asked. Some girls nearby noticed his accent and looked toward us.

"I'm incredible. I know that's immodest, but modesty isn't one of my strong points."

The guys laughed.

"You look like a wrestler," Grayson said.

"I wrestled in middle and high school. I played some football and tried other sports, but wrestling is my thing."

"We could use some more serious athletes in Alpha. We like to keep a balance between jocks and intellectuals. What G.P.A. did you have in high school?"

"Very close to 4.0."

"Really?"

"Yeah, don't let the blond hair fool you."

"That's great, if you can maintain it in college."

"It's early yet, but so far so good. My priorities are school, then wrestling, then working out."

"No girls?" Rhett asked.

"Well... yes and guys."

"You're bi?" Grayson asked.

"Yep."

Rhett gazed at me thoughtfully, but didn't comment.

"I'm surprised, but okay. It's cool. Any luck with the girls yet?" Grayson asked.

"Yeah, with a few. I had a make out session with a girl earlier, but it was kind of random."

"Random?"

"I was studying in The Rose Well House. She came in, started talking to me, and pretty soon we were going at it."

Grayson laughed.

"What about guys?"

"I'm focusing on a guy from Norway. His name is Haakon and he's awesome. We hook up as often as possible."

"How do you have time to study?" Grayson asked

"Hey, I don't hook up that much," I said laughing.

Our food arrived. Grayson must have liked milkshakes because he had two. Before I could comment, he moved one of them toward me.

"You have a try a milkshake here. That's an order," Grayson said.

"Yes sir." I did as I was told. "Damn, that's good."

"You're addicted now. One sip is all it takes."

"I can believe it."

My burger was delicious, but rather difficult to eat with so many toppings on it. The fries were great too, but the milkshake was the best.

We talked as we ate. I learned that Rhett was from Georgia and I told the guys about Verona and living in The Graymoor Mansion Bed & Breakfast. I also told them about Skye's awesome car and his threat to make me drive a Yugo. I had to explain what it was. Like me, they had never heard of one. I also told them about playing football with the physics majors and how it was as close as I'd ever get to being on *The Big Bang Theory*.

"I think you'll make a great addition to Alpha," Grayson said. "If anyone dares to blackball you, I'll hold them while Grant punches them."

I laughed. "Thanks. Since you bought me food today I'll be your friend forever."

"I see you are easily bought," Rhett said.

"Oh, you should see what I'll do for a chocolate chip cookie. Oh, that sounded really bad, didn't it?"

"Only if you don't like being known as a cheap whore," Grayson said. "Hmm, if you were a girl I'd go buy a case of cookies. Maybe if I was really drunk, but... nah."

Rhett and I laughed.

After we finished eating, we drove back to the house.

"It was great getting to know you, Colin. I look forward to having you in Alpha," Rhett said as we stood outside.

"I look forward to riding with you," Grayson said.

"I'm glad I had the opportunity to meet you both. Thank you again for taking me to Five Guys."

Grayson and Rhett went inside. I walked to my bike and then headed back to my dorm. I knew I'd have no trouble making it through the rest of the night. I even had my trail mix left.

It was too early to go to bed and too late to do much of anything, so I put in some time on a project due at the end of the semester. It wasn't exactly a fun use of my spare time, but what I did now I would not have to do later.

Chapter Eight

The night of the final test had come. I had no idea what it was, but I was not concerned. I had been instructed to come wearing my thinnest pair of shorts. I had no idea why, but as a pledge I did what I was told.

Eight of us gathered in the lounge. No one had been kicked out during pledge week and no one had backed out.

Flynn entered the room. His shirt was stretched tightly against his muscular chest, making me curious as to what he looked like shirtless.

"You have nearly reached the end of your pledge period. So far, all of you have done well. You face one final test and you will find it the most difficult of all. We are bending the rules on this one, but I think I can trust all of you to keep what happens here to yourself.

"When your name is called, you will proceed through that door, closing it behind you. Inside all the current brothers of Alpha Alpha Omega will judge how you deal with your final task. Any questions?"

No one spoke.

"Very well. Riley. You are first."

Riley stood and walked to the door, pausing only to take a deep breath before he opened it, stepped through, and closed it behind him. There were several moments of silence, followed by a loud smack, and a wail of pain. I maintained a dispassionate expression on my face, but most of the others looked slightly alarmed. There was another smack and another cry of pain. From the sound, I was almost sure Riley was getting his ass paddled.

Slade was next. He looked a little pale, but also determined to go on. He walked through the door and soon we heard a smack and a loud yelp. Flynn departed and left us alone.

"I thought they weren't allowed to hit us," Max said.

"Maybe smacking on the ass with a paddle doesn't count," Wes said. "You aren't going to back out now, are you?"

"Fuck no, but I didn't expect to get my ass paddled."

"Be a man."

"Oh, shut up."

I grinned. I wasn't looking forward to getting my ass blistered, but I'd experienced worse pain. The command to wear my thinnest shorts now made sense.

The guys around me were obviously nervous, but I was not. While I didn't enjoy pain and generally tried to avoid it, I could take it. I wasn't concerned with that would happen to me behind the door. I had faced situations far more frightening than this. There was no danger here, merely discomfort.

One by one those around me were summoned into the room, then came the smacks and the cries of pain. I was surprised at how much some of the guys cried out. The brothers must have really whaled on them to make them yelp like that. I hoped my ass wouldn't be too sore in the coming days. I was more concerned about the after effects than getting paddled.

I sat alone in the lounge as my last companion walked through the door. I listened to his cries of pain. I smiled as I thought about the things we did to get into the fraternity. Perhaps we were all just a bit insane.

"You're up, Colin," Flynn said.

I stood and walked to the door. I was ever so slightly nervous now, but even more curious. Flynn followed me in, but didn't close the door behind him. The current brothers of Alpha, each holding a paddle, stood before me and stared grimly at me. The pledges stood off to the side, watching. Damon smacked his paddle into his hand. I peered at the brothers closely.

"You guys are full of shit, aren't you?" I said.

Grant lost it and began laughing. Soon, the others joined him. I stood with my arms crossed and a slight grin on my face. Grant stepped toward me.

"When did you figure it out?"

"Just now, but I was slightly suspicious. I couldn't believe these guys were big enough pussies to scream and cry out like they did," I said, nodding toward the other pledges.

"I thought my performance was great," Riley said.

"You sounded like a girl," I said, causing the guys to laugh again.

"Congratulations, Colin. Welcome to Alpha Alpha Omega," Grant said. He shook my hand, then hugged me.

"Okay, men. Now it's time for a party. We will have pizza in the lounge as soon as Grant goes and picks it up," Flynn said.

"Help me?" Grant asked, looking at me.

"Sure. I don't have to walk this time, do I?"

"No, we'll take my car. We have an order waiting on us at Pizza Hut."

Grant and I walked outside and climbed into his red Nissan Twin Turbo.

"Nice," I said.

"It's a 1990, but it still runs great."

"It looks even better."

"You have a car?"

"No. It wouldn't make much sense to have one here since I'd have to park it by the stadium and then move it on game days."

"Now that you're an Alpha brother you can park a car at the house. You can also move in. Flynn handles the finances and room assignments so you'll have to talk to him. You'll also have to talk to residential services at IU about moving out of your room."

"I am eager to get out of my dorm. It's okay, but...

"It's a dorm," Grant said, then laughed.

"It will be like moving out of Motel 6 and into a Hilton."

"As long as you don't expect maid service."

"What? You're not going to make my bed and clean my room after I did yours?"

"Nope. You'll have to wait until next year to get your own little slave, I mean little brother."

I laughed.

The nearest Pizza Hut was located on Pete Ellis Drive, less than a block north off 3rd Street, so by the time our short conversation ended, we had arrived.

I couldn't wait to tell Skye I had been accepted into Alpha. He had already okayed the extra expense. I was eager to tell Marc too. I knew he'd be excited that we were now brothers.

I followed Grant inside. He paid with a debit card and then we carried tall stacks of pizzas out to the car. I climbed in, then Grant placed them on my lap so I could keep them safe.

"I hope you didn't have to pay for this," I said.

"No. I used the house debit card. Flynn is its guardian. Anytime we have house expenses we pay with it or Flynn writes out a check. We're very careful with finances."

We were back at Alpha in less than five minutes. We carried the pizzas into the lounge where the others had set up tables and chairs and brought out ice, plastic cups, paper plates, and two-liters of soft drinks.

Everyone attacked the pizza. There was very little talk for a few minutes, but then the conversations began. I smiled as I looked around at my new brothers talking and laughing. I had no intention of joining a fraternity when I came to IU, but I was glad Grant had talked me into it.

"I loved the look on your face when you figured out the whole paddling thing was a con job," Wes said. "Your expression clearly said, 'you assholes.'"

I laughed. "That is what I was thinking, but I also admired the deviousness of it."

"I was not looking forward to walking through that door. I was very relieved when they let me in on it," he said.

"What I want to know is who decided I should be last?"

"That was me," Flynn said. "I figured you were the least likely to crack under pressure."

"So you decided to torment me the longest?"

"Yes."

"You have an evil side I admire. Now, let's talk about my room," I said, putting my arm over his shoulder. "I think I deserve the best room available and the best roommate, don't you think?"

"I was thinking of putting you the broom closet, but I might be able to find something bigger."

"I already have a broom closet in Hershey Hall. My room is a single, which has its advantages, but I want a roommate."

"Roommates can be good or bad."

"True, but I figure there is less of a chance to get a bad one here."

"All the best rooms are taken, naturally, but there aren't actually any bad rooms in Alpha. Come upstairs and I'll show you the one I was thinking about for you. Hey, Wes, join us."

Wes and I followed Flynn upstairs and down a hallway. Flynn opened the door of an empty room and we entered. It wasn't large and yet it was much larger than my room in Hershey. There were two single beds, desks, and chairs, along with nice built in closets and dressers. The floor was carpeted and the walls looked freshly painted. A sizeable window offered a view of 3rd Street.

"It's nice," I said.

"What do you two think of being roommates?" Flynn asked.

"Sounds great to me," I said.

"Me too. Did we actually have a choice?" Wes asked.

"No," Flynn said, then laughed. "If you hated each other I would have reconsidered, but I doubted that was the case."

"My only question is: when can we move in?" Wes asked.

"As soon as you sign the papers and pay your dues. You can stop in tomorrow if you like."

"Oh, I will. I want to get away from my current roommate as fast as possible. He is so annoying that I fantasize about smothering him in his sleep."

"I will too. I'm eager to get into the house. This will be great," I said.

We returned to the party downstairs. It was much quieter than the last party, but this one included only the current Alpha brothers. During the evening, I had a chance to talk with most of them and meet the few I had not previously met.

I rode back to Hershey Hall thoroughly content. From the moment I was accepted as a pledge, I was reasonably sure I would get into Alpha, but it was a relief to know I was in. The first thing I did when I reached my room was call Skye and give him the news. The second thing I did was call Marc. Both were excited and happy for me.

***

"If you laugh at my car, I will hit you," Wes said.

"Hey, you are nice enough to haul my stuff to Alpha. Without you, I would be carrying it all across campus by the armload. I don't care if you drive a clown car, I will not laugh. Besides, I have a friend who drives a hearse. Nothing surprises me."

"He really drives a hearse?"

"Yeah, it's actually rather cool. I've ridden in it a few times. I've even slept in the back on trips."

"I might be too freaked out to do that."

"Things like that do not bother me." I didn't tell Wes about my encounters with the supernatural. I needed to know him much better before I did that, if I told him at all.

We exited the campus bus and walked across the stadium parking lot.

"There it is. My very own 10-year-old Chevy Lumina van," Wes said.

"Oh, I was expecting much worse. It looks like it's in good shape and hey, it's blue."

"It runs well, but on the coolness scale it rates about a zero."

"Oh, on a scale of one to ten, it's at least a two."

Wes laughed. I climbed in the passenger seat and we took off.

"One advantage is that it will haul a lot of stuff. Hell, you could hook up in the back of this thing," I said.

"I have."

"Yeah?"

"This was my high school love machine. I fucked six girls in the back of this van."

"That's awesome. Those girls obviously weren't put off by your ride."

"No. There were advantages to being a jock, but I'm sure I don't have to tell you that. I bet the girls were all over you."

"Yeah and quite a few guys too." Wes looked at me, but didn't say anything. "I'm bi. I hope that isn't a problem."

"No. I'm merely surprised. How does that work?"

"I hook up with girls sometimes and guys sometimes."

"Which do you like best?"

"I'd have to say guys, but it depends on my mood."

"Ever had both at once?"

"Yeah."

"Wow. This is a little personal, so you don't have to answer, but you let guys fuck you?"

"I have, but I'm much more of a top, like 90% more."

"Man, I could not do that. It has to hurt."

"It can hurt. It depends on the skill of the top. I happen to be so good that I can top a guy without hurting him at all. Mostly it feels amazing."

"Hey, stop hitting on me." Wes grinned.

"You should be so lucky!"

"As I'm sure you've guessed, I'm straight. Hey, you want to do the sock on the door thing if one of us is hooking up?"

"Sure, that works. I usually never hook up with more than three or four guys a day."

"Are you *serious*?"

"No."

"Jerk."

I laughed. "Actually, I don't have much time for hooking up. In addition to school I have wrestling practice and I want to ride with Alpha's Little 500 team."

"You are busy."

Wes found a parking spot not far from Hershey. We went inside and began bringing things out. I had three days to clear out before residential services put in someone new, but I wanted to move into Alpha as soon as possible.

I had already packed most everything up, except for what was in the fridge. When everything else was in the van, I emptied the contents of the fridge into a box and tossed a towel over it to help keep everything cool. I handed the box off to Wes, unplugged the fridge and carried it out to the van. I came back for one quick check to make sure I hadn't missed anything and then left my room in Hershey Hall for the last time.

There was plenty of room left in the van, so we headed to Wes' dorm, which turned out to be McNutt. His room was harder to get to and he had more stuff, but after several trips we had it all loaded.

After a short drive to Alpha we got out and opened up the back.

"I see why we loaded my stuff first. That way I have to help you carry your stuff in, but you can take off and leave me to carry mine alone."

"Would I do that to you?" Wes asked. "Besides, blondie, in case you didn't notice, there is a side door."

"Hey, don't be hating on the dumb blond."

"I love dumb blond girls."

"I bet you do."

"I haven't actually found a blond girl who is dumb."

"The dumb blond thing is a stereotype we blonds started as a ruse to hide our superior intelligence."

"Uh huh."

We made trip after trip up to our room, pausing only long enough to plug in our refrigerators and load them before continuing. With two of us it didn't take too long. Organizing everything was going to take considerably more time.

"Hey, I'm going to hit the SRSC. Want to come?" I asked.

"Sure. I spend a lot of time there."

"Me too. I think we're going to get along," I said, smacking him on the back. "You have a bike?"

"Yeah."

"Want to ride or be lazy and take the bus?"

"Let's ride."

"Perfect. I ride almost everywhere, except wrestling practice."

We went outside, climbed on our bikes, and headed across campus to the SRSC. It was quite a bit further from my new home than it was from Hershey, but still not far. Most things on campus were within easy walking distance.

Wes wasn't Haakon, but I enjoyed having a workout partner. I had a feeling we were a good match as roommates, unless...

"Do you like country and western?" I asked.

Wes wrinkled his nose.

"Whew. Opera?"

"I'd rather die."

"Good. I was suddenly stricken with fear that you have dreadful taste in music."

"Oh. What do you listen to? Show tunes?"

"Grr." I glared.

"I have a confession. I like some show tunes," Wes said.

"Homo!" I coughed.

"Hey, that is not politically correct."

"I like dick so I'm allowed. I can also say faggot, queer, fairy and several other words with impunity."

"What if I say them?"

"Then I'm entitled to kill you."

"Harsh."

"Hey, that's the way it is. Do you think I'm making up these rules as I go along?"

"That's exactly what I think."

"This is my chest and abs day. What about you?" I asked as we locked up our bikes.

"Upper body, so we are good."

Since we rode our bikes to the SRSC, we went straight to the main weight room instead of doing cardio first. It was crowded as usual, but we were able to get a bench press machine to share. Wes let me go first.

"God damn, you use a lot of weight!" Wes said after my first set.

"I started young and my uncle is a trainer. You should see the weight he uses."

"Bodybuilder?"

"No, just incredibly strong."

"Maybe you can teach me a few things."

"I'll try."

Wes went next. He used far less weight than me, but still a respectable amount. He was quite well built so I wasn't surprised.

"You are so lucky," Wes said, as we switched places again.

"Why?"

"Look around. It's like 95% guys in here."

"This is true."

"The girls who are here look like they could beat me up."

"Think of the rough sex you could have."

"Think they're lesbians?" Wes asked.

"Because they are working out? Forget the stereotypes; they are bullshit. Some of the most feminine girls you will ever meet are lesbians and some of the butchest are straight. You can almost never guess sexual orientation by the way someone looks or acts."

"What if a guy is checking out another guy's ass?"

"He could be comparing himself."

"What if he pops one while he's doing it?"

"Then he's probably gay or bi."

"I could learn a lot from you."

"Oh, you will. Since you're my roommate, you have access to my superior intellect."

"Do you give modesty lessons too?"

"Only on Tuesdays."

As we talked, I learned a lot of little things about my roommate such as the fact that he hated sushi and had never seen a single *Star Trek* or *Star Wars* film. I agreed about the sushi. I told him that we have a place back home called, "Joe's Bait Shop and Sushi Bar". I also told him he had to watch all the films. It was required for life.

"You want to swim?" I asked after we'd finished a great workout. "I have a locker. You can borrow my shower stuff. Oh wait, you don't have a swimsuit."

"Actually, I do. I have a locker here too."

"Cool. So you want to hit the pool next?"

"Sure, but I think you just want to shower with me so you can see me naked."

"I haven't been able to think of anything else since the moment we met. My every move since then has been with the single goal of seeing you naked. I arranged to have you accepted as a pledge for Alpha and then made sure you got in and that we'd be roommates, all so I could see what you've got."

"Ha! I knew it!" Wes said. "Hmm, there is a flaw in your story. We didn't meet until the pledges got together."

"Hey, I'm blond. Remember? You can't expect me to make up good lies on such short notice."

"Is being blond your excuse for everything?"

"Yes."

"I guess it works. With that light blond hair, you can't be too bright."

"Hmm, I'm beginning to suspect I'm being insulted."

"If you weren't blond you'd know you're being insulted."

"Get going," I said, giving Wes a rough shove in the direction of the locker room.

I made a show of checking Wes out as we stripped.

"Well damn, this is anticlimactic. All that work merely to see this," I said, indicating his body. "What a letdown."

"Hey! I look freaking fantastic."

"Not compared to me," I said, then flexed my arms and chest.

Wes was obviously working hard to think of something suitably insulting to say, but remained silent.

"Can't think of a comeback. Can you?"

"Shut up and go shower!"

I gave Wes my evil laugh and walked toward the shower. He was close behind me.

Wes did look good naked. If I'd met him randomly on campus and he was interested I might have hooked up with him, but he was my roommate and wasn't into guys. I preferred that. I didn't know how hooking up with a roommate would work. It sounded like a bad idea. I had a feeling Wes would be a great roommate. We had similar interests and he was completely cool with the fact that I swung both ways.

As always, I enjoyed the hot water of the showers and the scent of my soap and shampoo. I loved the sensual feel of a soapy washcloth as it glided over my bare skin. Showering could be an erotic experience, but this shower was about quickly cleaning away the sweat of my workout.

We returned to the locker room and slipped into our swimsuits.

"You're an exhibitionist, aren't you?" Wes said, looking at my Speedo.

"Would you quit checking out my dick? Try to control yourself, "straight" boy," I said, making air quotes.

"Everyone who looks at you will see your dick in that tiny thing. Hell, how do you even keep it in there?"

"Practice."

"I'd be self-conscious wearing a Speedo."

"That's because you have a huge ass."

"Hey!"

I laughed. The truth was that Wes had a hot ass.

"I don't even think about it. The singlets we wear for wrestling are nearly as revealing. If I don't wear a jock the outline of my dick is obvious."

"I couldn't wear a singlet. I'd be so embarrassed I couldn't wrestle."

"Most people don't pay that much attention. Those who notice only watch meets to check out wrestlers."

"Isn't it creepy knowing people are perving on you?"

"What do I care? I liked to be looked at."

"Yeah, I knew it. You're an exhibitionist."

We opened the door to the pool. I loved the humidity and the scent of chlorine in the air. We took lanes side-by-side, jumped in, and began to swim laps.

I swam quickly and pushed myself. I wasn't an expert swimmer, but I knew how to swim. I swam in the pool daily back home and came to the pool in the SRSC as often as I could. Wes swam at a slower pace, but this wasn't a race. He kept with it for a good long time, then got out and moved to the open area to mess around in the water. I kept going for another twenty minutes and then stopped. My chest heaved as I climbed out of the water. I joined Wes in the shallow end.

"What are you, a dolphin? You swim like one," Wes said.

"I'm good, but not that good."

"You should be on the swim team."

"I doubt I'm a match for those guys. Besides, I can't do everything."

"You seem like you're trying to do everything."

"Yeah and I hope I'm not taking on too much, but life is short and there is so much I want to do."

We didn't remain in the pool long after that. We soon returned to the locker room, rinsed off, changed, and headed out.

The ride to Alpha took only a few minutes. I wished I had time for a longer ride, but I need to unpack and do a little reading for classes. Time slipped away too quickly. I could almost swear time passed faster in Bloomington than it did back in Verona.

I began putting away my clothing when my ears were assaulted with a horrendous noise. I turned to Wes and glared. He laughed.

"You really don't like country music, do you?" Wes asked.

"No, and if you want to live you will turn that shit off."

Wes switched over to rock.

"That was foul, but it was worth it to see the look on your face," Wes said.

"I suppose I won't take revenge, since you suffered as well."

Even with a roommate, I had more space in my new room. The built-in wardrobe and shelves provided plenty of room for everything. I didn't feel as if I was trapped in a broom closet.

A knock on the doorframe drew my attention to the door.

"Hey, Colin. Want to begin riding with the team tomorrow?" Grant asked.

"I will if I can. Wrestling usually runs until six."

"Perfect. We usually meet about 6:15 or 6:30."

"Sweet. I will be there. If practice runs long I'll call to let you know I can't make it."

"Great. How do you like your room?"

"It's great, even with Wes in it."

"Ha ha. Colin thinks he's witty. I play along," Wes said.

"Hey. I am witty."

"Sure you are, buddy," Wes said, patting me on the shoulder.

"I see you two are getting along," Grant said.

"Yeah, but we can talk about that later. I don't want to say anything too nice about Wes when he can hear."

"Oh yeah. You must avoid that. How do you like Alpha so far, Wes?"

"I don't think I've spent an entire hour in the house yet, but so far, so good. As much as I hate to say this in front of Colin, he's a vast improvement over my last roommate."

"I have to run, but I'll see you tomorrow if not before, little brother."

I nodded. Grant disappeared. Wes and I kept talking while we unpacked. A little later, Wes listened to his music with his headphones while I read. I kept at it until the words didn't make

157

sense any more. By then, Wes was reading one of his textbooks in bed.

"I hope you don't mind, but I sleep naked," I said as I pulled off my shorts.

"It's okay if you want to take the risk I'll lose control and ravish you during the night."

"I'll take my chances. Good night, Wes."

"Good night, Colin."

I finished stripping and climbed into bed. I'd only had a roommate before on a very temporary basis, such as when the VHS wrestling team stayed overnight for an away game. There were often three or four of us sharing a room then and we usually didn't get much sleep. This was different. I could hear Wes breathing and quietly turning the pages of his book as I grew drowsier. I had a feeling I was going to like rooming with my new Alpha brother.

Chapter Nine

The next day was intense. When my alarm went off, I wasn't quite sure where I was. I grinned when I figured out that I was now an Alpha brother and living in the house.

Wes was still sleeping, so I quietly gathered my shower supplies, slipped out of the room, and walked down the hallway to the bathroom without bothering to put a towel around my waist.

I hung up my towel and stepped into the communal showers, which I much preferred over the stalls in Hershey. I wasn't completely awake but I began to come around as I shampooed my hair and soaped up.

I rinsed off and walked toward my towel. Grayson sleepily waved as he passed. I had a feeling he was not a morning person.

I dried off, then returned to my room. Wes was up and getting dressed.

"You snore," he said.

"You're such a liar."

"True and I'm glad you don't snore."

"I slept like I was in a coma. You could have violated me last night and I wouldn't have known."

"Maybe I did," Wes said, wiggling his eyebrows.

"You know, my ass is a little sore..."

Wes laughed and shook his head.

I stuck two strawberry Pop-Tarts in the toaster and grabbed a bottle of water from my fridge. One thing I loved about IU is that many of the water fountains included a water-bottle filling spout.

I dressed and stuffed books and notebooks into my backpack as I waited on my breakfast.

"Feel free to use my toaster," I said as my Pop-Tarts popped up.

"Thanks. I usually just eat a couple granola bars or get something in the IMU."

I quickly ate, slung my backpack over my shoulder, and headed for the door.

"See you later," I said.

"Later."

I walked outside and took my bike out of the rack. I had purposely set my alarm for an hour earlier than usual so I could get in some riding before my first class. This evening, I would tag along with the Alpha riders for the very first time and I needed all the practice I could get. I had grown accustomed to the single speed bike, but I had not been able to devote as much time to riding as I would have liked.

I rode down 3rd Street then headed up Indiana Avenue, quickly passing the Sample Gates and Dunn Meadow. I continued up 3rd to 17th, took a left, and then rode north on Dunn Street. Soon, I was out of town and riding in the country.

The morning air was cool, but that coolness was already giving way to warmth, indicating this would be a hot day. I breathed in the fresh air as I rode past trees and small open spaces. I passed plenty of houses, but they weren't packed together as they were in town. I was only a short distance from the actual town and yet felt as if I was out in the country.

The alarm on my phone sounded after a few minutes and I headed back. I had covered quite a distance in slightly less than half an hour. The hills were a bit of problem. With a multispeed bike I would have switched gears, but that wasn't an option on a Little 500 bike.

The weather had already changed from cool to warm by the time I returned to campus and parked my bike in a rack by Ballantine. I had just enough time to hit the restroom, get a drink, and walk to my first class before it began.

I did my best to focus during class. One thing that helped was taking notes. I had also found that writing things down helped me to remember them. I had read somewhere that the human brain was designed to discard information it didn't see as important after about 15 seconds. Maybe writing something down caused my mind to consider it important enough not to discard.

My cell vibrated, indicating I had a text, but I ignored it. One of my rules was not looking at my phone during classes. Some professors had that same rule and I could see why. A phone was a distraction.

My mind tried to wander to Haakon, wrestling, Alpha Alpha Omega, and the upcoming bike ride, but each time it veered off-topic, I pulled it back. There would be time to think about all the rest later.

Another distraction was a girl with sexy legs who sat below me and off to the left. For a moment, I pictured pulling her legs over my shoulders and.... A guy wearing a red tank top that showed off his muscled shoulders sat right in front of me. He had long, wavy black hair. He was another distraction.

Despite the many disruptions of my concentration, I actually gave the professor most of my attention. I was getting better and better at it each day.

I walked to The Rose Well House after class and sat down on one of the cool limestone benches inside. I checked my phone. I had a text from Haakon; *Lunch? Burger King? I'll let you touch my Whopper.* I quickly texted back; *Yes. 12:15? I wanna do more than just touch it, lol.*

I had a quiz in my next class, so I pulled out my notes and went over them. I did most of my studying well in advance, so this was only a last-minute review. I also took the time to enjoy the view of Dunn's Woods and to watch two chipmunks that visited me in the Well House.

I didn't have a lot of time, so I put away my notes and sat for a couple of minutes. I gazed at students walking past, at the statue of Herman Wells a few feet away, at the trees and at the squirrels nosing about. Doing so gave my mind a chance to clear.

Just as I was beginning to stand I received another text from Haakon; *You can do anything with my Whopper you desire, as long as you slip your foot-long between my buns. See you at 12:15.*

I had difficulty standing after reading that message. I had trouble walking too. A girl meeting me on the brick pathway noticed why and raised her eyebrow. I had to fight to keep from laughing.

My dick calmed down by the time I reached my next class. The professor started with the quiz, which helped me get my mind off Haakon's buns.

I had a dull ache in my balls all through class, but was still able to pay attention. I was accustomed to that dull ache. I seemed to have it more often than not.

I used the few spare minutes I had after class to get part of a reading assignment out of the way and soon it was time to head to The Commons in the IMU.

It seemed like only yesterday that I wandered the halls of the IMU during my visit when I was still a high school boy. It was on that visit that IU went to the top of the list of schools I was interested in attending. I considered others, but it wasn't much of a contest after that. Now, I wandered the same halls as a student and a frat boy.

I spotted Haakon standing near the Burger King. He was wearing a blue tank top and khaki shorts. I wanted to rip that tank off him and lick his chest.

Haakon nodded when he spotted me and we joined the long line. The Commons was always crowded at lunchtime.

"I liked your text," I said.

"Yeah?"

"Especially the part about buns. It made me very hungry."

"Oh, I'm hungry too, starving in fact."

I grinned.

I doubted anyone around us knew or cared what we were really talking about, but I wanted to forget lunch, take Haakon to my room and sink my wiener deep in his buns. Unfortunately, that would have to wait. While I would have spare time here and there later in the day, it was in such small amounts there was no way Haakon and I could hook up. I would have to content myself with the pleasure of anticipation. Besides, spending any time with Haakon was enjoyable.

It took us a while to order and get our food, but at last we stepped away from Burger King with our trays. The Commons was packed, but we claimed a recently vacated table for two along the wall.

"Busy day?" Haakon asked as he bit into his Whopper.

"Yeah. I got up early to ride, then I had classes. I have another class this afternoon, then wrestling practice, and then it's straight to Alpha to ride with the Little 500 guys."

"That's all? You aren't going to practice with the football and swim teams as well?"

"I have to take it easy now and then."

"Do you even have time to sleep?"

"Yeah. It's not as bad as it sounds. I'm very good with organizing my time. I do a great deal of studying between classes and during small blocks of time where I'm doing nothing but waiting. I have a good balance of physical and intellectual activities. One allows me to rest from the other."

"I couldn't handle your schedule."

"I'm sorry we haven't spent more time together."

"It's fine. We're both busy and we're together now. I'm sure we'll manage some more time together very soon."

"Yes we will, especially after that text."

Haakon laughed. "I called home yesterday. It was only 16 degrees there."

"Are you kidding? It's that cold in early September?"

"Oh, that's Celsius. That is about 60 or so in Fahrenheit, but that's about as warm as it gets in September."

"Damn, it was like 80 here and today will probably top 85."

"It is very warm here."

"The temperature will drop a lot later in the month I'm sure. These are more summer temperatures, but it is sometimes 100 in the hottest months."

"I would melt!"

"I have felt like I was melting before."

"You play sports when it is that hot?"

"Yes, but I drink lots and lots of water. I spend a lot of time sweating and peeing when it's extremely hot."

Haakon laughed. We talked so much it's a wonder we had time to eat. After we finished, we walked outside and took a stroll in Dunn's Woods. When we reached an area near the middle where there were benches, we sat down. I pulled Haakon close and gave him a long and lingering kiss. There were students walking past, but we ignored them. The sight of two guys making out might not be common on the IU campus, but it wasn't exactly shocking either. I didn't care. I wanted to kiss Haakon and I was going to kiss him. The only person who could stop me was him.

After a few minutes, Haakon pulled away and sat back.

"We have to stop so I'll have time to calm down before I walk to class," he said. I looked down at the big bulge in his shorts. I wanted to grasp it, but controlled myself.

"I'd like to bend you over this bench right now."

"Damn, don't talk like that or I'll never be able to go to class."

I laughed. "Hey, it affects me as much as it does you." It was true. I needed a couple of minutes to calm down before I could stand.

"Where is your next class?" I asked.

"Woodburn."

"Cool, I have time to walk you there if you're ready."

"Yeah, I'm not too obvious now."

"That thing you have in your shorts is so big it is rather obvious when it's hard," I said.

"Hell, yours is obvious when you aren't."

I laughed. "Sorry, genetics."

"Oh, don't apologize. I like it."

"I know you do."

"Stop or I'll have to sit down again."

"Okay, I'll be good, until we have some alone time; then I'll be very, very bad."

"Not helping!"

"Um. I like puppies!"

"You are a goof."

"Yeah, but it stopped you from thinking about other things. I do like puppies. There's a thing coming up in Dunn Meadow where you can rent one for half an hour."

"Rent a puppy?"

"Yes. It's to raise money for the shelter. I saw it in the IDS." Haakon looked perplexed. "The student newspaper: the *Indiana Daily Student*."

"Let me know when it is. I miss my dog."

"What kind do you have?"

"He's a mix, about twenty-five pounds, brown and shaggy. We call him Mop Top."

"I never had my own dog, but my Grandmother has an American Eskimo and it's almost like he's mine. We spend a lot of time together. I miss him."

"Oh, we have that breed in Norway. Pure white?"

"Yes. He's a bigger one. He weighs about 30 pounds."

"They are very friendly."

"Yeah. He's a big baby and loves everyone. I can't wait to see him again."

We soon arrived at Woodburn Hall.

"Text me when you have some free time so we can get together," Haakon said.

"Oh I will, and it will be as soon as possible."

Haakon grinned, turned, and walked toward the building. I turned toward the HPER, the Health, Physical Education, and Recreation building. The HPER is basically an older, less equipped version of the SRSC, but with classrooms.

It was difficult not to think about Haakon during class. I managed it, but he returned to my thoughts the moment it was over. I couldn't wait to hook up with him again. I'm so glad Haakon is a bottom. He was damned near perfect.

I rode my bike to Assembly Hall, found a quiet place on a bench, and began to study. I wanted to get as much done as possible before practice. Considering all that was going on, it's a wonder I was able to keep my mind on my work, but I did it for the most part. Haakon slipped into my thoughts a few times and renewed the ache in my nuts, but I didn't mind. I would use my sexual need to fuel my aggression during wrestling practice.

We didn't dress out in singlets during today's practice, but instead hit the weight room. I was glad because there is no way I could make it to the SRSC today.

Each wrestler had his own workout especially designed by the coaches after an evaluation. Mine was intense. I don't think it was any better than what Skye had designed for me, but it was a good variation that hit some of my muscles in a different way. I was getting stronger, but then I was always increasing my strength because I consistently worked out and pushed myself. I had learned from Skye how to push my body without going too far. Doing too much was a worse mistake than not doing enough.

I sat up after I completed my last set of bench presses to find Norman watching me.

"What?" I asked.

"You use more weight than I do."

I shrugged. "It's the weight I need to use."

"You know, you look extremely strong, but you're even stronger."

"Shh, don't tell anyone, but Colin is secretly a super hero," Evan whispered loudly enough for everyone near to hear.

"Yeah, he's disguised as his nerdy, pathetic alter ego right now so you can't tell by looking," Jackson said.

"Blow me, Jackson," I said, making him laugh.

Norman continued to eye me as I moved on to the military press. I suppose I could understand his confusion. Norman was massively built with almost bodybuilder size muscles. I was quite muscular, but considerably more compact and I did not look at all like a bodybuilder. The truth was that size wasn't as accurate a measure of strength as most thought. Bigger didn't always mean stronger. The workouts Skye had designed for me were intended to increase my strength, not my size. I looked strong, but I was much stronger than I looked.

Evan's super hero comment was a joke, but it made me think of Skye. Ever since I was very young, I suspected that my uncle really was a super hero. He couldn't fly like Superman or shoot out webs like Spiderman, but he was capable of feats that even someone as built as him should not be able to do. The day he rescued me from the automobile accident that took the lives of my mother and stepfather convinced me there was something to my belief beyond hero worship. The car we were in went into a lake and quickly sank to the bottom. Skye dove into the lake, swam down at least a dozen feet to the car and pushed it out of the lake onto the shore. It seems impossible, but that's exactly what happened. Sean and Marshal were there. They saw him do it. I talked to each of them separately about it months after. They didn't want to talk about it, but they both admitted what had happened. Skye wasn't from another planet. He didn't have superpowers like a comic book super hero and yet he could do things that should have been well beyond his physical abilities. He was as close to a real super hero as the world would ever get.

As I moved from the military press to butterflies I wondered if I was like Skye. I was stronger than I looked, stronger than I truly should have been. Had I inherited something that made me different from others? Skye wasn't my biological father, but we did share many of the same genes. I didn't think I was capable of pushing a car out of a lake, but if faced with the necessity like Skye, I would try. I was alive today because he tried. Knowing Skye, he likely never doubted he could do it.

I was soon dripping with sweat. I loved to sweat when I worked out, except that it made my hands slippery and I had to keep drying them off. Sweating made me feel like I was accomplishing something. I didn't think of a workout as work. I enjoyed it. I loved the way it made me feel. If I wasn't able to work out regularly my muscles cried out for it and that first bench press after being away was pure bliss. I suppose I had a workout addiction, but as addictions went it wasn't so bad.

"My ass is dragging," Fletcher said as the team walked toward the locker room.

"What does not kill you, makes you stronger, which is why I should now be the strongest man on Earth because that session nearly killed me. I'm going to my dorm and crashing right after I shower," Blake said.

"Good idea. I'll join you," Fletcher said.

"Hey, you crash in your own dorm room."

"That's what I mean, jerk."

I loved these guys.

"What are your plans, Colin? Are you crashing in your room or are you just going to stretch out on a bench in the locker room?" Fletcher asked.

"I'm riding my bike to Alpha to join the Little 500 guys on a 20-mile ride."

"You are shitting me."

"Nope."

"Why aren't you exhausted?"

"Hey, I'm tired. I'm just not a little pussy like you."

Fletcher smacked his fist into his palm, but smiled. The members of the team often talked shit, but we never meant any of it. The true competition among us was who could talk shit the best. The competition was fierce. We were all graduates of high school locker rooms, and the things said there would make mothers cringe.

I was tired, but my shower relaxed my muscles and reenergized me. Taking a shower was perhaps a waste of time, for chances were I'd soon be sweaty again, but as much as I loved to sweat during a workout, I hated stale sweat on me after I had a finished.

I left Assembly Hall and walked to my bike. I pedaled south and in only a few minutes arrived at Alpha. The riders were only beginning to assemble.

I hurried up to my room, grabbed a granola bar and a bottle of water and quickly ate.

"What's the hurry?" Wes asked as he entered. "Oh yeah, you're riding with us."

"Us?"

"Yes. I have decided to ride too. I want to see if I can keep up. If I like it you may have competition for a spot on the team next year."

"Great. You ready to go?"

"Yeah. I came in to dump my backpack."

I finished my granola bar and water and then we headed downstairs and outside.

"What kind of bike do you ride?" I asked.

"It's a 21-speed Trek street bike. You?"

"Mine is a Schwinn regulation Little 500 bike so it's single speed."

"I'll have to get a single speed if I get serious."

"Go to Peralta's Bike & Skate Shop on Kirkwood near KOK. Marc carries the Little 500 models. He's an Alpha brother so you'll get an extra discount."

"Sweet. I'll think about it after today's ride. Wait, didn't you just come from wrestling practice?"

"Yeah, we hit the weight room today."

"You're going to ride after that? Are you a masochist?"

"Ah, what's a little bike ride after a little workout?" I grinned.

"You obviously have mental problems."

"Yes, but they tell me I'm not violent."

"Hey, Colin," said Grant, gripping my shoulder. "Ready for your first ride with Alpha?"

"Oh yeah."

"Grant, I have a 21-speed. What gear is closest to a single-speed bike?" Wes asked.

Grant took the bike, set the speed, then returned it.

"There. That should be close."

168

"Thanks."

"Don't be cheating either. I'll have my eye on you," I said, pointing at Wes.

"Me? Your roommate? Cheat? I only cheat if I know I won't get caught."

I held my thumb up.

I gazed around at the assembled riders. Wes and I weren't the only freshmen; Max and Riley were riding too. Grant, Flynn, Grayson, Rhett, and several others were all older. There were a total of twelve of us.

"Since this is the first ride for some of you, we're going to do a fairly easy ride of fifteen miles today. We will increase the length and difficulty of our rides as time passes, working up to fifty and even sixty miles as our schedules permit. If anyone gets a flat or has another breakdown, call out, especially if you're in the rear of the pack. I'm pleased to have four freshmen join us. Grayson and I are the only two returning team members this year. The Alpha fraternity council will choose the riders for this year's team based on my recommendations since I am now the old guy. Any questions? No? Okay, let's go." Flynn said.

I was expecting twenty miles so this would be an easier ride than anticipated. I wished I had logged more hours on my bike, but I only had so much time and I didn't even know I was joining a frat until late in the game.

We rode down 3rd Street and soon turned north on Indiana Avenue, following the route I had that morning. We continued to follow it right past the stadium and out into the country. Riding with eleven others was different from riding alone. While I enjoyed my solo rides and the feeling of freedom, this was better. I enjoyed the companionship.

I was excited in a way I hadn't been in a long time. I had participated in a lot of sports, but bike racing was new to me. I had been riding bikes for years, but only as a means of transportation. This was something more.

Flynn and the older guys obviously took riding practice as seriously as my coaches did wrestling practice. We weren't merely out for a ride. We were training for a race that was quite a big deal at IU. As a freshman, I wouldn't have a real shot at making the team until next year, but I intended to train as if I would be racing in the next Little 500.

I was glad I had spent time getting accustomed to a single speed bike because it was a far greater challenge than riding a multi-speed. Wes was struggling, particularly going uphill. The inclines, especially the steep ones, were a challenge, but I didn't have much trouble with them. I had very strong legs.

Dunn Street became a winding, country road after a while. I wasn't even sure it was call Dunn Street anymore. Steep banks rose up on either side of us and then opened up so that we could see valleys below us. We passed under the intertwined branches of great oaks and then out into the sunshine. The scenery was ever changing.

Riding hit my leg muscles in a new way, which was exactly what I was seeking. I tried to challenge my body in different ways to better prepare myself for whatever challenges might lie ahead. I had picked up the Greek view of the well-rounded man from Skye. The ancient Greeks didn't believe in concentrating in one area, but instead sought to be proficient in many. I did focus on wrestling, but I was involved in many different sports as well, such as martial arts, gymnastics, swimming, and weight lifting. It was about more than the body too. The mind was just as important. For me, that was the greatest challenge. I was intelligent, but it took greater effort for me to sit down and study than it did to hit the SRSC. Riding would help me get closer to the Colin I wanted to be. Even if I never made the Little 500 team, my time would not be wasted.

I should have been more tired after a day of classes, then a workout that left most of my teammates exhausted, but riding was different enough it seemed like a break. Leg exercises were a part of my workout, but riding was not the same. As for studying, riding with the guys was a true break from that.

The miles passed by quickly and our route curved back around toward campus. I wasn't quite sure where we were most of the time, but Flynn was an experienced guide. The other freshmen were hurting as we neared the end of the ride, especially Wes. He had an impressive upper body, but his legs weren't as developed and it was costing him. Rhett was a sophomore, but he was struggling too. I could see why practice began months ahead of the Little 500, which would not take place until next April.

Wes grimaced as he climbed off his bike in the Alpha parking lot. He walked a couple of paces and then promptly dropped down on the pavement and grabbed his left calve with an expression of pain on his face.

"Flex your toes back toward you," I said.

Wes slowly relaxed. "Yeah, that helps."

"A leg cramp is a bitch. If you flex your toes back toward you it stretches the calf muscles, which eases the muscle spasms and lessens the pain."

"How do you know all this?"

"Among other things, I'm studying to be an athletic trainer, but I picked that up playing football. My coach told me. Better?" I asked.

Wes nodded. I gave him a hand up.

"I don't know if I'm cut out for this," he said.

"Hey, there is no shame in admitting you are a wussy. I'll represent our room if you can't hack it."

"You jerk."

I laughed. "Seriously, maybe it's not your thing, but you should stick with it for at least a couple more rides to be sure. Your legs will adjust. I've already put in quite a bit of time on a single-speed. It was difficult at first, but it gets easier."

"You okay, Wes?" Flynn asked.

"Yeah, it was only a leg cramp. Dr. Stoffel here healed me."

"Great. Hang in there; you'll get it. Great job today, Colin."

"Thanks."

Wes crossed his arms and glared at me. I smiled and shrugged.

"Need help inside?" I asked.

"Nah. I'm good. Thanks for teaching me that toe thing. I'll remember it when I get a leg cramp at night."

"Oh, I hate those! That hurts worse than getting punched in the face."

Wes departed. I picked up my bike and put it in the rack.

"You ride like a pro," Grant said.

"Hardly."

"You're damned good for someone who isn't an experienced rider. You're good for an experienced rider, better than you should be. You're in incredible shape, which is probably why you excel at this."

"Hey, what did I tell you about hitting on me?" I teased.

"Why can no one take a compliment?"

"Oh, I can take a compliment. I'm merely getting a little revenge for that pledge initiation."

"Hey, you're supposed to take it out on next year's pledges."

"Oh, I'll do that too. So you think I'll have a good shot at making the team next year?"

"Definitely. You might even make it this year."

"Seriously? Do freshman ever make the team?"

"Almost never, but like I said, you're good."

"I'd hate to steal an older rider's spot."

"At this point, none of us is guaranteed a spot. The council will pick the top four riders to race, plus a couple of alternates. The racing team is usually composed of the more experienced riders, but not always. What matters is that Alpha has the strongest team possible. We are known for being one of the toughest Little 500 teams and we intend to stay that way. The alumni are counting on us. Winning the Little 500 is as important to them as it is to us."

"Tell me the truth, Grant. You just want to impress girls, don't you?"

"No, but it's a great fringe benefit."

"Yeah, I thought so."

"How did you like riding today?"

"I loved it. I enjoy riding alone, but riding with the guys is way better. Thank you for getting me into this."

"Hey, recruiting you has made me look very good."

We walked inside. I joined Wes in our room. He was lying on his bed.

"Want to go for a run?" I asked.

"Please tell me you're kidding."

"I'm kidding."

"If you weren't I would have you committed."

"It wasn't that bad."

"Maybe not for you, Mr. Super Jock."

"Oh, I like that name. I think I'll keep it. Does it come with a cape?"

Wes groaned. "I have created a monster."

"Don't feel guilty. I've been awesome and known it for a long time."

Wes threw his pillow at me. I kindly tossed it back.

"So have you finished whining and decided to join us again tomorrow?" I asked.

"Maybe."

"Come on. You know you want to. You'll consider yourself as a wussy if you don't. Think of it as a challenge."

"Okay! Okay! I'll ride again tomorrow. I think you just like to see me suffer."

"I love it, but I think you can do this and I think you'll like it once you get into it."

"You sound almost like a drug dealer; *Psst, hey buddy, want to train for a bike race?*"

"Ride with us two more times and then if you want to quit I won't say a word."

"If I don't like it, I'm blaming you and I will complain loudly."

"I can deal with that."

Chapter Ten

I sat across from Haakon at a table on the patio in front of the IMU. The scent of wood smoke drifted toward us from the fire pit where flames crackled merrily. It wasn't exactly a romantic meal, but the Baja Burritos, chips & salsa, and Cokes from Baja Fresh in The Commons were delicious.

It had been another eventful day. Classes, wrestling practice and then another ride with the Alpha Little 500 riders had kept me busy. I had taken only enough time to shower before I hurried to the IMU to meet Haakon.

It was past 8 p.m., but there was still plenty of light. Haakon looked especially handsome this evening, and as always, I enjoyed his company, but I was filled with a sense of anticipation. Tonight we were going all the way. We hooked up fairly often, but rarely had time to truly go at it.

"Are you as horny as I am right now?" Haakon asked, nearly making me spew a mouthful of Coke all over the table. It was not a question I was expecting, but then Haakon was a guy and all guys thought about sex several times a minute.

"How horny are you?"

"I think my dick is going to rip through my shorts."

"Yeah, I'm as horny as you are then."

"Don't you love our romantic meals?" Haakon asked with a twinkle in his eye.

"They are the best."

"Tonight you get a special dessert."

I groaned.

"You know if we keep talking like this neither of us will ever be able to stand."

"True, but we have time yet. So... how is the riding?"

"Great. I love it. We're up to 25 miles and I'm ready for more."

"How is Wes doing?"

"He's doing pretty well actually."

"So he's no longer thinking of quitting?"

"No, he's addicted now. He won't quit."

"Hearing you talk about it almost makes me wish I could ride."

"Well, you could probably ride with us."

"For 25 miles? I don't think so."

"You could do it."

"Maybe, but I am not used to riding such long distances. I think I'll stick to listening to you talk about it."

"As long as I don't bore you."

"Hey, you know I'm as into sports as you are, and bike racing is new to me."

"That's one of the things I love about you."

"There are others?"

"How long do you have? It would take an hour merely to list what I love about your body and that's just the beginning. I wish you weren't here for such a short time. It just figures that the most awesome guy on campus is only here for one semester."

"You're only here for one semester?" Haakon asked, grinning goofily at me.

"It goes without saying that *I'm* awesome, but I'm talking about *you.*"

"I wish I could stay longer too, but I must return to Norway. We have until the middle of December."

"A few weeks is better than none."

"True and we will both have Christmas to distract us soon after. I'll send you some photos of Norway when I return home and I want to see photos of Verona."

"Deal."

We continued talking while we ate near the fire. When we finished we took our trays inside and dumped our trash in one of the bins in The Commons.

I took Haakon's hand and we cut through the IMU and departed through the south entrance. We passed the seated statue of Herman Wells and then The Rose Well House as we walked along the edge of Dunn's Woods toward Alpha. Holding Haakon's hand almost made me feel as if he was my boyfriend. That could not be, but my feelings for him made me realize that I might someday fall for another guy, or a girl, whether I planned it, wanted it, or not.

Two guys met us on the path. They noticed us holding hands, but didn't look as if they cared. That's something I liked about Bloomington. There was a great deal of diversity and acceptance here. Indiana was a rather backward state. There was a lot of bigotry, ignorance, and prejudice, but not here. I often saw girls holding hands as they walked and even kissing and no one paid much attention, except for horny boys who probably fantasized about hooking up with them. There were Asians, Muslims, and students from several different countries in my classes and no one thought of them as Asians, Muslims, Hispanics or whatever. They were just people. Here I was holding hands with a boy from Norway who spoke a different language at home. His nationality and native language didn't matter. I wished the entire state could be like Bloomington and Verona. There were islands of intelligence and acceptance in a sea of bigotry, hate, and stupidity.

"What about your roommate?" Haakon asked as we crossed over 3rd Street and walked toward Alpha.

"Oh, he's going to watch."

"Works for me."

"Really?"

"Seriously, it wouldn't bother me, but I would prefer to be alone with you."

"I told him to be out of the room unless he wants to watch us go at it. He said he would gladly stay away. Straight boys are weird." Haakon laughed.

We entered Alpha and I took Haakon up to my room. I tied a sock around the doorknob so Wes would know we were inside if he returned. It would also let everyone in the house know that someone was getting it on in the room, but I didn't care.

"This is much nicer than your old room and nicer than mine."

"I'm glad you like it," I said, wrapping my arms around Haakon.

I kissed him deeply and he immediately responded. We stood in the middle of my room making out for the longest time before I pulled his shirt over his head and ran my hands over his smooth, firm torso.

Haakon pulled my shirt off and guided me onto my back on the bed. He climbed on top of me, straddled my crotch, and began to caress and massage my shoulders, chest, and abs. Soon, he leaned over and kissed me, then nibbled on my neck, and kissed and licked all over my torso, giving special attention to my nipples. My dick was ready to rip through my shorts.

I pulled Haakon down on top of me and then rolled him onto his back. I lay full-length on top of him while I kissed him. I explored his body as he had mine, but went further. I unbuttoned and unzipped his shorts and pulled them off, then pulled down his boxer briefs with great difficulty. He was so hard I almost couldn't get them off.

I leaned down and took Haakon in my mouth. I worked him right to the edge and stopped. It made him aggressive. He stripped my remaining clothing away and went down on me.

Soon, we worked into a sixty-nine position. Our muffled moans filled the room and could likely be heard in the hallway. I didn't care. I had walked by rooms in Alpha before and heard the unmistakable sound of sex.

Haakon lost control first, which made me go off like a shotgun. We both moaned louder than ever as we released our pent-up need.

We weren't finished yet, but Haakon scooted around until I could hold him in my arms. We slowly made out as we recharged for the next round.

I climbed on top of Haakon and rubbed against him as we made out. He kissed me more urgently as I did so, and soon began to pant.

"Let's do it," he said.

I climbed off him, put on a Trojan, took out my bottle of lube, and returned to Haakon.

"Start slow, like last time," he said.

"I will."

I pulled Haakon's legs over my shoulders and pressed against him. I encountered a great deal of resistance, but I was patient. I knew if I wasn't careful I'd sink in several inches all at once when that resistance gave away which was not at all pleasant for the bottom. I carefully applied pressure. The key was patience. It took a while, but when I finally slipped in only the head was inside Haakon. He grimaced slightly.

I eased myself in very, very slowly. Haakon began to breathe harder. I applied easy, but steady pressure until I was all the way in. I leaned over and kissed him.

"Fuck me."

I smiled. Guys who normally weren't vulgar in the least changed completely during sex. I won't even repeat some of what I've heard uttered during sex, but it never failed to turn me on.

I pulled out slowly, then pressed myself in again. I went a little faster this time, but still slowly. I pumped myself into Haakon over and over, maintaining the same slow and easy pace until he began to moan. That was the signal. I began to go at it faster and harder.

This is the point where a lot of tops lost control, but not me. I had amazing control over my body. Topping was one of the most exquisite sensations ever, which is why many guys cannot go the distance. Topping simply feels too good, but by maintaining control, that sensation can be extended for minute after minute. I could cut loose quickly or hold out for nearly an hour.

"Harder! Please! Harder!" Haakon panted.

I obliged and went at it hard and fast. There was no need to use care now. Haakon was beyond feeling pain. He was in a state of bliss.

Haakon cried out and shot all over his chest. I buried myself balls deep and cut loose. Our moans and groans were so loud they could probably be heard downstairs.

I pulled out slowly when our orgasms dissipated. When sex was over pulling out too quickly could be painful for the bottom. Haakon showed no sign of pain as his chest heaved and he grinned at me.

"Damn, I needed that. We have got to do this more often," he said.

"I love the way you think."

"That was incredible, Colin," Haakon said, pulling me down on top of him and kissing me. "Thank you."

"No. Thank you." I grinned. "Let's go get cleaned up."

Haakon and I stepped into the hallway, wearing only towels. We started to walk to the bathroom when we heard clapping behind us. We turned to see Grant, Rhett, and Grayson applauding. Haakon and I took a bow, which made the guys laugh. We turned and continued toward the bathroom.

We hung up our towels and walked into the shower room. I always showered after sex. Lube felt good while I was doing it, but sticky and nasty after.

We shampooed and soaped up. I took the opportunity to admire Haakon's form. I love the contours of his body. The female form was beautiful, but the male even more so. Haakon was beautifully sculpted and his skin so smooth. I had been with quite a few hot guys, but Haakon was one of the hottest.

We rinsed off, dried, and then returned to my room and dressed. I had already taken the sock off the door, but we were still alone.

"I hope you won't be too sore tomorrow," I said.

"If I am it will be a pleasant reminder of tonight. You're amazing. Each time with you is better than the last."

"Does that mean you might want to do it again?" I asked.

"I want to do it daily. I'd do it again right now, but I'm not sure I could handle it. Maybe tomorrow..."

"You are damn near perfect," I said. Haakon laughed.

"Yes, I'm aware of that," Wes said as he entered.

"I wasn't talking to you."

"You had to be talking to me. Perfect doesn't fit anyone else in this room. No offense," he said, looking at Haakon.

"Haakon, this is my roommate, Wes." Haakon stood and shook his hand. "I *was* talking about Haakon. You'd agree if you saw his hot, hot ass."

"Sorry, a guy's ass doesn't do anything for me. Now, a girl's..."

"This is interesting. You're straight, I'm gay, and Colin is bi," Haakon said.

"You know there is another word for bi—slut," Wes said grinning. I crossed my arms and glared at him. "Seriously, Haakon. You don't know what you're getting into. I barely get to spend any time in the room because Colin has the sock on the door day and night. Guys, girls, couples, groups; it's a constant orgy in here."

Haakon laughed.

"You are so full of shit, Wes," I said.

"I'm trying to be entertaining. I truly hate to say this in front of Colin, but he's a great guy. I don't mean any of the bad stuff I say about him, but I enjoy seeing him glare at me."

"I know he's great. He's absolutely wonderful," Haakon said.

"So which one of you just got fucked? There is no other explanation for that level of happiness and contentment."

"Guess," I said.

"Hmm, while it would please me to think you're an insatiable bottom boy, I'd have to say Haakon."

"Correct," Haakon said.

"I could never do that."

"Don't knock it until you're tried it," I said.

"You forget, the only dick I like is mine. A girl wanted me to try it. She had a strap-on. I simply could not make myself do it."

"You poor, pathetic straight boy," I said.

"Hey, we can't all be sluts... I mean bi."

"He's a jerk, but I still like him," I said to Haakon.

"I should get going," Haakon said.

"Can't stand Wes, huh?"

"He's very nice."

"That is not the response I wanted."

"Sorry."

"I'll walk you to your dorm."

"It was nice meeting you, Wes."

"You too."

Haakon and I departed. We crossed the street and walked up the sidewalk toward Forest Quad. It was quite a beautiful night, but it was a little chilly. September was getting on so cooler temperatures would soon be the norm.

Haakon and I talked quietly all the way to Forest, which wasn't all that far. I kissed him outside his dorm and then smiled all the way back to Alpha. I loved IU, but so far Haakon was my best college experience.

***

"You didn't," I said as I sat across the table from Marc in The Tudor Room.

"Yes, and it drove my teammates crazy. After a while, they threatened to beat me if I sang in fake Italian again. I sang less after that, but I still kept up my bad Italian accent. I spent weeks pretending to be Dave Stoller from *Breaking Away*."

"I bet you could do a real Italian accent now."

"Yes, after living with Alessio and making several trips to Italy I'm sure I could. I envy you, Colin. There is nothing like training for the Little 500, except actually racing in it."

"I won't be racing this year, but I love training."

"Back in my day, we picked the riders months before the race. I think picking them only weeks before is better. It makes for a stronger team. No more than four guys are out there on the track, but everyone who trains is a part of the team and most of them will race someday."

"I hope next year will be my year. There is a chance I might race this year, but it's not good."

"Freshmen race for other teams, but there is usually so much competition for a spot at Alpha that freshmen don't have much of a chance."

"If I get a spot this year it will be awesome, but if I don't perhaps it's for the best. I'll be that much stronger a rider next year. I want the four strongest riders out there, whether I'm one of them or not."

"I see you're already dedicated to Alpha and the team."

"Yes. I'm accustomed to being dedicated to a team. Wrestling is more solitary, but there's still a feeling of team there. I actually like riding better. Maybe it's because it's a fraternity team, but there is much more of a team feeling."

"You'll learn a lot you didn't know about riding. Racing in particular is far more complicated than outsiders imagine. Being stuck back in the pack can be nerve racking. You're riding inches, and I mean often two or three inches away from other riders, and if anyone in front of you makes the slightest error you're toast."

"Yeah. I've watched videos of past races. It's tight in the pack. Some of the wrecks are horrific."

"That's why getting a good place during quals is key and so is breaking out in front. The more bikes behind; the less chance of being in a wreck.

"Being behind a rider can also be an advantage. Getting into just the right position in a rider's wake makes for easier riding. That's one reason 1st place changes so many times during the course of the race. The goal of most teams is to be as close to the front as possible, but not necessarily in the lead until near the end of the race."

"I never thought of that."

"You'll learn a lot of little tricks. Training is only beginning now. Later, you'll get into exchanges, strategies, and everything else involved in racing. Experience is the best teacher. No matter how much you train, nothing can truly prepare a rider for being out on the track with 32 other riders. That's why it's so important for a team to have experienced riders."

"Why aren't you still coaching the team?" I asked.

"That position belongs to someone who is in Alpha now. I've stepped in to coach when requested, but it was always during years when there wasn't a current brother who could handle the job. Flynn has it covered. This will be his 3rd race. He's experienced. Alpha has faith in him and so do I."

"I bet you miss it."

"Very much, but I wouldn't want to go back to actual racing. I don't think I'd fare so well against the younger riders."

"You could take them. You're a legend."

"I intend to remain a legend by not racing again. Besides, I'd have to build a team from scratch. I couldn't race for Alpha since I'm alumni."

"I sometimes wonder how I will deal with leaving school when I graduate. Leaving high school was difficult. I was the top athlete at VHS, but here I'm one among many. That's okay, but I'm afraid it will be rough when I can no longer be on a team."

"It's a change. At first, I missed being on the Little 500 team so much I couldn't stand it. The team continued to ride together after the race my senior year, but even that wasn't the same. Graduating and actually moving out of Alpha was extremely difficult for me, but I went back home and started the next phase of my life. Luckily, it brought me back to Bloomington. Being an

Alpha brother gives me a solid connection to IU. It's not the same as being a student, but I'm a part of things."

"Skye doesn't seem to mind not being a part of a team."

"No and he was the top dog in his day too. Your life will change a lot, Colin. One part ends and then another begins. You're a freshman. The years will go quickly, but you have a lot of them left. I wouldn't concern myself with what comes after if I was you. Enjoy what you have while you've got it."

"I intend to. You should try this vegetable lasagna. It's great," I said.

"I would but then I wouldn't have room for dessert and that would be tragic. Is it as good as the chicken with roasted red peppers?"

"It's even better."

"Oh, you are cruel. I'll have to console myself with chocolate cake when I finish this."

"Thanks for lunch. You know I can pay for my own."

"Yes, but I invited you and I'm buying. Save your money for another trip to the Tudor Room."

"I do eat here now and then. It's not much more than a lot of other places."

"True. Alessio and I eat here often. How is your uncle?"

"You have to ask? He's always great. Nothing seems to get to him and he loves running the gym and Natatorium at Graymoor."

"Yeah, I'd say he's exactly where he belongs."

We hit the dessert bar. Marc chose chocolate cake, as well as a piece of lemon meringue pie. I picked pecan pie, a cupcake with vanilla icing, and a no-bake cookie.

"Let me guess, you can eat whatever you want and never gain weight," Marc said.

"Pretty much, but I'm very active. I do try to mostly avoid junk food and limit the amount of fast food I eat."

"You almost make me wish I was your age again, but to be perfectly honest, it's more fun being my age."

"I never bought into the idea that my teen years were the best of my life."

"They aren't. There are too many problems and uncertainties at that age. I do recommend getting the most out of them you can, but I think you're already doing that."

"Yeah, Skye says I should do as much of what I want as I can and have as much fun as possible because one never knows when life will drastically change or end. I'm sure you know he had a friend drop dead right beside him when he was a teen."

"Yeah. Jimmy Kerstadd. I'm considerably older than Skye, but still remember when it happened. It was front-page news in *The Verona Citizen*. Everyone was shocked because Jimmy was a very fit sixteen-year-old. Later, it came out he was on steroids."

"Yeah, Skye told me he actually tried steroids, but when Jimmy dropped dead beside him as they ran together he never touched them again. I would never use them. Skye talked to me early on about steroids and how stupid he was to try them. That's one thing I love about Skye. He doesn't hesitate to tell me about his mistakes."

"He is a rather awesome guy, but don't tell him I said that," Marc said and grinned.

"Yeah, I try not to compliment him too often at least not to his face."

"I'm very pleased you've joined Alpha and are riding. I can live vicariously through you for a few years."

"You seem pretty connected to the fraternity."

"I am and it's great. I love being in a position to help and we live so close Alessio and I can attend any event that includes alumni. Alessio says I've never grown up, but why should I?"

"I don't plan to grow up. Skye never has and it works for him."

"I know it's months away, but you make sure to bring your bike into the shop right before the Little 500. Every year, I service the bikes of the Alpha Little 500 team for free to make sure they are in top shape."

"That's great."

"We service a lot of Little 500 bikes at the shop, but everyone else has to pay. We actually sell most of those used in the race, mainly because we offer really good deals on them. Members of Alpha get an extra discount so all the Alpha bikes come from the shop."

We started talking about bikes again and did so until I had to leave for class and Marc had to return to his shop. It was a great lunch. Marc was much older than me, even older than Skye, and yet as we talked he seemed like another guy from the frat.

I thought about that as I walked to class. Maybe when I looked at Marc, I was looking at my own future. I don't mean owning a bike shop, but rather keeping in touch with Alpha and helping out the new generation of brothers. I liked that idea. It made me feel that someday when I graduated, my time at IU wouldn't truly be over.

Chapter Eleven

"Are you guys physically attached to each other? Every time I see you on campus you're together and I hardly get to spend any time in my own room because you two are always getting it on," Wes said as Haakon and I entered my room at Alpha.

"We do spend a lot of time together, but we only have until December you know," I said.

"I'll have to deal with Colin after you leave, Haakon. He'll probably cry himself to sleep every night and he'll get so horny I won't be able to sleep for fear of being violated."

"I can't picture Colin as the crying type and I'm sure he can find plenty of guys to hook up with when I've gone back to Norway."

"You have nothing to fear, Wes. You're just not hot enough to make the cut. I would never be desperate enough to go after you," I said.

Wes gave me the finger and I laughed.

"Do you guys want the room?" he asked.

"No. Haakon is joining us on our ride. I asked Flynn if it was okay and said it's fine."

"Oh, shit, yeah. I didn't know it was getting that late. Hmm, you don't look like a spy from another team," Wes said, eyeing Haakon.

"It would be difficult since I'm not a member of a team."

"How are you going to keep up us? We're pretty hardcore. We're up to 35 miles already and we don't take it easy."

"I will be riding a 21-speed."

"Yes, that will help. The single speed almost killed me at first," Wes said.

"I enjoyed watching him suffer. It was fun while it lasted," I said.

"We'd better go. Flynn will be up our asses if we're late," Wes said.

Most of the guys knew Haakon already. He was in Alpha house so often he was practically a brother. I'm sure everyone knew I was bi by now too. I never made an effort to keep it secret. Why should I? The guys were totally cool with it.

We took off and headed up 3rd Street as usual. It was one of the busier streets in Bloomington, but drivers were accustomed to bikers. The large number of us made it even safer. It's much easier to see several riders than one.

Haakon didn't have much trouble keeping up. He was very fit and his multi-speed bike gave him a huge advantage. He kept extra distance from the nearest bike when we closed in and rode close together. Flynn instructed us to bunch up and ride as if we were racing on some of the long level stretches. It gave us some idea of what it would be like riding in a close pack during a race.

It was late October now and the air was cool. I hoped the weather would allow us to ride as long as possible before winter hit. Riding a bike inside on a trainer wouldn't be nearly as fun.

We passed beneath orange-golden leaves as we pedaled through the countryside. The ride was challenging and yet also relaxing. It was a time I could get away from all the studying and reading. I could let my mind relax in a way I couldn't during wrestling practice or my workouts in the SRSC.

My time with Haakon was slipping away and I didn't like it. I tried not to think about it. We spent most of our free time together now. We met for lunch almost daily and even studied together in my room, The Rose Well House, or the Well's Library. We got the least done when we studied at Alpha, at least if Wes was out. It was never long before we began making out and that always led to more. Once we kissed, the sock was soon tied around the doorknob.

Haakon was beautiful with his hair flying in the wind, but I didn't look at him at all if we were riding in a close pack and tried not to gaze at him too often even when we weren't. I had started wearing bicycling shorts and jerseys. The shorts left almost as little to the imagination as my wrestling singlet and if I gazed at Haakon too often the front would be uncomfortably tight.

Haakon was sweaty and flushed at the end of the ride, but he handled it well. If he was around longer I could have turned him into a racer. There was so much more we could do if he wasn't leaving so soon, but that was life. There was never enough time.

"Want to shower and then grab something to eat?" I asked.

"I'd love to," Wes said.

"I didn't ask you, but I suppose we could endure your company."

"I was kidding."

"No, really, join us. It'll be fun," Haakon said.

"Eh, you don't want a third-wheel."

"Sure we do. It's only eating. You have to get lost if we get it on."

"You're going to do that in a restaurant?"

"Grr."

"Okay, I will join you, but keep your hands to yourself in the showers."

"We were planning to take advantage, but we'll try to control ourselves," I said.

"He has a very high opinion of himself. Doesn't he?" Haakon asked.

"Yes, and I have no idea why; just look at him."

"Hey, I'm standing right here you know!"

"Come on, let's go," I said, putting my arms over Wes and Haakon's shoulders.

We walked inside and upstairs and then began to undress in my room.

"I feel like we're getting ready to have a 3-way," Wes said when we were all mostly naked.

"Just how many 3-ways have you had with other guys? Is there something you want to tell us, Wes?" I asked.

"Hmm, let's see." Wes started counting on his fingers. "Zero."

"It took you that long to count to zero?" Haakon said.

"Hey, there will be no ganging up on the straight boy."

"Oh, nice ass," Haakon said, running his hand lightly over one of Wes's butt cheeks.

"Hey, if you want some ass go after Colin. He will give it up to *anyone*."

"Don't make me spank you," I said.

Wes made a show of quickly covering his ass with his towel.

"Come on, let's go shower together. Want me to wash your back, Wes?" I asked.

"Um, no. If I didn't know you were kidding, I'd be a little frightened right now."

"Kidding. Yeah. That's what I was doing. Kidding," I said, trying to make it sound as if I was covering up.

"I wish my roommate was this much fun," Haakon said.

"Oh, Wes is a lot of fun. He can sleep through anything if you know what I mean." I made a circle with my fingers and stuck my index finger in and out.

"You're really scary sometimes, Colin. You know that, right?" Wes asked.

"It's one of my charms."

We hung up our towels and entered the showers. Haakon and I shared soap and shampoo as always. I relaxed under the hot water. Getting the sweat off felt great.

"You did very well, Haakon. If you were sticking around you could join a team," Wes said.

"Don't forget I was riding a 21-speed."

"I don't think many guys could keep up with us for 35 miles even on a 21-speed."

"Haakon is a stud."

We kept talking while we showered. I wanted to fool around with Haakon, but it was not an option. Besides, there was no time. We rinsed off, dried, returned to the room, and dressed.

"Where do you want to eat?" Wes said.

"Let's go off campus," I said.

"Okay, as long as it isn't expensive."

"How about Fazoli's?" Haakon asked.

"Perfect," I said.

"Yeah," Wes said.

"Want to walk? It will probably be faster than taking the bus," I said.

"Sure."

Fazoli's was only a few blocks away, just this side of College Mall. The three of us walked up the sidewalk, talking about our bike ride and whatever else came to mind. At first, we passed fraternity and sorority houses on our right and campus to our left. After a short time, the houses gave way to businesses and then individual homes, most of them rented out to college students, but campus still continued on our left. It wasn't until we were halfway there that we left campus behind.

We cut across Eastland Plaza, which contained the China Buffet, Dollar Tree, Petco, and other businesses, then crossed College Mall Road. The Fazoli's was just to our right.

"You want to share an ultimate sampler?" I asked Haakon.

"Sure."

"Okay, you paid last time so I'll get it this time." We usually each paid our own way, but the last time we were in Taco Bell I didn't have my wallet so Haakon took care of it.

Wes ordered lasagna. Our platter came with lasagna, spaghetti, fettuccine Alfredo, and penne. The portions of each were smaller, but there was plenty for both of us.

"Awe, ain't it sweet?" Wes said when we were seated and Haakon and I ate off the same plate.

"Want to beat him up later?" I asked Haakon.

"No. I might bruise my knuckles. I hate that."

"You two make a great couple. You're both jocks and you're exactly the kind of guys I expect to see together, gay guys anyway."

"We are a great couple, but since I have to leave in December a serious relationship isn't an option. Besides, neither of us wants to get too serious," Haakon said.

"So you're both sluts, huh?"

"I couldn't be a slut even if I wanted. I don't have the time!" I said. Haakon and Wes laughed.

"I'm glad we're rooming together. I've never spent time around bi or gay guys before. You're really not that different," Wes said.

"You've probably spent a lot of time around gay and bi guys. You just didn't know it."

"True. I'd never take you for anything but straight."

"Hey, let's not get insulting," I said, pointing my fork at Wes.

"Funny."

"Seriously, it's an interesting experience for me. I think I might do a paper on it; something along the lines of societal expectations versus reality."

"You know you're not supposed to use big words around us blonds," I said.

"Yeah right. I've seen some of the grades on your English composition essays. You're obviously very intelligent," Wes said.

"Oh, let me get my phone out. You can say that again and I'll record it."

"Not a chance, but I will let you record me saying that you're smarter than you look. You almost have to be."

"I think I've been insulted."

"See? If you truly were a dumb blond you would have no idea I insulted you," Wes said.

"Seriously, between my blond hair and being a jock, most people assume I'm not very bright. It sometimes gives me an edge," I said.

"It must suck to have people assume things about you."

"Everyone has to deal with that. Don't they?" Haakon asked.

"I suppose they do. I had to deal with the dumb jock thing in high school. A lot of girls wouldn't go out with me because they assumed all I wanted was to get into their pants. I did want that, but I wanted to go out and have fun too. I would have been perfectly fine with hanging out and doing no more than making out or even hanging out without making out, but a lot of girls never gave me the chance."

"Oh, you poor little straight boy," I said.

"Shut up."

I laughed. "Guys in general have a reputation. If you're gay it can be an advantage."

"Sure, gay guys have it made."

"Hardly," Haakon said.

"Well the bi guys do."

I said nothing, but grinned broadly.

"You know, I really missed my friends from high school and didn't know if I'd like it here or not when I started at IU, but college is way better than high school. Joining Alpha and being around you guys has made a big difference," Wes said.

"Yeah, I really like being in Alpha too," I said.

"Says the guy who had no interest in joining a fraternity," Haakon said.

"It's true. Grant lured me in."

"Yeah, I guess a bi guy would find Grant hot."

"That's not what I meant, jerk," I said. Wes laughed.

"I'll say one thing for our training sessions, I have much stronger and sexier legs than when I started," Wes said.

"Eh-eh," Haakon said.

"Hey, I know my legs are stronger and seriously, don't you guys think I have sexy legs?" Wes actually got up and displayed his legs for us. I made a so-so gesture with my hand, but a girl at a nearby table smiled at Wes and gave him a thumbs up.

"Do you show your legs to all the guys you meet?" I asked.

"Only those who are gay and half-gay."

Wes was distracted during the rest of our meal by the girl who had approved of his legs. She was sitting with two friends and I noticed all of them looking in our direction now and then. Wes kept smiling at them.

"Why don't you go sit with them?" Haakon asked when we'd finished.

"You guys don't mind?"

"We're big boys. We'll get over it," I said.

Wes smiled and stepped over to the girl's table. "Mind if I sit down?"

"You ready to head out? This could be painful to watch," I said.

"Yeah, let's go."

We nodded to Wes as we passed and then walked outside.

"Think they'll end up having a four-way?" Haakon asked with a grin.

"You never know. My guess is Wes will flirt with the girl who likes his legs, get her number, and then go on a solo date with her later."

"Maybe we should start a pool."

We walked back the way we'd come, but were in no hurry. It was dark now and the moon was out. It was harder to see the stars here than in Verona because of all the lights, but I could still make them out.

"My legs are tired. I bet riding a single-speed really hits your leg muscles," Haakon said.

"Yes, but I've already grown accustomed to it. I took a lot of shorter rides in the beginning and that helped. It's like weight lifting. It's best to ease into it."

"I wish we could go back to your room, but I have way too much work waiting on me," Haakon said.

"Yeah, I have quite a bit to get done too. There is always tomorrow."

"Yes there is."

I stopped and kissed Haakon deeply, then we walked on toward campus. I couldn't wait until tomorrow.

***

October slipped into November far too quickly, but Haakon and I made the most of it. We saw each other daily and managed some alone time most of those days. I didn't meet with any other guys now. I was so busy I didn't have time, and I had Haakon, so why bother? I didn't hook up with any girls either. I had no more time for them than for boys.

The best thing about the arrival of November is that our first wrestling meet was upon us. The locker room in the Intercollegiate Athletics Gymnasium was much smaller than that in Assembly Hall, but then the gym itself was much smaller. It was even smaller than the VHS gym back in Verona.

I felt a sense of anticipation as I pulled on my singlet. We were going up against Purdue, the archrival of IU. Purdue had an excellent wrestling program, so I expected stiff competition. Haakon, Grant, Wes, and some of the Alpha brothers would be in the bleachers watching. Skye had even driven down to watch my first meet. I couldn't wait to introduce him to Haakon and show him Alpha house.

I located the guys in the stands and nodded to them as I walked toward the bleachers. It took me a bit longer to spot Skye in the small crowd, but when I did he waved at me. I was glad he was here. I wanted to share this with him.

I watched the matches before mine with great interest. This was my first ever college wrestling meet. I shouted encouragement to our guy on the mat along with my teammates. This was when we truly came together as a team. We were each out there on the mat alone, but every member of the team as well as much of the crowd cheered us on.

I sized up my opponent as we walked onto the mat. He was a considerably shorter than me, but compact and very muscular. He wouldn't be a pushover, but then I didn't expect to face any pushovers in college.

We took our positions. The ref blew his whistle and we exploded into action. I immediately earned a point for an escape, but when I clashed with the Purdue boy it was not an easy battle. He was skilled as well as strong.

My opponent was giving me some trouble, but before long I had the upper hand. I took him down and forced him onto this back.

Getting him pinned wasn't easy, but not as hard as I expected. I countered his attempts to escape and soon had one of his shoulders on the mat; a few seconds later the other went down. The ref slapped the mat and held my hand in the air. Skye, my teammates, and my friends in the stands cheered for me. It was a great beginning to my college wrestling career.

I looked into the stands as I walked back to the bench, first to Skye who gave me a thumbs up, then to Haakon and the others who all raised their fists into the air. When I reached the bench, my teammates patted me on the back.

I cheered on my teammates during the remaining matches. We kicked Purdue's ass by winning all but four. Our coaches were ecstatic. We walked into the locker room listening to the cheers of the IU supporters.

I stripped off my sweaty singlet, showered, then dressed and headed out into the gym where I knew Skye and Haakon would be waiting.

Skye walked toward me when he spotted me and hugged me.

"You were even more formidable on the mat today than you were in high school," he said.

"Thanks. There's someone I want you meet."

I took Skye over to where Haakon waited and introduced them.

"So this is Haakon. You're right, he's gorgeous," Skye said.

"You'll have to get used to Skye. He's not shy," I said.

"I like that," Haakon said, taking in my uncle's buff body.

"Why don't you join us, Haakon? I'll take you both out to eat," Skye said.

"Yes, please come," I said.

"I would like that."

"How about Bucceto's?" I asked. "It's really close and I hear it's great."

"Anywhere you two want to go," Skye said.

I looked at Haakon. "Anywhere is fine with me."

"You didn't drive the Auburn, did you?" I asked Skye.

"No. It's too cold. I brought my new car."

"You bought a new car?"

"A used car, but I think you'll like it."

We walked out into the parking lot. I was curious to see what Skye had purchased. My heart began to beat faster as Skye walked toward a red and white '57 Chevy coupe.

"What do you think?" Skye asked.

"I think you should take a bus back and leave this for me to drive!"

"Keep dreaming."

"This car is beautiful," Haakon said.

"Climb in."

"You take the front," I told Haakon. I knew I'd have plenty of opportunities to sit up front in the future.

We got in. Skye started up the car. I loved the sound of the powerful engine. We turned left on 10th and then right on Pete Ellis Drive soon after. In less than a minute, Skye turned right and passed Barnes & Noble and Best Buy among other businesses. Bucceto's was located near the west end of a small strip of stores and restaurants.

Bucceto's was crowded, but we were able to score a booth.

"What do you guys want? Pasta or would you prefer pizza?"

"Pizza," we both said, then laughed.

"Let's get a couple of larges. You guys can take the leftovers, if there are any. Pick what you want," Skye said.

Haakon and I each picked a pizza. Haakon chose the sweet lil' razorback, which had pepperoni, smoked sausage, bacon, basil, and garlic. I picked the bar 20, with barbeque chicken & sauce, red onions & smoked gouda.

"You were incredible," Haakon said as we sipped our Cokes.

"Thanks. I thought that Purdue guy was going to be tougher, but he turned out to be not too difficult to pin. The hard part was taking him down."

Haakon looked back and forth between Skye and me. "You two look a lot alike."

"Well, Skye is my uncle."

"Yeah, but he looks like he could be your dad, except he's too young."

"Skye is ancient. He's an old, old man!" I said.

"Hey, I'm thirty."

"Like I said, ancient."

"Watch it, Colin or we'll go back to that gym and wrestle and I'll kick your butt in front of Haakon," Skye said.

"You delude yourself, Obi Wan. I was the student. Now I am the master," I said.

"You keep telling yourself that," Skye said, making Haakon laugh.

The truth was that I was no match for Skye on the mat. I didn't know anyone who could successfully challenge him.

Most of the girls near us, even those with guys, eyed our table. I wasn't surprised. Skye and I drew attention wherever we went and especially when we were together. That sounds conceited, but it's true. While my face was the gift of genetics, my body was the result of a ton of sports and a lot of work. Part of my body was thanks to genetics too, but if I sat on my ass and watched TV all day instead of getting out and doing things I would not look the same. Haakon was incredibly good looking and had an awesome bod so why wouldn't girls check us all out?

Haakon told Skye about his interests and Skye talked about playing football and wrestling in his high school days.

"I can see why you and Colin get along so well. You are a lot alike, but not so much alike as to cause friction," Haakon said before excusing himself to use the bathroom.

"Why don't you invite Haakon to come to Verona for Thanksgiving?" Skye asked as soon as Haakon was gone. "It would be much better than him staying on campus, and he might like to see what an American Thanksgiving is like."

"I was going to ask about that," I said.

"He can share your room or we can get him his own."

"Oh, we can share."

"Why am I not in the least surprised?"

"Because you used to be me?"

"If that's true I'm locking you in your room and never letting you out. You should not do the things I did."

I laughed.

Our pizzas arrived and Skye and I attacked them. Haakon came back soon after.

"We thought about waiting for you, but then decided not to," Skye said.

"Actually, we didn't even think about waiting," I said. Haakon grinned and grabbed a piece of the pizza he had selected.

"Oh, this is good!" he said.

We talked and laughed, but mostly ate as the pizzas slowly disappeared. I waited until we slowed down before I popped the question.

"Haakon, would you like to come home with me for Thanksgiving? We live in a hotel so it's not your typical Thanksgiving, but the food is incredible. I would love to show you around."

"We would love to have you," Skye added.

"Yes! I would love that! I wasn't looking forward to being stuck on campus. I'm sure it will be dead."

"Great. Skye can pick us both up at the beginning of break."

We continued our conversation. There was only about a fourth of each pizza left when we finished. Skye had them boxed up for us.

Skye paid, left a tip, and then we departed.

"Where to?" Skye asked as he started up the Chevy.

"I want to show you the house and introduce you to some of my brothers, if they're around. Want to come, Haakon?"

"No. I have some work to do and I'm sure you two would like some time to talk. Thanks very much for the pizza."

"You're welcome," Skye said.

"You sure?"

"Yeah. I'll see you soon."

"We can drop you off at Forest. You know where that is, right Skye?"

"Yep."

A very few minutes later Skye pulled into the half-circle drive in front of Forest.

"Thank you again for the pizza. It was very nice meeting you," Haakon said.

"It was great meeting you. I'll see you later this month."

"I look forward to it. Bye, Colin."

"Bye."

I got out to take the front seat and give Haakon a hug and a quick kiss. I hopped in the passenger seat and Skye pulled back onto 3rd Street.

"Isn't he incredible?" I asked.

"Yes he is. I have a feeling you two would become a couple if he wasn't leaving so soon."

"Yeah, that's not what I'm seeking right now, but if he was sticking around I think it would happen."

"Some of the best things in life aren't planned."

"True. I don't want him to leave, but I'm doing my best to enjoy the time we have."

"That's all any of us can do."

"Get into the left lane. Alpha House is coming up soon."

In less than a minute, Skye pulled into the parking lot. Damon and Federico, who were coming out of the house, immediately set upon us, or rather upon the car.

"Sweet car," Damon said.

"Thanks," Skye said.

"Guys, this is my Uncle Skye. This is Damon and Federico," I said pointing them out.

"Where did you get this?" Damon asked.

"A car auction. My other car is a convertible and only seats two, so it's not practical sometimes."

"I am in love with your car," Federico said.

"Try not to drool on it," I said.

"Feel free to check it out," Skye said as I led him toward the front door.

I first took him into the lounge.

"Nice place. This is quite a step up from Hershey Hall. Oh, here is the shrine to Marc," Skye said, walking to the wall of photos and trophies.

"It almost is. He's pretty much revered as a god here."

"I can see why. That's quite a legacy."

"I never thought of bike racing before I came to IU. Grant, my big brother that I told you about, is the one who got me hooked. I'm glad he did."

"It's something I never did. We had nothing like that at USC as far as I know."

"I feel it's something of my own. I've always felt like I was living in your shadow and it's a long shadow."

"Colin. You are the most remarkable young man I have ever known. I know I'm biased, but it's true. You aren't standing in anyone's shadow. Every father hopes his son will surpass him and you have surpassed me."

My face paled as I looked at Skye. He meant it. I hugged him.

"Thanks, Skye. I love you."

"I love you too. I wish your mom could see you now, but then she was always proud of you."

I almost felt as if I could cry but I did not cry easily. That wasn't because of some macho bullshit. It just took a lot to bring tears to my eyes. If something bad happened or I was in pain I usually sucked it up. It was different when my mom died, but for the most part I almost never cried.

I gave Skye a tour of the downstairs. He met Grayson and Riley along the way. I showed him around the upstairs next. Grant was in his room so I was able to introduce him to Skye.

"Last on our tour is my room," I said, walking in.

"Excuse me, *our* room," Wes said.

"Eh, like you matter." I grinned. "Wes, this is my Uncle Skye."

"So tell me, does Colin snore at home?" Wes asked.

"He keeps the whole house up."

"Here too. He snorts like a hog."

"You are the biggest liars!" I said, but laughed.

"This is a lot nicer than your dorm room, or any I had for that matter."

"It's one of the perks of joining a frat."

"This isn't even one of the better rooms. First year brothers get the crappiest rooms," Wes said.

"The best rooms must really be something then. Maybe I should have joined a fraternity," Skye said.

"Did you go to IU?" Wes asked.

"No. I went to USC. I wanted to get out of Indiana for a while and get away from the winter cold."

"That must have been nice."

"It was, but after school a great job opportunity opened up back home and I was not sorry to return."

"Maybe you should retire when I graduate and hand your job over to me," I suggested.

"Keep dreaming, kid. I should head out. I have a long drive back and I'm sure you're busy."

"Thanks for coming to watch my match."

"I couldn't miss your first college match. I might be a little biased, but you were the best wrestler out there."

"You're a lot biased," I said, but grinned.

I walked Skye downstairs and we hugged before he stepped out the door. I missed him as soon as he was out of sight.

"How old is your uncle?" Wes asked as soon as I returned to my room.

"Thirty. Why?"

"Shit. I thought he was twenty-two or twenty-three. He looks more like your older brother than your uncle. Damn, he's buff!"

"Are you hot for my uncle, Wes?"

"No, but if I was going to hook up with a guy, I'd want him."

"Hmm, I think you have a little gay in you, Wes."

"Hey, no guy has ever been in me and no guy ever will be."

"Are you sure about that? You sleep pretty soundly you know."

"Not funny, Colin."

I laughed. My phone chimed, indicating I had a text. I looked at my phone.

"Oh, man."

"What?" Wes asked.

"It's a text from Haakon. It says, "Your uncle is smoking hot! I'd do him in a heartbeat.""

"Maybe you guys can have a three-way."

"Uh, no."

"Haven't you at least thought about hooking up with your uncle?" I hesitated for a moment too long. "You have!"

"I had a serious case of hero worship for him when I was younger and I'd be lying if I said I didn't find him attractive. If he had initiated something with me, I wouldn't have resisted, but nothing like that ever happened and I'm glad. He's my uncle, but he's like a brother and a dad. I don't think of him in a sexual way."

Wes nodded. "I understand. My older sister is smoking hot."

"Hey, I don't want to hear your incest stories," I said, interrupting him.

"Oh fuck you, Colin."

"I don't want to hear about your repressed homosexual desires either."

"Grr!"

"I'm only messing with you. I want to stay on your good side. I might need your van someday."

"You're a pal, Colin."

I smiled and texted Haakon back.

Chapter Twelve

It seemed like no time at all passed before Skye returned to pick Haakon and me up for Thanksgiving break. It was, in fact, less than three weeks since his visit, but it seemed like only three days. I lived a busy life at IU.

Haakon and I were sitting on my bed talking when Skye knocked on the doorframe.

"Your ride is here."

"Well, I should hope so. I called for a taxi over an hour ago. There will be no tip for you," I said.

"Yeah. Yeah. Get your stuff. I'm hungry. Where would you like to eat?"

"How about Casa Brava? I want some Mexican," I said.

"Is that okay with you, Haakon?" Skye asked.

"Sounds great."

"Casa Brava it is then."

Haakon and I each grabbed our bags and followed Skye downstairs. The house was practically empty since most of the brothers had already departed. Only a very few would remain over break.

We put our stuff in the trunk of the Chevy and then I directed Skye to Casa Brava, which was located in Eastland Plaza across the street from College Mall.

A few minutes later we were in a booth munching on chips & salsa and browsing the menu. When our waiter arrived, Skye ordered Fajitas Lulu; Haakon ordered quesadillas, and I ordered the Burrito Casa Brava.

"I bet you guys are ready for a break," Skye said.

"Yes, if I read anymore my head will explode," Haakon said.

"I plan to sleep a lot."

"Really? I volunteered you to vacuum the entire house," Skye said.

"Not funny."

I loved chips & salsa and had to be careful not to eat so many chips I couldn't finish what I'd ordered. Our food arrived soon. I looked at Skye's plate strangely as he assembled a fajita.

"Ham and pineapple? What kind of fajita is that?"

"I'll soon find out. I thought it looked interesting."

"It's some weird Mexican/Hawaiian hybrid," I said.

"Then it should be great."

"My quesadillas are incredible," Haakon said.

I tasted my burrito. It was so good I knew I'd have no trouble devouring it and the refried beans and Spanish rice.

"How is it?" I asked when Skye had tried his fajita.

"It's different, but really, really good. I wonder if I could get Martha to make something like this."

"Martha?" Haakon asked.

"She's the head chef at the mansion."

"It must be different living in a hotel."

"It is, but I love it," I said.

We grew quieter as we ate, which was not at all unusual. It had been a long time since I'd eaten Mexican food, unless I counted Taco Bell, but that wasn't real Mexican.

We hit the restroom before leaving and soon we were headed north. It wasn't long before I dozed off and as a result the trip seemed to take no time at all. I didn't awaken until we arrived in Verona.

"Colin's awake. I have to stop telling you embarrassing stories about him now, but we'll pick up where we left off later," Skye said to Haakon, who sat in the seat beside him.

"Yeah, right," I said.

"Wow," Haakon said as we pulled through the gates of Graymoor Mansion. "It's huge!"

"Wait until you see the inside," I said.

Skye drove around to the carriage house. He pulled the Chevy inside and parked next to his Auburn and Marshall's hearse. Haakon stared at them both when he got out.

"That's Skye's 1935 Auburn Speedster. The hearse belongs to Marshall. He's a paranormal investigator and does ghost tours of the house."

"You live an interesting life," Haakon said.

"You have no idea," Skye said. "I'll let you show Haakon to your room. I'm going to check on the Natatorium."

Haakon and I grabbed our bags and carried them around to the main entrance.

"Whoa," Haakon said as we stepped into the vast lobby.

"Big huh? You haven't seen anything yet. Let's head upstairs."

Haakon took in the paintings, antique furniture, and other oddities of Graymoor as we ascended the stairs. The entrance to our suite was on the fourth floor so we had quite a climb.

"Wow, it's like Harry Potter," Haakon said when I pressed the hidden latch on the painting that covered the entrance to our suite and it swung out.

"Yeah, it kind of is. Graymoor is an unusual place. Just don't expect the paintings to talk or move."

We walked up the wide, but short flight of stairs and entered the suite I shared with Skye.

"This is so cool!"

"Thanks. My room is in here," I said, moving off to the left.

"You live in a palace," Haakon said when as he took in the enormous canopy bed, the paintings, and the stained glass.

"The entire suite is the interior of part of a house in England. It was shipped here and reassembled over a century ago. It's really old, like 500 years old."

"This is beautiful, Colin."

"Yeah, so you can imagine what I thought of my dorm room."

Haakon laughed.

"I will have to take a lot of photos. My family will never believe me otherwise."

"There are plenty of things to photograph here. Um, I might as well tell you, the mansion is haunted. The chances that you will see or hear a ghost are high."

"Seriously?"

"Yes."

"That's so cool. I'm very interested in ghosts."

"You will love Graymoor then. I mean it when I say there are ghosts. There is one in particular..."

"Hey!" Haakon said, jumping.

"Etienne, behave yourself," I said.

A boyish giggle filled the air. Haakon swallowed hard and his eyes widened.

"You said you were interested in ghosts. Haakon, I'd like you to meet Etienne."

"Hello," said Etienne.

"Um. Hi?"

Etienne giggled again.

"He's pretty, almost as pretty as you," said Etienne.

I looked at Haakon and smiled. He looked around, but of course could not see Etienne.

"He's rarely visible, except around Marshall. He's thirteen. I can show you what he looks like later. There's a painting of him in the mansion."

"I'll see you again soon," Etienne said.

A moment later, Haakon jumped again. "He groped my butt!"

"He's known for that."

"Is he still here?"

"I don't think so."

"Did that really just happen?"

"Yes," I said, laughing.

"Why didn't you tell me you knew a ghost?"

"You never asked."

"Who asks something like that?"

"Who is crazy enough to go around telling people he knows a ghost?"

"I see your point," Haakon said. "What other surprises await me here?"

"You'll have to wait and see, but there is nothing dangerous here."

"You sure?"

"I'm sure. This was a very dangerous house years ago, but thanks to Marshall it's safe now."

"I have a feeling there is a story to tell about that."

"Yes. I'll tell you some of it later, but you don't have time to hear everything and I don't know everything either."

"I have a feeling I won't be bored during this trip."

"No you won't," I said closing the door.

I pulled Haakon to me and kissed him deeply. We began to strip each other and soon we were writhing naked on the bed. We didn't leave my room again for over an hour.

When we did leave, I gave Haakon a tour of house. Well, I showed him part of the house. We could have spent hours looking around without coming close to seeing everything.

"This is incredible," Haakon said as we stepped into the Natatorium. That was the usual reaction to the Olympic-size pool surrounded by lush plants and statues that looked like they came from ancient Greece. Perhaps they did. The Natatorium was constructed almost entirely of glass and on a bright day like this one it was stunning.

"Back here is the gym," I said, leading the way.

"Wow."

A forest of exercise machines spread out before us. There were not as many as in the SRSC at IU, but there was every machine imaginable, as well as a hot tub.

"Why do you ever leave home?" Haakon asked.

"I do like to go outside sometimes. Besides, if I never left home, I would not have met you. Come on, I'll show you the Solarium next."

There was a great deal to see in the hallways on the way to the Solarium, so it took us a while to get there. The mansion was rather like a museum. Many guests stayed just so they could spend time looking around. There was easily enough inside the mansion to keep one occupied for days.

"This is even more impressive than the Natatorium," Haakon said taking in a deep breath.

"I love it here. I often come here to think. You have no idea how wonderful it is to come and walk here during the winter when everything is bleak outside."

We walked along the paths, which took us past vastly different types of vegetation. One path immersed us in a familiar fragrant world of roses, azaleas, petunias and other plants one might see outside if it was summer. Another was tropical, with orange, lemon, kumquat, and banana trees. There were other paths with still different types of vegetation, but like the rest of Graymoor, it was hard to take in everything.

"The Solarium is big, but there seems to be more in here than is possible," Haakon said.

"Graymoor is like that, although I think the layout of the paths has something to do with it."

"It's easier to breath in here."

"This many plants put out a lot of oxygen. I wish I could capture it and breath it while I'm riding."

"It smells wonderful too. I liked the chlorine scent of the Natatorium, but this smells like orange blossoms, lilac, and lavender. The scent keeps changing as we move around."

I paused by a large angel's trumpet tree, leaned in, and kissed Haakon. I pulled him close and we made out for a few moments.

"I like that even better," Haakon said.

"There is a lot more of that upstairs."

"Good."

It was a long time before we departed from the Solarium. I showed Haakon more and more of the sights of Graymoor until we finally arrived at one of the points I definitely wanted him to see.

"That is Etienne Blackford," I said, pointing to a full-length portrait of our resident boy ghost, painted hundreds of years before when he was alive.

"He's beautiful. This reminds me of Gainsborough's *Blue Boy.*"

"Yes, but this was painted in the 14th century."

"Etienne is far prettier than the boy in Gainsborough's painting. He's almost too pretty to be a boy. I love his blond hair. I like the way it curls down to his shoulders. His family must have been very wealthy. That purple suit looks like crushed velvet."

"They owned an estate in England. You've actually walked through part of Blackford Manor. The entire manor is inside Graymoor Mansion. It was moved here long ago."

"This place is fantastic."

"You don't know the half of it."

We continued with the tour until we tired of walking. It wasn't possible to see everything in Graymoor. I'd lived there for years and I hadn't even been in all the rooms yet. Haakon was quite thoroughly impressed.

"Wow," Haakon said, repeating a word he frequently uttered during his stay in Graymoor Mansion. He drew in a deep breath. "It smells heavenly."

"It will taste even better. Come on," I said, pulling him toward the buffet spread out in the main dining room.

This was not our first meal in the dining room. We had eaten here several times in the last few days, but Thanksgiving was something special at Graymoor Mansion. Many people stayed at Graymoor on Thanksgiving just for the excellent meal.

A member of Martha's kitchen staff put out a new turkey as we approached. It was well after noon so lots of guests had already come and gone.

We helped ourselves to turkey, dressing, sweet potato casserole, mashed potatoes, cranberry sauce and more, then found ourselves a small table off to one side of the room. The enormous dining table, which seated more than two-dozen, was full. I liked the small intimate table with the candle in the center better anyway.

"How do you live here and remain fit? I bet I've gained five pounds already and I may gain another five after I hit the desserts."

"I swim and work out a lot. I've also learned to eat in moderation, although today I'm eating everything I want."

"I love the mirrors at the ends of the room. It makes it look infinite."

"Yeah, although the reflection of a reflection of a reflection gets disorientating if you look into one of the mirrors too long."

"I'm sure, but nothing like that ball room you showed me. That mirrored floor freaked me out."

"It does most people at first."

"It's a good thing you were beside me. I couldn't keep my balance at first and I thought I was going to fall up."

"That's why you shouldn't look down while you're walking in that room. It messes with your mind."

"Is it me or is the food even better today?"

"It seems better, but it's hard to say. This is only my second Thanksgiving Dinner here. Skye and I used to go to Grandmother's for Thanksgiving."

"Did she die?"

"No, but she decided she was too old to prepare all the food. I'm sure it's an enormous amount of work. She's supposed to be here a little later. I'll introduce you."

It was only about ten minutes later that my grandmother and her husband entered.

"There she is," I said standing.

I walked toward them and gave my grandmother a hug.

"Hi, Grandmother. Hi, Josh. We're already eating, but grab a plate and we'll join you," I said.

I returned to Haakon.

"Let's move to the big table. There's enough space for us on the end now," I said.

"Who is that guy with your grandmother, another uncle?" Haakon asked.

"Actually, that's my grandfather, although I never call him that."

"Your grandfather? How is that possible? How old is he?"

"Josh is thirty. Grandmother is fifty-one. "

"He can't be Skye's dad."

"No, they were actually best friends until Josh ran off with Grandmother. I'm told it was quite the scandal back then. Skye and Josh have made up so it's all cool now."

"Wow, your grandmother is edgy."

"Yeah, I love to watch the reaction of people when they find out Josh is her husband."

We moved to the larger table. I introduced everyone when Grandmother and Josh returned. Skye showed up soon after and joined us as well.

Haakon and I finished our turkey and dressing first, so we moved on to hot tea and dessert. I told Haakon he had to try some pumpkin pie because it was the traditional Thanksgiving dessert. I had a small piece too, as well as a piece of pecan pie and a cranberry and white chocolate chip cookie. I planned to sample other desserts later.

We talked as we ate. Grandmother asked Haakon and me a lot of questions about college. I hadn't talked to her since I started school, but I was sure Skye kept her informed. He must have or she would not have known to ask about Alpha or bike racing.

The others eventually caught up with Haakon and me, but we graciously went back for more dessert. This time, I had banana cream pie and peach cheesecake. Haakon tried key lime pie and chocolate cake.

Grandmother hugged me again before we parted. She hugged Skye as well. Josh merely shook our hands.

"Can you just roll me up the stairs. I don't think I've ever eaten that much in my entire life," Haakon said.

"I was going to take you guys out for ice cream," Skye said with the mischievous twinkle that often appeared in his eyes.

"Don't mention food," I said.

"I will see you guys later. I'm hitting the gym to work off some of the blackberry cobbler I ate," Skye said.

"That's not a bad idea. What do you think, Haakon?"

"Yeah, let's do it."

"We'll meet you in the gym in a few," I said.

Haakon and I walked upstairs to change into tank tops and shorts for working out. I told him to bring his swimsuit along in case we swam after.

Skye was doing military presses when we entered the mostly empty gymnasium. Thanksgiving was not a big workout day for most. Currently, there were only two other guys in the gym.

Haakon stared at Skye for a few moments until he realized he was gaping.

"See something you like?" I asked with a grin.

He nodded. "I think you should reconsider that three-way idea."

"That's a definite no, but if you have the balls you can hit on him."

"I don't think I do," Haakon said, making me laugh.

"Come on. Let's get started."

Haakon kept stealing glances of Skye as we worked out. I was accustomed to my friends lusting after my uncle. I didn't mind, although I was tired of the inevitable, 'Have you guys ever messed around?' question. I once thought about making up a detailed incest story as a joke for Sam Slayer, one of my friends who had the hots for Skye, but didn't because even making up a tale about Skye and me was somewhat disturbing. I was also afraid Sam might believe it.

By the time we finished our workout I was feeling much less like a slug. Haakon and I decided we wanted to swim so I led him to the locker room.

"This is nice. Everything here is nice," Haakon said as we stripped and tossed our clothes in the locker.

"Yes, living here doesn't suck."

I smiled when two older women checked Haakon and me out as we walked out of the locker room to the pool. Like me, Haakon wore a tiny swimsuit that was almost like wearing nothing. I was one of the rare few that wore such a swimsuit here, but Haakon was from Europe where they were more common.

We dove in, swam a few lengths, and then treaded water.

"Oh, this feels good," Haakon said.

"It feels even better if you look outside," I said.

Beyond the glass walls and roof, it had begun to rain and the very last of the autumn leaves tumbled and twirled on the wind. It was quite chilly outside, but the Natatorium was warm and slightly humid.

"I wish I could be here when it was snowing outside," Haakon said.

"I wish you could too."

Our time together was short. We had less than a month now. In the middle of December Haakon would go home and it was likely I would never see him again. I was not looking forward to that day.

***

"How was your break?" Wes asked as he entered our room.

"Great, but I ate too much."

"What did Haakon think of Thanksgiving?"

"He liked it. We ate so much we had to work out after."

"I bet you guys worked out every night in bed too. Didn't you?"

"Oh yeah, every night and some mornings and afternoons."

"Lucky. I didn't get any over break."

"I can put in a good word with Haakon for you if you want, but I don't think you're his type."

"Ha! Of course I am! I bet you guys fantasize about me. I'm his type. I am every girl's and gay boy's type, but he's not my type."

I grinned. Wes was a great roommate and brother.

Thanksgiving break had passed too quickly, but I was glad to be back. I had missed my frat brothers, riding, the SRSC, and even classes.

There would not be much outdoor riding now as the temperatures fell, but soon we would begin to work out on trainers. It was a good way to keep in shape, but it was nothing like riding through the streets and countryside. I had used the exercise bikes in the gymnasium in Graymoor daily, so I had maintained my riding fitness. I wasn't about to let up because I could not ride outside.

Finals were coming up, but I was in good shape. I had turned in all required papers and projects before Thanksgiving break. Some of my brothers were not nearly as organized and on top of things. They scurried around trying to complete everything before the end of the semester. I was glad I had worked ahead.

I quickly got back into the routine of classes, wrestling practice, wrestling meets, and training for the Little 500. While I was curious about what the future held for me, I also wished I could remain in my freshman year of college forever. High school was great, but nothing compared to this.

Haakon and I spent as much time together as we could. Wes actually called us "the twins" because we were together more than apart. Poor Wes had to spend a lot of time studying for tests in the library because Haakon and I were getting it on in the room.

With so much going on, time slipped away more quickly than ever. There was precious little time between Thanksgiving break and the end of the semester and it seemed as if each day passed in an hour. Almost before it seemed possible, finals week was upon us.

I had quite a bit of spare time during finals week. That was the week Haakon and I spent the most time together. We studied a great deal for our final exams, but usually did so together. Since we were both freshman we were taking some of the same tests. We didn't share a single class, but we did share professors.

My last exam was on Thursday, but I wasn't leaving then because Haakon wouldn't depart until Friday. His last exam was at 10 a.m. that day and then he departed by shuttle to the airport in Indy at 2 p.m. I almost couldn't believe it. In 48 hours he would be gone.

I felt rather queer when I walked out of Wiley Hall after taking my last final exam. I actually had nothing to do. The semester was over for me. There were no reading assignments, no papers due, and there would not be another wrestling practice or meet until next semester. There were no scheduled Little 500 team workouts either. Free time had been a luxury all semester, but now I would rather have been busy. Haakon still had exams so I wouldn't be able to see him until tonight. He might even need to study then.

It was too cool to ride my bike outside, but I did so anyway. Riding alone in the bleak cold of December wasn't exactly cheerful, especially since I was feeling lonely, but the physical exertion helped me get my mind off Haakon's imminent departure. I reminded myself that I would see him tonight. That helped to cheer me up.

Life was hard sometimes. Many thought I lived a charmed existence, but everyone had problems. Everyone experienced sadness, loss, and pain. I was usually able to maintain a positive outlook, but it was more difficult sometimes than others. The most difficult time in my life was right after my mom died. My entire world shifted. If it had not been for Skye I don't know how I could have handled it. Haakon returning to Norway was a small thing compared to the loss of my mother, and yet it was more difficult for me than anything I had faced since her death.

I felt somewhat better when I returned from my ride, but I couldn't quite shake my sadness. I knew the best thing I could do was keep busy, so I caught a bus to the SRSC.

Working out helped me forget that my time with Haakon was fast slipping away. Each exercise was familiar and while the SRSC was only sparsely populated, there were a few other guys working out too. I was not alone.

After my workout, I changed into my swimsuit in the locker room and headed to the pool. As the scent of chlorine hit my nostrils I was reminded of all the times Haakon and I swam here together.

I climbed into the pool and did laps until I was able to do no more, then returned to the locker room, showered, dressed, and caught a bus to the IMU.

I was hungry, so I walked up the steps and entered the building. I walked through The Commons to Burger King and ordered myself a Whopper, fries, and a Coke.

It was nearly closing time for Burger King and Baja Fresh, but there were still many students seated at the tables. Most of them weren't eating, but instead were studying for exams. I was glad mine were over and yet I almost wished I had studying to do.

After I ate, I walked across the old part of campus to Alpha house. There, I played Foosball with Grayson, Damon, and Rhett. This was one of those times that I was especially glad to have brothers.

I went upstairs to find a note from Wes stating he was secluding himself in Wells Library to study for his last exam. Apparently, there were too many distractions for him here in the house. I had escaped to the library, the south lounge in the IMU, and in warmer weather The Rose Well house to study in peace many times this semester myself.

I thought about packing, but I wasn't taking much with me other than my dirty laundry. Instead, I got on my iPad and watched a streaming video of last year's Little 500 race.

I had always been more interested in participating in sports than watching them, but I was pulled into the race. With luck, I would be racing on that track someday.

I was keenly interested in every aspect of the race, but the wrecks most dramatically caught my attention. Observing them clearly demonstrated the necessity of remaining near the front of the pack. The riders were so closely packed together that when one went down most of those behind went down as well. All it took was one error or one slip on the cinder track to cause a crash that could easily involve a dozen or more riders.

Seeing the accidents that occurred during the race likely discouraged some, but not me. There was risk in everything. I never ignored risk, but I never let that stop me either. A big part of life was managing risk and knowing when a risk was acceptable and when it was not.

Was all the training and effort worth it when one accident could destroy a team's chance to win? I thought about that as I watched the hopes of even strong teams dashed by mishap, but never once did I doubt that all the hard work was worth it. If I knew in advance that Alpha Alpha Omega would come in dead last, I would still train and ride my hardest just to be out there on that track.

I was interrupted by a knock at the door. Haakon smiled at me as I opened it. I pulled him inside and kissed him deeply, paused to tie a sock around the doorknob, and then kissed him again.

"I've missed you. Have you finished studying already?" I asked.

"If I study anymore my head will explode. I'm finished with studying. What I need now is relaxation."

"Oh, I'll relax you. I'll relax you until you moan."

Haakon grabbed me, kissed me hard, then ripped my shirt over my head. A few moments later we were naked on my bed.

We knew each other's bodies intimately, but were always eager to explore. Our hands, lips, and tongues wandered over each other's hard, smooth body. We worked each other into a frenzy of need and then we ended as we usually did, with me on top of Haakon thrusting as he urged me to go harder and faster. We filled the room with our moans and groans and then lie still.

"Want to stay the night?" I asked.

"What about Wes?"

"I think he can handle being in the room while we sleep together."

"I would love to stay. My roommate is already gone. It's lonely in my room."

We stayed up late talking, but not too late because Haakon had a test the next morning. Wes came in about 10 p.m. The three of us talked, laughed, and ate junk food.

I slept with Haakon in my arms. I liked the feeling. I wished I could keep him with me forever, but I had to content myself with one last night.

The next morning Haakon dressed and left for Forest Quad so he could prepare for his last day at IU. I felt lonely after he departed, even though Wes was still sleeping in his bed. This was my last day at IU for a while too so I showered, dressed, and then walked over to the IMU for breakfast. Haakon and I were having a goodbye lunch in The Tudor Room at noon, so I didn't want to eat too much. I thought about Burger King for breakfast, but instead bought a blueberry muffin and a cup of hot tea at Sugar & Spice. I walked to the very sparsely populated food court and sat at a table.

The food court and The Commons were always the least busy in the mornings even when the campus was full of students, but with the university quickly emptying it was almost deserted. Most of the students who had finished their exams were already gone and nearly everyone would depart by the weekend. Most of the dorms would close up on Sunday. Only some international students, a few fraternity brothers, sorority sisters, and students who lived off campus would remain.

After I finished breakfast I roamed the IMU, gazing at paintings by T.E. Steele and other artists. On the 2nd floor I found a painting of the first capital of Indiana painted by Hoagy Carmichael. I didn't know a great deal about him, but I knew he lived in Bloomington, wrote *Stardust* and a lot of other songs, and was in a lot of movies way back. I didn't know he was a painter too. It was amazing that one man could do so much. I excelled at about any type of athletics, but I doubted I could paint stick figures and I was sure no one would want to hear any song I wrote.

I returned to Alpha house, stripped my bed, and gathered my dirty laundry. Once Haakon was free I intended to spend every moment with him I could. Skye was supposed to arrive to pick me up at 2:30 so I wouldn't have much time to get ready to depart after Haakon got on his bus. The timing was no accident. I did not want to remain on campus any longer than necessary once Haakon was gone.

I stayed in my room because Haakon was coming here as soon as he finished his exam. He appeared at my door at 11:15. We hugged and kissed.

"Hey, watch the homo stuff," Wes said, but then grinned. My roommate had roused himself only a half hour earlier.

"Yeah, Haakon. We can't make out in front of Wes. You know how it turns him on," I said.

"Yeah, right. Hold me back," Wes said.

"I still have some things to pack. Let's go to my room," Haakon said.

"Sure."

"It was nice meeting you, Haakon, despite the disgusting homosexual displays," Wes said, shaking his hand.

"It was nice meet you too, Wes. Try to keep Colin in line when I'm gone."

"Yeah, like anyone can do that."

"See you later, Wes," I said and then Haakon and I departed.

Snow began to fall as we stepped onto the sidewalk and walked toward Forest Quad. The fluffy white flakes stuck in Haakon's hair and landed on his nose.

"I feel like I'm home already," Haakon said.

"It snows a lot there, huh?"

"It's not rare."

"It snows quite a bit in Verona too, much more than it does here. How was your exam?"

"Difficult, but I believe I did well. I can't believe my semester here is over."

"Me either. I'm going to miss you. It will be hard to return next semester knowing you won't be here."

"Think of it this way. You didn't even know me when this semester began."

"True, but now that I do, I'll miss you."

"I'll miss you too and I will miss being here. We'll keep in touch. We already have each other's email address. I know it won't be the same, but it's something. I'll send you photos of Norway and you can send me photos of Verona."

"I'd like that."

We entered Forest Quad and rode the elevator up to Haakon's room. His half was nearly bare.

"I only have a few things left to pack. I didn't bring much with me, but I bought a few things while I was here, mostly IU clothing. Oh, this box is for you. It's mainly shampoo and stuff I can't take with me that I thought you could use. It will make up for all your stuff I used at the SRSC."

I laughed. "I don't think you used that much, but thanks."

"I also used your locker so I'm getting the better end of the deal."

Soon, Haakon was packed. He had only a large backpack and two bags.

"Alpha is closer to the IMU than Forest. Why don't we take your bags there before we go to lunch?" I said.

"That will be great. I'll turn my key into the R.A. so I won't have to return. I'll be right back."

I waited in Haakon's room for only a few minutes before he returned.

"Okay, let's go," he said.

I grabbed one of his bags and the box he'd given me and walked out into the hallway. Haakon followed, paused a moment as he looked at his room one last time, and then closed the door.

"Partings are difficult," Haakon said.

"Yes. Leaving high school was hard for me."

"Probably because you were a god there," Haakon said and laughed.

"Well, I was popular and a top athlete, but not quite a god. Almost, but not quite." Haakon bumped his shoulder into me since he couldn't punch me with his hands full.

"I have good memories of this place. I will take those with me and I am excited to go to my new school."

"I'll be excited to get back to wrestling and eventually riding with the team outside again. I rode my bike a little yesterday, but it was cold."

"You rode yesterday? You must be part Norwegian to ride in the winter."

"I might be. I have the blond hair."

We carried everything into Alpha and up to my room. Wes was gone so there was no need for goodbyes again. It was very nearly noon so we immediately left and walked across the street to campus.

Dunn's Woods looked different now that the leaves were gone. The snow continued to fall and began to cover the ground with a blanket of white. I took Haakon's hand as we walked between the woods and the old limestone buildings of IU.

We were glad to escape from the cold when we entered the IMU. We stopped in the South Lounge to warm ourselves by the fire for a few moments before continuing on the short distance to The Tudor Room.

The hostess escorted us to a small table by a window. We ordered our drinks and then hit the buffet.

I put spinach and artichoke chicken, baked ham, and mashed potatoes on a plate, then returned to our table.

I tried not to think about Haakon's rapidly approaching departure because I wanted to enjoy what time I had left with him. I was largely successful in doing that as we ate, talked, and took in the ambiance in The Tudor Room.

It was a good day for soup, so after we finished what was on our plates we checked out what the salad and soup bar had to offer. The choices were chicken and black bean or broccoli and cheddar. I chose the former and Haakon the latter. We also made a trip to the coffee and tea bar so our jasmine green tea would have time to steep before we had dessert.

"If I could take you and The Tudor Room with me I don't think I'd mind leaving so much," Haakon said.

"It is nice, although sometimes I'm more in the mood for a taco or a burger."

"You must keep me informed about the Alpha Little 500 team, especially if you get to race," Haakon said.

"I will, although my chances of getting to race are slim. A lot of teams use freshman, but Alpha has such a strong Little 500 tradition that a freshman rarely makes the cut. The team is picked on merit so I have a shot. I'm going to work my ass off trying to be one of the four who race, but if not, then there is always next year. What's important is that we field the strongest team possible."

"No one can ever say you aren't a team player."

"I've become very dedicated to Alpha."

"No? Really?" Haakon asked. I stuck out my tongue.

Dessert was next. The choices were numerous as always. I picked a piece of chocolate cake with creamy icing and a piece of chocolate turtle cake. Haakon picked chocolate cake as well and a piece of pecan pie.

"I could live in here," Haakon said.

"Me too, but if I did I'd eventually become so fat I'd have no choice but to live here because I wouldn't be able to fit through the door."

"There is that danger."

"Yes, I love to eat here, but I limit my visits. I think even with the desserts it's healthier than fast food."

"No doubt."

"That means we can have more dessert. As soon as I finish this, I am returning to the dessert bar."

"You are a bad influence, Colin."

"Yes, in more ways than you know."

We left our table for more tea and then for more dessert. This time I had pecan pie and a toffee chocolate bar. Haakon had apple and blueberry pie.

"This is fruit so it doesn't count as dessert," Haakon said.

"I like your logic."

We lingered in The Tudor room until after one, then walked through the IMU. Haakon eyed me as if I might be crazy when I entered Sugar & Spice and purchased some chocolate chip and no bake cookies.

"You cannot possibly be hungry," he said.

"No. I bought these for you as a going away present. Later today, you can eat them on the plane," I said, handing him the bag.

"Thank you, Colin. It will be like having a bit of IU with me, at least until I eat them all."

We returned to the South Lounge and sat by the fire until our time was truly growing short, then we walked hand-in-hand back to Alpha.

We only had time for a very short make out session before we grabbed Haakon's bags and headed back to the IMU. We walked through the building and then down to the lobby of The Biddle Hotel and out the front entrance. Haakon's shuttle to the airport in Indianapolis was already waiting.

Haakon gave his bags to the attendant, then gazed at me as we stood under the portico.

"I'll never forget you," he said.

"Nor I you."

We hugged, then kissed, then held hands for a moment as we gazed into each other's eyes.

"I'll contact you and let you know I arrived home safely and you'd better do the same," he said.

"I will."

"Goodbye."

"Goodbye."

I watched as Haakon climbed on the shuttle and then stood there until it began to pull away. The last sight I had of Haakon was him waving. I turned and walked back into the IMU, fighting to keep the tears that welled up in my eyes from running down my cheeks.

Chapter Thirteen
January 2011

The snow slowly disappeared until there was none at all as Skye drove me back to Bloomington. The spring semester didn't begin until Monday, but I was returning a little early because I'd promised Haakon to show his brother around campus.

I was more than ready to return to school, wrestling practice, and Little 500 training. Christmas in Verona was as beautiful and enjoyable as always, but it was hard to keep myself as busy as I wished. Buying and wrapping gifts took up some time. I worked out, swam, and trained on the exercise bikes in the gym daily, but none of that was enough to keep Haakon from my mind.

I put in some time at the gay youth center during break to use up a few more hours. One of the interests I hadn't been able to pursue much recently was gymnastics. At the center, I worked out on the parallel bars, the pommel horse, and the rings. The rings were the hardest by far, but I was fairly proficient on them. I'd never be an Olympic gymnast, but because that was not one of my goals it didn't matter. I also spent a lot of time at the center instructing and helping out the kids who went there for classes.

When we arrived in Bloomington, Skye drove us straight to the China Buffet. It was after 1 p.m. and we were both hungry. Skye was driving straight back to Verona after dropping me off at Alpha, so it was a good break for him.

I loved Chinese food, especially Gen Tso's chicken and honey chicken. I tried Indian food during the fall semester, but didn't care for it much. It was good enough, but I was never quite sure what I was eating. The tastes of Indian food were so different I couldn't get into it.

Skye and I filled plates with our favorites, as well as kung pao chicken, crab Rangoon, beef terakihi, and other items off the buffet.

"You know, I think I just might move in with you. It's warmer down here and I love all the restaurants," Skye said.

"Sorry, you're not a member of Alpha Alpha Omega."

"Oh, I see how it is. When I was in school I had no desire to join a fraternity, but judging from how much you like it, I guess I missed out."

"I wasn't enthused either. Grant lured me in with The Little 500."

"If he's studying business he will make a great businessman someday. He knows how to sell."

"I like getting involved with something you have never done. At VHS I always heard; 'Your uncle was an incredible football player' and 'Your uncle was one of the best wrestlers ever at VHS'. I feel like I've always lived in your shadow."

"I cast a long shadow, but you stepped out from it long ago, Colin. You are most certainly forging your own path now. You are doing things I didn't even think of doing. I'm very proud of you, but I always have been."

"Thanks. I was concerned I was taking on too much, but I've handled it well so far."

"Definitely. When are you meeting Haakon's brother? What's his name?"

"Hamlet. I'm meeting him tomorrow at noon."

"Hamlet? He's seriously named Hamlet?"

"Keep in mind he's Norwegian. Did you expect him to be named Bob?"

"True. It's an interesting name at least. It's nice of you to show him around."

"Haakon thought it would be a good idea. Hamlet doesn't know anyone here and has never been to the U.S. before. I thought we'd have lunch, I'll show him around, and clue him in to the way things are done here."

"I'm sure having a guide will be a big relief for him."

"I'm not certain when he arrived on campus. I'm sure he has completed orientation and has taken the freshman campus tour, but it's a lot to take in all at once. IU is a big place."

"You're an expert now."

"Hardly. I haven't even been inside all the buildings."

"It was like that for me at USC."

Skye and I talked all through lunch, which took us quite a while because we ate a lot. We continued talking as we traveled to Target and Kroger and bought my supplies for the spring semester.

When we arrived at Alpha, Skye got out and opened the trunk, then helped me carry in our purchases and my enormous bag of clean laundry. It took two trips to bring in everything, even with both of us carrying huge armloads.

"If you need anything, call me," Skye said, giving me a hug as we stood in my room. I hugged him back. We said our goodbyes then Skye departed.

It was quiet inside the house. I was sure at least a few brothers were around and more would arrive soon, but I had not seen nor heard any of them as Skye and I brought my things inside. There was no sign of Wes either. I looked forward to seeing my roommate again.

I put my clothes and the items we'd purchased at Target and Kroger away, then changed into workout clothes and headed downstairs to the Little 500 training room. I climbed on a bike and began to ride.

***

I missed Haakon. I felt like he should be here. It didn't seem right that he wasn't. I reminded myself that he hadn't died. He was merely attending school in Norway. I had never fallen for anyone like I had Haakon. I'd had lots of relationships with guys and girls, but none of those relationships was as intense. If Haakon had remained at IU, I'm almost certain we would have seriously dated.

It was what it was. At least his brother would be here this semester. He wasn't Haakon, but he was a connection to him at least. I was looking forward to meeting him and discovering how much he was like his brother. He could be similar or a complete opposite. I would find out soon enough because I was meeting him in in the lobby of The Biddle Hotel in the IMU at noon and it was nearly noon now.

I entered the building through the south entrance and soon passed through the South Lounge. Memories of sitting in front of the fire with Haakon entered my mind. It seemed like both ages ago and yesterday.

I continued through the lounge and out into the hallway, passing The Tudor Room and then the bookstore around the corner. I walked down the stairs and past Sugar & Spice. Each location awakened more memories of Haakon.

Campus was slowly coming to life. Several of my Alpha brothers had arrived and there were a fair number of students in the IMU. The number of people in the union was nothing like a busy day during the semester, but it was far from empty.

I walked down the wide stairs that led to the lobby of The Biddle Hotel and then stopped. Haakon was standing only a few feet away. My heart began pounding and I grinned.

"Haakon?" I said as I approached. I couldn't believe it. He was back!

"No. I'm Hamlet. You must be Colin." My confusion must have shown on my face because Hamlet smiled and said, "Didn't my brother tell you? We're identical twins."

"He left out that little piece of information, but he didn't actually tell me much about you at all," I said, trying to mask my extreme disappointment.

"Well, I'm glad to meet you. Haakon talked about you too much. He showed me pictures of you, but you're even more handsome in person."

"Thanks. This is... weird. I wasn't prepared for this, but I'm glad to meet you. Would you like to get something to eat before I show you around?"

"I am always ready to eat."

"You are identical," I said with a grin. "Come on and I will introduce you to the food court and The Commons."

I kept glancing at Hamlet as we walked back up the stairs and down the long hallway. I could have sworn I was walking next to Haakon. My mind couldn't quite grasp that this was not him. It was just like Haakon to not tell me his brother was his identical twin. His mischievousness made me miss him all the more.

"Straight ahead is the bookstore. Did you pick up your texts already?"

"Yes, I did."

"Then you already know it's the bookstore. I promise, some of the information I give you will actually be useful. On our right is Sugar & Spice. It has the best cupcakes and cookies anywhere in Bloomington."

We followed the hallway to the right and then back to the left.

"This is the food court. It includes Pizza Hut, Cyclone Salads, Sakura Sushi & Hot Bowl, and Charleston Market. It's open later than The Commons which is right down here," I said as we entered the next area. "As you can see there's a Burger King and at the other end of all the tables is Baja Fresh, which serves Mexican. Around the other side of the hallway is Freshens, which has smoothies and frozen yogurt. Downstairs is the Dunn Meadow Café. What do you feel like eating?"

"What do you like?"

"Don't worry about me. I eat here a lot. Besides, we don't have to get our food the same place anyway. That's the beauty of the food court and The Commons."

"Burger King would be great."

"I'm a big Burger King fan so let's do it."

A very few minutes later Haakon... I mean Hamlet and I were seated at a table with our Whoppers, fries, and drinks.

"It's usually much more crowded in here. Tomorrow around lunch time there will be lines everywhere and it will be very difficult to find a seat."

"I think IU is much bigger than The University of Oslo. We have about 16,000 students there."

"We have close to 50,000 here."

"Wow."

"Yes, and that's just the Bloomington campus. There are smaller IU campuses at different locations in the state."

"This will be an adjustment."

"I'm sure, but everyone is generally friendly and we have a big international population. I sometimes hear languages I can't even identify."

"Haakon said you are a fraternity brother."

"Yes, Alpha Alpha Omega."

Talking about Alpha led to talking about bike racing and the Little 500. Hamlet asked a lot of questions and was genuinely interested in my answers. We didn't stop talking all through lunch.

"What would you like me to show you? One thing we can do is scout out the locations of your classes and then look at whatever else you want as we go. Do you have your schedule with you?"

"No. It is in my dorm."

"Why don't we grab it and then I'll show you where your classes will be tomorrow? I scouted the locations of all my classes before my first day the fall semester. It helps."

"Great. I live in Wright Quad."

"Okay cool. I was in Hershey Hall before I joined Alpha. It's close to Wright. Did you check out the food court in Wright? It's big."

"Yes, I found it."

"I ate there sometimes when I lived in Hershey. The food is good. Ready to head out?"

"Yeah, let's go."

I pointed out buildings like the HPER, the art museum, The Lily Library, The IU Auditorium, and others as we walked east toward Wright Quad.

Hamlet told me about his interests and The University of Oslo when I wasn't pointing out buildings. He had interests very much like his brother, including a strong one in athletics. He began asking me questions about wrestling, which took up the rest of our walk to Wright.

"Wright isn't air conditioned, but I don't think that will be a problem during the spring semester. The beginning of the fall semester is when it gets hot here," I said as we entered Hamlet's dorm.

"I am accustomed to cool, but I would not mind some hot weather."

"Me either, but we won't be getting any of that in January."

Hamlet's roommate was out, but his room was about what I expected; two loft beds, two desks, and built-in shelves and wardrobes. It was a bit cramped, but not bad and had a nice view of Jordan Avenue and the Wells Library across the street.

"Do you think we might have time to work out in the gym?" Hamlet asked.

"Yeah, that would be great. Make sure you have your student ID so you can get into the SRSC."

"Haakon said you like to work out. I'll take my workout clothes with me."

"Oh yeah. I've already rented a locker there. We can stop by Alpha and I'll pick up my clothes and shower stuff."

We headed out once more, with Hamlet now wearing a backpack. I gave him a short tour of the Wells Library first since it was a building he would no doubt use often, then we visited each of the buildings where he had a class and even tracked down the exact room numbers. I scouted out some of my classes at the same time.

"I wish I had time to join a fraternity," Hamlet said as we entered Alpha house.

"It is much nicer than the dorms. It's one of the perks. Wait until you see my room."

I led Hamlet upstairs. The door to my room was open, which meant Wes had finally showed up.

"I want to move in," Hamlet said when he entered.

"Haakon?" Wes asked.

"This is Hamlet, Haakon's twin brother. He neglected to tell me he had a twin. This is my roommate and fraternity brother, Wes."

"Wow, you guys look exactly alike," Wes said.

"Really? I suppose Colin and I look somewhat alike, but not exactly." Hamlet grinned.

"Oh god, you are exactly like your brother."

"Oh no. I am much stronger, more intelligent, and better looking."

"Now you sound like Colin."

"That's an extreme compliment," I said quickly.

"Yeah, right," Wes said.

"We are heading to the SRSC to work out. Want to join us?"

"No. I still have to unpack and go shopping. I'll join you some other time. It was nice to meet you Hamlet."

"You too."

Hamlet and I walked to the nearest bus stop and caught a campus bus. I was able to point out several more buildings on the way. When we arrived at the SRSC we walked down to the locker room. I loaded my new locker with my stuff and we changed into tank tops and shorts.

I had a chance to check out Hamlet's body as he stripped down to boxer briefs. It was the same body I knew so intimately. I had to keep reminding myself that this was not Haakon. They looked alike, spoke alike, walked alike, and even laughed alike. It was as if they were two copies of the same person. Hamlet smiled at me when he caught me looking at him.

"I can't get over how much you are like Haakon."

"Yes, we freak out a lot of people. Sometimes our family cannot even tell us apart. It's very useful at times."

"I'll bet."

When we had dressed we headed upstairs to the cardio area and put in some time on the bikes. After we warmed up, we walked to the main weight room and got down to some serious working out.

I felt slightly guilty because the sight of Hamlet's bulging muscles turned me on as he did curls, military presses, and lats, but how could it not? He looked exactly like the boy I'd had incredible sex with on numerous occasions.

Hamlet checked me out as well and I wondered what that meant. Guys checked me out all the time in the gym and locker room, even straight guys so it didn't always mean what most would assume. What if Hamlet was interested in me? How did I feel about that? I couldn't help but be attracted to him, but he was Haakon's brother.

I didn't think about it too much. There was no point in pondering possibilities. I would think about it when the situation became clearer. After today, I might not even see him again. He looked like Haakon, but he was not Haakon. I had to keep reminding myself of that.

Hamlet and I had a great workout. He was definitely the equal of his brother in the gym. That's one of the things I'd loved about Haakon. He could keep up with me when it came to physical activity.

"Do we have time for a swim?" Hamlet asked as we walked downstairs to the locker room.

"Sure. I reserved today to show you around IU."

We stripped in the locker room and walked into the showers. I took advantage of the opportunity to check out the parts of Hamlet I had not yet seen. He was truly identical to Haakon.

We changed into swimsuits after washing off the sweat of our workout and walked to the pool. I loved the scent of chlorine in the air. It reminded me of the Natatorium in Graymoor, but there the chlorine scent was mixed with that of blooming plants. There were no plants here.

There were not a lot of swimmers, which wasn't surprising. The SRSC was the least crowded before classes began. At present, there were only three girls and three guys messing about in the shallow end. I noticed the girls eyeing us, much to the annoyance of the boys.

Hamlet and I swam laps for several minutes. I loved to swim. It was vastly different from most of the physical activity I indulged in. I loved the feel of gliding through the water. I wished I could experience some parts of my life more than once. If I could, I'd live an alternate version of high school and perhaps this time I'd join the swim team. I wish I could do that. I never had enough time to do everything I wanted.

Hamlet and I moved to the shallow end where we received a chilly reception from the boys. Now that we were closer, the girls couldn't stop looking at us. Hamlet grinned at me. He knew what was happening.

We floated on our backs and took it easy for a while. I was lucky that I had access to a pool almost all the time. I took advantage of it. I would not live in Graymoor Mansion or attend IU forever. Who knew where I'd end up in the future?

I winked at the girls when we departed a few minutes later.

"You like to cause trouble, don't you?" Hamlet asked with a grin as we walked back to the locker room.

"Only a little."

"Those boys were getting seriously annoyed."

"They can relax now. Maybe the girls will settle for mere mortals now that we're gone. It's difficult being a god, isn't it?"

"Haakon warned me about your sense of humor. He said not to take you too seriously when you acted conceited."

I smiled. Hamlet's brother knew me well.

We dressed and headed out of the SRSC.

"I'm getting hungry again," I said.

"Me too."

"Hmm, let me think of a good place. The Tudor Room is awesome, but it's closed right now. How do you feel about Mexican?"

"I love Mexican."

"Let's go to Casa Brava. It's over by the mall and I can show you the mall too. We'd better go to the mall first because it closes at six on Sunday."

We walked to 10th Street, caught a city bus, and then rode the short distance to a bus stop near the mall. In nice weather we could have walked, but it was rather cold out.

"This is College Mall," I said as we walked toward it. "It's not huge, but it's plenty big enough. A couple of blocks to the south is Kroger, which is an enormous grocery store. It's almost like a mall itself."

We entered near Sears, passed the small food court and then walked toward Dick's Sporting Goods, passing Old Navy, Abercrombie & Fitch, and lots of other stores along the way. Just before Dick's we turned left into the longest section of the mall.

"This is quite nice and it's close to the university," Hamlet said.

"It's easy to ride the bus over. I usually walk or ride my bike. The street we crossed over just before the bus stop is 3rd Street. Alpha is located on 3rd only a few blocks to the west."

"I like Bloomington and it is much warmer than home."

"This is our coldest time of year, so just wait until spring."

We walked all the way up to Macy's and then headed back. The only store we entered was Target. I had been inside only the day before with Skye, but I thought of a few things I needed to pick up and Hamlet wanted to purchase a few items as well.

Several minutes later we exited the mall, walked across the parking lot, and crossed College Mall Road. Casa Brava was located on the near end of the strip mall that included The China Buffet.

We were soon seated in a booth eating chips & salsa. When our waiter returned with our Cokes, Hamlet ordered a beef Chimichanga Casa Brava and I ordered a fajita taco salad, which came in a tortilla shell bowl.

"Thank you so much for showing me around today. Haakon told me a lot about campus and has lots of photos, but I was still lost. It's also nice to know someone here. This is the first time I've been out of Norway."

"It's probably quite a culture shock."

"It is very different here. The main adjustment I have to make is speaking English. I think in Norwegian so I have to translate."

"You speak English extremely well."

"I learned when I was very young so it is not difficult for me, but I'm accustomed to speaking it only occasionally, not all the time."

"I'm sure it's difficult. Foreign languages confuse me. When it comes to other languages I am a dumb blond."

Haakon... I mean Hamlet laughed.

"I'm having a hard time remembering you aren't Haakon. I have to keep correcting myself."

"We are frighteningly similar. You have an advantage over me. He told me much about you, but you basically already knew me before we met."

"I could kick Haakon's butt for not telling me he was an identical twin."

"We are both just a little evil."

"I always liked that about your brother."

"Yes. He told me. He told me everything."

"Everything?"

"*Everything*," Hamlet said and grinned.

Our food arrived. I didn't eat salad as often as I should, but most salads weren't enough for me. This one was an exception. It had a lot of fajita steak, cheese, guacamole, and sour cream. It was also huge. With the chips & salsa I would be stuffed.

"There are tons of places to eat in Bloomington. I usually grab something in my room for breakfast, eat cheap for one meal and get something better for the other," I said.

"I will have to watch how much I spend. Coming here was very expensive."

"Your travel expenses are certainly much higher than mine."

"Our parents wanted us to experience another culture and study abroad, but couldn't afford to send either of us for four years, let alone both of us. Coming one semester each was a compromise."

"I've never been outside of the U.S."

"You can come visit us in Norway someday."

"I would like that, but only during the warmest part of the year."

"I do not know if you would have made a good Viking."

"You have Viking ancestors?"

"Oh yes. My ancestors raped and pillaged, although the Vikings are misunderstood. Many were traders and craftsmen. Everyone was raping and pillaging back then, but the Vikings got all the bad press so to speak."

"I've learned that in history classes. There has always been a great deal of warfare everywhere."

"The world is filled with barbarians, but my people are the best known for violence."

I laughed. "I have Scandinavian ancestors myself."

"Yes, you look like you belong in Norway."

"Not until you turn the heat up!"

Conversation came so easily with Hamlet. I hoped we could be friends. I had my Alpha brothers and others, but one could never have too many friends and I especially liked Hamlet.

After supper, we gathered our bags and headed for the bus stop. Only minutes later, we stepped off the bus near Alpha House so I could take my things inside, then walked to Wright so Hamlet could dump his.

"*Percy Jackson & The Olympians: The Lightning Thief* is playing in the Whittenberger Auditorium in the IMU at 8 p.m. Want to go? It's free with a student ID," I said.

"Yeah, I missed it last summer when it came out."

"Me too."

We walked over to the IMU. I pointed out a few more things to Hamlet since it was not yet 8 p.m. When show time neared we got some popcorn and entered the auditorium. It was not large, but plenty big enough and as big as the smaller screens in theatres like Showplace.

I couldn't shake the feeling that I was on a date with Haakon. It was as if I was in an alternate reality where he had never left

IU. When I began to slip into that fantasy I pulled back. It wasn't fair to Hamlet and it wasn't true. Hamlet was a unique individual. He was identical in many ways to Haakon and yet he was an entirely separate being. His feelings and thoughts might be similar to those of his brother, but they were his own.

I actually knew some of the Greek history presented in the film. I had taken a World Civilization class last semester and the professor spent quite a bit of time on Greek culture. My paper for the class was a comparison of Bronze Age and Classical Greece, which were separated by a thousand years. I was not the dumb blond many believed me to be.

I gazed at Hamlet a few times during the film. He was so very handsome and I yearned to kiss the lips I knew so well. Being near him was wonderful and yet confusing and frustrating. It was as if I was plagued by a recurring illusion.

I did what I tried to do in all difficult situations; I enjoyed myself as best I could. Hamlet was not Haakon, but he was most of what I loved about his brother. Perhaps Hamlet and I would become friends and I could enjoy one part of the relationship I'd had with his brother.

"That was awesome. I want to read the book," Hamlet said as we left the auditorium after the movie.

"You know what I liked the best? The pen."

"I gathered that when you cracked up when Chiron was telling Percy the pen was a powerful weapon and Percy kept saying, "It's a pen!""

I began laughing again.

"You *really* like that."

"Yeah, it gets to me."

"I had a very nice time today. Thanks for showing me around. I know it's not what you probably wanted to do on your last free day before classes."

"I agreed to show you around as a favor to your brother, but today was awesome. I would very much like to hang out again. As Haakon likely told you I'm very busy, but maybe we can hit the SRSC again, eat out, or whatever. Do you have a phone yet?"

"Yes, and you have my number. Haakon gave me his phone since it's not much use in Norway."

"Okay, cool. Text me. The first week will likely be especially hectic, but after that it will be easier to find time when we're both free."

"I will do that. Thanks. I'd better get to my room. I still haven't unpacked everything. Have a good night." Hamlet leaned in and kissed me on the cheek.

"Good night."

I watched for a few moments as he walked away and then turned and headed toward the South Lounge and out the rear entrance of the IMU. I had a feeling my life had just become a lot more complicated.

Chapter Fourteen

My left shoulder was almost on the mat, but I wasn't going down. I absolutely refused. My opponent from Maryland was tougher than any I'd faced so far, but I was going to win this match.

The University Gym was filled with shouts of encouragement from my teammates. I centered myself mentally and then broke free. I glimpsed the astonished expression on my opponent's face for only a moment as I forced him onto his back. I moved quickly before he had time to recover. Less than five seconds later I pinned him. We stood and the ref held my wrist in the air.

My teammates patted me on the back as I sipped water and watched the next match begin. That was the closest I'd come to losing against an opponent in my weight class in as long as I could remember. I felt energized as I always did when I faced a serious challenge.

I headed to the locker room with my teammates after the meet. We peeled off our sweat-soaked singlets and hit the showers.

Wrestling always made me horny. My thoughts were not on sex while I wrestled. If they were I might never win a match, but wrestling caused an ache in my groin that gave me an extra edge of power. It was still there when a match ended and the feeling only intensified as I showered with my teammates. If I didn't have exceptional control I would have been rock-hard. As it was I was only mildly stiff.

I didn't let my eyes wander much in the showers because the sight of my teammates soaping up only increased my torment. Instead, I focused on the luxurious feel of the soapy washcloth gliding over my skin and the delicious warmth of the water.

I rinsed off and headed back to the locker room, quickly dressed, and then headed out into the gym where Hamlet and Wes awaited me.

"We've been waiting forever. I'm starved!" Wes said.

"It didn't take me that long to shower, Wes."

"Well, I'm glad you're here. Wes keeps trying to make out with me," Hamlet said. Wes growled.

"You could do worse, Wes," I said.

"You guys just don't get the concept for heterosexual, do you? I mean, you are a homo like Colin. Right, Hamlet?"

"Oh yes. I belong to the superior branch of humanity. I am gay," Hamlet said.

I had wondered about Hamlet. Since he was so much like Haakon I figured he was gay, but that was by no means certain, until now.

"Technically, I'm only half-homo," I said.

"You like dick, so to me that makes you a homo."

"Who said you're allowed to say homo?" I asked.

"My roommate is a homo so I'm entitled."

"I'll have to check the rulebook on that one. So, you're starving. Where are you taking me to eat?"

"I'm not taking you. You're paying for your own."

"It was worth a try."

"How about Dagwood's? I'm in a sub kind of mood."

I looked at Hamlet.

"Too easy," he said.

"That's not what I meant! Grr! Stop picking on the straight boy," Wes growled.

"I could go for a sub," Hamlet said.

"Come on, you guys can ride on the team bus."

"I don't know. I've heard stories about wrestlers. What if they try to molest me?" Wes asked.

"Enjoy it?" Hamlet suggested.

"Now I know why there are no great Norwegian comedians," Wes said.

We had to wait a while for all my teammates to come out of the locker room, but soon we were on our way to Assembly Hall. There, we caught a campus bus that dropped us off by The Sample Gates, only half a block from Dagwood's on Indiana Avenue.

Hamlet and I gazed at the menu as Wes ordered a Genoa Salami and Swiss sub. Hamlet decided on a turkey wrap. I ordered a Dagwood Supreme, which included roast beef, ham, turkey, provolone, Colby, lettuce, tomato, onions, and Dagwood's special sauce. I was hungry!

We sat at a table by the window. The day was sunny, but the cold of January made its presence known. It was warmer here than in Verona so I didn't mind much, but I preferred weather warm enough I could wear shorts.

Our sandwiches soon arrived. Wes stared at mine for a moment.

"Do you plan to eat that alone or will you be taking it back to the house to share with the brothers?"

"It's not that big and wrestling uses a lot of energy."

"I thought your ass was pinned for a while there," Wes said.

"I was merely toying with him."

"Liar."

I laughed. "He was tough. He was the toughest opponent I've ever faced."

"I wouldn't want to face him," Hamlet said.

"Oh, I would... if you and Colin were with me," Wes said.

"Three on one hardly seems fair," I said.

"Sounds fair to me."

"Uh huh. He did come close to pinning me, but that only made me more determined that he wasn't going to succeed. I don't like to lose."

"Does this mean you'll throw yourself on the ground and kick and scream if you aren't chosen to race in The Little 500 this year?" Wes asked.

"No, unless you think that would change the council's mind." Hamlet laughed. "I only started riding last semester. I don't expect to race this year. A part of me hopes for it, sure, but I'm working toward next year."

"I'll be picked to race this year. There is no doubt," Wes said.

"Wes has a lot of fantasies," I said to Hamlet.

"Hey!"

"You should ride with us sometime, Hamlet, once we start riding again."

"I doubt I could keep up. Haakon told me you guys are serious riders."

"You can ride a 21-speed like Haakon did when he rode with us. That will give you a huge advantage. Our bikes are fixed gear."

"You actually race on a fixed gear bike? Haakon said the race is 50 miles."

"That is the way it has been done since the race started in 1951. It evens the odds. Everyone rides the same bike. The alterations that are allowed are so minor they are insignificant. If teams could use any bike, some would end up with a huge advantage. All bikes are not created equal."

"I might ride with you, but only after I put in a lot of time on the bikes in the SRSC. I rarely bike at home."

"We will be happy to have you join us."

"Unless... what if the Norwegians are sending a team and he's a spy... Are you a spy?" Wes asked.

"I'm, uh... not allowed to say," Hamlet said.

I laughed.

"You are as much fun as Haakon said," Hamlet said.

"Oh, Colin and Haakon had *a lot* of fun," Wes said.

"Wes..." I warned.

"It's fine. As I said earlier, Haakon and I tell each other *everything*."

"So you know Colin and your brother..."

"Yes, I know," Hamlet said.

"It's a good thing he does or I'd beat you, Wes."

Wes smiled smugly.

"Haakon and I have no secrets. We can practically read each other's mind, so it would be hard to hide anything even if we wished, and why would we? I think our openness with each other is part of why we are so close. There are no misunderstandings."

"So you're both gay. Have you guys ever...?" Wes asked.

"Don't go there, Wes," I said.

"I bet you're curious."

"Wes," I growled.

"Okay. Okay!"

"You'll have to forgive, Wes. He sometimes asks questions that are far too personal and makes inappropriate comments."

"I find him interesting, sort of like a specimen on display."

"In a freak show?" I asked.

"Hey! I'm sitting right here!"

"He also whines if he doesn't get enough attention," I said.

"See what I have to live with?" Wes asked, but smiled.

"My roommate has turned out to be fun too, but he keeps asking me what life is like in St. Olaf. I keep telling him I do not know where that is and he laughs," Haakon said.

Wes and I began laughing.

"What?"

"Have you never watched *The Golden Girls*?" I asked. Hamlet shook his head.

"I thought all homos watched that show," Wes said.

"I'll show you an episode sometime, but there is a character named Rose from St. Olaf, Minnesota. She's very naïve and not terribly bright and she tells ridiculous stories about life in St. Olaf using a lot of Scandinavian names and words. I think a lot of them are made up, but I'm not sure."

"I must see that. Maybe I will torment my roommate by making up my own ridiculous stories."

"That will teach him," Wes said.

We talked while we ate. Wes slipped in a few more inappropriate comments about Haakon and me, but he didn't go too far. I would get him back someday. I wasn't sure how, but I would do so.

"I'm going to get out of here before Colin begins regaling us with his latest athletic triumph. You might as well know, he's a huge bragger."

"Get lost, Wes," I said.

"I can see I'm not properly appreciated here, but I'll still get lost if you two want to get it on in the room later."

"Wes..."

"I'm going. I'm going."

I shook my head as Wes departed.

"As you can see I have an interesting roommate."

"He's funny."

"Yes, and he knows just how far to push without quite getting punched. I am sorry about that question he asked about you and Haakon."

"Oh, I've been asked that a lot."

"I suppose it goes along with being a twin and with both of you being gay. I wonder if you would be asked as often if you were hetero and had a twin sister."

"I bet not, but I'd still get asked. If Wes asks again I'll make up a story that will make him blush."

I loved the mischievous glint in Hamlet's eyes. "It will take a lot to make Wes blush."

"I will do my best."

As I gazed at Hamlet across the table I very much wanted to take him back to my room, but I didn't know how he'd feel about that and a part of me would've felt like I was cheating on Haakon. That was ridiculous, but Hamlet was his brother. I was so powerfully attracted to Hamlet because he was so much like Haakon. It was difficult to even think of them as separate individuals. That made me wonder if I truly liked Hamlet or I was merely trying to get back what I'd lost when Haakon went home. Identical twins were confusing!

"I should return to my dorm and get some work done," Hamlet said.

"Me too. Would you like to go to brunch tomorrow? I'll pay. I promise you will love it."

"That sounds nice, but you don't have to pay."

"I want to this time."

"Okay, but I will pay another time then."

"Deal. Meet me at The Tudor Room at say... 11 a.m.? You remember where it is, right?"

"Yes. I will be there. You know we eat out a lot together."

"We do, but we have to eat so why not together?"

"True. I'll see you tomorrow then."

Hamlet leaned in and kissed my cheek as he had more than once before. I wished I could figure out what that meant.

I dumped my trash, walked outside and headed toward Alpha. I was already looking forward to tomorrow.

***

I did not get up early on Sunday morning. Weekends were my only real chance to sleep in and I had plenty of time to do everything I needed to get done after brunch.

I could hear the piano music before I entered The Tudor Room just before 11 a.m. Hamlet was already there.

"This looks very expensive," he said when I walked up to him.

"It's not nearly as much as you think and we get a student discount."

"It looks like we'll have to wait a while for a table."

"No. I'm special. I don't have to wait." I walked up to the podium. "I have a reservation for Colin Stoffel."

"Yeah, you're special *and* you have a reservation," Hamlet said as we followed the hostess to a table by a window.

"I'm also smart enough to plan ahead."

Our waiter, Evan, appeared and asked what we'd like to drink. I ordered cranberry juice and Hamlet ordered orange juice.

"If you want an omelet, follow me. There is often a long line but there isn't right now. If you don't, hit the buffet."

Hamlet followed. I ordered an omelet with everything. He ordered one with bacon, onion, and green peppers.

"I'm going to get some tea while we wait for our omelets. There is a coffee and tea bar up front."

I chose jasmine green tea and Hamlet picked English breakfast. By the time we dropped off our cups at our table, our drinks had arrived and our omelets were finished.

Hamlet went straight for the main buffet, but I stopped at the French toast and waffle area and added some French toast, syrup, strawberries, and blueberries to my plate before following. From the buffet I chose Tudor Room casserole, bacon, and eggs Benedict.

"This is very nice. Are you sure it doesn't cost too much?" Hamlet said.

"Relax. After our student discount it's $12.95."

"Wow, that's cheap for this. If I had plenty of money I would eat here every Sunday."

"Students likely get a discount because few of us have plenty of money."

"Your French toast looks good, but I couldn't possibly try everything."

"Yes, and don't forget dessert. The Tudor Room has the best desserts."

The piano music, the linen table cloth and napkins, and the upscale ambiance made for a very pleasant brunch. There was a family eating near us at a large round table, several other students alone or in groups, and lots of other couples and individuals. Even when I came here alone, I never felt alone, but it was nicer to have a companion.

"You know where all the cool stuff is on campus," Hamlet said.

"I doubt I know where all of it is, but I have had an entire semester to explore. I know a lot of older people back home who went here, including one of my coaches, so I knew quite a bit before I arrived."

"What secrets have you not shared with me yet?"

"Hmm, I already told you Sugar & Spice has great desserts, but they also have huge soft drinks, so does the food court. If you follow the hallways into The Biddle Hotel, there are ice machines that few know about. In the back of The Commons, off to the left of The Back Alley, there are microwaves, which can be useful. That's all I can think of at the moment. Did you let Haakon in on the secrets of The University of Oslo?"

"Yes, I gave him a list and showed him around over winter break. He knows a lot more than I did when I started."

"Do you think you guys will room together when you go back?"

"No. We live together at home and will see each other plenty without living together. We both want to meet new people."

"That makes sense. Are there a lot of hot guys at UO?"

"Yeah. There is some good scenery, but not as good as here. I hooked up with a few. College provides some fun opportunities."

"Yes it does."

"It must especially for you since you're bi."

"Yes, and college girls aren't as shy about hitting on a guy as they are in high school. I sometimes get offers from girls I don't know."

"I can imagine; you are exceptionally attractive."

"So are you."

"I am no match for you. I almost did not believe Haakon when he told me about you until he showed me photos of you."

"You're going to inflate my ego, and most believe it's quite big enough."

Hamlet laughed.

"I'm not hung up on looks, but who doesn't appreciate beauty?" Hamlet asked.

"I know, and everyone has their own idea of what is attractive."

"True. In Oslo there was a boy with spiky black hair and green eyes that I found very hot, but he rejected me because I was too slim and muscular. He liked boys who were pudgy."

"Yeah, everyone has their own thing. I knew a girl in high school who always wanted me to wear my Nikes when we got it on."

"Oh, I'm getting a nice visual image."

"She was totally turned on if I wore my shoes and nothing else."

"Maybe that could be your outfit for classes."

"I don't think so, especially not in January!"

"Come on, be bold."

"Bold is one thing, cold is another."

I had a wonderful time talking with Hamlet over brunch. He possessed the same quirky, flirty humor as Haakon. I could not help but like him and be attracted to him. I wanted so badly to kiss him and take him back to my room.

We moved on to dessert. I didn't have much room left, but I did select a piece of key lime pie and a no bake cookie. Hamlet had vanilla cake with icing and coconut cream pie.

We lingered over dessert and hot tea. There were a lot of people in The Tudor Room, but no one was waiting on a table so there was no need to hurry. It was an excellent place to sit and talk.

I left Evan a tip and paid the bill when we departed. I was seriously tempted to kiss Hamlet and very much feared that if I remained with him much longer that I would do so.

"I should get going. I have a lot to do before classes tomorrow," I said.

"Yes, I want to run to Kroger and get some other things done while I have the time," Hamlet said.

"This will be another busy week for both of us, but text me. We can have lunch together or work out at the SRSC or whatever."

"I will text you. Count on it," Hamlet said.

As always, he kissed me on the cheek before departing. I very nearly grabbed him and kissed him on the lips, but I managed to control myself.

I walked through The South Lounge and out into the cold of January. I was seriously worked up. I was hard enough I even had a little trouble walking. I wanted Hamlet and I wanted him bad. If he had been anyone else I would have gone for it, but he was Haakon's brother and that made things complicated.

Falling snow blanketed the floor of Dunn's Woods and covered the roof of the Rose Well House. I yearned for the season when the forest was green and the air warm, but January possessed its own quiet beauty. What struck me most was the silence. I could hear almost nothing, but the sound of my own footsteps on the snow.

It was a short, but cold walk to Alpha. The cold should have calmed me down, but I was as worked up when I entered the house as I was when I departed from the IMU.

"You look frustrated," Wes said the moment I entered our room.

"I am."

"What's wrong? Did The Tudor Room run out of donuts?"

"They don't have donuts. I'm frustrated because of Hamlet."

"Ah."

"What?"

"You're hot for him, aren't you?"

"Yes, and I very nearly kissed him just now."

"Why didn't you?"

"Haakon."

"Listen, I know you guys were close, but you'll probably never see him again. Your relationship with him is over. Hamlet is here now. If you want him, you should jump on him."

"It's not quite that easy."

"Of course it is. Make a move on him. If he's into it, go for it. If not, back off."

"I don't want to hurt Haakon."

"Why should hooking up with his brother hurt him? You're not dating him. It's not like you would be cheating on him with his brother."

"I know, but it doesn't feel right."

"Well, if you aren't going to jump on Hamlet, jump on someone else or I won't feel safe at night."

"Funny."

"I do my best."

"I'm going to go work out."

"That's your answer to every problem."

"Hey it works."

"Oh wait, I know... You're going to hook up with random guys in the showers in the SRSC, aren't you?"

"Have you been following me again?" I asked with a grin.

"Hey, I have better things to do with my time."

"Sure you do. Later, Wes."

"Don't come back until you get some. Later."

I smiled as I departed. Wes was a great roommate.

Chapter Fifteen

I hit send and almost immediately wished I could take it back. It was February and we were more than a month into the spring semester. I had spent quite a lot of time with Hamlet and the sexual tension between us was intense. I had just sent a long email to Haakon explaining my feelings for his brother. I hoped he didn't hate me for it.

I rushed off to class. Wrestling was nearly over until the fall, but there were still a few practices and meets. So far I had done extremely well. I was one of a handful on the team who had not lost a match. While wrestling was winding down, preparations for the Little 500 were revving up and our practices were growing more intense. We spent most of our time on the trainers, pedaling until the sweat dripped off us. My eagerness for April grew daily.

I didn't receive a response from Haakon for two days. I tried not to think about the implications, but it wasn't easy. He often took a day or two to answer. Like me, he was extremely busy.

I hesitated before opening his email when it finally arrived. I had such wonderful memories of my months with Haakon. I hoped I had not ruined everything. There was no use in tormenting myself. I clicked on the email.

> Colin, I'm not surprised you have feelings for my brother. We are very nearly the same person. I would be surprised if you did not feel something for him and be attracted to him. I knew this would likely happen when you met and if I had any objections I would not have asked you to show him around IU. Don't feel guilty. What we had will always be special to me, but it will not be ruined by any relationship you have with Hamlet. I did not tell you this, but we have shared boys before. I have stronger feelings for you than I've ever had for anyone, but thinking of you with Hamlet does not bother me in the least. You do not need it, but you have my approval, as long as you do not hurt him and I know you would never do that. Love, Haakon.

I grinned. Why did I feel as if I should have known?

I hit reply and wrote Haakon another email. This time I had no regrets at all when I sent it.

My schedule in the days following the receipt of Haakon's email were especially packed so it was three days before I was able to see Hamlet again.

I was anxious as I walked toward the IMU where we were meeting. That wasn't like me, but Hamlet, like his brother, affected me in a way other boys did not.

Hamlet smiled as I approached Sugar & Spice. We entered together and both ordered hot tea, which we carried down to The Commons. We found an out of the way table. It was late enough in the evening that The Commons was sparsely inhabited.

"I emailed your brother," I said before I even took a sip of tea.

"I know. Haakon and I tell each other everything. Remember?" Hamlet reached across the table and took my hand. "The feeling is mutual."

I smiled.

"I'm usually far more outgoing, but this is an unusual situation."

"Really? You've never hooked up with twins before?" Hamlet asked, releasing my hand.

"Well... not male twins."

"Oh, I sense a story."

"I'll tell you that one later. I didn't want to upset Haakon. He means a lot to me."

"I know he does. I like that you are the kind of guy who cares. A lot of guys wouldn't."

"It's been very hard not to pounce on you."

"Oh, I like that."

"I'll warn you, now that I've heard back from your brother you are in great danger."

"Good. I like danger."

I stood, walked around the table, pulled Hamlet to his feet, and kissed him deeply.

"Want to go to my room?" I asked.

"More than anything."

We picked up our tea and walked to the closest southern exit from the IMU. We kept gazing at each other and smiling as we walked along the edge of Dunn's Woods.

A very few minutes later we arrived at Alpha and walked up to my room. Wes was reading.

"Get out," I said.

Wes looked at me, then Hamlet, and then he grinned.

"It's about time," he said, pulling on his coat and grabbing his book. "I'll be back in a couple of hours. I do hope you'll be finished by then."

Wes departed. I pulled Hamlet to me and kissed him deeply again, then stepped back and ripped his shirt over his head.

Our shoes and all our clothing were in a pile on the floor in under a minute. I shoved Hamlet back on my bed and then pounced on him.

We were all over each other from that moment on. Our fingers, lips, and tongues were everywhere. We explored each other for minute after minute while our sexual need intensified. Finally, we couldn't stand it a moment more and moved into a sixty-nine position. Only moments later, we both groaned with ecstasy as we released our pent-up passion. As soon as we caught our breath we went at it again.

Haakon and I had waited a long time to go all the way, but I didn't want to wait with Hamlet. He didn't object when I pulled out a Trojan, so I pulled his legs over my shoulders and entered him. It was every bit as good as it had been with his brother.

We were still laying on my bed when Wes returned. He hesitated at the door.

"Uh, are you guys finished?"

"Yeah, you can come in," I said.

"Will you be putting on clothes soon?"

"You've seen naked guys before."

"Yeah, but... I feel like I shouldn't be here."

I laughed. Hamlet and I got up and dressed.

"There. Better?"

"Yes."

"He has trouble controlling himself around me," I told Hamlet.

251

"Yeah, hold me back," Wes said with zero enthusiasm.

"I should go. See you soon?" Hamlet asked.

"You can count on it."

We kissed at the door and then Hamlet departed.

"So, was it worth the wait?"

"Yes."

"Hamlet and Haakon don't happen to have a sister, do they?"

"More than one, but they are in Norway."

"Damn, I bet they are hot."

"I'm sure. Thanks for getting lost."

"I left for self-preservation. I feared I might get hurt if I stuck around. I overheard you having sex with Haakon once. If I didn't know better I would have thought you were fighting."

"Listening at the door, huh? You pervert."

"No. I heard you while I was coming upstairs. I didn't even have to see the sock on the doorknob to know what you were doing. You know your nickname in Alpha is Animal."

"It is?"

"Yes, and it comes from what the guys hear when you are having sex."

I laughed.

"I do get a little rough."

"A little? Damn. I wish more girls liked it like that. What I need is a girl that is like a guy, but... no that doesn't make sense."

"I get it. You want a girl who is as consumed with lust and as aggressive as a guy. They are out there. I've met them. You'll find one and when you do I will get lost."

"You'd better."

"I'm going to take a walk. I need to think."

"You're going to relive your wild sex session, aren't you?"

"Yeah, but you know, telling you about it would be more fun. As soon as you left..."

"No! I do not want to hear about it."

"Even when I pushed Hamlet down, pulled his legs up over..."

"No!"

I laughed. "I'll see you later."

I walked downstairs and outside. I wasn't sure how I felt now that Hamlet and I had hooked up. It felt slightly wrong, but how could it be? Haakon knew about us. It didn't bother him so why should it bother me?

I sighed as I crossed 3rd Street and walked onto the old part of campus with its massive limestone buildings. Having a relationship with twins was complicated. Quite often when I was with Hamlet, I felt as if I was with Haakon. Even just now while we were having sex I didn't feel as if Hamlet and I were hooking up for the first time. He was so much like his brother that sex with him felt familiar and comfortable. The same things turned them on and they even moaned alike.

My main concern had been that I was transferring my feelings for Haakon to Hamlet. I'm sure I did that in the beginning, but since they were so much alike it was more likely that I simply liked Hamlet in the same way. If they were both here at the same time that could have been a problem, unless they didn't mind sharing a boyfriend. From a sexual standpoint the idea was intriguing, but from an emotional one it might be disorientating.

I didn't need to think about that. They were not both here and it was extremely unlikely I would ever see either of them again after Hamlet returned to Norway.

I was overthinking the entire situation. I did that sometimes. The facts were simple. I liked Haakon so much I would have dated him if he wasn't going home so soon. Our one-semester fling was intense and incredible, but it was over. Now, I felt the same about Hamlet. They were both fine with the situation so there was no need to analyze it further. Discussion over.

I smiled. I was incredibly lucky. I feared I would return to IU and feel the absence of Haakon keenly, but instead I had his brother. I intended to enjoy my time with Hamlet as much as I did my months with Haakon.

***

Unseasonably warm weather arrived with March. I gazed at Hamlet riding near me. He had taken me up on my offer to ride with the Alpha team during practice. We were doing at least 30 miles today, but Hamlet was riding a 21-speed and he was an athletic guy so I had little doubt he could keep up.

The long winter of practicing on trainers was definitely over. This was not the first time we had trained outside, but it was the first time it was comfortable. I didn't mind the cold too much while I was riding, but slick roads could be hazardous. Only two weeks earlier we were caught in a snowstorm while riding. More than one member of the team, including me, went down on the slick pavement.

Today, the pavement was dry and the weather pleasantly warm. We headed out of town and into the country, riding miles on winding roads, up hills, and down into valleys. One of my favorite parts of the ride was following the old highway that passed by Cascades Park with its large stream and many small waterfalls. In the hot months, the valley was at least ten degrees cooler, but now there wasn't much variation in temperature, which was fine by me. I liked warmth!

My work on the trainers had kept me in shape. I had no trouble at all handing our rides. I had been slightly concerned that I'd have difficulty in the beginning, but I had worried about nothing.

Hamlet fell back when Flynn instructed us to close in and ride as closely together as possible. It was somewhat dangerous to do so, but we would often find ourselves in even tighter situations during a race. It was better to make mistakes now instead of then, and we sometimes did. We had experienced more than one mini-pileup when we first started riding in close formation last fall.

I could tell Hamlet was tiring as the miles added up, but he kept up well. If he was on a single-speed like the rest of us he could not have managed it, but then few who weren't Little 500 riders could.

I smiled at Hamlet as the team pulled back into the Alpha parking lot.

"What do you think?" I asked as I climbed off my Schwinn.

"I think I have jelly legs and that you guys are insane."

Wes and Rhett laughed.

"Does that mean you don't want to ride with us regularly?"

"I'm not a masochist. How the hell do you ride on those fixed-gear bikes? That close quarters riding is crazy too."

"Wait until you see the race," Grant said.

"I have a new respect for you guys, but I still think you're mental," Hamlet said.

We walked inside and up to my room.

"Want to shower?" I asked.

"Any excuse to get naked together, huh?" Wes said as he entered behind us and pulled off his shirt.

"I see you're eager to join us."

"I'm eager to stop smelling like an arm pit."

"I wasn't going to say anything..." I began.

"Oh, like you smell any better."

"I always smell real pretty."

"Oh, hot ass, Wes. You want to join us later?" Hamlet asked with a grin.

"Not on your life. I am an anal virgin and I intend to stay that way."

"At least until he meets a girl who wants to do him with a strap on," I said.

"Not even that. I do not get why you guys get into that. It's got to hurt."

"Don't knock it until you've tried it and if you try it you will be addicted," Hamlet said.

"Not likely!"

We all headed for the showers. Several members of the team were there when we arrived or came in soon after. Showering with guys who were into guys didn't bother any of them. Everyone knew I was bi and that Hamlet and I hooked up regularly. There were few secrets in Alpha.

The sight of Hamlet wet and naked always made me want him more than usual, but I controlled myself in the showers. I waited until we were back in the room before I pulled Hamlet to me and kissed him.

"Can you guys wait until I'm out of the room before you get into the heavy stuff?" Wes said, pulling on his boxer-briefs.

"Are you sure? You might learn something," I said.

"I might, but it wouldn't be anything I want to learn."

"We would appreciate it if you could get lost for a while."

"Can you guys be done and out of here by 9 p.m.? I'm meeting a girl and I feel lucky."

"The room is all yours at nine. I'll go study in the library," I said.

"Perfect."

Wes soon departed. Hamlet and I hadn't bothered to dress, so we dropped our towels and began to explore with our fingers, lips, and tongues. Hamlet had a very talented tongue.

Our time was a bit limited so we dropped onto my bed. Before long I was on top of Hamlet thrusting, and both of us were moaning and groaning. When I unloaded in Hamlet several minutes later he shot all over his chest.

"You are incredible. You are the best I have ever been with," Hamlet said.

"You're rather talented yourself."

"I am so glad you are a top. I do not know about here, but everyone is a bottom in Norway."

I laughed.

"There is no shortage of bottoms here either and I don't mind at all."

"You wouldn't."

"Come on. Let's get out of here."

I pulled Hamlet to his feet and kissed him. We wrapped towels around our waists and returned to the showers to clean up. We were soon back in the room. After we dressed, I quickly straightened my bed so the room would look nice for Wes' girl, then Hamlet and I departed.

"This has been a good day. The bike ride was great and sex with you was better."

"Want to do it again?"

"The ride no. The sex, over and over and over."

"Are you busy tomorrow?" I asked with a grin.

"If I am, I will make time."

We talked until we reached Wells Library, then Hamlet headed across the street to Wright Quad and I walked up the steps and went inside. I hoped Wes made good use of our room.

I used my forced exile to get some work done. I had brought along my laptop and the books I needed. I found myself a table and set to work.

I discovered that college course work was not that hard if I kept up with it. I knew a lot of guys that were completely overwhelmed, but that was because they procrastinated and put off assignments until the last minute. With my busy schedule there were days when I didn't have enough time to study, but most days I could not only complete what needed to be done before the next day, but also had time to work on projects that were not due until the end of the semester.

It was nearly midnight when I put away laptop and books, shouldered my backpack, and walked across campus. When I arrived at my room the sock was still on the door and I could hear the unmistakable sounds of a couple getting it on.

I yawned. I was too tired to go out again, so I walked downstairs to the lounge, dropped my backpack on the floor, took off my shoes, and lay on one of the couches. Soon, I was asleep.

***

I waited anxiously in the lounge with the other riders. Today was the day we discovered which four of us would be chosen to race in The Little 500 this year. As a freshman, my chances weren't good, but I couldn't help but hope that I would make the team. If I didn't, I was determined to go right on riding with those who did, attend all the pre-race events, and learn as much as I could for next year.

Flynn walked into the room carrying a sheet of paper. Everyone grew quiet.

"We've all worked very hard and each of us deserves a spot on the team. I mean that. Any four of us would make a very strong race team. The four who have been selected are the best of the best. Those representing Alpha in the Little 500 this year are Me, Grant, Grayson, and Colin."

My eyes widened and I grinned. I made the team? I was a freshman and I made the team? If this was a dream and I woke up soon I was going to be pissed.

I looked at Rhett. He was a sophomore and he didn't get a spot on the team. As happy as I was for myself, I felt bad for him. He smiled at me wanly and nodded his head.

"I know not making the team is a disappointment. We've all worked very hard, but we need to field the strongest team possible to uphold the Alpha Little 500 tradition. We're brothers and those racing represent us all.

"I hope all of you will continue training with those who are racing. One of you may have to step in for a racer if something makes one of us unable to compete before Quals. No matter what, we are all members of the Alpha Little 500 team. Those who are racing represent us all, as well as all the brothers of Alpha, past and present.

"Today, we are heading back to the track where we will continue to work on exchanges and prepare for the pre-race events so get your helmets and bikes and meet me in the parking lot in five."

Several guys patted me on the back and congratulated me. I walked over to Rhett and started to open my mouth, but he stopped me.

"You deserve to be on the team, Colin. I want you to be on the team. You're better than me. Hell, you may be the best."

"I feel like I took your spot."

"Spots are earned and you earned yours. I did my best, but the truth is I'm not as good as those who were chosen. I'm not surprised that I didn't make the team, but there is always next year."

"Thanks, Rhett."

"Let's go. You know how Flynn bitches if everyone isn't on time."

I smiled. I couldn't believe it. I was going to race in The Little 500.

We rode our bikes up to the Bill Armstrong Stadium where The Little 500 race was held each year. We had already been on the track practicing exchanges and getting a feel for the surface, but now for the first time I stepped out on it as a racer.

The track was cinder, but was kept level and packed for racing. Marc had told me that weather conditions could vastly affect the track so it might be quite a different track on race day than it was now.

We practiced two types of exchanges; the single-bike and the bike-to-bike. The single bike is more difficult and involves the rider coming in hopping off and the next rider hopping on without the bike stopping, but it is also quicker. For a bike-to-bike exchange, the outgoing bike must be lined up on the back line of the pit and the incoming rider must tag him before he can move. It might not seem that the small amount of inertia in a single-bike exchange would make that much difference, but it's much harder to get a bike up to speed when starting at zero than it is when the bike is already moving.

The first time we practiced exchanges in February I royally screwed up my first two attempts at a single-bike exchange. I wasn't alone. Everyone who had never done it before ended up falling off the bike or wiping out. I succeeded on my 3rd attempt and improved after that, but I was eager for more practice. The bike-to-bike exchange was easy in comparison, but it was hard to remain in place until properly tagged. Most teams preferred the faster single-bike exchange. In The Little 500, seconds, and even fractions of seconds counted. Marc told me that his first year of racing the first, second, and third place teams crossed the line within the same second.

I stood ready when it was my turn. Max came in fast. He hopped off but caught his foot and went down on the track, nearly taking the bike with him, but I already had my hands on the bars, jerked it away, hopped on and took off. Despite the fact that Max fell it was a good exchange because we didn't lose any time or speed. If the bike had fallen or I had fallen it would have been a different story.

I raced around the track. Grayson had warned us that the cinders were a bit loose on the second turn and he wasn't kidding. I could feel the tires slide, but kept the bike under control. I accelerated and raced around the track. Practicing on the track was easy because mine was the only bike out there. On race day there would be 32 others, which was quite a different story.

I pushed harder as the pit came in sight. I gave it everything I had. Grant stood ready. I came in fast, braked, and hopped off the bike as Grant hopped on.

"Nice, Colin. Your time was 28 seconds. That's about as fast as it's possible to go around the track."

"Great, but I'm sure the absence of other bikes helped a bit."

I grinned. I was very pleased with my time. The race was about far more than speed, but speed was an important and significant factor.

We continued practicing both types of exchanges. It was unlikely we would use the bike-to-bike exchange much, but it was useful at times, especially when a bike was damaged and needed to be replaced. We would likely use the same bike for the entire race, but if something happened to it, we could bring in another.

I was looking forward to Qualifications, better known as Quals to racers. Quals was where teams succeeded or failed in earning a spot in the race. There could only be 33 teams and I was told 40 or more sometimes tried out for one of those spots. Quals was also where teams earned their starting position. Getting as near the front as possible was extremely important because the further a rider was back in the pack, the more likely he was to be involved in an accident. A single accident could ruin a team's chances of placing.

I was also looking forward to other pre-race events, such as Individual Time Trials (ITT's), Miss-n-Out, and the practice race. None of those events affected the starting place for a team, but they were important.

Practicing exchanges wasn't as tiring as riding fifty or more miles, but it took even more concentration. I was pleased that we made very few mistakes. I felt like I had both types of exchanges down, but I wasn't going to get cocky. I intended to keep working on both types right up until race day.

After practice, we rode back to Alpha. I showered, then dressed in clean clothes and called Hamlet. I arranged to meet him in The Commons for a late supper. I couldn't wait to tell him I'd made the team, but there were two others I wanted to tell before him. I called Skye first. He was delighted and excited for me. Next, I called Marc. He was thrilled and insisted that we meet soon so he could give me some more racing tips. I couldn't wait, but first I was going to have a nice supper with Hamlet and then get a good night's rest.

Chapter Sixteen

"I'm a little edgy about the close quarters riding. It's tricky enough when we practice, but with 33 teams on the track it's going to be much worse. How do you deal with that?" I asked Marc as I sat with him and Alessio in The Tudor Room.

"You try not to get stuck back in the pack, and if you do get stuck there, you try to get around and away from the pack the first chance you get. The problem is, once you're stuck it's hard to break away," Alessio said.

"That's why Quals are so critical. If Alpha can get into the top six it will greatly reduce the likelihood of getting caught in the pack. Every rider is nervous about close quarters riding within a pack because all it takes is a front tire rubbing on a back tire to cause a pileup. The pre-race events will introduce the riders from the other teams to you and you'll have a chance to get to know them. By race day, you'll know who the experts are and who you want to avoid. The skill level of the riders varies greatly," Marc said.

"Yeah, I've met a lot of riders from other teams already."

"There is a brotherhood among riders. It's like a fraternity itself. You're all out there for the same reason. On race day, it's every team for itself, but at all other times the Little 500 riders are brothers, or sisters in the case of the women's teams," Alessio said.

"I mainly don't want to ruin our chances of winning."

"A single accident can do that, but they are often unavoidable. There's not much a rider can do when the bikes in front of him go down and he's hemmed in."

"I saw a tape of you avoiding a wreck," I told Alessio.

"That was the one when I was on the outside right of the pack, right?"

"Yes."

"I wasn't hemmed in so I was able escape, but only barely. I nearly went into the pits."

"Yes, but you didn't," I said.

I was lucky that I had access to two experienced Little 500 riders. Marc had even coached for years. Experience was something I lacked and could only get by riding in a race.

"This grilled chipotle barbeque chicken is great. You should make this at home, Alessio," Marc said.

"It is good and this honey Dijon glazed ham is delicious, but I have yet to try anything here I didn't like. The chili came close once. It was way too spicy!" I said.

"I thought this was a nice place for us to get together and discuss racing. The Commons and the food court would be way too crowded for us to talk, plus the food is much better here," Marc said.

"There are also great desserts," Alessio added.

"Back to what we were talking about. The race is part skill and part luck. Great teams are taken down by accidents and small miscalculations. That's one thing that makes the race so exciting. Every team has a shot at winning because a team that seems unbeatable may be defeated by simple bad luck or miscalculation," Marc said.

"True. One of the years I raced, Forest Quad dominated the track. We could not get past those guys, but then they did an exchange with only two laps to go. It was a mistake that cost them first place," Alessio said.

"An exchange that late doesn't seem like a good idea," I said.

"It depends on the situation. When I was coach I'd put in a fresh rider with as few as four laps to go, but never less than that. It has been done successfully when the team has enough of a gap built up. Racing is far more complex that it appears."

"I've learned that, especially this semester. The experienced riders have taught us new guys a lot."

"Experience is key," Marc said.

"I still can't believe I'm racing this year. Flynn says he thinks I'll work best as a power horse who gets out there and eats up a lot of laps, then the sprinters can come in and really fly."

"Yeah, you look like you have the power and stamina to get on the track and keep going," Alessio said.

"Yeah, I won't be the one who crosses the finish line, but I hope I can put my teammates into position to cross it first."

"It takes every member of the team. It's fifty hard and fast miles. One person cannot do it alone, Marc said.

"You nearly did," I said.

Marc laughed. "I rode most of a race myself, but not all of it. I still can't believe we won that year. That was not a good situation and I just about killed myself."

"Ah, but now you are a legend."

"No autographs please."

I laughed. We kept talking racing while we ate lunch. We continued talking over dessert. I couldn't resist the chocolate cake, apple pie, or peach cheesecake. Luckily, I was putting in lots of time riding at present so I would burn off all the calories.

"If we don't see you again before the race, we will be at the Alpha party after. We'll also be in the stands. We already have our tickets," Marc said.

"I'd say I'll look for you at the race, but I'll be too busy."

"Yeah, you concentrate on the race. Skye is coming, isn't he?"

"He already has a ticket."

"Cool. I'll contact him and maybe we can go together."

"Thank you so much for lunch and all the racing tips."

"You're welcome. I almost wish I was racing, but it's a sport for the young. We'll live vicariously through you."

I grinned, thanked them again, and then we went our separate ways.

***

The rest of March and early April was filled with training, workouts, and strategy sessions. I was more anxious about the upcoming race than I'd ever been about a wrestling meet, including sectionals and regionals. I felt more a part of a team than I ever had before. Perhaps it was because I was racing for a fraternity team. It was a team within a team. For whatever reason, I cared more about the outcome of this race that I'd ever cared about any sporting event.

I managed to see plenty of Hamlet. He didn't ride with the team again, but he joined me in the SRSC whenever his schedule permitted and we hooked up often. We also managed to eat lunch together quite a few times, usually in the food court, The Commons, or in the Wright Dining Hall, but at other spots on campus too. Being with Hamlet helped me relax and I was always happy when I was with him.

I felt the pressure as I walked onto the field at Armstrong Stadium for Quals. The four of us racing were down on the field, the rest of our team and several other Alpha brothers were in the stands. The crowd was nothing compared to what it would be on race day, but there were a lot of students and others present to support their teams. Quals were a big deal.

Today could make or break us. If our time wasn't good enough, we wouldn't even get to race. I wasn't too concerned about that since we had three tries. What most preyed on my mind was our position. We needed to get in the top six in order to have a serious shot at winning. We might win starting further back in the pack, but it would be more difficult and in this race fractions of a second counted.

We watched Delta Tau Delta as they took their turn. They were one of the top teams. They raced around the track and their exchanges were nearly flawless. Their posted time was going to be hard to beat. I was willing to bet they would not try again for a better time. They had no need so why risk it?

We observed a few other teams and then The Cutters were up. The Cutters were a very strong team and had won the last three years. They were the team we had to beat if we were going to win.

"Damn, they're good," Grayson said as we observed their first exchange.

"Yeah, just imagine how good it will feel when we beat them," I said.

Grayson smiled at me.

Our turn finally arrived. Teams could qualify with two, three, or four riders, but whatever number used was the greatest number of riders who could race. We were using four, which would allow us to compete even if one or two of us were too ill to do so on race day.

I was our 3rd rider. Flynn was up first. He flew around the track. His exchange to Grayson was beautiful and his time excellent. If we could keep it up and not screw up we'd qualify for sure and earn a good spot. Grayson was slower, but still ate up the track. I stood ready on our line. Grayson sailed in. The tip of his right shoe caught the frame as he dismounted, but I was already mostly on the bike by then and it didn't affect the exchange at all. I took off with excellent momentum and accelerated as fast as I could while my brothers cheered me on. I didn't hold anything back. This was a sprint. I was free to use everything I had and I did. The lap flew by in seconds, but seemed to pass even quicker.

I raced into our pit where Grant, my big brother and the reason I was here, stood ready. I almost felt as if the bike barely slowed as I jumped off and Grant hopped on. By the time I looked down the track he was already approaching the first turn.

All of us watched the clock. The Alpha bike was almost a streak as it raced around the track. Grant rode into the last stretch and then crossed the finish line. We waited for our time and cheered when it was posted. We were currently 2nd. Only The Cutters had a better time.

"We're sticking with that time," Flynn announced. There was no argument. Flynn was our coach and captain. I thought his decision wise. We might beat our own time if we tried again, but then again we might do worse. As in the race itself, one mishap could spell disaster during Quals.

We stayed to watch the remainder of the teams. Some made two attempts and a couple even three, so Quals took quite a while. I didn't mind. I loved bike racing and even Quals were exciting.

The Black Key Bulls knocked us out of second place, but no other team could best us. Flynn pumped his fist in the air when the starting positions were announced. We were 3rd, which put us on the front row.

We returned to Alpha, where then entire frat celebrated with pizza. We had performed exceedingly well at Quals. All of us would have preferred to be in the pole position, but 3rd put us in an excellent position to win the race.

I celebrated again that night with Hamlet. Wes was ever so kind in getting lost so we could. He was a great roommate.

A few days later the first pre-race event, the ITT's or Individual Time Trials, came up. This was a four-lap event like Quals, but there were no exchanges. Each rider rode the four laps by himself. The ITT's were a test of speed and sprint endurance. I was not a sprinter, but I was confident I could sprint for four laps.

For this event, four riders competed against the clock simultaneously. One was placed on a starting line at each of the four turns of the track, which meant we were spaced out from each other. It was possible for a fast rider to overtake another, but Flynn warned us more than once to avoid drafting off another rider, which meant we could not get behind another rider and ride in his wake to make our riding easier. Drafting was allowed in the race and was a desirable tactic, but here it would get a rider instantly disqualified.

My turn came up after about forty-five minutes. I pushed my bike to my starting position. An official placed it on the line and positioned himself behind me to steady the bike. ITT's were started from a dead stop and each rider had both his feet on the pedals when starting, which is why it was necessary for someone to hold the bike.

When everyone was in position, the starter fired his pistol and we were off.

Just as I had during Quals, I held nothing back. I tore around the track on my bike while my teammates and a few other brothers cheered. I came up on the Sigma rider in front of me and took care not to get behind him. Instead, I moved over just enough to safely pass him and then raced on.

Riding four laps full-out isn't easy, but I kept going. One lap passed, then two, then three. I passed the Black Key Bulls rider with only half a lap to go.

I was suffering a bit as I raced down the final stretch, but didn't let up. I sailed over the finish line, then coasted to a stop, and climbed off my bike.

My chest heaved and I panted, but I knew I'd done well. I had passed two riders. Perhaps the Sigma rider was a slower rider, but the other was a member of the Black Key Bulls and those guys were tough.

Cheers erupted from my teammates and I quickly looked toward the board. My time was 1.82 minutes.

"You broke the record," Flynn said as he stared at me in amazement.

"I did?"

"Anything under two minutes is incredible. The previous record was 1.97 minutes."

"I suppose I should have really tried then instead of slacking off," I said, then grinned.

"Let's let Colin do the entire 200 laps on race day. You can keep that pace for the whole 50 miles, can't you?" asked Grant.

"Oh, I couldn't manage 200 laps at that speed; maybe 185 laps, but not 200. Let's not get crazy."

The guys laughed.

I sat and watched the remainder of the ITT's. A few riders came close to two minutes, but I was the only rider who went under. When the ITT's finished the second-best time was 2.14.

"There will be no living with him now," Wes said as we departed with the rest of the Alpha team.

"You can handle it. You are in the presence of my awesomeness all the time."

"If I didn't know you were kidding, I'd punch you."

"Kidding... yeah... that's what I was doing..." I said, trying to sound as insincere as possible.

"You're such a jerk," Wes said, putting me in a headlock before releasing me.

"Isn't that what you like about me the most?"

"Yeah, sure. Why not?"

As soon as I was alone, I called Skye, then Hamlet, and then Marc.

"You did what? Are you *serious*?" Marc asked.

"Yes. My time was 1.82."

"Holy shit. How did you do that?"

"I, uh... rode as fast as I could for four laps."

"Damn, Colin. My best time ever for the ITT's was 1.99 and that was the record for several years."

"So it's that big of a deal? I mean, it doesn't count toward the race."

"It's a very big deal to Little 500 riders. Only a handful who aren't riders will pay any attention at all, but it marks you as a very strong rider and one to watch."

"Awesome. I did my best, but I didn't know I was even close to setting a record. I rode as fast as I could since it was only four laps. If it was much more than that I would have paced myself."

"Good job. I'm impressed. I wish I could have been there to see it."

I smiled when I disconnected. Marc was a hard-core bike enthusiast. The thing is, I was becoming one too.

"Your shoulders are tight," Hamlet said as he massaged them.

"I have a lot going on, especially the race."

"You're not worried about it, are you?"

"No. I don't get worried, but there is a lot of pressure. It's a huge deal, especially to my Alpha brothers. It's so easy to make a mistake when riding and one mistake can cost a team the race."

"That is a lot of pressure. I don't think I could handle it, but I'm sure you can."

"Why are you sure?"

"I know you. I've watched you wrestle. When shit gets real you don't get rattled. Instead, you focus and go into Superman mode."

I laughed. "Superman mode? I don't leap over tall buildings and in case you haven't noticed I can't fly."

"You know what I mean. It's like... you're physically superior to everyone else. I suspect genetic modification."

"You know this could go to my head."

"No, it won't. You pretend to be conceited, but you're not. I wish I was more like you."

"I think you're a lot like me."

"We have similar interests, but I'm not as confident as you. I'm not calm and focused like you are when a situation is intense. I get nervous and even shaky. You're fearless."

"I'm not fearless. Watch me when a wasp dive-bombs me. I scream like a girl."

Hamlet laughed. "Oh, you do not."

"Oh my god. Are you guys getting it on again? There's no sock on the door," Wes said as he entered.

"We're not getting it on," I said.

"Well, you're half naked and Hamlet has his hands all over you."

"I have my shirt off and he's giving me a shoulder rub."

"Yeah, we're not hooking up. Colin was just telling me about when he screams like a girl."

"What? I have to hear this. I want details!" Wes said.

"Hamlet thinks I'm always calm and fearless. I told him he should see me when a wasp is after me. I scream like a girl."

"I bet he doesn't," Hamlet said.

"I hate wasps and yellow jackets. I'm fine with any other bee, but those bastards go out of their way to sting. I would love to see one after Colin. I want to hear him scream like a little bitch."

"Uh oh. Wes knows my weakness now."

"I wonder how I can lay my hands on some wasps..."

"Funny."

"You two go on with your homo activities. I'll try to ignore you," Wes said, picking up a textbook.

I turned my head and Hamlet kissed me, but Wes didn't react. He was no fun when he was busy studying.

***

Miss-n-Out was the first pre-race event where riders raced against each other instead of the clock. While I won the ITT's, I was more excited about participating in this event since I would be racing for real for the very first time.

The Miss-N-Out event isn't mandatory, but most of the Little 500 riders participate. When I arrived with the Alpha team it looked to me like every team was on the field.

I looked toward the stands where Hamlet sat with Marc and Alessio. There were a fair number of other spectators as well.

This year's Miss-n-Out was run in heats of six riders. The rules were simple. All riders start on the same line and are given one lap to gain the position they desire and gain speed. Once they cross the start line again, the race begins. The riders race around the track and each time the pack crosses the start/finish line, the last one to cross is cut. Riders keep racing until there are only three left. Those three riders move up a bracket. The process continues until the final heat of six. In this heat, riders race until all but three are cut and then they commence a one-lap full-out sprint for first, second, and third place.

I couldn't wait to get out on the track. I was at a disadvantage to those riders who had participated in previous years, but I liked my chances. If nothing else, the race would be fun, and I had my own little group to cheer me on in addition to my teammates and Alpha brothers.

I watched carefully as the first group raced. From the cheering and shouting one would have thought this was The Little 500 itself. I loved how everyone got into it.

One rider after another was eliminated and then the three survivors rode off the track. The field was slowly thinned and then finally it was my turn to race.

The six of us jockeyed for position as we did our first lap. I was able to move in close to the gutter with only two other riders on my left. We crossed the line and the race began. The Black Key Bull rider shot out ahead and I let him. In this race, finishing first didn't matter. The only thing that mattered was not being last.

I paced myself, making sure that I had one rider behind me. From the stands it probably looked like I wasn't trying terribly hard until we neared the line. That's when the rider behind me tried to take me, but I didn't allow it. He was out.

The pack had pulled away a bit so I sped up and worked my way into fourth place. Another rider was cut, which left only four of us. This was the lap that truly counted and each of us knew it. The Black Key Rider sprinted and the rest of us followed. I didn't want to take any chances so I powered into second place. Thanks to taking it a bit easy early in the race I had plenty of power left. I crossed the finish line in second, which in this race was a win.

I watched others race as I waited my turn again. Flynn and Grant easily survived their races. Grayson was nearly knocked out, but finished third so Alpha was still going strong.

I returned to the track pitted against the other two survivors from my first race and three new opponents. I knew this race would be more challenging because the weaker riders were slowly being eliminated.

My goal was to come in fourth on our first lap, then third, then second, which kept two riders behind me and gave me a margin for error. My strategy served me well again and I finished second once more.

I knew I needed to change my tactics for the next round because I was becoming predictable. My strategy was also not without risk because staying further back increased my chances of being last and being involved in an accident. I decided to alter my tactic by keeping a bit further up in the pack.

My next race went well and so did the following, but the competition was growing consistently stiffer. We were near the end now so my new strategy was to stick very close to the front. For the first time, I was racing against a member of the Alpha team. I didn't like that, but it was part of Miss-N-Out.

I did well until the final lap when I miscalculated and my front wheel rubbed the back tire of The Cutter rider in front of me. He swerved before regaining control, which forced me to the right, nearly colliding with Grant. I jerked back too hard and went down. It all happened so quickly, and that was the end of me competing in Miss-n-Out.

"Tough break," Flynn said as I returned to the team.

"I screwed up, twice. I could have recovered if I hadn't cut so hard to the left to avoid Grant."

"Split-second calculations are always tricky. Don't worry about it. Think of it as valuable racing experience."

"Easy for you to say, you're still in the running."

"Hey, you can't win everything, Colin."

"But why not?" I asked, trying to sound like a whiny brat. The guys laughed.

Grayson was knocked out in his next race and Flynn was eliminated soon after. Only Grant made it to the final race. We all cheered ourselves crazy. He came in second, which was excellent.

I still felt like kicking myself as the teams and small crowd began to disperse, but I was well aware that I was not perfect, despite what I sometimes claimed.

Marc, Alessio, and Hamlet came down from the stands to join the Alpha riders.

"Are you guys ready?" Marc asked.

"Yeah, let's head out. I'm starving," I said.

"We will meet you there," Flynn said.

Marc and Alessio were taking Hamlet and the Alpha riders to Bucceto's for supper. Hamlet and I rode with Marc, while Flynn and Wes took the others.

A few minutes later we were seated in the east side Bucceto's placing drink orders and browsing menus.

"Order anything you want. We're paying, so take advantage," Marc said.

"All right! A large pizza just for me," Grayson said.

"Order it if you want it," Marc said grinning.

"Oh god, I was kidding, besides the pasta is great here."

"We really appreciate you taking us out for supper," Flynn said. Everyone echoed Flynn's gratitude.

"I was a broke college boy once so I know what it's like. Besides, it lets me hang out with riders again. You guys did a great job today."

"At least I was the only one who wrecked," I said.

"I was watching you when it happened. There is no way you could have avoided that collision without taking out Grant," Alessio said.

"Yeah, but I think I could have kept from going down if I hadn't cut back to the left so sharply."

"I don't think so. There wasn't enough room."

"I wiped out once during the practice race and ruined our chances to win," Marc said. "I hit a loose patch of cinders and I went down. I kept analyzing how I could have kept my bike under control and all I did was drive myself crazy."

"He drove the rest of us crazy too. We were ready to beat him up," Alessio said.

"It's fine to analyze accidents but only up to a point. If you think about it for more than ten minutes you are wasting your time. It's worse for an accident that costs the team a win, but even then you have to let it go. When you're out on that track you have to make split-second decisions. Some of those decisions will be wrong. That's part of being a rider," Marc said.

"You also have to acknowledge that sometimes, no matter what you do, you are screwed," Flynn said.

The Cutter's team entered and greeted us. Each of them stopped to talk to Marc. He was obviously a Little 500 legend outside of Alpha too.

When the waitress came I ordered chicken piccata. I loved the slightly lemony taste of that pasta. Others ordered ravioli, lasagna, rosemary cream chicken, calzones, and more.

As we waited for our orders and then ate, bikes and bike racing dominated our conversation. The Cutters sat at the next table and frequently joined in. One thing I had grown to love about racing is that outside of race day all riders formed a fraternity. We would each do our best to win, but once the race was over we would return to being brothers. I hadn't experienced that in other sports.

"I love the food here, but it isn't nearly as good as Alessio's," Marc said. "Unfortunately for you guys, it was my night to cook."

"I couldn't cook and watch Miss-N-Out too," Alessio said.

"This is incredible," I said, pointing to my chicken piccata.

"If you have any left, take it home. Chicken piccata is actually better the second day. It allows time for the chicken and pasta to marinate in the lemon-butter," Alessio said.

"You're making me hungry while I'm eating!" I said.

"Alessio is a master chef. His entire family are great cooks, so is everyone in the whole of Italy for that matter. At least that is my experience," Marc said.

"Greece has wonderful food too, but we're getting off topic," Alessio said.

"True, so back to bike racing..." Marc said.

Marc had lots of stories. He had raced and coached and had attended every single Little 500 since he was in college. Thanks to his bike shop, he knew almost every current rider. I envied him and his life in a way. He was doing what he loved and he had Alessio. I wondered if I would ever find someone like that. I had found Haakon and Hamlet, but my relationships with them were doomed to be short. Maybe someday...

Marc insisted everyone have dessert. Others ordered carrot cake, tiramisu, and chocolate torte, but Marc, Hamlet, and I ordered cheesecake, which was actually made by the NYC Carnegie Deli.

My cheesecake was almost too good, but even so the slice was too big. If I hadn't saved half of my chicken piccata to take home I could not have finished it.

I didn't even want to think about the size of the bill. We all thanked Marc and Alessio profusely for taking us out to eat and then went our separate ways.

Hamlet, Marc, Alessio and I continued to talk about bike racing during the short ride to Alpha. Biking enthusiasts never tired of talking about bikes. Thanks to Grant, I had become one.

"That was wonderful. It was so nice of them to invite me too," Hamlet said after Marc dropped us off.

"Well you are an honorary member of the Alpha Little 500 team."

"Since when?"

"Since now."

"As long as I don't have to race. After watching today, I am certain you guys are crazy."

"A mild case of insanity does help."

"Your wreck didn't look enjoyable."

"It wasn't, but mostly because it took me out of the competition. I'm lucky I didn't get scraped up."

Hamlet and I walked inside and up to my room.

"You guys have to get lost soon," Wes said the moment we entered.

"You have a girl coming over?" I asked.

"Two."

"Whoa! Are you sure you can handle two?"

"I will or I'll die trying."

"Will this be another all-nighter?" I asked.

"It's possible."

"If the sock is on the door knob when I return, I'll sleep in the lounge again. The couch is comfy."

"You're a pal."

"It's the least I can do after all the times you've made yourself scarce for us," I said.

"How many times has it been fifty, a hundred?"

"We have not hooked up that many times."

"I know you guys have hooked up at least twenty times."

"We only have one semester together. We have to make good use of our time."

"I think you're both part rabbit."

"You know you'd hook up daily, probably several times a day if you could," I said.

"Of course, I'm a guy."

"I'll see you later tonight or more likely tomorrow," I said.

"If you find me dead, remember that I died happy."

I smiled and shook my head as Hamlet and I departed.

"It's too late to catch the movie in the IMU. Want to take a walk?" Hamlet asked.

"Sure. I'm too tired for much else."

We crossed 3rd Street and entered campus. Winter was not far behind us, but it was only a memory now. The snow was long gone and spring would soon awaken the trees and other plants. In fact, spring flowers were already beginning to pop through the earth. Back in Verona, it was probably still too cold for even the earliest flowers, but here the cold weather was all but over.

We slowly strolled along the paths. We had no particular destination, so we wandered aimlessly through campus. It was quiet at this time of night.

"I can't believe how my time here has slipped away. I leave in less than a month," Hamlet said.

"I've been trying not to think about that. It was hard when your brother left and it will be just as hard when you do."

"Would you have rather never met us?"

"No. My time with each of you is something I'll always remember. I never thought much about a relationship with a guy before. I assumed I'd end up with a girl someday and start a family, but now I'm not so sure."

"You could still have a family with a guy."

"True, but you know what I mean. I'll be honest, I could get into a serious relationship with you or your brother."

"You could move to Norway and date us both."

"That would be incredible, but this is my home. I could never live so far away from Skye, or give up attending IU, and I don't speak Norwegian."

"I know. It was only wishful thinking. I hope that someday I will meet someone like you," Hamlet said.

"Me too, except... well, you know what I mean."

"At least we have now."

"Yes, and as my Uncle Skye taught me years ago, now is always the most important time of all.

Chapter Seventeen

"Our goal is not to win this race, but to gain experience so we can win the race that counts," Flynn said as we stood in our pit at the side of the track. "This is the first chance for those of you who have never participated in a Little 500 to experience what it's really like. This is the day to learn and to make mistakes. Ride this race as if the goal is to win, but don't get upset over errors. Today is the day we want to make our mistakes so that we won't repeat them during The Little 500."

The practice race was 50 laps, only one-quarter of the actual race, but it was long enough to give all of us new guys a chance to see what racing is really like. We had practiced for months, but I had never been on the track with 32 other teams before. This would be a new experience.

Grayson was leading off for us. He was an experienced rider and would hopefully create a gap so that we wouldn't fall too far back when he came in for an exchange.

I watched as the sea of bikes followed the pace car around the track. There were so many of them. Right now, they were staying in rows of three, but after a lap behind the pace car the starter would wave the green flag and the situation would change drastically.

I kept my eye on the racers as the pace car sped up and left the track. As the bikes neared the start line, the official waved the green flag and they were off.

The Cutters quickly pulled head. The Black Key Bulls fell in behind and Grayson moved in beside the Bulls rider. The Cutters set a fast pace. They and the next five teams pulled away from the main pack, but not by much. This was the beginning of the race and all the riders were fresh.

What attracted my attention the most was the main pack of riders. A good twenty riders rode in a tight pack that left little chance for error. A few others rode in front of the pack and behind, but most of the riders were in one large group. That pack was exactly where I did not want to be when my turn came.

By the 5th lap, the first half a dozen riders had created a gap of a few yards between themselves and the main pack. The pack had thinned out somewhat and looked less dangerous. Just as that thought passed through my mind, the riders for Sigma Pi and Phi Sigma Kappa collided and went down, quickly followed by seven riders behind them. No one was seriously hurt. All the riders quickly got up and took off again and the officials did not wave the yellow flag, but just like that nine teams had lost valuable time, decreasing their chances of winning.

Grayson signaled he was going to come in on the next lap. I took up my position. Grayson had created a nice gap. My job was get us back in the race without falling back into the pack.

Flynn didn't say anything to me. He merely nodded. There was nothing left to be said. This was still only a practice race, but this is where all the work I put in was put to the test.

Grayson came in fast. My hands went on the bars as his came off and my butt replaced his in the saddle in under a second. The bike was still moving quickly as I began to pedal.

Our exchange was near perfect, but even so most of the gap Grayson had created was gone by the time I built up speed. I slid in behind the Cutters rider who was now in the draft of the rider for the Black Key Bulls. I paced the Cutters rider. My job was eat up laps even if I had to fall back a few places to do so.

The pace was fast, but I was fresh and could handle it. The task would grow more difficult as the laps passed, but I was confident I could keep us near the front.

I was tempted to try to pull out in front, but it was easier riding in the draft created by the two riders in front of me. My task was not to get us into first place. It was to ride lap after lap and eat up the miles so the sprinters could come in and put us in a position to win.

I was certain that riding near the front was far easier than riding back in the pack. At present, there were only two riders ahead of me. Either of them could go down causing me to wipe out, but I only had to be concerned with two riders instead of more than a dozen. The riders in front of me were from some of the most experienced teams in the race, so that made it less likely they would have an accident.

My back tire slid slightly as I came around the third turn. The cinder track was loose there. I made a mental note to be wary. I rode five laps without incident, then ten. I maintained our position. As I passed our pit on my 11th lap Flynn signaled me to come in. If this was the actual race it would have been too early. I wasn't tired, but this race was only 50 laps and I knew he wanted to get everyone out on the track.

Since I had plenty of power left I used my last lap to pass the Cutters. I came up on the Bulls as the 3rd turn approached, but waited. I didn't trust the track. I felt both tires began to slide as I made the turn, but I was ready for it and maintained control of the bike. I heard a commotion behind me and knew at least one rider had gone down, but my focus was ahead.

I closed in on the Bulls rider and pulled up just behind and to the side of him as we came out of the 4th turn. I increased my speed and drew even with him, then veered slightly to the right and increased my speed further. The Bulls rider veered to the right as well. He knew I was coming in for an exchange and was using the opportunity to make an exchange at the same time. Teams often played off each other like that.

I sped toward our pit, slowing at only the last moment. My big brother Grant slid into the saddle as I hopped off. My inertia made me stumble, but I didn't fall. By the time I looked up Grant was well down the track. It was another successful exchange.

I didn't get another turn on the bike because Flynn wanted to concentrate on our sprinters, but the experience I had gained made me feel more confident. I carefully observed the rest of the race, noting the mistakes of the riders. That 3rd turn had become treacherous. There were three more wrecks during the race and all of them took place there. Each time, a bike slid out from underneath a rider. Once, it was the Gray Goat rider who was in 4th place that went down. Close to 15 other riders went down behind him and the others scattered to avoid the wreck. Most managed it, but a couple were hemmed in and went down too.

Flynn went in for only the last seven laps. He was a senior and the most experienced so he didn't need practice like the rest of us. Flynn was a sprinter. We had fallen back to 5th place, but Flynn slowly brought us up to 4th, then 3rd. That was as far as he advanced. He put in a mighty effort, but so did the riders for The Cutters and Forest Quad. Forest won the practice race. The Cutters were 2nd and we came in 3rd. That wasn't bad for a race where winning was not our main goal.

"Great job guys," Flynn said after he caught his breath. "I'm very pleased with our performance. We didn't make any mistakes and were able to keep close enough to the front we avoided the accidents. I know none of us got to stay on the track as long as we wanted, but the next race will be 200 laps and we'll all get plenty of track time, especially Grant and Colin who will power through the laps leaving Grayson and me to fly.

"I'm sure you all noticed the loose cinders on the 3rd turn. That's one of the dangers of a cinder track. Depending on the weather, we may not have any problems with the track during the race. Then again, there may be one or more problem areas. It's something we have to keep in mind. No matter how good you are, a loose area, especially on a turn, can take you down."

We discussed our performance a bit more and Flynn mounted his bike and instructed us to follow. I wasn't sure where we were going. He took us west on 17th Street and then south on Indiana until it became a one-way street headed in the opposite direction. We followed him past the Grant Street Inn, across 3rd Street, and kept riding south. Soon, we were on Lincoln and after a few minutes, Flynn coasted to a stop. The rest of us halted behind him. I wasn't sure why for a moment, but then I spotted it.

"It's Dave Stoller's house from *Breaking Away*," I said.

"Everything in *Breaking Away* was filmed on location in or near Bloomington. Visiting the house before the race is an Alpha tradition."

As I gazed at the house, I half expected Dave to come out of the door or around the side of the house on his bike. I hoped Alpha did as well as the Cutters in the movie. I wanted to win more than anything.

***

"Are you nervous about tomorrow?"

"Why would I be nervous?"

"Oh, I don't know. You're racing in THE sporting event of the year. Thousands of people will be watching you from the stands and maybe hundreds of thousands on TV. Your frat brothers are depending on you. That's a lot of pressure," Hamlet said.

"Oh, I see. So your goal is to make me nervous?"

"I'm sorry."

"I'm messing with you. I'm not nervous. I'm excited and restless, but not nervous."

"How can you not be? Sorry."

I laughed. "Listen. Months of work are riding on this race and there won't be another for a year. The race is a huge deal, but I'm ready. I've done all I can do to prepare. I'm going to do my best tomorrow. That's all I can do. If worrying would improve my performance, I'd worry, but it won't."

"You're always so damn calm under pressure."

"Um... sorry?"

"Shut up," Hamlet said, then grabbed me and kissed me. Our kiss deepened and then I pulled away.

"I should tie the sock on the door," I said.

"Yes, you definitely should."

Sex with Hamlet was intense and familiar. I knew exactly what turned him on the most. I knew before I even met him because he was identical to his brother. Sometimes even now I momentarily forgot I was with Hamlet, and thought I was with Haakon instead. Dating twins was confusing!

Our moans and groans filled the room. One thing I loved about both brothers is that they were bottoms and could take it as long as I wanted to give it. I had exceptional control and I could hold back my orgasm for over an hour, even when I was on top of Hamlet, thrusting hard.

I could tell when Hamlet was ready to pop. I let my control slip when I knew he was close and I could usually time my orgasm to coincide with his.

We both groaned louder than ever and then we were still. I rolled off Hamlet and lay by his side.

"I feel the same way about you that Haakon does," Hamlet said.

"How's that?"

"You have ruined all other guys for me. No one will ever come close."

"Yep. When you've had the best the only direction to go is down." I laughed and Hamlet slapped my abs.

"Ow! Jerk!"

Hamlet grinned. "Come on, let's shower."

We each wrapped a towel around our waist. I untied the sock and tossed it on my bed, then we headed down the hallway. Grayson nodded to us as he passed. My brothers were accustomed to seeing Hamlet. He was a frequent visitor to Alpha.

We soaped each other up and made out a little since no one else was using the showers, then rinsed and dried off. We walked back to my room feeling much cleaner.

"Are you guys naked together again?" Wes asked as we entered.

"We're not naked. We're wearing towels," I said. We dropped our towels together and reached for our shorts. "Now we're naked."

Hamlet and I dressed and sat back on the bed, using it as a couch as we talked to Wes.

"I hope you don't need the room," Wes said.

"No, we just finished. I hope you don't mind. We used your bed this time."

"If I thought that was true I'd pound you."

"Hey, your bed needs to see some action."

"Have you forgotten the girl I had here last night?"

"Oh yeah! If you need the room we can get lost."

"I have things I need to do, but you don't have to get lost."

"Cool. I'm all mellow so it's time to relax."

"Sex does put one in a mellow mood, doesn't it? Hamlet said.

"Yes, and right after sex is one of the only times I'm not thinking about sex."

"Really? I think about it even right after I've had sex," Wes said.

"I guess you'll just have to hook up more often or get a girlfriend who wants to do it all the time," I said.

"Do such girls exist?"

"Yes," I said, grinning.

"Grr. I'm sure you've met them. Why is it so easy for you? Wait, don't answer that," Wes said as I began to open my mouth. "Never get him started on how awesome he is, Hamlet. He will never shut up."

"Oh, he's awesome, and when we do it he can keep going and going and going..."

"Okay, new topic! You shouldn't be hooking up today anyway. You're racing tomorrow."

"Wrong, hooking up is exactly what I needed to prepare for tomorrow.'"

"Sex helps you prepare for a race?"

"I'm all relaxed now. I'm going to go to bed early so that I'll be rested up for tomorrow. Today is all about chilling out."

"Well, you're certainly good at that."

"You should take notes. You'll probably be racing next year."

"I hope so. Just remember tomorrow when you're on the track you are not only representing Alpha, but our dorm room."

"Are you making a special banner?"

"I was going to, but I couldn't fit 'The 3rd door down from the top of the stairs on the 2nd floor' on it."

"Uh huh."

Hamlet leaned his head against my shoulder.

"Aww, don't you two make such a sweet couple," Wes said.

"Hey, Hamlet is mine. You find your own boy."

"You keep forgetting. I'm not bi."

"Everyone is bi to some degree."

"Well, my degree doesn't extend to dating guys."

"Come on. What about our bromance?"

"I prefer to call it friendship."

"He cops a feel of my ass when we hug," I said to Hamlet, who laughed.

"You big liar," Wes said.

"I should probably go so you can rest up for tomorrow," Hamlet said.

"Yeah, if you stay the two of you will end up having sex again," Wes said.

"He does have a point. I'll walk you to your dorm."

"Are you sitting with us tomorrow, Hamlet? You are an honorary Alpha brother," Wes said.

"Yeah, I'll be there wearing purple."

Hamlet and I departed and crossed the street onto campus. I took Hamlet's hand and enjoyed the closeness. I wasn't a huge fan of relationships, but there were advantages over mere hookups.

We didn't speak as we walked together, but we didn't always need to talk. Merely being together was enough sometimes.

I hugged and kissed Hamlet at the door to his dorm. He smiled at me, turned, and walked inside.

I strolled around campus slowly and aimlessly. Tomorrow was the day. Racing in The Little 500 wasn't like participating in other sports. Everything came down to one single event and luck played a big part in whether a team won or lost. Outsiders no doubt wondered why teams that barely qualified bothered racing at all, but I knew. They raced for the experience of being a Little 500 rider. Even the team members like Wes, who wouldn't actually be on the track, were a part of the experience. That's what The Little 500 was about for those who participated. The experience, not only the actual race, but all the other events, the training, and the time spent with those who loved racing and loved to ride. Marc had even returned to coach after his college days. He wasn't paid for it. He received nothing tangible for his efforts, but he returned because he wanted to be a part of things once more. Being a part of things. That's what The Little 500 was all about.

I grinned to myself as I walked. I held myself in this moment when I was still a freshman and poised before what would likely be one of the most exciting events of my life. One thing I had learned from the sudden and unexpected death of my mom and my step dad when I was young is that every moment is precious, no matter how mundane or uninteresting it might be. I very nearly died in the car crash that took my mother and step dad from me. In fact, I did die, but Skye brought me back. If he hadn't been there to save me, that would have been it. I would have never experienced these last few years or what was yet to come. I could die tomorrow or today and so each moment was something truly special.

I returned to my dorm room. Wes was out, which was fine by me at the moment. I made myself a mug of hot cocoa in the microwave, then took it downstairs with me and gazed at all the Little 500 photos and trophies in the lounge. There was a lot of history there, history that most would never know about or even care about it, but it was important to those involved and to my fraternity. I was now a part of it.

I turned in early. I didn't fall asleep for quite a while, but I lay there and relaxed. I had learned long ago that the best way to fall asleep was not to try. At some point, I don't know when, my thoughts turned into dreams.

Chapter Eighteen

I began the day of the race by sleeping in, but not too long because Skye was arriving at 10 a.m. to take me to breakfast. I got up shortly before that, showered, shaved, and dressed, then headed downstairs where most of the frat was already working on setting up for the cookout that would take place after The Little 500. The party would actually begin mid-to-late morning, but the grills would be fired up after the race.

I walked downstairs to wait for Skye. I didn't have long to wait. He walked in the front door only a couple of minutes after I entered the lounge.

My uncle gave me a hug. Skye being here for the race was more important to me than anything. I wished my mom could be here too. Maybe she was.

"Hungry?" Skye asked.

"Always."

"Okay, stupid question. Let's go."

We walked out to Skye's Auburn boattail speedster, which was surrounded by my brothers and others.

"I've never seen a car like this before," said Max.

"What? I thought everyone had one," I said.

"When was this made?" Rhett asked.

"1935," Skye said.

"Wow."

"Okay guys. Back off. I want to go to breakfast. You can drool over my uncle's car later. It will be here a lot today."

We climbed in. Skye started it up and we departed.

"How about The Bakehouse on the east side?" Skye asked.

"Sounds good to me. They have great pancakes."

The Bakehouse was only a few blocks away. We arrived in less than five minutes. I browsed the menu behind the counter for only seconds before I decided. I ordered pancakes with blueberries and strawberries, bacon, sausage, and hash browns. Skye ordered a three-cheese omelet, which came with toast.

We got our drinks and sat near one of the many windows.

"Excited?"

"Yes."

"I'm excited and I'll only be watching. I'm going to sit with Marc and Alessio. I'm sure they plan to sit with your frat brothers."

"You'll be their god now that they've seen your car."

Skye laughed. "I'm going to leave it parked at the frat. You don't think anyone will mind, do you?"

"Are you kidding? They would probably pay you to park the Auburn there."

"Marc said they would meet me at Alpha and we'll walk from there. It will be easier than trying to find parking."

"True."

"I'll admit I'm envious. I have never done anything like what you're doing today."

"Wow. I don't think I've ever heard you say that before."

"It's true. Nothing I have done comes close."

"Come on. Your life would make a great series of comic books. I don't know anyone who does more exciting things than you."

"True, but I have never raced in The Little 500 and I never will, so I envy you today. I'm also very happy for you and very proud of you, but then I'm always proud of you."

"Keep going and I'll expect my own statue."

We talked until our food arrived and continued to talk a little while we ate. This was another moment that was special to me; sitting with my Uncle Skye, who was also my father, my brother, and my best friend. I hoped he would be in my life for as long as possible.

We returned to Alpha and mingled with brothers and guests in the side yard where tables, chairs, and tents were set up. A lot of Alpha Alumni returned for The Little 500.

Skye wished me luck when I departed with the team for Armstrong Stadium. I knew he would be in the stands cheering for me, along with Hamlet, Marc, Alessio, and all of my brothers.

The race didn't begin until 2 p.m. but fans were already in the stands when Flynn, Grant, Grayson, and I entered the stadium.

We signed in and picked up our bikes, which had been carefully checked over by the officials for any sign of illegal alterations. We pushed our bikes to the Alpha pit, which was just past the center of the stretch where most of the crowd would be seated. As the 3rd place team for Quals, we'd had third choice of pits and color. Flynn chose this pit location because there was plenty of space for the incoming rider to sail in and stop and plenty for the outgoing rider to get his speed up before hitting the first turn.

We intended to use only one bike during the race, but we didn't want to take any chances. Having three backups might seem extreme, but this was The Little 500. The extra bikes were not only backups but were set up as trainers behind our pit so that we could keep warmed up when we weren't on the track.

"This is our pit," Flynn said when we arrived. "That line and that one are our boundary lines. The exchanges must take place within those lines. If we go to a bike-to-bike exchange, remember that the bike must be on the rear line and that you cannot move before you are tagged. We don't want to get a penalty.

"Any time you are out in the pit, make sure you do not get in the way of a rider. If you do we will draw an impeding penalty of five to ten seconds. If that happens, our chances of winning will be severely lessened. We've trained long and hard for this and we don't want to lose the race because of a foolish mistake."

Flynn kept talking. Virtually everything he told us was a review, but we all listened as if our lives depended on it. No one wanted to be the one who screwed up and cost Alpha the race.

The stands began to fill, with members of the various fraternities who had teams in the race coming in the earliest to get spots behind their pits. Soon, most of my Alpha brothers were in the stands behind our pit, including Skye, Hamlet, Marc and Alessio, all wearing our team color of purple.

I felt like time had slowed and that we would never get to 2 p.m., but at last we did. There were several announcements and then I knew the race was truly getting close when the teams were told to take their places on the track. The announcer named each team in order and its riders and then the teams walked once around the track. I have to admit to a certain thrill when I heard "Colin Stoffel" over the loudspeakers. I could swear I heard Skye cheering for me.

Next was an a cappella performance of *On the Banks of the Wabash*, and then the singing of the National Anthem, during which two skydivers, one trailing an American flag, each landed in the exact center of the field. I wasn't sure how a skydiver could do it. It had to take incredible skill.

I had a great vantage point for everything, including the release of hundreds, perhaps thousands of balloons, which the announcer told the crowd were biodegradable.

There was an amazing number of people in the stands. Armstrong Stadium wasn't enormous like the football stadium, but it was plenty big. Much of the crowd were IU students, but there were plenty of others as well. All the fraternities who had teams were well represented, most of them wearing their team color.

I thought our team looked sharp in our purple jerseys and riding shorts. The jersey and shorts reminded me of the singlet I wore during wrestling season, because they were so close fitting.

The cinder track was firmly packed, but the riding surface had been somewhat hazardous yesterday for the riders in the Women's Little 500. Loose areas had caused a few wrecks. I know the guy in charge of the track had worked hard since yesterday's race to pack and smooth the track, but the weather conditions had not changed, so we were likely to have difficulties today as well. I didn't realize it until we started riding on the track a handful of weeks ago, but it varied a great deal from day to day. Whatever the conditions today, all riders would face the same hazards.

The officials took the bike each team was using and positioned it on the track. Flynn was our most experienced rider and also one of our sprinters so he would start the race for Alpha. The plan was for him to maintain our third-place starting position and perhaps advance in order to create a good gap so that when we did our first exchange the next rider, me, could rejoin the race without falling back too far.

I watched with excitement as the opening preliminaries were finished, the riders took their places beside their bikes, and the announcer said, "Riders, mount your bikes."

The pace car started around the track, followed by 33 riders. The pace was considerably slower than racing speed and yet the excitement began to build as the car and riders went around the track three times. Near the end of the third lap, the car speeded up and exited the track. A few moments later the bikes approached the starting line. The official starter waved the green flag and the 2011 Little 500 Race was on.

The Cutters started the race in the pole position, with the Black Key Bulls 2nd, Alpha Alpha Omega 3rd, and Delta Tau Delta 4th. The Cutters immediately took the lead with the Bulls pulling in close behind, followed by Flynn for Alpha.

The Cutters set a fast pace from the beginning, which stretched the first eight riders out and distanced them slightly from the pack. That was exactly what the leaders wanted.

Bikes don't make a great deal of noise, but as the riders completed the first lap and 33 bikes passed my position within a few seconds the whir of the chains and tires was surprisingly loud.

The leaders pulled out farther ahead of the pack during the next few laps, but most of the riders managed to keep the gap from widening too far. At this point in the race all the riders were fresh. Later, the weaker riders would tire and would be unable to keep up a fast pace. There was a great deal of strategy concerning what riders to use, when to use them, and how many laps they should stay on the track. Racing wasn't merely about riding fast; it was about timing, stamina, pacing, and avoiding mishaps.

I warmed up on a trainer as I watched the race. I was going in next. The plan was for Flynn to ride only a few laps before coming off the track, but the plan might change without notice. The rider on the track was the best judge of when he should come off.

On the 10th lap, Flynn gave the signal that he was coming in on the next lap. Each team had to do a minimum of 10 exchanges during the race. We had an actual chart on a clipboard with 10 squares to cross out as we did exchanges to be absolutely sure we did 10. The name of the incoming rider was recorded as well to avoid any possible confusion. Grayson recorded the exchange as I checked my helmet and gloves.

I took up my position as Flynn came into the stretch. He angled off, sped toward the pit and braked only when he was on top of me. He jumped off and I replaced him in a near-perfect exchange. I say near-perfect because I'm not exactly sure what I'd call a perfect exchange.

The bike still had considerable momentum as my feet hit the pedals and I took off. It did not take me long at all to come up to speed. Thanks to the gap Flynn built and the gap from the pack, I was able to slide smoothly into 5th. That might not sound so good, but at this point in the race it was a good place to be. I could draft off the riders in front of me, but I was not stuck back in the pack.

My job was not to try to get out in front. My job was to keep us in a good position and ride lap after lap. Flynn was a sprinter and had only stayed on for 11 laps. I was a horse and I would ride a far greater number. I'd keep going until I began to tire enough that I could not maintain our position. It was fine for a horse to wear himself out. The sprinters had to remain fresh.

The sun was shining and the temperature high enough I was soon sweating, but I was comfortable. I'm not sure I would have wanted to race in the hot summer months, but April offered fine racing weather. Some years it was rainy, chilly, or both; other years it was downright cold; this year the weather was quite nice for racing.

I maintained my position until lap 27 when I spotted my opportunity to move up to 4th with minimal risk and effort. A single lap later I passed the Delta Tau Delta rider who was obviously tiring and moved in behind the Cutter rider who was currently in 2nd. I put us back in 3rd place, not by sprinting, but by taking advantage of the opportunities that presented themselves. I was very pleased.

The first wreck occurred on lap 34 and it was bad enough the officials, who were posted at intervals all around the track, waved the yellow flags. The yellow flag meant a rider was down and that no team could change position. The race slowed and we stayed in formation for an entire lap until the officials waved the green flags and we were off again.

I don't know which team went down or how many others were involved, but no one wanted to see the yellow flag come out. When a rider went down, he got back up and on the bike as fast as possible. If he couldn't get back on the bike, he was hurt badly enough he was out of the race.

The accident did not adversely affect those in the front, which is the main reason teams wanted to be near the front. Riding in the pack was risky.

Flynn signaled for me to come in on lap 45, but I signaled I wanted to stay on. I had plenty of power left and felt it was in the best interest of the team for me to eat up more laps before I rested.

I could feel myself beginning to tire on lap 59 and signaled that I was coming in. I had maintained our position well so our second horse, Grant, was coming in.

I hurtled toward our pit, braked, and jumped off. Grant replaced me so quickly we momentarily touched. I stumbled slightly, but didn't fall. Grant took off like a shot.

My chest heaved and sweat ran down my face in rivulets as Flynn handed me some water. I needed to rest before I could go in again, but I wouldn't be needed for some time.

"Good job, man. I knew you had stamina, but damn," Flynn said.

I smiled and looked up into the stands. There was my personal cheering section; Skye, Hamlet, Marc, and Alessio. Skye gave me a thumbs-up.

I took a seat and rested. My breathing slowly returned to normal and I cooled down. It was my turn to watch the race while my big brother Grant did his best for the team. So far, we had performed well, but there was still a lot of race to go.

The race began to go badly for us on lap 68. Grant was riding in 6th place when the front wheel of the Forest rider in 5th rubbed the back tire of the Gray Goat rider in 4th. The Grey Goat rider was able to remain upright, but the Forest rider when down. Grant swung wide but the front wheel of the Forest bike slid into his path and Grant hit the cinders as well. The downed bikes caused others to crash behind them and still others to swing wide to avoid the pileup. Everyone was able to get up and mount his bike, but by the time Grant was once again moving we had dropped back to 16th place.

"Grayson, get ready," Flynn said.

I wasn't sure what the plan was, but as Grant came into the stretch he veered off toward the pit. He had not signaled he was coming in so he was obviously hurt. He stumbled and fell as he got off the bike, nearly taking it down, but Grayson had a firm hold. He wrenched the bike upright and took off.

I feared Grant was hurt badly, but he stood and walked toward us. He was limping slightly and bleeding.

"Do you need help to the first aid tent?" Flynn asked.

"No. I'm not hurt that badly. I can go in again later after I'm bandaged up. I just need some time."

"Good job on recovering," Flynn said.

"I thought I had avoided the downed bikes."

"You would have if the Forest bike hadn't slid under you as you passed," Flynn said. "You did everything you could."

"Yeah, but now we're in 16th place."

"We'll catch it up. Go get yourself patched up."

Grant waited until the track was clear then crossed and limped to the first aid tent.

"This is not good, but we can still come back," Flynn said.

"Grayson has already moved us up to 14th," I said looking at the board.

"Be ready to go in for him. Hopefully he can recapture some of our lost ground. You eat up some laps, then I'll go back in."

"Sounds like an excellent plan."

One of the reasons spectators found The Little 500 so exciting is that everything could change in a moment. We were doing extremely well and then suddenly we were pushed back into the pack. We weren't alone. Forest and the Grey Goats, among others, had lost considerable ground too.

I wasn't as rested as I would have liked when Grayson came in, but Grant's time on the track had been vastly reduced due to the accident. Grayson had managed to pull us up into 10th place, but I didn't like where I was riding.

I had recuperated quite a bit so I focused on maintaining our position while I watched for chances to advance. I was not a sprinter, but if I could move us up even a place or two we'd be in much better position for the sprinters to take us back near the front.

On lap 68 I moved into 9th place. I was having trouble maneuvering. I wasn't stuck way back in the pack, but there were too many bikes around for me to easily move up. What concerned me more was that the frontrunners were pulling away further from the pack.

A handful of teams had already been lapped. When that happened, the officials moved them far enough to the right side of the track that they would not obstruct the other riders. That meant they had virtually no chance to place, but then they had no chance anyway. It's far too difficult to catch up an entire lap.

I moved us into 8th place on lap 73. I was quite pleased with my progress. I had taken advantage of two opportunities to move up without expending much extra energy. When Flynn came in for me, he would be in that much better of a position to move up. I still had plenty of power left to eat up lots of laps before I needed to come off the track.

I considered moving up again on the backstretch on the very next lap, but the Beta Theta Pi rider moved up on my right side and the opportunity was gone. Moments later, the 5th place rider, from Sigma Chi, went down causing a chain reaction. I had absolutely no room to maneuver and nowhere to go. I couldn't even swerve without hitting another rider. I rammed into a downed bike and felt myself sailing through the air. I thought I saw my bike above me for a moment, but then I slammed into the track hard and everything went black.

I opened my eyes. I could hear bikes whizzing past. I began to sit up but I felt dizzy and my entire body hurt. I tried to sit up again, but a hand on my chest prevented it.

"Don't try to get up."

I don't know who had spoken, but in moments a woman wearing a bright yellow vest leaned over me. Two others helped me move me onto a stretcher and I was carried off the track, onto the field, and inside the first aid tent. I had barely been set down when Skye appeared above me.

"How do you feel?" he asked.

"Never better," I lied then grinned.

An EMT looked me over, then shined a light in both of my eyes.

"How many fingers am I holding up?"

"Two."

"Do you know where you are?"

"I'm in the first aid tent."

"What's your name?"

"Colin Stoffel."

"Can you sit up?"

I tried and this time I wasn't dizzy, but a sharp pain shot through my right leg and the backs of my arms and the right side of my right leg stung.

"The good news is you don't have a concussion. Tell me what hurts."

"My right leg."

He examined my leg. I winced when he probed a particular area of my lower thigh.

"You've pulled a muscle, but it doesn't look too bad. There's no serious damage."

"Can I ride?"

"You won't harm yourself further by riding, but I don't think you'll be able to do so. That leg will cause you some pain for a few days and the scraps are going to sting for a couple of hours. We'll bandage you up and give you some Tylenol, but you're not in good enough shape to get back on a bike. I'm sorry."

That's when I came close to crying. I could take pain, but the thought of not being able to ride anymore and of letting my team and the whole fraternity down was about more than I could take.

I winced slightly as my scrapes were cleaned. Why did they always put stinging medicine on scrapes? I sat impatiently as the race continued outside. I wondered how much the accident had cost us. Our chance of winning was surely gone now.

"You are free to go," the EMT said after I was cleaned up and bandaged.

"Thank you."

I slipped off the gurney and winced as I began to walk. The scraped areas on my arms and legs stung, but it was my leg that hurt the most. Hopefully, the Tylenol would kick in and help. I limped slightly as I exited the tent.

"I hate letting the team down," I said as Skye walked beside me.

"You didn't let anyone down. There was no way out of that wreck. You couldn't go left or right and since you didn't have a basket on your bike with E.T. sitting in it you couldn't fly over the bikes in front of you, although you did fly several feet. I'm just glad you weren't seriously hurt."

"You know, right before I hit the track I thought I saw my bike above me."

"It was. You flew through the air for about ten feet and your bike went further, then skidded across the track."

"I guess there wasn't much I could do."

"There was nothing you could do. You had no options. I know you're disappointed, but most riders never get to ride in a

Little 500. You have and there are three more years of riding ahead."

"Yeah. It still sucks."

"Yes, it does. I'll let you go back to the team. I'll rejoin Marc, Alessio, and Hamlet. They'll be happy to know you are okay."

"Thanks."

"I'll see you back at Alpha."

We crossed the track when it was clear. Grant and Grayson climbed off the trainers and approached. My brothers in the stands actually cheered for me.

"Are you okay? Shit. We were afraid they'd take you off in an ambulance," Grant said.

"I'm not seriously hurt."

"You look hurt," Grayson said.

My leg hurts and all the scrapes sting, but I'm tough."

"Listen, little bro, just because I wrecked doesn't mean you had to wreck too. You don't have to do everything I do," Grant said and grinned.

"I guess we're pretty much screwed for this year," I said.

"We're not giving up. Flynn is out there now. I'm going in for him soon."

"Are you up to it?"

"Yeah. I've rested and recovered. My wreck wasn't as bad as yours. It's not going to be much fun, but I can do it."

"Shit, I'm sorry Grant."

"There is nothing to be sorry about. This is the kind of thing that happens in the Little 500. It's all part of the race."

"So, where are we?" I asked.

"We are currently on lap 97 and in 14th place."

"Not good, but I'm surprised we aren't a lot further back."

"The wreck you were in took down 16 riders and most of them were near the front. You were down and so were two others, so the yellow flag came out."

"So we're not totally screwed, just mostly screwed."

"That about sizes it up, but we won't give up."

"No. We won't," I said. "Where's my bike?"

Grant took me to it. The front rim was badly dented and several spokes broken. The chains were dangling and some spokes on the back wheel were broken as well. My bike was fairly well mangled. After looking at it, I realized I was lucky I wasn't more seriously hurt.

"Damn. It's a mess. With yours damaged that puts us down to two bikes."

"True, but we only need one."

Grant soon went in for Flynn, who joined me where I was seated as soon as he caught his breath.

"I'm glad to see you upright."

"Thanks. It took me a while to get this way. I was a little dizzy."

"I bet. The impact ripped the straps from your helmet."

"Hell, I never even thought about the helmet."

"It was a good thing you were wearing one."

"That's pretty much everything wrecked then, my bike, my helmet, and shorts and jersey, although they aren't ripped up too much."

"I'm glad you weren't seriously hurt. You're lucky to be sitting here instead of lying in a hospital bed. At least you can watch the rest of the race. Grant, Grayson, and I will handle the riding."

"Are you sure Grant can do it?"

"He's not going to be as fast as usual or be able to go as many laps, but he'll be good for short stretches. It will help."

"Damn, I wish I could ride."

"I know, but you did a damn good job."

"Except for wrecking."

"That was beyond your control. You can analyze it to death, but it was an unavoidable accident. That's part of the race."

"That's what Grant said."

"He was right."

Grant wasn't up to his usual level, but he kept us in 14th place and allowed Grayson a chance to rest up before he went back in.

I wished more than anything I could get back out there and ride. Even if Grant wasn't in a weakened state he couldn't do the work of two. Flynn and Grayson were excellent sprinters, but now they would have to make up both for Grant's lesser performance and my complete absence. That meant neither of them would have anything left for the end of the race.

Now I knew how a rider benched by an injury felt. I wanted to be out on the track doing my part to help the team, but instead I was stuck watching from the sideline. I stood up and took a couple tentative steps, but the pain in my thigh intensified. I sat back down. It was so frustrating to watch while Grant, Grayson, and Flynn tried to make up for the distance I had lost.

Grant came in on lap 119. If he was in top form he would have stayed on the track for much longer. Accidents had not been kind to us today.

The exchange was a good one, but we still dropped back to 16th place before Grayson was up to speed. Within three laps Grayson moved us back into 14th and then advanced to 13th. He was a great sprinter, but he was using too much energy too early in the race. We were no longer able to follow our strategy.

I sat and watched as Flynn went in for Grayson, Grant went in for Flynn, and then Grayson went back out on the track once more. There were teams with only three members and in very rare cases only two, but those teams rarely placed well. Teams racing with fewer than four members usually did so because they had no choice.

I closed my eyes and calmed myself. I focused on relaxing my muscles, especially those in my right leg. I pictured all my problems and concerns flowing away from me as if they were steam rising up off my body.

Now was always the most important time. I could focus on what I did not have or instead focus on what I did. My mom wasn't here, but Skye was with me. Haakon was far away in Norway, but Hamlet was behind me in the stands. I was injured, but I was still part of the team and I was here at The Little 500, where I had so long dreamed of being.

I focused on my thigh and imagined the area that hurt growing warmer. I willed the muscles to relax and heal. I told my subconscious mind to keep those muscles warm and relaxed and then I opened my eyes.

The riders zipped past the Alpha pit. It was now lap 150 and we were in 8th place. My teammates had put in an amazing effort to bring us back that far, but it had cost them. Grant was back out on the track again. Flynn and Grayson both looked like they needed a good long rest, but they wouldn't get one unless I did something.

I stood up and walked slowly to the trainers at the rear of our pit. My leg didn't hurt as much as it had. I climbed on a trainer and began to slowly pedal. The scrapes under the bandages stung and my thigh still hurt, but I was able to do it. Flynn and Grayson were watching me. I gave them my best confident smirk.

I slowly warmed up on the trainer. I was not miraculously healed, but I was in better shape than when I limped back to the pit. I was most certainly not in top form, but I focused on what I had instead of what I didn't.

Grant signaled that he was coming in on the next lap. Flynn moved into position for the exchange. I climbed off the trainer, walked over to him, and put my hand on his shoulder.

"I'm going in."

"Are you sure?"

"I'm sure."

Flynn nodded. He trusted my judgment.

Grant looked surprised when he spotted me, but there was no time to talk during an exchange. I replaced him on the bike and I was off.

I was in pain, but I could handle it. I didn't try to will the pain away. Instead, I drew it into myself and used it to power my determination. We were on lap 155 now. There were only 45 left to go and all my teammates needed a rest.

As I came back around to the Alpha pit, I could hear what must have been the entire fraternity chanting "Colin. Colin." It made me smile, but I kept my focus on the race.

My thigh hurt a lot, but I didn't let that stop me. My various scrapes stung like hell, but I could deal with that. I focused on keeping up with the other riders and then on lap 160 I moved us into 7th place.

I began to tire much more quickly than I should have, but I was going to do the best I could on partial power. I wasn't going to back off.

It took me until lap 170, but I moved us into 6th place. My leg was beginning to really hurt, but I kept going and on lap 177, I moved into 5th.

I pushed myself as I had never pushed myself before. This wasn't the first time I had fought my way through a difficult situation. The pain was only physical this time, not emotional. This was nothing compared to those days after my mom had died. Those were the worst, most painful days of my life. I smiled when I thought of my mom. I felt like she was watching me. I knew she would be proud of me. She had always been proud of me and she had always known I loved her. I missed her, but I had no regrets.

I picked up my pace even as I tired. On lap 185 I moved into 4th place. I maintained that position, but the pain in my leg was increasing and my breath came fast and hard. I remained on the bike. Each exchange cost us 2-4 seconds and could cost us much more if it didn't go down well. As much as I wanted to let Grant eat up some of the remaining laps I didn't dare.

I couldn't move up any further. The pace was too fast and I was using everything I had to keep up. I wasn't sure how close the 5th and 6th place riders were behind me, but I couldn't hear them.

The Cutters were right in front of me, Forest Quad was in 2nd, and Sigma Alpha Epsilon was 1st. They were all strong teams and none of them would be easy to take.

The pain in my leg grew worse, but I maintained the pace. By lap 190 my heart was pounding in my chest. By lap 193, I was gasping for breath, but I had achieved my goal. I had eaten up the laps as I was meant to do and I had even put us in striking distance of 1st.

I shot toward the pit. Flynn stood ready. I was in enough pain I felt like crying. Sweat poured off me and I gasped for breath. I braked hard and half jumped/half fell off the bike. Flynn had it firmly under control and took off like a flash.

I grimaced with pain as I breathed hard and fast. Grant and Grayson helped me up and then to a seat. I was slightly dizzy, but sipping some water helped me to cool down. By the time Flynn flew past on lap 195 my breathing was already returning to normal.

Alpha went crazy in the stands behind us as Flynn moved into 3rd place on lap 197. The race was almost over. There were now less than three laps to go.

The Cutters made their move and Flynn fell back into 4th for a moment, but then passed Sigma Alpha Epsilon to regain 3rd. On lap 199 Flynn took Forest. Alpha was now in 2nd place.

The cheering in the stands was deafening and the riders came around into the final stretch. Flynn moved to the outside and pedaled like a madman. His front tire drew even with back tire of The Cutters rider. He began to inch up, but the finish line was only yards away. Flynn gave it everything he had. For a few moments I thought we might actually pull off an astonishing comeback, but The Cutters raced over the finish line a fraction of a second before Flynn. Alpha failed to win The Little 500, but all things considered it was amazing we managed to pull off 2nd.

The Cutters fans poured onto the track and surrounded the winners. Flynn pushed the bike back toward us looking upset and downcast.

I was feeling more than a little down myself. We tried so hard and came so close only to fail at the very end. Grant and Grayson joined me as I walked to meet Flynn.

"Second place sucks ass," Flynn said.

I burst out laughing. I couldn't help it. The expression on Flynn's face and his tone of voice struck me as funny. Laughing wasn't the correct response, but soon Grant, Grayson, and finally Flynn lost it as well. I had a feeling that, "Second place sucks ass" might become our new motto.

By the time our Alpha brothers reached us we were smiling. Flynn put his arm around my neck and put me in a momentary headlock. Our teammates and every member of Alpha soon surrounded us. All of them congratulated us on 2nd place.

We were called to the stand where we received our 2nd Place Trophy. Standing up there, holding that trophy with our brothers cheering for us, I almost felt as if we had won.

We shook hands with The Cutters as we came down the stairs. Their coach pulled me in close and said, "You coming back and riding after that accident was the most amazing fucking thing I have ever seen in my life."

I smiled. "Thanks."

We stood near as The Cutters posed with the enormous Borg-Warner trophy and received the trophy they would take home. They held their bike over their heads as the crowd cheered.

As we made our way back to the pit, riders from several other teams patted us on the back and congratulated us as if we'd won.

"That was incredible, Colin. All of you were amazing," Skye said as he finally reached me.

"That was the most amazing effort I've ever seen. You guys should be extremely proud," Marc said.

Flynn, Grant, Grayson, and I immediately felt much better about coming in 2nd. Marc was a Little 500 racing legend. His words were the equal of any trophy.

"Every one of you gave it everything you had. Most teams would have given up," Alessio said. "This year was a lot like the year when Marc had to ride most of the race himself. Believe me, I know the effort it takes and Marc knows even better. You should be very proud of yourselves. Your 2nd place is better than many of the 1sts won by Alpha."

We posed for a lot of photos. I felt like a celebrity even without winning. I could only imagine what it would feel like to actually win the race.

Skye, Marc, and Alessio headed back to Alpha, as did most of our brothers, but Hamlet remained behind with the team.

"You were amazing. I was so scared when you crashed. I thought you were hurt badly."

"Me? Never. I'm practically indestructible."

"I'm beginning to believe that."

"You were magnificent." Hamlet hugged me close, then kissed me.

"Oh my god. What is it with you two?" Wes said as he approached. "Good job, roomy."

"Thanks. You like the way we kiss, huh?"

"Not that!"

I laughed.

We remained talking with members of other teams and racing fans until Armstrong Stadium began to clear out, then we headed back to Alpha. I, for one, was starving.

Smoke wafted off the grills sending a delicious scent our way as we arrived at Alpha, making me hungrier still. As eager as I was to eat, I needed to clean up. I was sweaty and dirty.

I didn't want to shower and get my bandages wet, so I washed off in a sink with a washcloth, put on new deodorant and some Burberry Brit and then dressed in clean clothes. I was sore and my body ached so I took a couple more Tylenol before I joined the party.

There was quite a crowd under and around the tents. In addition to all the current Alpha brothers, there were lots of Alpha alumni, guests, and some parents. I received congratulations from so many people I had a hard time making my way to the grills.

Damon and Federico were currently in charge of the grills and they were kept busy. I walked away with both a hamburger and a brat.

I hit the tables of food and added potato salad, baked beans, and barbecue potato chips to my plate, then grabbed a Coke from the ice filled cooler. Once I had everything, I joined Skye, Hamlet, Marc, and Alessio who were already eating.

"We would have waited for you, but we didn't want to," Skye said. I grinned.

"I am starving!"

That was the last thing I said for quite a while, but I listened to the others while I ate. Everyone was talking about their utter amazement that we were able to come back and take 2nd place.

I limped as I headed for the dessert table. I felt like I was getting sorer by the minute. My impact with the track and my overexertion were catching up with me. I didn't even want to think about how sore I'd be in the morning.

The vanilla cupcake with buttercream icing and brownie I brought back to the table were definitely worth the trip.

"Want to see your wreck?" Marc asked. "I uploaded it to YouTube when we got back."

"Yeah."

He handed me his phone. I hit play and watched my wipe out.

"Damn!" I said.

"It already has 10,000 views," Hamlet said, checking it out on his phone.

"Guys, check out Colin on YouTube," Wes said as he watched it on his phone too.

"It just went up to 14,000 views. I think you're going viral Colin," Wes said.

"Great. The whole world can watch me crash and burn."

I gave Marc back his phone and watched it on mine. Skye had told me that I flew several feet into the air and that my bike had gone even further. He wasn't kidding. After looking at the video I was surprised I was still alive.

"You are definitely going on the wall for having the most spectacular Little 500 crash ever," Flynn said.

"It's not the fame I was seeking, but I'll take it," I said.

"What's your bike look like?" Marc asked.

"Not good. You may cry when you see it," I said.

"I'll grab it," Grayson said.

He retrieved my bike and carried it over. It was such a mess the wheels wouldn't even turn.

"Maybe we should display your bike on the wall too," Flynn said.

"You can if you want. It's no good for riding."

"I'll give you a new one," Marc said.

"You don't have to do that."

"I want to. You deserve it. Besides, I know a guy. I can get it wholesale."

I grinned. "Thanks!"

At first, coming in 2nd to The Cutters was hard to take. It was only natural that we feel disappointed, but the feeling was quickly dissipating. I'm sure each of us would always regret not winning, but we had accomplished something rather incredible. I would have felt a little conceited thinking that, but I knew it was true. If I had any doubts, the 50 or so people who told me we did an amazing job would have erased them.

"So, was it worth it, Colin? Was all the riding and training for one single race worth all the effort you put in?" Alessio asked.

"Yes, but you already knew the answer to that since you were a rider."

"True and I didn't even make the team my first year like you."

"I hoped I would, but I was surprised I made it."

"I like the way things are done now better. In my day, the team was set early in the fall," Alessio said.

"Thank you," Marc said.

"That was your idea?" I asked Marc.

"Yes, it occurred to me the second year I coached that it made more sense to pick the riders for the race after everyone had a few months to train and improve. I don't know why no one thought of it before."

"What was amazing was the number of riders who kept on training even though they didn't make the team," Alessio said.

"I would have. My focus was on next year. Oww," I said as I moved my leg.

"Sore?" Marc asked.

"Yeah, but I figure I'm lucky that I don't have any broken bones."

"Or a concussion," Skye added.

We lingered at the table and then I mingled with the guests. A lot of the alumni wanted to meet me. My teammates and I even signed a few Little 500 programs and posed for photos with the children of alumni. They acted as if we were celebrities. I suppose we were for today, but it would not last. Even the winners would soon fade into the background and the rest of us would be forgotten. It didn't matter. Now was the only time that counted.

The party lasted for a few hours and it was nearly dark before everyone cleared out. Skye stayed until late. Before he departed we hugged and he told me once again how proud he was of me.

I went up to my room while the guys were still cleaning up. The day was catching up to me. I felt as if a truck had hit me.

"I am wiped out," I said.

"Did signing all those autographs wear you out?" Wes asked.

"It is tough being famous."

"Oh lord. Maybe it's a good thing you didn't win. You would have been impossible to live with."

"Every part of my body aches."

"I have a remedy for that. Go to sleep."

"I think I will after I take another Tylenol."

"I think you're developing a drug problem."

"If you think I'm getting out of control, you can take the bottle away from me."

I took just one, then lay back on my bed.

"Aren't you going to take your shoes off?"

"I'm too tired."

"You're such a baby."

Wes walked over, untied my shoes and removed them and my socks. I fell asleep before he finished and began to dream about the race.

Chapter Nineteen

"This is nice," I said as I lay on the grass in Dunn Meadow with my eyes closed. The warmth of the sun felt as good as a hot tub.

"I didn't think you'd be up for anything too strenuous today," Hamlet said.

"I'm too sore to work out and swimming would get my bandages wet. There's one strenuous thing I might manage..."

"We'll get to *that* later." I could almost hear the smile in Hamlet's voice. "I can't believe the spring semester is almost over."

"Don't remind me. I'm not looking forward to saying goodbye. It was rough when your brother left. It's almost worse this time."

"I knew you liked me better," Hamlet teased.

"No. I like you both exactly the same amount. You are identical twins."

"It's really not fair. There should be two of you as well."

"Um, sorry?"

"You should be. What were you thinking? You should have been born twins."

"Oh, I doubt the world could put up with two of me."

"Mmm, I could."

"Having a twin fantasy?"

"Yes. I'm thinking about getting it on with two of you."

"Pervert."

Hamlet laughed. "Have you ever thought of being with Haakon and me at the same time?"

"I refuse to answer because my response will incriminate me."

"Ha! I already knew the answer. Most guys have twin fantasies."

"You've shared guys, right?"

"Not many, but yes."

"Was it awkward or... sorry if I'm getting too personal."

"It's okay. It wasn't awkward at all. My brother and I don't get it on together as many might assume."

"Or fantasize about," I said with a laugh.

"Yeah. We've only been with three different guys together. Each of them wanted to watch us together so we kissed and messed around, but that's it. What made it hot for us was turning on the boy watching. We're not really sexually attracted to each other. We have messed around, but not much. Sometimes we sleep together, especially when one of us is upset or worried about something, but it's not sexual."

"You are lucky to have each other."

"Yes, we are. I sometimes feel sorry for those who don't have a twin. It's hard for me to imagine."

"I guess it would be."

"I don't know what I'd do if something happened to him, but I'm not going to worry about that."

"Yeah. You shouldn't. I sometimes worried about what would happen if I lost my mom. Worrying about it didn't make dealing with her death one bit easier."

"There's too much shit to worry about. Doing so would be a full-time job and I have better things to do."

"I think Haakon and you should both return and go to school here full-time."

"You just want to see us kiss."

"Well yeah, but you can do that for me on FaceTime." Hamlet punched my shoulder. "It would be great if you were both here, as long as you were willing to share me. I could never choose between you."

"Hey, I'm clearly more awesome than my brother."

"Right, anyway... It's good to have dreams. I'm going to miss you."

"I'm going to miss you too."

"I bet you'll also be glad to be back home."

"Yes, I miss Haakon and the rest of my family. I miss my familiar life there, although some of this place has become familiar to me too."

"I feel like I've always been here."

"I bet you'll be glad to get home too."

"Part of me will. I have friends I miss and, of course, I miss Skye. It will be nice to be back in a room that is significantly larger than a closet."

"Says the frat boy who has a larger and nicer room than any freshman living in a dorm."

"It's still small and when it comes to rooms, size does matter."

"It matters in other things too."

"Yes, although talent counts for a lot."

"True."

"You have both."

"So do you."

"I'll have so much studying to do going into finals week. It's going to be hard for us to get together," I said.

"Yeah, I know, but we'll manage."

"Our race training sessions will be lighter now so that will help."

"You're still training?"

"We never stop. The next Little 500 will be here before you know it. I'll miss practices if necessary to spend time with you."

"Wow, I am important."

"Yes, you are." I leaned over and gave Hamlet a kiss on the lips. "I wish I could have met you later in my life."

"Maybe you will."

"You and your brother need to move here."

"One never knows what the future will bring."

"True."

We both sat up. I was beginning to get a little too warm.

"Are you hungry?" Hamlet asked.

"Yeah."

"Come on, since you managed to take 2nd place yesterday, I'll buy you lunch at Burger King."

"Where would you have taken me if we'd come in 1st?"

"Brunch at The Tudor Room."

"Oh man. You should have told me before the race. I would have tried harder."

"I don't think that's possible."

Hamlet gave me a hand up. I appreciated it. I limped a little as we walked across Dunn Meadow. I had been terribly sore when I got up this morning. I was still sore now, but not as much. Moving helped.

We went inside the IMU and ordered from Burger King. Since it was a fine late April day we took our Whoppers and fries out to the large patio just below The Commons and sat at a table with an umbrella.

"I'll be leaving just as the weather is getting really nice here," Hamlet said.

"Okay, I'll let you stay if you want."

"I wish. Haakon said it was wonderfully warm and even hot here when he arrived last year."

"August can be extremely hot and September quite warm."

"One thing I do not like about Norway is the climate. I'm accustomed to cold, but I prefer warmth."

"I love heat!"

"I bet you just like running around shirtless for all the attention it gets you."

"That is merely a fringe benefit. Someday, I will be old and wrinkled and everyone will want me to keep my shirt on. I'm going to enjoy this body while it's still fairly new. It already has several miles on it."

"Your body may be slightly used, but it's in like new condition. I should know."

I gazed out over the eastern end of Dunn Meadow toward 7th Street where a biker was riding past.

"You're already thinking about next year's Little 500, aren't you?"

"Too soon?"

"I suppose not. Thinking about next year's Little 500 the day before this year's race would have been too soon."

"I definitely was not thinking about it then."

"What are you going to do this summer?" Hamlet asked.

"I'm going to do a lot of bike riding, working out, martial arts training, and sword training."

"Sword training?"

"Yes. My Uncle Skye has been teaching me how to fight with a sword for a few years now."

"He knows how to fight with a sword? That's unusual."

"Skye is an unusual guy. I am as well for that matter."

"Oh, I knew that already. Sometimes, I think you are Thor reborn."

"He's a Norse god, right?"

"Yes. He is the god of sky, thunder, and fertility."

"Fertility, huh?

"Yeah and you've got fertility to spare, or perhaps I should say virility."

"You're turning me on."

"Everything turns you on."

"We gods are easily aroused."

Hamlet shook his head.

We took our time eating our Whoppers and fries. Today was a rare occasion. Normally Hamlet or I usually had something to do or somewhere we needed to be. Today, we were both free.

Finals were coming up fast and that would keep us both busy, but I hoped we could still find time to be together. My schedule was lighter. Wrestling season ended weeks ago and while the Alpha Little 500 team would still train, our sessions would not be as intense as they were leading up to the race. There were also no more pre-race events to keep me busy.

When we finished eating we dumped our trash, then walked down the steps to Dunn Meadow and strolled toward the east with no particular destination in mind.

We visited the art museum where we gazed at Greek vases, artifacts from Egyptian tombs, and paintings by Monet, Picasso, and Jackson Pollack. We also checked out the Lily Library where extremely old books were on display, including an actual Gutenberg Bible. There was also a desk Abraham Lincoln had used in his law office in Springfield, Illinois, an Oscar won by John Ford, and an Action Comics #1. I was far more into sports and fitness than old stuff and yet it was still cool to see things I could see nowhere else.

Hamlet and I spent the day wandering all over campus and downtown, going wherever we felt like going and doing whatever we felt like doing. We talked and laughed and enjoyed our time together.

We ended up back in my room. Wes was out so we put a sock around the doorknob, stripped each other naked, and went at it hard and rough as we had so often before. By the time we finished I was slick with sweat and out of breath. Sex is best when it leaves one exhausted.

Hamlet and I spent the entire afternoon and evening together. It was approaching midnight before I walked him to his dorm and kissed him at the entrance. Our time from now on would be limited, but we had made excellent use of this day.

***

Time accelerated as the end of the semester approached. It was a repeat of the end of the fall semester. I was attending classes, hanging out with my brothers, and training as if none of it would ever end and then suddenly the end was near. I felt as if the day of Hamlet's departure was speeding toward me like a locomotive.

Hamlet and I had lunch together when we could and studied together whenever possible. Usually, we studied in my room. Hamlet was around so much all the guys knew his name. It had been the same with Haakon the semester before.

We hooked up as often as possible. I wasn't interested in other guys. I wasn't even interested in girls. My only sexual thoughts were of Hamlet. This must be what it felt like to be in love, but it seemed odd that I could be in love with one twin and then the other. Perhaps it was not so odd since they were practically identical in every way. I had a feeling that I would always love them both.

I had finished all the required papers and reports for my classes well ahead so all I had to do during finals week was study. I tended to study as I went along so even that wasn't too taxing. School came fairly easily to me. I was blond, but not dumb.

Alpha threw an end of the semester party on Wednesday night during finals week. Hamlet and I both studied ahead for our Thursday finals so we could attend.

The party began at six p.m. It was limited to members of Alpha and invited friends. Most of the friends were girls, which

I'm sure surprised no one. Frat boys are a rather horny lot and are almost always looking to score. There were a couple of brothers with steady girlfriends, but they were the exception to the rule.

The grills were fired up and the scent of roasting hot dogs drifted over the Alpha side-lawn where we held all of our outdoor parties. There were no tents this time, but plenty of tables and places to sit. In addition to hot dogs there were several different kinds of chips, soft drinks, and a keg.

Hamlet and I talked and laughed with the other guys as well as the girls. I noticed one of the girls eyeing both Hamlet and me until Rhett whispered in her ear. I knew he'd told her we were a couple. If Hamlet had not been in my life I would have been interested in her. She was hot.

Good music played, but not too loudly because some of the brothers were studying for finals inside during at least some of the party. I imagine most put studying aside for the evening, but we were serious about school. Alpha had one of the highest G.P.A.'s of the Greek community at IU. My brothers liked to party, but we were not an animal house.

After we ate, Hamlet and I danced together and with others who were dancing around us. A couple of girls rubbed up against us as they danced. I was quite sure we could have taken them up to my room, but Hamlet had no interest in girls and my only sexual interest at present was Hamlet.

We had a great time at the party. Unlike most, we didn't drink. I had never been much into alcohol. I viewed it as the enemy of staying fit and keeping myself in great shape was one of my priorities. Besides, it was damned expensive. I had better things to spend my money on. Even when it was free, I preferred not to drink. My brothers understood. The fact that I did not disapprove of others drinking probably increased their understanding.

Hamlet and I danced closely together and even made out a while. Some of the girls nearby watched us, but none of my brothers thought anything about it. I was sure a lot of fraternities were not so accepting, but Alpha most certainly was. That was another thing I liked about my fraternity. My brothers didn't think of me as the bi guy. I was Colin.

Hamlet headed back to his dorm about 11, but not before we kissed goodnight. The party was still going, but beginning to wind down. Most Alpha parties went much later, but this was finals week.

When I went inside I could still hear the music, but just barely. I undressed and lay back on my bed. I wasn't very sleepy or tired, but I had two finals tomorrow so I wanted to be well rested.

I gazed at the ceiling, thinking about my freshmen year at IU. I did not want it to end. I wished I could create a loop in time so the entire year would repeat over and over. I slowly drifted off with that thought in my head.

Chapter Twenty

Hamlet sat across from me at a table in The Commons. We were having a farewell lunch of Whoppers and fries, as well as cupcakes and no bake cookies we picked up at Sugar & Spice on the way. It seemed fitting that our last meal together should be in the place where we'd eaten so often, with our predictable orders from Burger King.

"I feel so strange. I have absolutely nothing I have to do. I hardly know what to do with myself," I said.

"Oh, you'll think of something. You'll hop on your new bike or hit the SRSC or run around campus shirtless and drive most of the girls and some of the guys insane with lust."

"Would I do that?"

"Yes!"

I laughed, but then grew quieter.

"I'm going to miss you," I said.

"I'll miss you and I'll pay for that when I get home."

"What do you mean?"

"Haakon pined for you something terrible when he returned. You were all he could talk about. I might have... teased him about it a little."

"You are terrible."

"Only a little, mostly I kept him busy so he wouldn't think about you so much. Now he will get his revenge."

"Yes, but he will also be there to keep you busy. Don't forget, we'll email and we can do FaceTime. I'm sure Haakon told you we talk on FaceTime."

"Yes, but it's not the same."

"I know." We grew quiet. Our time had grown very, very short.

"I'm glad I came and I'm glad I met you. Everything Haakon said about you was true," Hamlet said and grinned mischievously.

"I'm glad you came too. I was not looking forward to the spring semester. I knew it would be lonely without Haakon."

"I'm sure you would have survived and with all your interests and activities you would still have had a great semester."

"Maybe, but I would still have missed Haakon. Please understand that I never saw you as a stand-in for him. The two of you are identical in almost every way, but I like you for you, not because you remind me of your brother. I'm so glad I got to meet you and get to know you."

"Let's try not to be too sad when we part. Instead, let's remember all the fun we had together. Remembering is like experiencing something all over again so in way, we can be together whenever we want."

"I will be sad, but happy too because of what we've shared. Who knows? Maybe we will all meet again someday. Even if we don't, we'll keep track of each other on Facebook and we'll keep in touch."

"Yeah," Hamlet said.

We both knew it would not be the same. Saying goodbye would hurt, but after a while we would be left with only pleasant memories of our time together.

We remained in The Commons eating and talking until our time grew short and then I walked hand-in-hand with Hamlet to his room in Wright Quad.

His room was practically empty. His roommate was already gone. Only Hamlet's packed bags sat on his bed. We hugged and then kissed deeply.

"I'm going to miss that for sure," Hamlet said.

"Me too."

I gave Hamlet another kiss, then we picked up his bags and walked back toward the IMU where he was catching the shuttle to the Indy Airport.

We waited for his shuttle in a small courtyard just to the left of the Biddle Hotel entrance to the IMU. A fountain and beautiful plants made it a very pleasant location. We sat on one of the stone benches and reminisced about our semester together, often laughing, then growing quiet again.

All too soon, Hamlet's shuttle pulled up. We stood, hugged, and kissed once more. I helped Hamlet carry his bags to the shuttle where we handed them to an attendant. We hugged once more and Hamlet turned and boarded the shuttle.

I stood and waited until Hamlet departed, waving until the shuttle turned and hid him from view. In a few moments more the shuttle was out of sight.

I choked back a sob as I turned and entered the IMU. I did not cry, but I came close. Saying goodbye to Hamlet was as hard as saying goodbye to Haakon. It was perhaps even worse this time, because when the fall semester began neither of them would be here.

By the time I walked through the IMU and out the south entrance I was no longer in danger of crying. I was tough and I'd faced greater hardships. Instead of dwelling on my loss, I would remember all the good times I'd had with Haakon and Hamlet. When the fall semester rolled around they would be a pleasant memory. I'd once again train for The Little 500, hang out with my brothers, work out in the SRSC, and enjoy all that college life had to offer. Life wasn't for looking back; it was for looking forward and enjoying every moment as it came. If future moments were anything like those of the last two semesters, I had a great deal to anticipate. I could not wait.

Made in the USA
Middletown, DE
13 April 2018